Code FFF series

Book 1:

Fearless

By: Terri Luckey

D1712808

From the Code FFF series (Fearless, Fallen & Forgotten)

Book 1: **Fearless**
By Terri Luckey
© 2018 Terri Luckey

ISBN-13: 978-1718866874
ISBN-10: 1718866879

Cover by Art 4 Artists (http://www.art4artists.com.au)

For more information about the book contact:
www.terriluckey.com

Acknowledgments:
I'd like to thank God for giving me the strength and inspiration to write this book, and I wish to thank my family, my critique group, my proofreader, and my cover artist for their assistance, without which this novel wouldn't have come to pass.

Table of Contents

Prologue: Shamed…......... 06

Ch.1: Taking Risks….......08

Ch. 2: Freed…................ 12

Ch. 3: Accusations………17

Ch. 4: Suspect…............. 26

Ch. 5: Friendless…..........33

Ch. 6: Alone…............... 40

Ch. 7: Assault…............. 46

Ch. 8: Homesick………...53

Ch. 9: Fallentier…..........58

Ch. 10: Beloved Family…64

Ch. 11: Disappointed…... 70

Ch. 12: Unwanted……….74

Ch. 13: For Nothing…….78

Ch. 14: Prowlers………...81

Ch. 15: Reconnaissance…85

Ch. 16: Hard Choices…... 91

Ch. 17: Blending in…....... 94

Ch. 18: Aspirations…...... 101

Ch. 19: Choices………… 107

Ch. 20: Not Alone……... 110

Ch. 21: Sparring……….. 115

Ch. 22: Nosy…………...118

Ch. 23: Consequence…... 121

Ch. 24: Revelations…...... 124

Ch. 25: Stuck up…........... 130

Ch. 26: Surprises………...135

Ch. 27: Battling a War…..140

Ch. 28: Right Thing……..146

Ch. 29: Caught…………..150

Ch. 30: Negotiations…….156

Ch. 31: Evaluations…….162

Ch. 32: Failing………... 172

Ch. 33: Firsts………….. 180

Ch. 34: Chances……….. 185

Ch. 35: Blood Rubies…..189

Ch. 36: Bizarre………... 198

Ch. 37: Celebration……..204

Ch. 38: Threats………...210

Ch. 39: Busted………... 217

Ch. 40: Silence………...221

Ch. 41: The Deal…........224

Ch. 42: Abandoned…….229

Ch. 43: Jungle…………232

Ch. 44: Extreme Risks....236

Ch. 45: Cutting Strings... 242

Ch. 46: Babying………..248

Ch. 47: Tested…...........251

Ch. 48: The Mission…...256

Ch. 49: Shark Bite…..... 263

Ch. 50: Expansion……..268

Ch. 51: Fishing………...272

Ch. 52: Nerves………... 276

Ch. 53: Traitor…...........279

Ch. 54: Searching……...285

Ch. 55: Hopeless……... 288

Ch. 56: Stipulations…... 291

Ch. 57: Mascot………...297

Ch. 58: Goodbyes……... 301

Ch. 59: Above us……... 304

Ch. 60: Answer………...306

Prologue

Shamed

Derrick

Warm air from our captor's breath penetrated the cloth of the black hood over my face and moistened my ear.

"Derrick, I already know you're both spies," he snarled. "Admit it and save yourselves some pain."

I tried to control my fear as I struggled against the rough ropes that bound my hands behind my back and to the chair. Beads of sweat dripped into my eyes.

"We're not sp-ies," I declared, but my voice betrayed me with a quiver. I had to get the ropes undone before…

Thump. Thump. Was the chair next to me scraping against the floor? Kurt must be trying to escape too.

A cramp shot through my shoulders as I pulled against my bonds, but they wouldn't budge.

My gut clenched. To control the panic, I focused on breathing. Inhale, exhale. Hold it for the count. 1, 2…

Zap! Pain seared me, and every nerve jumped. Even tied, I flopped around in the chair while the electricity jolted my body. I tasted blood as I bit my lip. The pain consumed me.

I screamed and sobbed. I'd beg him to stop if I could only form the words.

Kurt swore at him and called him obscene names. The excruciating pain suddenly cut off, leaving me breathless.

A crackle sounded on my right. The stun gun. Kurt's chair jumped against the floor as he flailed, but only a gasp came from him.

Not one scream. Kurt stayed strong.

Shame filled me. My own weakness disgusted me. How long would it take before I'd reveal anything to stop the torture?

Would I fail the R2I, Resistance to Interrogation Training?

Chapter 1

Taking Risks

"There's no such thing as safe." Connor (Family friend)

Derrick

Everyone thinks being rich guarantees happiness. It doesn't.

Dad's wealth wasn't making him happy. He worried all the time. One of his worries was someone kidnapping me—like they took my sister.

I was a prisoner here. I wasn't even supposed to leave the mansion to tread the grounds without informing our guards. But I wanted to prove myself—not just to Dad—to me. I needed to be fearless.

My heart drummed like a jackhammer ran inside as I jogged to the back of our estate. The mid-morning sun left few shadows to hide in. If our guards mistook me for a trespasser, they had orders to shoot.

Taking risks never concerned me before. I loved the furious pounding of my heart—didn't I? I yearned to feel invincible again.

I stopped at the gate. The tall fence of wrought iron rails with black mosaic panels blocked my view of what lay inside. The shiny panels caught my reflection, giving my medium height and build a much taller and thinner fun-house effect. My black hair, brown eyes, and the muscles I'd worked so hard to develop disappeared in the blurry image.

With today's heat, it didn't seem as if fall had replaced summer. Between my sweaty hands and shaky fingers, punching in the security code wasn't easy. I finally opened the gate to the separately fenced training compound.

When I stepped inside, I snorted at the sight of the first obstacle in the course—a tin dinosaur head, its mouth wide open to show the tunnel beyond.

Even with his wealth, Dad liked to repurpose things. The mechanical dinosaur used to be on the pee-wee golf course he built on our grounds after I asked to visit one, only it hadn't been fun to play alone. This obstacle course wouldn't be as easy as pee-wee golf—it was to be an agent's final test.

After my performance in R2I training last month, Dad likely doubted whether I had the skills necessary to realize my dreams. Ever since I was a kid and heard Dad's best friend, Connor, talking about some unsung heroes foiling a terrorist attack, I wanted to be one of those heroes. I'd imagined them as silent ninjas moving in the shadows to protect the innocent. Innocents like my sister. After ten long years, law enforcement had given up on finding her, but Dad hadn't. I wanted to do more than miss her every day.

At age seventeen, I had to wait before I could apply to be a secret agent. If the CIA didn't hire me, plan B was working for the FBI, but neither would consider me until I was eighteen and had a bachelor's degree. And first, I had to convince Dad I could do the job.

I walked toward the dinosaur.

The custom foam bags to pad the new obstacle course weren't delivered yet. I could get hurt. A cold fist squeezed my heart.

I pushed the button on the pole next to the dinosaur. A tinny voice came out of the speaker, "To pass this course, overcome fifteen obstacles in fifteen minutes, starting now."

The hum of motors whirred to life. *Clang.* The dinosaur's teeth had crashed together. Those jaws opened again. I counted one, two, three. *Clang.* The mouth slammed shut. None of this was tested yet. Could I be crushed?

I sucked in some courage and raced toward the dinosaur. Timing the jaws, I dove through the mouth into the tunnel. A jagged tooth caught my pant leg. *No.* I kicked frantically, scratching myself. Blood trickled down my calf. My jeans ripped. I yanked my feet out of the mouth right before the teeth slammed together. Relief flooded me.

Inside the tunnel, the mid-morning sun didn't penetrate very far.

Ahead, it was as dark as a moonless night. The tinny, mechanical voice echoed in the tunnel from another speaker. "One minute elapsed, fourteen remaining."

I needed to hurry to finish the remaining obstacles in time. I hit the button on my watch. A blue light bathed the concrete tunnel with an eerie glow. Without room to stand up, I scrambled forward on my hands and knees.

The grade of the tunnel rose steeply, so I wedged both feet against the sides to keep from sliding back. The tunnel leveled out, and light appeared ahead. Was I close to the exit? I turned off my watch light as the tunnel grew brighter. *Clack, clack, clack.* A giant fan with spinning blades split the sunlight. The metal blades whirled too fast to dive through them.

The tinny voice reported, "Two minutes elapsed. Thirteen remaining."

I needed out. *Now.* But how?

There. Mounted on the tunnel wall was a gray electrical box. I threw open the lid. A slide of the heel of my boot and *click*, a compartment popped out that held a multi-function tool. I used the screwdriver to unscrew the top of the panel and reveal wires. I cut them. The fan stopped. I maneuvered my body through one of the gaps, careful not to touch the sharp fan blades, blinking as my eyes adjusted to the sunlight.

I was on a ledge, perched at the top of a wooden climbing wall with rock holds mounted on it. Grrr. Descending a wall was more difficult than scaling one.

I carefully lowered myself to each hold, my shoulders burning under the strain. A third of the way down, a *whoosh* parted the air. What was that? A knife thunked into a wooden plank so close, it scratched my hand. My jaw dropped open.

The obstacle course wasn't supposed to be *that* risky once the padding was installed. Why would Dad put knives into the program?

Wait. Where was the hum of motors and the tinny voice? A minute must have elapsed.

I gasped as the revelation hit me. Someone must be in here to silence them. Our guards would yell and use guns, not knives. It had to be someone else.

Someone who wanted to kill me.

My mouth dried. Dad's wealth presented a motive for kidnapping, but why would anybody want to kill me? My mind screamed, *why didn't matter now*. The response to a threat was D-E-C. Determine. Evade. Counter pursue.

Determine—the threat came from an unknown suspect wielding weapons. Evade—I was too exposed on this wall. I needed down ASAP, but it must be an eight-foot drop with no cushioning. I could break bones.

Another *whoosh* sounded. Another knife? My heart hitched as I flung myself back from the wall.

I plummeted toward the ground.

Chapter 2

Freed

"The greatest things in life aren't paid for with cash, but tears."
Victor Costa (Derrick's dad)

Derrick

The ground rushed toward me. I flexed my knees to soften the shock. My feet hit, and I flung myself in a roll to ease my landing. "Oomph," escaped me when my breath flew out at the impact.

However dazed, I needed to move. Counter pursue. I lunged for my ankle holster, pulling out my 38 snub-nosed revolver, and jumped to my feet. In the shadow cast by the wall, I caught a movement.

I aimed my gun. "Freeze, or I'll shoot."

A laugh rang out. There was no mistaking that laugh.

"Okay, you have me," Dad called.

I lowered my gun and moved toward his disembodied voice. Dad excelled at remaining unseen—a great asset for a spy. His dark hair, brown eyes, and medium skin tone blended into the shadows and most ethnic groups. When I drew near, his arms snaked out to wrap me in a strong hug.

He said softly, "You shouldn't be taking this test yet."

My cheeks warmed as my relief turned to frustration, and I stepped back. "I wanted to prove I could be fearless, again, but I couldn't even convince myself."

He shook his head. "You were naïve. It's not fearless when you don't recognize the risk. Fear's a natural reaction to danger. Only if an agent doesn't let the fear stop them do we name them fearless." He caught sight of the blood on my hand and grabbed it to examine the injury. "You should have moved when you heard the knife coming."

For Dad to throw a knife at me was really crazy. "I might have been seriously hurt, or shot you, thinking you were an enemy."

Dad's chin jutted out. "You needed to learn you can't relax your guard anymore. There are threats."

Not this again. When Mom died, Dad had withdrawn from us. But after Deidra was kidnapped, he went to the other extreme. He hovered and made the grounds much more difficult to enter or escape.

"I'll be eighteen next year. You can't keep me fenced in forever."

"You won't be anymore. I'm leaving, and it might be a while before I come back."

Wait. My stomach knotted. I didn't want Dad gone indefinitely. Other than disagreeing about his restrictions, we got along great.

"Can't you take me with you?" I asked.

"No, and I don't have time for explanations."

Had Dad decided to spy again? He hadn't been on a mission since Mom's death, eleven years ago. According to him, his business kept him too busy after he added the civilian division. With his launch of the *I-Spy* cameras during the dot-com revolution, consumer sales exploded. The little camera that looked like a glass eye and used an application that connected to a cell phone to watch property, kids, or cheating spouses. It came in everything from stuffed animals to garden gnomes.

Dad hadn't completely left spy work. He still made toys for other agents and helped train them. That wasn't very risky since no one but agents knew of his involvement. Usually family didn't even know. I only did because I was great at eavesdropping and had confronted him and Connor.

"Are you going to do a black op?" I asked.

"Something like that."

I knew better than to expect him to divulge any details of a covert operation. My phone's ringtone sounded. I pulled it out of my pocket to look at the screen.

"It's the guard shack at the gate," I explained.

"Put it on speaker, but I'm not here."

I punched the button. "Yes."

"Derrick, it's Ivan. The system's down—every camera and microphone. I'll call someone to work on it. And Jake's here. Do you want me to send him in?"

I'd rather talk more to Dad and learn what was going on. Jake and I had a shaky friendship at best.

Dad mouthed, "Act normal. Let him come back."

"Yeah, tell Jake to go to the training compound." I hung up the phone and asked Dad, "I take it you took down the system?"

Dad smiled. "Where's Angela?"

If my latest tutor was here, I'd be stuck inside studying. "She left early this morning. She said she had a family emergency." Dad said something in Italian I didn't recognize. "Are those swear words?"

"Yes," he admitted.

I'd never heard him swear. What happened to his "*no-one needed swear words if they had a good enough vocabulary to think of something intelligent to say.*"

My gut churned. "What's going on?"

"Coincidences don't exist. I shouldn't have trusted Angela, and neither should you. In fact, don't trust anyone but Connor." The tension lines in Dad's brow revealed his concern.

If I had to choose one person to trust besides Dad, it would be his best friend, Connor. He'd been like an uncle to me.

"I've got to go. Remember, I love you, and you know who I am." Dad took a step away. "Keep Jake out of the mansion for fifteen minutes."

"Wait, is there any way I can contact you?"

He turned back to whisper, "Music at 12A, QSO CW PL 94.8 Use K-24. I'll be N-14. No one else but you."

He'd listen for radio tones in Morse code, using the private frequency at 12 a.m. tonight. It would be an illegal transmission since I'd be using a call sign not registered to me, but it was better than nothing.

"Derrick, are you in there?" It was Jake.

"Go," Dad mouthed, then he jogged deeper into the course.

I shook off my worry for him. Dad's skills were considerable. That's why he'd been asked to train so many other agents.

"I'm coming, Jake," I yelled as I ran down the far side of the course to avoid the obstacles.

When I reached the gate, it was open, and Jake stood framed in it. Not even a tuft of hair dared to stick out from Jake's short military cut, and his clothes looked freshly pressed. Some agents called Jake "golden boy." He appeared "golden" this morning with the sunlight framing his blonde hair and light complexion.

My thick black hair and brown eyes would never be called golden. Not that I wanted that, but it might be nice if I didn't have to work as hard to impress agents. Everyone seemed to believe Jake would succeed while they doubted me.

He pointed to the course. "I thought it wasn't finished."

"It only lacks the foam bags, but I wanted to do it before we leave for the FBI's leadership camp."

Jake turned up his nose. "Leadership camp is nothing compared to tradecraft."

Dad's tradecraft camp was secret since it was for agents. He wouldn't have let me and Jake attend if we hadn't been aware of our fathers' roles in the CIA, and weren't well on the path to becoming agents ourselves.

Jake's lip curled. "I can't believe you're doing the course without cushions. You never see the difference between challenge and recklessness."

Jake's superiority complex grated on me. If he'd been locked behind gates all the years I had, he might have done some reckless things too. Jake even attended school—a private school—but he went. One of the few places Dad considered safe enough for me to go was the Bureau's camp.

Now I could go anywhere. A chill of foreboding ran through me. I shook it off. I'd be all right. Hadn't I shot a pellet gun before I learned to ride a bike?

When Deputy Director Johnson called, he'd said Jake needed something to do besides worry about his older brother, who was on his first black-op assignment, and overdue checking in.

I was concerned about Jake's brother too. "Have you heard anything more about Kurt?"

"No. And now he's two days late. There's no way he went rogue."

Rogue—an agent who left an assignment uncompleted, or who defected to another country. Kurt wouldn't have done either.

"He might be surrounded by people and unable to make contact without revealing himself." Even as I tried to convince us both, my gut churned.

Jake nodded. "Yeah, that's got to be it."

Tires squealed somewhere close, an engine raced. I pushed past Jake to see a white pickup truck and a black SUV leave the driveway and go off-road, careening around the mansion and the trees on the grounds to speed toward us. One of our security jeeps chased them both. The white pickup truck tried to pass the black SUV. The SUV swerved into it, but the white pickup broke free and pulled in front.

My ring tone pierced the air. I answered my phone to hear Ivan's voice. "Before we could close the gates, an unidentified pickup raced through behind Connor and Parker. E and E if you can. Shoot if necessary. We're pursuing."

I reached down and pulled my revolver from my ankle holster.

"What's happening?" Jake shouted.

"The pickup's a gate crasher! We're to evade and escape!"

Jake pulled his pistol as I scrambled to the side.

"We should spread out. Find a tree for cover," Jake yelled.

"That's what I'm doing." I slipped on the leaves under the maple I pivoted behind and recovered my balance. Jake ducked behind an oak as the vehicles approached my tree. The pickup truck slammed on its brakes. I leveled my gun.

The SUV careened into the driver's side door of the pickup with its nose, blocking the driver in. The passenger side door of the pickup truck cracked open.

I slid my safety off.

Chapter 3

Accusations

"Great nations aren't formed or kept without sacrifices, and our nation is the greatest." Victor

Derrick

Something inside the white pickup truck glinted—a gun. The trespassers were armed.

As CIA agents, Connor and Parker should be prepared to face anything, but I still yelled a warning,

"They have a gun."

They ducked, leaving only a shock of Connor's red hair visible, then vaulted out of the SUV.

Two of our guards, Luis and Ivan, raced up in a jeep to the other side of the trespassers' pickup truck.

"Put your hands up." Ivan barked into a bullhorn while Luis aimed an assault rifle at them.

"We're licensed bounty hunters," one of the trespassers shouted as both of them raised their arms inside the pickup truck. "We don't have to be on opposite sides. We can split the reward."

What were they talking about?

"Unless you have a warrant, you're trespassing. We'll shoot if you don't do exactly as told." Ivan's tone rang with menace. "Exit the vehicle slowly." When they did, he grabbed them and zip-tied their hands behind their backs.

Relief flooded me. I lowered my pistol, slid on the safety, and holstered it. As Ivan led them to the jeep, he glanced over at me.

"We'll call the police to pick up these perps. There may be more, so stay alert."

What did Ivan mean? I shouldn't demand answers in front of the trespassers. After our guards loaded them into the jeep and drove off, I turned to Connor.

"What's going on?"

"A lot. Where is everyone?"

"It's the maids' day off, our cook's grocery shopping, and my tutor had a family emergency."

"What about your dad?" he asked.

Dad said to only trust Connor, and Jake and Parker were listening. "He should be at work."

Jake rushed to ask, "Is there some news about Kurt?"

Connor's eyelids lowered for a millisecond. Not even good agents could hide every micro-expression. When Connor didn't want to tell me something, his lids dropped a fraction.

He waved at the SUV. "Everyone get in."

I blew out my breath. I wanted explanations, but everybody else was climbing in. Parker was buckling up in the front passenger side. Jake scooted over in the backseat, leaving me room. When I jumped in, Connor started the SUV. It sounded fine even though it had a big dent.

Connor did a U-turn and stepped on the gas. My head slammed into the roof when we hit a bump, so I grabbed the handle above the door to stop my bouncing as we raced over the lawn. When we reached the front of the mansion, Connor skidded into the driveway near Jake's Corvette and shifted into park.

He looked over his shoulder at Jake. "Parker will drive you to meet your dad. I'll follow shortly with Derrick."

Parker got out, but Jake just sat there. His face had paled. "Is it bad news?"

Connor removed his key from the ignition. "The Deputy Director ordered us not to say anything before he sees you."

My heart lurched. Who waited to reveal good news? Jake's hands shook as he reached for the door and climbed out.

"I'll see you later, Derrick," his voice cracked with strain.
"Sure, Jake."

As Parker drove off with Jake, Connor removed his seatbelt. "We should go inside, lad. You need to pack anything you can't live without."

Connor spoke a dozen different languages, but when he reverted to using an Irish term, and called me *lad*, it usually meant he was upset.

My gut churned as I jumped out of the SUV. "Tell me what's going on."

"It's teeyou," Connor answered as we moved toward the mansion.

A chill raced through me. T.U. meant turned upside down. Something bad. Unexpected. I'd heard him use the term once before, the day Deidra was kidnapped.

Connor's shoulders drooped. "PD raided a house after they received a tip about someone being tortured." His voice lowered. "They found Kurt dead and evidence incriminating your dad as a mole."

Pain stabbed my heart. Even though Kurt was four years older, we'd trained together, and I considered him a friend. Unlike Jake, he was quick to offer help, and his skills were impressive. Could he really be dead? And why would anyone believe Dad was a mole? That was crazy.

"Dad would never do anything to harm operatives." I punched in the alarm code and opened the door. "And we don't need money."

Connor trailed me in. "Supposedly, it wasn't just for money. They were blackmailing him to keep Deidra from being harmed."

Our steps clicked against the marble tiles as we walked through the grand salon with its inlaid ceiling and crystal chandeliers. "Dad wouldn't sell out Kurt, even for my sister. You don't believe that, do you?"

Connor blew out his breath. "Not really, but it looks bad. There's a lot of incriminating evidence, videos, the works."

"That proves it wasn't Dad. If he'd done it, there wouldn't be any evidence." We passed the formal crème chairs and divan to go over to the steps. "Someone has to be framing him."

"Who? After the Bureau's agents were killed investigating this terrorist group, Deputy Director Johnson kept Kurt's assignment secret. Your dad and I are the only ones who knew because I was his handler and Vic trained him."

I grabbed the banister and started up the steps. "You weren't the only ones. I knew since I trained with him, and Kurt told Jake."

Connor's voice sharpened as he followed me up the stairs. "Did you or Jake tell anyone?"

"I didn't. And I can't believe Jake would, knowing the risk to Kurt. What about Angela? Was she informed?"

"No. Now you see why the Deputy Director believes Vic's the mole?"

My breath caught. "We have to convince him Dad's innocent."

"I don't think we can. Not without proof. And Vic didn't help anything by disappearing. The Deputy Director's assigned me to bring him in."

"What?" My gut lurched, and I hesitated on the landing of the wide sweeping stairway before continuing to climb. "You'd do that?"

"Victor trained most of our operatives, so he can identify them. No one wants to risk him blowing their cover. But that's not the worst of it. When PD raided the house, news crews were there, so the Company couldn't keep it under wraps."

The CIA rarely let details of operations emerge, and they were good at containing that information. Hard to believe they'd failed. It all seemed unreal. Could I be dreaming? I'd never dreamt something this crazy. I reached the second floor and turned down the hallway.

"Is that why those bounty hunters came here?"

"Yes. A reward's been posted, along with your dad's picture. They're calling Vic a terrorist, so there will be plenty more after him." He glanced at me. "Derrick, I have to be the one to bring him in. I'm probably the only one who won't shoot him on sight."

My heart ached, and my feet faltered. Connor put a hand on my shoulder. "If you know how to contact him, you need to let me know."

Dad had said no one, but me. Besides, with what I knew now, I'd rather trust in Dad's ability to hide than agents who wanted to see him dead. Connor couldn't guard him 24-7. Hard to get away with lying when agents look for revealing tells, so I stuck to the truth.

"I don't know any way of contacting him right now." *I only know how to reach him tonight.*

I opened the door and walked into my spacious room. My huge bed, desk, chair, computer, and small replica of the mansion didn't even come close to filling it.

"Why can't I stay here?" I asked.

Connor sat in the chair. "Under the law known as civil asset forfeiture, the government can seize anything used in a criminal activity. The Company believes Victor trained agents here to learn their identities. Plus, money they assume was pay-offs was deposited in his accounts. Even you and Deidra's trust has suspicious deposits. Everything's already frozen."

My neck felt uncomfortably warm as my anger surged. "How can they do that? Dad hasn't been convicted."

"It doesn't require a conviction for the government to do it. I'm sorry."

I punched the wall, and pain slammed through my fingers. Dumb move. It didn't relieve my anger.

I spit out, "It sure seems like someone doesn't want Dad to have the resources to clear his name."

My head spun with everything. Like I was trying to swim in an ocean with huge waves pummeling me, and I couldn't reach the calm water. What would Dad say? *Focus on one task. Prioritize.* What was first? *Packing.* I tromped to my walk-in closet and took out my duffel with the clothing and toiletries I'd planned to take to the FBI's leadership camp.

I'd need my suit for Kurt's funeral. I packed it and my sunglasses. I looked at the replica of the mansion on the floor.

"This isn't going to fit in my duffel."

Connor shook his head. "I don't think you want to be carrying around a dollhouse."

What dollhouse had perches inside? "It's not a dollhouse."

"I know, but other people don't. Just put Pip in his shoebox."

I patted my leg. My pet Sugar Glider came running out of his house to me. His five-inch length and four-ounce weight were barely noticeable as he climbed up my leg to where I could reach him. "The shoebox is for when he eats, and there's a hole so he can get out. I don't like being caged, and I don't cage Pip."

I slipped the elastic translucent band with gray polka dots over Pip's head and under his chin. The dots blended into his coloring and held a camera lens, a receiver, and the new protocol of an undetectable bug Dad developed. When I gently placed Pip in my duffel, he disappeared under the clothes as I stuffed his box with bowls, pellets, vitamins, and an apple slice inside.

I dug through my dresser drawer for my cash. A quick count revealed $49. Not much. I crammed it in my jean's pocket. I slipped my radio and the rods for my Slim-Jim antenna inside my bag.

"Will the government be upset about you letting me take this stuff?" I asked.

"Probably, but I don't suspect it will harm the country if we lose a few of your things before they secure the mansion." Connor motioned to my bag. "You won't be able to get in again, so is that everything?"

What else did I want? My family. Our family portrait was sitting on my desk. I slipped it out of the frame and into the front compartment of my bag.

I zipped my duffel partially shut, leaving an opening so Pip could look out. "So what's going to happen to me?"

"We'll discuss it, but first I need to go to your dad's office. The Company wants his computer and files secured." He moved out of the room.

I slung the duffel over my shoulder and followed him. "So someone can plant more stuff to frame Dad?"

Connor practically jogged down the hall to the steps. "I have to follow my orders, but I'll backup the hard drive. If anyone tampers with it, there will be evidence to the contrary."

"Okay. Dad said I could trust you."

Connor's feet froze on the steps, and his eyes flickered once.

There was that tell again. "Can't I?"

Connor blinked a couple of times. "Whatever happens, I hope you'll remember I love you and your dad."

I tensed. Connor was acting weird, and he wanted to bring Dad in. I couldn't warn Dad until tonight. Meanwhile, I needed to do everything I could to convince the Deputy Director of Dad's innocence.

We turned into the hallway off the grand parlor and hurried into the office. Connor pressed the separate code on the key panel beside the steel doors. They slid open to reveal the cherry paneling lined with shelves of books, Dad's desk and computer, and his business files.

Connor rushed to the desk. After pushing the button underneath to release the floor bolts, he shoved the desk aside. He pulled the rug back and tapped a sequence with his foot. He checked his watch before tapping the next sequence. They had to be timed right. The panel slid open, revealing a bare safe. He shut the panel and put the desk back.

"Have you been in here?" he asked.

"You're the only one Dad gave the codes to."

He snorted. "Like that's ever stopped you."

I gave him a smirk. "I didn't clean out the safe."

"Then it had to be Victor." He strode to the computer and pushed the power button. Nothing happened, so he turned it around. "The hard drive's missing." He re-engaged the office alarm. "Okay, let's go."

In the foyer, I took one last look back before I left the mansion, the only home I remembered. At times, I'd believed it a prison, only now I couldn't return. Despair rose up, and a lump formed in my throat. Dad was in danger, and we'd lost a place to call home.

I trailed Connor outside. "I wonder how Dad will feel when he finds out the country he risked his life for is taking everything he worked so hard to get."

Connor frowned. "What's your dad say about material things?"

"They're like catsup. Nice to add flavor, but catsup's not good on its own. People are more important than things."

Connor moved onto the driveway. "Wherever Victor is, he isn't going to be upset about losing this stuff. He'll be more worried about you. And he wouldn't blame the country he loves for the actions of a few."

He was right. Dad wouldn't. And he wouldn't want me to either. Connor motioned to his car. "Jump in the passenger side. There's more I need to tell you."

More? I wasn't sure how much more I could take. Dad was

always saying to be adaptable, to expect the unexpected. He'd throw surprises at us during training exercises to see whether we could cope. Could this be a test, and not real—a fabricated scenario? I wanted to believe it, but the grim set to Connor's face dashed my hope. I dragged myself to the other side of the vehicle and reluctantly climbed in.

Connor shifted the SUV into drive and peeled away from the mansion. As we approached the gate, the guards raised it, and Connor drove the SUV down the lane and onto the main road.

"With your dad gone, you've become a ward of the state. Since I'm your family by love, not blood, and I'm out of the country so much, they wouldn't agree to you staying with me." Connor turned onto the entrance ramp to the Fred Washington Parkway. "Kids without family normally go to a foster home. Unfortunately, few want teens, and no-one wants those labeled unadoptable since that name's also assigned to kids with behavioral issues. Victor hasn't relinquished his parental rights, so you'll be sent to Fallentier group home."

"Can't I be emancipated and live on my own?"

"If you could prove you can support yourself, but that's not going to happen with your trust frozen. At least it's only a year before you age out. Just keep your head down. Are you still packing?"

"Of course. Dad said to always wear my weapons."

"On your property. This won't be like your last visit to headquarters. Everyone's on edge. They won't allow weapons at the group home, either, so you'd better let me hold onto them."

I handed my sheathed knife and holstered gun to Connor. He opened the SUV's glove department and pressed his thumb against a small panel. The side of the glove slid open, revealing a hidden compartment. He stuck my weapons inside and closed the panel.

A lot of agents didn't even carry a gun, but I felt as exposed as if I'd stripped my clothes off.

"Would you make a dead drop for me?" I asked.

"Some nut could target you to get to Victor, so I'll do it. Remember, your weapons are a last resort."

As we drove along the Potomac, the brilliant sunshine and stunning scenery mocked me. It felt as if my world had burned down, so the sky should be gray at least. Connor took the 123 exit, and we drove on what appeared to be a suburban street. Before we reached the strip mall, Connor turned onto the almost tree-covered, nondescript private drive, which led to the CIA's headquarters. We came to the barred gates and guard shack. A group of Marines stood in front of the gates, preventing entrance.

Vans, cars, and SUV's with big letters painted on the sides—WJLA, WUSA, and plenty more—crowded the lot. Was every news agency in the country here? People flocked around the gates, many holding cameras—reporters.

"Connor, what is this?"

"Trouble," he answered.

Chapter 4

Suspect

"Innocent until proven guilty doesn't exist in the minds of the CIA."
Victor

Derrick

My spirits plummeted even further. The reporters crowding Langley's gate settled any doubt about whether this could some kind of elaborate training test. No training exercise would involve the press. The Company didn't want their attention. This was real, no matter how much I wished it weren't.

The press had a long-standing arrangement with the CIA not to broadcast agent's pictures, but I didn't have that protection. A future spy didn't need his face known. How could I avoid the cameras?

"Since you're a juvenile, your name hasn't been released to the press." Connor's tone was cold and professional. "Do you have anything to cover your face?"

"I have my sunglasses and my sweatshirt hood."

"Use them," Connor ordered.

Why was Connor acting so distant? I grabbed my modified sunglasses and put them on. Connor pulled the SUV behind two other cars waiting in line as I yanked my hood up.

"Am I going to be treated like a suspect?"

Connor shifted into park. "They believe your father was working with terrorists who recruit kids. So, of course, they assume you might be involved."

My stomach did a somersault. The CIA couldn't legally investigate Americans, but there were ways around that. The Company could claim they suspected me of planning terrorist strikes in foreign countries, or they might work jointly with another agency like the Bureau and *loan* them agents.

A chill raced through me. I'd read about the CIA's dark history, which included forced disappearances and even executions of those considered a threat to our nation. As a terrorist suspect, could I *disappear* and get taken to one of the CIA's secret prisons where they used torture?

Maybe I was overreacting, but Americans had been held at Gitmo and on carriers. Gitmo had suspects as young as age thirteen. Should I jump out and flee? Not yet. I needed to try to help Dad.

Connor lowered his head to speak into his phone. "We're here."

I couldn't hear the other side of the conversation, but a second later, Connor said, "I understood you were leaving, sir." After another pause, he said, "As soon as we get through the gates." He hung up and pocketed his phone.

"Will I be able to see Deputy Director Johnson?" I asked.

"Yes. He wants to meet with you now since it might be awhile before he returns."

Good. Even if I couldn't convince him of Dad's innocence, I needed more information to learn who did this to us.

"Should I leave my duffel in here?"

Connor's face softened a little. "That's fine, but they'll probably search it."

I grabbed Pip out, then pressed his ear and motioned under the front seat. When I released him, he scurried underneath. Would he follow the signal to stay hidden? If the guards found him, they might consider him some kind of risk.

Connor took his ID badge out of his pocket and clipped it to the front of his suit. Under his name were the initials, SOG CMD.

When had Connor moved up to Special Operations Group Command? SOG carried out the CIA's most covert ops. The S should really stand for 'secret' rather than 'special'.

The cars in front of us moved through the gate, and Connor closed the gap. Surveillance cameras mounted on the fence and guard shack watched us. One of the half dozen Marines stationed there touched his ear where an earpiece dangled before striding toward our vehicle.

Reporters swarmed toward us too. I pulled my hood tighter as Connor lowered the window.

The Marine asked Connor, "You have Victor Costa's kid?"

"Yes." Connor motioned toward me.

The reporters aimed their camera at me while they shouted questions. "Did you know your father's a terrorist?"

"Do you know where your father is hiding?"

Their shouts came as rapid as fists flew in a boxing match, and it felt as if each scored a punch. They weren't even saying "alleged." The media had already convicted Dad.

One shoved his microphone through Connor's window at me. "What's it like to live with a terrorist?"

Anger flooded me, and I grabbed the mic.

Connor barked, "Let go."

I felt like breaking his Mic., but then what would they presume? I took a calming breath and released it.

The Marine at our window waved us forward as the line of Marines parted. "Follow the jeep to the second gate."

The Marines closed their line, and a Jeep pulled out in front of us. When Connor drove through the gate, a second Jeep maneuvered behind us. Dread rose in me. Why were they sandwiching us between them? The base of my neck tingled in response to feeling trapped.

We drove for several minutes before coming to a second gate with a guard shack and surveillance cameras. Six more armed security officers stood around it, but they wore the uniform of the SPS, the Security Protective Services employed by the CIA.

It was rare for the SPS to allow a member of the public into the 258-acre campus of the CIA headquarters. I'd been inside once after I learned about Dad and Connor's involvement with the Company. I only got to the memorial wall where Deputy Director Johnson met me to warn if I told anyone what I knew, it would risk Dad and Connor's safety and they could get killed. Both jeeps with the Marines turned around, going back the way we'd come when Connor pulled up to the second guard shack.

He unclipped his ID and handed it to one of the SPS guards. "Deputy Director Johnson wants to see Derrick."

The guy examined Connor's identification, then said, "We'll need to screen and fingerprint him, so exit the vehicle."

Why would they need my fingerprints? Were they going to arrest me? An icy chill raced up my spine. Connor switched off the vehicle, but he left the keys in the ignition when we got out.

As one of the SPS guards searched the car and rifled through my duffel, another handed me a basket. "Place anything metal you have inside this."

I put in my watch, my phone, and my belt. My glasses weren't metal. I hopped around to pull off my boots, then stood on the asphalt in my socks.

When the guard snorted, I explained, "My boots have metal studs."

I sure wasn't telling him about the hidden compartments. The boots barely fit in the basket, so I wedged them on top.

Another of the guards brought out a wand to run it in front of my body. A loud buzz sounded from the wand.

Three of the SPS guards drew their guns to aim them at me.

My heart pounded. My muscles tensed. My training kicked in.

The nearest guard brandishing a gun had the telltale bulk of a bullet-proof vest. I leaped behind him and grabbed his arm to pull it behind his back. When I gave it a quick twist, he dropped his pistol into my waiting hand.

The grip of the Glock-45 felt comfortable. I wrapped my other arm around his neck. His hands flew to my arm to keep me from choking him.

I stuck the gun to his temple so everyone could see it. "Holster your weapons. Now!"

They hesitated. Connor took a position between us. "Do it."

They sheathed their weapons. I backed with my hostage toward the SUV to make my escape.

Connor moved toward the vehicle too. Would he try to intervene?

"Stop, Connor." My voice cracked.

His feet froze. "Let him go, Derrick."

"So they can arrest me?"

Connor's nose wrinkled. "The Company doesn't arrest people.

It's policy to confirm a visitor's identity with an iris scan and fingerprints."

"Is it policy to draw a weapon?"

"No. They overreacted, but think before this goes further. I know you're scared, but how could this affect you?"

Headlines of a terrorist suspect holding a hostage at the CIA headquarters wouldn't look real good.

"I'm not scared." But I couldn't keep the gun in my hand from trembling.

Connor's gaze flicked to the gun. "Petrified would be a normal reaction to having all this happen."

Inside, I was shaking like the tail of a rattlesnake, but I wasn't going to admit it. "I'm concerned."

"Understandable, but I won't let anyone abduct you." Connor held out his hand. "Give me the weapon and stand down. I'll make it so this incident never occurred."

Could Connor do that? With him in division command, yeah. I let go of the guard's neck and lowered the pistol to place it in Connor's palm. "The safety's still on."

When I released the gun, the SPS guard I was holding turned around and shoved me against the SUV. Hard.

My temper flared, and I snarled, "Do you want another lesson?"

Connor yelled, "Knock it off!"

Was he talking to the SPS guy or me? Another guard closed in to frisk me. He found my necklace and examined it.

The necklace was such a part of me I hadn't even thought about it setting off their metal detector. "I never take that off."

"Real stupid, kid," the SPS guy whispered as he clutched my arms. They ran the wand over me again, but it didn't buzz.

"Release him," Connor ordered. When they let go, Connor glanced at me. "If you changed your mind about seeing the Deputy Director, I can take you to the group home. Otherwise, we need fingerprints and an iris scan. It's your choice."

My determination to help Dad wouldn't allow me to leave. "All right, I'll sign your permission form."

Connor's eyes twinkled. "You're underage. If we needed a

signature, it would have to come from your guardian. You know who that is."

Right, a ward of the state. The government already owned me. I just hadn't signed up.

Another of the guards aimed what looked like a large boxy cell phone at me. Was that a HIDE—the iris scanner and fingerprint imager the military used to identify terror suspects in Iraq? This looked more advanced than the pictures I'd seen.

"Lift your glasses," the guard ordered.

When I did, he pointed the HIDE at my face. Then he turned the thing over. My picture was displayed, and my eyes were highlighted. The words, "Iris scan completed, ready for Fingerprint Identification," flashed on the screen, so I dropped my glasses back over my eyes.

"Press your fingers one at a time on the imager," the guy instructed.

I put them in the indented area until he was satisfied, then I asked, "Can I have my stuff back?"

"On your way out," he answered curtly.

I didn't want to walk around in my socks or leave some of the few things I owned, but arguing wasn't going to change it. At least they left my eyeglasses alone. They probably assumed I needed them to see. Not with 20/20 vision.

A guard passed Connor back his ID. We got in the vehicle, and I tucked my glasses inside my duffel. They raised the bar of the gate, and Connor drove through.

The spacing of the buildings gave the headquarters the feel of a college quad. The sleek stone and glass structures with their rows of windows featured several inspiring architectural details.

Connor parked in the lot of the main building. Three columns with a shelf above stood in front, like a sculpture. I got out and, following Connor inside the glass doors, ogled the huge arches we walked under. Gleaming marble pillars lined the lobby. The virtual tour didn't compare to seeing it in person. I gasped. My feet stood within the CIA's seal on the floor.

Connor smiled. "You like it?"

"It's breathtaking."

We moved across the giant lobby, through another door, and down a corridor. The look changed to that of many other office buildings, work areas separated by dividers. Employees dressed in suits stood at the files or sat at the desks typing.

The scents that all government offices seemed to share blasted me—paper, ink, metal, coffee, and something else—did bureaucracy have a smell? It felt stuffy, and sweat trickled down my back.

I unzipped my sweatshirt. "I see why the government confiscated my trust account if they're too broke to run the A/C."

Connor chuckled. "You found us out."

As employees spotted me, a hush came over the place. Even the few I recognized looked at me with hostility.

We came to a bank of elevators. A too familiar scream pierced the air from a room just beyond.

Connor startled, then raced toward the sound. I rushed after him, but paused inside the entrance. Employees sat watching a television mounted on the wall. *Must be a break room.* The sobbing came from the television screen, which showed a person bound to a chair, a black hood covering his face. My dad stood over him with a stun gun in his hand. Could it be? Words scrolled across the bottom. "Warning: This segment should not be viewed by children."

My cheeks heated, and sweat moistened my palms as shame engulfed me. This was unbelievable.

Chapter 5

Friendless

"To be right is lonely when everyone else disagrees." Derrick

Derrick

Heat crept up my cheeks as I blushed. How did the news agency get that video?

The television image flashed to a ranch house, and an announcer's voice rattled excitedly, "If you're just turning in, the police raided a house this morning with terrorist activity. A law enforcement agent was found dead inside, and a video of his ordeal was recovered." They showed a press photo of Dad. "Victor Costa, millionaire founder of the 'I-Spy' company, is the prime suspect in the murder. There is a reward of $100,000 for aid in his apprehension."

The picture on the screen changed to the gate in front of the CIA headquarters. "Law enforcement agencies are combining their efforts to bring these terrorists to justice." They showed me in the car with my hood over my head. "This is Victor Costa's son being brought in for questioning."

The image flashed to the CIA's public affairs officer, Gerard, being interviewed.

"Is Victor Costa's son also a terrorist?" a woman reporter asked.

Gerard frowned. "He's definitely a person of interest."

My breath caught. Grrr. This kept getting worse. The people in the break room turned to stare menacingly at me. No one claimed to have a shred of evidence, yet they all believed me guilty? I glared back at them. Connor tugged on my arm and I followed him out. We moved past the elevator bank to a plain door with a plaque hanging above it that said "Private use only."

Connor inserted his badge into a slot next to it and placed his thumb on a plate. The lock clicked and Connor opened the door. I trailed him into a hall with another elevator. Hmmm. How many employees even knew of this elevator's existence? Connor punched a code into the numbered panel beside it, and put his eye up to the circular lens of an Iris scanner where a beam of light flickered. The elevator doors opened.

When we got on, it descended into the depths of the building, stopping at a hall lined with doors. Unlike upstairs, there were no cubicles here. A few of the doors had blue laser beams crossing in front of them.

"Why the lasers?" I asked as we walked past them.

"It's how these offices are locked if they're not occupied at the moment." Connor didn't slow until the last door. "This is where the Deputy Director will meet you."

We entered a room with a few wooden chairs, a small desk, and bare walls. Kind of plain for a Deputy Director's office. An older, petite woman dressed in a blue suit sat behind the desk.

"This is Alice, the Deputy Director's secretary," Connor explained.

"He's expecting you." Alice's tone was crusty. "Go on in."

We traipsed past her to another door. Connor knocked twice before opening it. This inner office was nicer. Several art prints, displaying scenes from around the grounds, lined the walls. The furniture was leather, and the lamps were brass.

Deputy Director Johnson and Jake shared the same tall frame, blue eyes, and blonde hair, only the Deputy Director's hair appeared more gray than blonde today. His face was drawn, and his body sagged in the chair behind his large desk. Not surprising with the news of Kurt's death.

Jake was sprawled out on the couch. He sat up as Deputy Director Johnson motioned to a couple of chairs.

"Connor, Derrick, take a seat."

I needed to say something, but what? Maybe the truth?

"I'm really sorry about Kurt, Sir."

The Deputy Director's sad eyes locked onto me. "Me too. So what do you know about these terrorists?"

"Nothing."

He scrutinized me. "If that's true, I won't blame you for Victor's actions."

"My Dad wouldn't do this, Sir." Somehow, I had to prove it. "That clip on the news was when Dad trained Kurt and me on Resistance to Interrogation."

The Deputy Director's lips pinched. "You're not on the tape."

"They must have cut me out." My cheeks warmed. I hated to admit it. "Except for the screams. Those were mine, not Kurt's. He never broke." Deputy Director Johnson's brow arched. My heart sank. "You don't believe me?"

"I'd never ask an agent to give R2I training to their son because most couldn't. But regardless, that clip is one thing in a huge stack of evidence." He rested his arms on the desk. "Your dad will receive a fair trial, but regardless of the outcome, agencies won't forget those images. A cloud of suspicion will hang over you both, and the career you wanted won't happen." He leaned forward. "I can erase that cloud over you and release your trust so you don't have to go to a group home. All I need is for you to prove you're not involved—by helping us bring your dad in."

A trial would make Dad a 'graymail', a defendant who could divulge intelligence secrets. I wasn't naïve enough to believe the Company would risk that. "Why did you allow this to go public? Are you trying to justify authorizing a forced disappearance so you can detain Dad, or are you hoping he'll be gunned down?"

A muscle in the Deputy Director's jaw ticked. He frowned.

It appeared as if I could be right. My spirits sank. "I'll do anything I can to prove Dad's innocence, but I won't help you kill him."

Jake moved forward to perch on the edge of the couch. "I told you. Derrick's always been a maverick. He thinks he knows everything, but he's just a spoiled rich kid who doesn't know squat."

Jealous much, Jake? To turn on me now. What a jerk.

"You're not exactly poor." I met the Deputy Director's stony gaze. "If you took our possessions because you resent what we have, I've got news for you. You could put Dad naked on a desert island, and he'd still be wealthier than you."

The Deputy Director removed a picture from his wallet and slammed it on the desk face-up. It was Kurt. "I'm not letting your dad live like a king while we bury Kurt in the ground."

My heart squeezed as I thought of Kurt. "Accusing the innocent doesn't serve justice."

A pulse throbbed in Jake's neck as he stood and shouted, "Your sister's lucky she was kidnapped." Spittle flew from his mouth. "At least she escaped you and your dad."

Blood pounded in my ears. I rose and took a step toward Jake. The nails of my clenched fists pricked my palms. "If you hadn't just lost Kurt, I'd feed those words back to you with a straw after I broke your jaw."

"Enough!" The Deputy Director pointed to the couch and barked, "Sit down, Jake."

Jake collapsed, slumping into the leather. The Deputy Director's eyes hardened as he turned back to me. "Law enforcement agencies consider you a person of interest, so you won't be allowed admittance to the Bureau's camp or Kurt's funeral."

Wait. I couldn't even tell Kurt goodbye? The ache in my heart sharpened. Did he really believe I was a threat?

"Are you adding me to the terrorist watch list?"

The Deputy Director's posture stiffened. "Since you're refusing to cooperate, you've left me no choice. Your dad's already on it."

My gut clenched. Would Dad's alias hold up?

"It could be a while before a social worker comes for you." The Deputy Director pointed to the door. "You can wait at the front gate."

Should I go to that group home? It might allow me to gather more Intel if I did.

Connor stood. "I can take Derrick to Fallentier."

The Deputy Director shook his head. "You need to go to Costa's home since you know his employees. Make it clear they won't be needed anymore."

My heart flopped. Our cook, Shen, our maid, Maria, our

groundskeeper, Omar, and our guards, Ivan and Luis, weren't only staff, they were friends. What would happen to them and their families without jobs? And what about Dad's other employees? Would the government dismantle his company?

Dad had good attorneys, but would he want me to sue the government? No, and that's not what I needed to focus on. I had to find out who framed him and gather the evidence to clear him. If I helped Dad, that would help our employees.

I opened the door and glanced back. "When Dad's name's cleared, I'll expect all of our things returned and an apology." I slammed the door and rushed past the secretary into the hall.

A lump rose in my throat, and tears threatened to fall. I didn't want to give them the satisfaction of seeing me fall apart on the security cameras. I drew a few deep breaths and pushed down my emotions. A little calmness returned, enough to straighten my face.

While I waited for the elevator, Connor caught up and followed me on. "I'll take you to the guard shack, and if you're still here when I get back, I'll drive you to Fallentier,"

After the elevator dinged and the doors opened, I followed Connor back through the halls to the lobby. As we walked through, I didn't gape. It had lost its sheen for me. This would probably be the last time I came here, but I only felt relief as we left the building and moved toward the SUV.

Connor shot me a smile as he unlocked his vehicle. Now he wanted to act friendly? I needed a friend back there. He hadn't helped me defend Dad at all.

I climbed into the back seat as Connor got under the wheel. My pet Sugar Glider, Pip, poked his head out from under the seat and scurried up my pants to my pocket. I petted him.

Whoever framed Dad had to be someone close to us to get their hands on that video footage. Could Connor be involved? Pip could find out more, but I'd need to make sure I'd see Connor later so I could retrieve my pet.

"If I leave my duffle in here, can you bring it to that home if I'm gone?"

"Sure." Connor took his cell phone from his inside shirt pocket.

"Thanks."

While Connor scrolled through his contacts, I pressed the spot on Pip's collar to turn his bug on, snaked my hand for surveillance, gently squeezed his ear for stealth mode, pointed to Connor, and put him on the floor. Pip scurried up the seat and beside Connor.

Connor was talking on his phone. "I'm bringing Derrick Costa back to wait for a ride."

Pip made his move, climbing into Connor's suit pocket. I fished my sunglasses out of my duffel and stuck one of Pip's food pellets on top before zipping it. If anyone rifled through it, they'd dislodge the pellet.

Connor hung up, and brought the SUV to a stop at the SPS post. He lowered the windows to talk to an SPS officer. "We need Derrick's things."

The officer handed me my necklace, belt, and boots. "Our policy is to confiscate weapons, so your multi-tool won't be returned."

I wouldn't consider it much of a weapon. They must have x-rayed my boots to find my heel compartment. Since I was a person of interest, now, I better expect them to exert themselves. They probably planted at least one GPS tracker in my things, and they'd be tracing my phone.

As I shoved my feet in my boots, Connor drove to Langley's front gate where the Marines were stationed.

"I'll drop you here," he said.

Two Marines moved toward the car. I put my sunglasses on and climbed out. As the Marines flanked me, Connor drove away. They escorted me to a chair they set inside the guard shack, and took positions next to me. I tried to analyze what information I'd learned. Hard to concentrate with people standing over me. The minutes crept by, each one too long.

I wanted to leave. Maybe I should call a taxi. Wouldn't that put a big dent in my cash? It would be worth it to get out of here. I retrieved my phone from my pocket, switched on the Wi-Fi and locator, and spoke into it.

"Siri, call the closest taxi company."

My screen faded to black. It was fully charged, so why did it do that?

I punched the three digits for our provider and got a recording. "This account is closed. To reactivate service, please hold for a representative."

The government shut off my phone? I hung up. With my service off, they could still hack me, so I switched off the locator before shoving it in my pocket. I'd have to walk and find a bus stop.

What if the press swarmed me again? Did it matter now? No law enforcement agency would hire someone on the watch list. My future as a spy was over.

"If someone will open the gate, I'll leave." When I walked out of the shack, a big burly man pulled up to the gate in a sedan.

"I'm here for Derrick Costa," he announced.

With his unlined face, I'd estimate him in his mid-twenties, but the rigid posture, short hair, and calloused hands seemed wrong for a social worker. What did he want with me?

Chapter 6

Alone

"Nothing lasts. Everything's temporary." Gina

Gina

You never get something for nothing. I sat alone on the school bus. Friends cost too high a price—tears. I wouldn't pay the cost of involvement anymore—the heartache of being torn from someone I cared about. I'd take lonely over heartbreak.

Most of the other kids were jabbering excitedly. They were happy school dismissed early today. I wasn't. School was better than spending more time at my foster home.

I slung my book bag over my shoulder as the bus pulled over and stopped. The driver let me out at the corner since my foster home was on a dead end street. I rose and walked down the aisle.

A kid stuck his foot out into the lane, and I stumbled over it. I shot him a glare. "Jerk."

He laughed. "Are all foster kids clumsy?"

Why did foster parents broadcast to everyone their good deed? I kicked his shin.

"Crap." He grabbed his leg.

"Oops. Sorry, I'm so clumsy."

The driver hollered, "Hurry it up, Gina."

"I'm coming."

I got off the bus and walked up the deserted street. The neighborhood only held decrepit homes with peeling paint and sagging roofs. The houses had been decent once, but those days were long past. Now only a few were occupied, like the yellow ranch that was my foster home.

Two cars were parked in the driveway. Not good. Mary's boyfriend, Fred, worked at a factory, and his hours must have been cut again for him to be home this early. Mary hadn't worked since he moved in because he was too controlling and didn't let her. The money the state paid her wasn't enough to cure their financial woes, so I'd probably be moving soon.

Technically, she wasn't even supposed to have a boyfriend living with us without the state doing a background check on him, but I wasn't going to rat her out. There would be no point anyway. I'd just lose a foster home. No one picked a foster kid over their significant other.

At a whimpering sound, I stopped in my tracks. Was something in trouble?

Another pleading whine came. Desperate. Was it coming from the storm grate? I bent to check. It was dark inside the drain, but I made out a lumpy shadow. Part of the shadow lifted—the head of a puppy. Sad, soulful eyes locked on me as its body shook with fright or excitement.

"Poor thing. How did you get in there?"

The puppy looked maybe two or three months old. It whimpered again, but it didn't rise to its feet. Was it hurt?

I tried to lift the grate, but it was either locked or stuck. There was a narrow opening between it and the curb. I lay next to it and reached in with my arm. What if a snake was down there too? I shuddered but kept searching. My hand brushed a soft paw.

The foot jerked back from me.

I'd extended my arm as far as I could. "I won't hurt you, little guy. Come here, and I'll get you out," I crooned.

Some scrabbling sounded, then a damp nose sniffed my hand. "Good puppy."

It whined, then inched up. I petted it reassuringly, slid my hand under its damp belly, and lifted it out. The nasty odor of something rotten mixed with wet dog assaulted my nose. I moved back from the road to put the puppy on the overgrown lawn.

He was a male and had a short, scruffy coat that was a mishmash of different colors. There were shades of brown with gray and silver mottling that blended in with some white patches on his feet, chest, and nose.

One of my foster moms owned a couple of show poodles. When she figured out kids didn't easily follow commands and there'd be no ribbons, she stopped fostering, but I learned a little about dogs.

I didn't think he'd get very big. His paws weren't, and his length was only a little more than my foot. When I ran my hands over his bony body, I didn't feel anything broken. I found a few scratches, but nothing looked serious. Probably just weak from lack of food. Obviously, he hadn't had much care.

"Were you unwanted too?"

My heart tugged at me to help him, but how? Mary and Fred wouldn't let me keep him, but maybe I could hide him long enough to find him a home.

I picked him up again and cut through the yard to the garage off the alley. The overhead door was damaged and didn't open. One of the projects Fred claimed he'd get to, but hadn't yet. The side door didn't work much better. I turned the handle and shoved the door with my shoulder. It opened enough to let me slide inside to the gloom of the interior.

The scents of oil, gasoline, and fertilizer wafted to me. The smell seemed to come from the boxes stacked on wire shelves. Hmmm. Last time I snooped in them, I only found junk like broken remotes and old clocks. Nothing else was in the garage except for a work bench with some tools on it. The fumes weren't so strong as to be unsafe for the puppy and since Fred seldom left his computer, he shouldn't find him in here.

I sat the puppy down. "Stay here. I'll be back as soon as I get some stuff for you."

I brushed off my clothing, but much of the soil from the puppy remained. After I cut around the yard to the front of the house, I steeled myself and plodded inside. The living room's furniture revealed the home's decline. The black vinyl couch showed wear cracks, stains marred the wooden desk, and the coffee table in front of the couch had a wobbly leg—the result of Fred's last drinking bout. Only the flat screen computer on the desk was new—bought with the check Mary had received from the state for my care.

Fred sat at the desk. His cheap cologne didn't mask the choking odor of smoke coming from the overflowing ashtray. He took a swig of his beer, licked his thin black mustache, then glanced at me before waving at his monitor.

"Look at that. Someone else the government took advantage of."

I didn't bother to find out what he was going on about. Fred seemed to expect the internet to make him happy, but it only gave him more to gripe about. His rants included a ton of subjects, everything from politics to the way women dressed. I tuned it all out.

My petite foster mother came bustling in, carrying a sack. "Oh good, Gina. You're home. Look what I found shopping." Mary reached into a sack from a local thrift store and pulled out a pink dress with lacy frills.

Mary wore plain blouses and skirts, and that dress would be too long for her short frame. It must be for me.

I groaned to myself. With my dark black hair, green eyes, and tanned skin, wearing pink would look like Pepto Bismol spilled on a Graham cracker.

"I told you I don't wear dresses."

She waved the dress in front of me. "But the homecoming dance is Saturday. You have to wear one to that."

I crossed my arms. "I'm not going."

Mary had a face that was too long, and it dropped even farther as her chin fell. "Not going?"

Why did people think foster kids were one size fits all, and we could fulfill all their dreams? Whether they wanted an athlete, a genius, or something else, we'd be that thing. Was there as a foster kid catalog I wasn't aware of? Had Mary ordered a pageant girl?

Faking being something I wasn't never worked, so I didn't bother anymore. I never even unpacked. Foster kids were exchangeable.

Fred held out his empty bottle. "Mary, I need a refill."

Mary's voice quaked. "That was the last."

"You can spend money on dresses for your foster kid, but not pick up my beer?" he barked.

"I'll get some." She grabbed her purse.

I shook my head. Why did Mary act like a mouse and do whatever Fred told her? As she left the house, I hurried to my bedroom.

I wrinkled my nose at the pink walls, the narrow bed, and small white dresser. Had Mary thought she'd be getting a five-year-old?

I was long past wanting replacement parents, but I couldn't afford to be stupid. The streets weren't a good place to live. Every month, I received another $50—the state mandated allowance—from the funds Mary received for my care. I saved almost all of it. When I aged out, I'd have enough to pay for an apartment until I could get a job.

I rifled through my garbage bag with my belongings until I found the thread worn blanket I'd dragged around for years. The only thing I had left from when I lived with Mom. Maybe it was time to let go of it. I emptied my book bag, stuffed the blanket inside, and crept out to the living room. There was a knock at the door. Fred stomped over, cracked open the door, and began to talk to whoever was there. While he was distracted, I slipped into the kitchen.

I opened the refrigerator to examine the skimpy contents. Milk, condiments, and some Jell-O. Nothing good for a puppy. A quick search in the cupboards found a half loaf of bread and some canned goods. One was spam. A puppy should be able to eat that. I grabbed the can and two plastic bowls that used to hold whipped cream. I filled one with water. After using the metal piece on top to fold the spam lid back, I dumped the meat in the other bowl, put the lids on the bowls, placed them in my rucksack, and snuck out the back door.

When I opened the side door of the garage, the puppy waddled weakly to me. I sat the bowls down for him. He dived into the spam, gulping it up. When he finished the meat, he lapped up the water, then scampered around me.

"You sure sprang back fast. You're a toughie, aren't you?"

He gave me a little yip.

"You like that? All right, I'll call you Tuffy."

When I took the blanket out of my rucksack, I couldn't resist rubbing it against my face. Any scent from Mom had disappeared long ago. Tuffy grabbed a corner of the blanket in his teeth and tugged.

"Okay, Tuffy. I guess you need this more than me."

Tuffy released the blanket and gave me another little joyful yip as if to say, "Thanks."

I spread the blanket under the tool bench for him and put his bowls at the top. He scooted under the bench to sniff and paw them. Since he didn't act half-dead anymore, would he get himself into trouble? Maybe I could fix up something to put in front of the bench so he'd be confined and hidden if anyone came in.

I heard muffled words from outside. A couple of male voices. One sounded like Fred's. Was he coming in?

The door rattled. Shoot. He'd want to know what I was doing in here. I rolled under the workbench with Tuffy. The door flew open.

"...a killing," Fred said as I heard his heavy tread. The smell of his cheap cologne wafted to me.

All I could see from under the bench was his work boots, then a pair of men's black shoes as someone followed him inside.

"That should eliminate any trouble," the stranger said.

My spine tingled. It sounded as if they were discussing a murder. I had enough street smarts to know certain things will get you killed—like ripping off a drug dealer, getting between a pimp and his prostitute, or letting a gang catch you in their territory. Oh yeah, and knowing too much about a murder. If Fred or this other guy discovered me in here, I could end up dead.

My heart sped up and hammered in my chest. Tuffy whined.

Oh no! I grabbed his muzzle, trying to keep him quiet

"Did you hear something?" Fred asked.

Chapter 7

Assault

"I fight to survive so there's only one rule—to win." Gina

Gina

My heart was in my throat. If Fred and his friend searched, they'd find me and the puppy. There wasn't anywhere but under the workbench someone could hide. I petted Tuffy's head, hoping he'd keep quiet. The gasoline fumes should mask his odor.

"Fred," Mary hollered.

"It's my old lady." Fred's boots clomped toward the side door. "I'll get rid of her." A thunk revealed he opened it. "What?"

"I got your beer," she answered.

"Well, it's about time," Fred barked. "I'm busy. Put it in the fridge."

Mary harrumphed, then the screen door slammed closed at the house.

Fred's boots turned back to the guy with the black shoes. "You have the money?" he asked.

"Yeah." I heard the soft sound of paper rustling. "It's all there." The guy in the black shoes moved around Fred then stopped. "I'll be in touch."

Then the guy in the shoes left. A second later, Fred tromped outside too.

Whew. That was a close call. I released Tuffy and rolled out from under the workbench. If Fred was conducting illicit meetings in this garage, I didn't want to be hanging around in here. I'd have to hide

Tuffy somewhere else. I packed Tuffy's bowls in my book bag as he ran around me. I picked him up, opened the door, and began to sidle out.

Something slammed into me from the other side. Fred. Tuffy was thrown out of my arms, landing outside. The puppy scrambled away as I stumbled back into the garage, crashing into the workbench.

Fred rushed in after me. "I thought I heard someone." His thick arms shot out on both sides of me, trapping me against the workbench. His breath gagged me as he leaned closer. "Being too nosy is a problem that needs solved."

Would he kill me? I couldn't get much leverage with him practically on top of me, but I kneed him.

He hollered, then wrapped his fingers in my hair and yanked me to the floor. He jumped on top of me, straddling me.

I twisted and bucked, clawed at his arms, and pummeled his back with my knees. Then I heard the screen door of the house.

Mary hollered, "Gina."

With Fred's weight squashing my breath from me, my scream, "Mary," came out muffled.

Even if she heard me, would she help me against Fred? Doubtful, and he might kill her too. I had to help myself. I flailed my hands and feet, but to no avail.

I desperately searched for anything I could use. There was a cord hanging down from the bench. I reached over and pulled it. A metal power drill crashed onto the floor. I grabbed it, then swung it at Fred with all my might. The shock reverberated up my arm as the drill hit Fred's head with a thud. He collapsed on top of me. Struggling to breathe, I pushed him with all my strength. He fell on the floor with a thump. Blood oozed from a gash on his head, but his chest was rising and falling. Must be knocked out. As the shock wore off, I shook with relief. I was safe and I hadn't killed anyone.

Mary rushed in the garage and hurried to Fred. Her eyes flashed angrily at me.

"What did you do to him?"

"He… he came after me," I breathlessly gasped. "So I defended myself."

Mary gave me a desperate, defeated look. "He might kill us both."

My mind spun as I picked myself off the floor. "I'm leaving. You should get away from him too."

I fled out of the garage with my heart pounding. I looked for Tuffy, but I didn't see him anywhere. Poor little guy must be frightened.

"Here Tuffy, here," I called. "Come here, puppy."

Not even a whimper sounded. I checked the storm drain, but Tuffy wasn't there. My heart ached for him, but I didn't dare waste more time searching. Fred could wake any second. Hopefully, Tuffy would find someone else to care for him.

I ran to the house and then to my room. My mind screamed at me. *Get out of here fast.* I grabbed my garbage bag that held my belongings and raced back outside.

After running for three blocks, I checked over my shoulder again, but no one pursued me. There still wasn't any sign of Tuffy. I stopped to catch my breath and pulled out my cell phone. I'd try not to rat Mary out. I wouldn't tell my social worker about Fred living there, but I had to tell her the rest. I needed out of here.

When I called, I got her recording, so I left a message. "Lila, its Gina. This guy Mary knows, Fred, he tried to kill me. You need to come get me at the convenience store on the corner of 8th and Elm."

***

My butt was getting sore sitting on the concrete sidewalk with my back propped against the side of the convenience store. Ouch. I took my fingers out of my mouth. I'd chewed my nails to the quick while I waited. It wasn't the first time my social worker took over an hour to come.

Worry gnawed at my gut as I replayed the incident over and over in my mind. Maybe I shouldn't have left Mary there alone. What would Fred do to her? Police cars and an ambulance had screamed past a while ago. Mary must have called them. I sure hadn't.

A skinny guy that worked at the store came out with a bag of trash and, after throwing it in the dumpster, looked over at me.

I took another sip of my fountain drink. I only bought it because he said I had to buy something to wait here. Would he say I had to purchase something else? I didn't want to waste more money. I wiggled my toes and felt the rolls of cash stuffed above my size seven feet in my size eight shoes.

"Still waiting for your ride?" he asked.

"Yeah, she must have gotten held up, but she'll be here."

He frowned, but shuffled back in. A police cruiser turned into the convenience store. My breath caught. Were they after me? They didn't have their siren on. Maybe they needed coffee?

The police car pulled up right next to me, and two cops climbed out. "Are you Gina?" the closest asked.

I nodded. "My case worker shouldn't have called you. I'm not going to press charges against Fred."

If I did that, they might go after Mary for child endangerment. I didn't want to cause her more problems.

The cop's forehead creased. "Uh, okay." His tone became authoritative. "We still need you to come with us. Your caseworker will meet us at the station when she can."

Lila probably had more than one emergency, but I'd have waited longer. She didn't have to send these guys to get me. I hated hanging out with cops.

I stood and, after picking up my garbage bag, took a couple of steps toward them. When I got close, he grabbed my arm and pushed me against the cruiser's door.

"Hey, what are you doing?"

"Drop the bag and put your hands up," he ordered.

I dropped my stuff and placed my hands on the car. "That bag has all my belongings in it, and they better not be damaged."

The other cop came over and frisked me. My heart pounded in my chest so hard it hurt, but I refused to show my fear.

Instead, I blasted them. "Did you enjoy feeling me up?"

"Shut up," he said and grabbed my wrists to zip-tie them together.

"Is this how you usually treat victims?" I asked sarcastically.

He pulled me back by my arms, then opened the door of the cruiser. "You're under arrest for felony assault with malicious wounding. You have the right to remain silent. Anything you say can be used against you in a court of law…"

I tuned him out. I'd heard the fairy tale before. Rights only worked for those with the money to ensure them, and hope was for saps with real families. Ugh. I was in for it.

***

When we arrived at the police station, one of the cops escorted me to a door with a sign, "Interview room 3." He tugged me inside. Fluorescent lights spotlighted a few metal chairs around a steel table, all bolted to the floor. A camera and huge mirror hung on opposite walls. Was the mirror one of those two-way ones that allowed other cops to watch the room?

He barked at me, "Turn around."

When I did, he removed my handcuffs and pointed to a chair. "Sit down."

"Didn't anyone ever teach you to say please?" I snapped.

"Please," he snarled.

I sat. He motioned toward the door. "When someone's ready to talk to you, they'll be in." Then he left.

When I sprang up to check the door, it was locked. I must have fidgeted for an hour before a balding cop with a mustache and glasses finally came into the interview room carrying a folder.

Something about him looked familiar. He seated himself on the other side of the table and said, "My name is Detective Brown."

Was anyone else watching us? I waved at the mirror.

The detective snorted. "No one cares about seeing me interview another punk kid." He opened his folder and shuffled through it. "This isn't the first time you've had assault charges leveled against you. You seem to have made a habit of it."

I crossed my arms. "I make a habit of defending myself from people who want to murder me."

"So that's your story?" he asked.

"It's the truth. I overheard him discussing a murder, so he wanted to off me."

"Humph." He flipped a page. "The victim was conscious at the hospital and gave a statement before he was rushed into surgery. According to him, he and his friend were discussing making a *'killing'* at work when he won their gambling pool, not a murder. He said he was trying to explain to you that it was wrong to eavesdrop when you went crazy and attacked him."

"He was the one who dragged me to the floor."

"He claimed he was trying to restrain you from hurting him further. The only marks I see on you is bruising on your fists. Do you have any other injuries?"

"My back's sore."

"He has scratches, bruises, and a bashed head to support his story."

I shook my head. "He was going to kill me."

His eyebrow arched. "I think you were mistaken about his intent."

Could I have messed up? I was good at reading people, so I didn't think so.

He leaned forward. "Before I became a detective, I was a patrol officer. We were at your old house a lot, but you were much younger."

My stomach flopped. That's why he looked familiar. "I'm not like my mom. I don't do drugs that make me paranoid so I think people are after me."

"Mental illness isn't always drug related. Sometimes it's genetic."

I knew that, and it terrified me to think I could go nuts too. Could my sanity be slipping? No. I wasn't going to believe that.

Anger rushed up in me. "I'm. Not. Crazy."

"I didn't say you were."

"You implied it." I leaned back in the chair and changed the subject. "So why did Fred need surgery?"

"His brain swelled. Now he's in a coma. You better hope he recovers, because even though you're sixteen, they could decide to try you as an adult. And with your record—" He slammed the folder down on the table. "—there's a good chance you'll get prison time."

My heart fell to my toes. A knock came at the door.

The detective walked over to open it. Two guys stood there. One was a few inches taller than the other, but both wore dark suits and sunglasses.

"I'm conducting an interview," the detective snarled.

The taller guy in the suit flashed him a badge. "We'll take over.

You can go."

The detective said to the other guys as he left, "Good luck finding out the truth."

"Gina?" The taller one asked as they came in and shut the door.

"Yeah. Who are you?"

"You can call me Parker." He motioned to the other guy. "And this is Jax. But it's not who we are that's important. What *is* important is that we can make the charges against you disappear if you're willing to help us."

I'd known kids who had worked with cops, even made up stuff to save themselves. That had never been me. "I hate Narcs."

"Maybe you think you'd like prison?" The shorter guy asked.

The thought of being caged was making my skin crawl. "No."

"We'll give you some time to consult a lawyer and talk to your cell mates about what prison is like. We'll come back tomorrow for an answer." He strode to the door and spoke to the detective. "Lock her up."

My spine curled, and my body turned to rubber as dread flooded through me. I sagged in my chair. Then I got angry at myself. I was tough, wasn't I? Couldn't I handle anything?

Chapter 8

Homesick

"Home isn't a place, but a sense of security. I'll always be homeless now." Derrick

Derrick

I cracked open my window, letting warm air flood into the rear seat of the black sedan.

The burly stranger who'd introduced himself as Sam Becker spun his chiseled jaw to glance at me. His body could pass for a football lineman's, but his square face and short nose gave him a bulldog look. He claimed he was my new cottage father, whatever that was.

"What are you doing?" he asked.

"I'm feeling a little sick." Like in *sick* of the CIA ripping up my stuff. I'd already removed a GPS tracker and listening bug from slits they'd cut in my boots and belt.

"Are you nauseous? Should I pull over?" Sam probably thought I'd been holding my gut as I worked the tracker out of my belt.

"I just need a few minutes of fresh air."

When Sam returned his scrutiny to the road, I stuck my arm out long enough to toss the bug and tracker onto the flatbed truck passing us, then closed my window.

The CIA wasn't the only ones who could play the eavesdrop game. I reached inside the arm of my sunglasses to pull down a smaller extension that held my earpiece. If Sam spotted the flexible arm, he wouldn't know what it did. I adjusted it over my ear to listen to the bug my pet Sugar Glider, Pip, carried.

Connor's smooth voice poured into my ear. "You needed me?"

he asked someone.

"Yes," responded an unfamiliar, gravelly voice. "Come in, and take a seat."

I heard footsteps, then the creak of a chair. "Do you think Costa's son is a threat?" the rough voice asked.

"No," Connor responded. "I'm certain Derrick was as shocked as I was to learn about the allegations."

"Then this could be an opportunity to acquire the asset we need," the other man said.

My heart leapt. Was I still being considered by an agency? Maybe my career as a spy wasn't over.

"I don't think he's a good choice," Connor retorted.

What? Why would Connor say that?

I heard papers shuffling. "His tradecraft impressed the Bureau instructors at camp," the rough voice said.

"His skills aren't the problem," Connor replied. "He's too independent. We need a team player. Besides, the CIA considers him persona non grata."

Grrr. Connor was shooting down any chance I had.

"It's not the CIA's call," the other guy said.

Was Connor working for another agency?

The guy's voice crackled in my ear again. "Maybe you're too close to him."

"I admit there's a conflict of interest," came Connor's soft reply.

"Don't work directly with him, then, but we still need to know where his loyalties will lie. Inform his family."

"That could destroy our relationship. He's already lost so much." Connor's clipped words left no doubt he felt angry.

"I wouldn't ask for me, but it's for the country."

"Fine," Connor snapped. "Are we through here, Director?"

A director. Of what?

"For now."

A chair scraped, followed by steps. A car door opened and shut, an engine started. Connor must be headed elsewhere. Their conversation had been bewildering. I'd caught someone's interest, but to what end?

I tucked my ear piece back into my sunglasses as we came to the outskirts of the city. Sam exited the highway.

"Do you have any questions about the rules?" he asked as we passed a truck stop.

I looked at the paper he'd given me. *Respect and obey the staff. No drug or alcohol use. No stealing. No fighting. No weapons. No swearing. No gang involvement. No leaving the grounds without approval.* The last one could be a problem.

I folded the paper and stuck it in my back pocket. "I don't have questions."

"Good," he said as we passed a neighborhood. "Fallentier is the last stop before Juvie since every kid here has a string of offenses on their record."

"I don't have a record."

"No, but you're a terror suspect. There are places worse than Juvie, so follow the rules. Three violations or strikes as we say, and you're out. Only, I don't know where they'd send you."

How much did he know? Was he trying to imply I'd end up in a CIA prison? I'd run first. Sam turned the car onto a lane with a dead end sign and slowed considerably on the narrow road lined with trees. As he twisted the wheel back and forth to maneuver around potholes, his rigid shoulders screamed to me military background. Should I ask? Patience wasn't one of my strengths.

I leaned forward over the seat so I could watch him. "How does a guy with a military background end up as a cottage father, or is that a front for you?"

His eyes widened, and his mouth dropped open. With that reaction, it appeared as if I'd called it right. Cottage father wasn't his only job.

He chuckled, but it seemed forced. "No. After shrapnel from an IUD messed up my left leg, I was discharged. I took this job because when I lived in a group home, a veteran on the staff tutored me so I'd pass my ASVAB test and get accepted in the military. When I asked how I could pay him back, he said pass it on. I'm trying to do that."

His sincerity convinced me that part was true, but was there more to the story? "So you think you can get some Fallentier kids in the military?"

He snorted. "Not with their records. The standards are stricter now."

We'd traveled down the rough road a couple miles. Right before it dead ended, a drive wound to the left. A dilapidated gray sign marked it with Fallentier group home printed in brown lettering, but someone painted a black stripe over 'tier' so the sign read Fallen group home.

Sam turned into the drive. A fence with coiled wire on the top enclosed the grounds. Lights and cameras were mounted near the gate. For something that was supposed to be a group home, it sure looked like a prison.

Sam pulled the car to a stop near a brick column with a camera lens and speaker. He lowered his window. Warm air blasted us as he stuck his hand out and pushed the button. "It's Sam with the new kid, Derrick Costa."

The speaker crackled with static. A voice squawked, "I'll open up."

The gates slowly swung back to reveal a guard shack. Beyond it, a long drive led to an imposing older, two-story, brick building with black shuttered windows. Several smaller concrete-block buildings squatted around the bigger one. The only thing that didn't look dismal were the trees and grass on the grounds.

"For safety reasons, the guards need to search you," Sam said.

Yup, a prison all right. A lanky guy wearing a blue uniform with a security badge came out of the guard shack. A side arm and stun gun were attached to his belt.

"Get out of the car and place your hands on the hood," he ordered.

I opened the door and scooted out slowly to reluctantly comply.

After the guard patted me down, he said, "You can get back in."

As soon as I closed my door, Sam drove to one of the concrete bunker-like buildings. "This is cottage five. Your new home."

Chilly needles of apprehension prickled me. A longing for my old home hit me with such force that my eyes misted. I ducked my head, breathed in deep, then exhaled a few counts longer to calm myself.

Sam stiffly climbed out, betraying his leg injury. "You'll be fine as long as you follow those rules." He stuck his head back in. "Coming?"

What choice did I have? Sitting in the car wouldn't change anything. How bad could it be?

FEARLESS   by Terri Luckey   p57

Chapter 9

Fallentier

"Anywhere that restricts freedom is a prison." Derrick.

Derrick

When I jumped out of Sam's sedan, the day's heat blasted me. A whirr sounded as the fan of the air-conditioner alongside the concrete building sprang to life. At least the place had air-conditioning.

I followed Sam as he strode quickly inside. His limp didn't seem to slow him much.

He waved a hand at the room. "This is the common area for television and computer use. There aren't any kitchens in the cottages. Meals are eaten in the main building's cafeteria."

Cheap wood paneling covered most of the walls. Did someone actually try to make this look like an awful imitation of a cabin? On my right, some orange plastic chairs circled an old-fashioned console box television. To the left, two computers that looked like they came from the age of Atari sat at a work station consisting of two planks attached to the wall with L brackets. Four folding chairs were pushed underneath.

Sam shuffled through the common area to a hall with several doors. "There are six bedrooms with two bunks for you kids..." he pointed to the first door on the left ...and this one's my room." He waved down the hall. "There's an emergency exit at the end, but it's alarmed. Bathrooms are in the middle of two rooms, so four kids share them." He flung open the first door on the right. "This is your room."

More like a cell. The room couldn't be larger than eight by eight.

Pushed up against the longer walls were beds the size of cots with a thin mattress. Those took up most of the room, leaving a small walkway. Two metal lockers were crammed between the top of the beds. Beneath the beds, only three-feet of space lay before the wall, where another door stood slightly ajar. I glimpsed a tiny bathroom with a standing shower, toilet, clothes hamper, and an adjoining door to the other kid's room.

"Uh hum."

At the sound of a throat clearing, I pivoted. A white kid with brown hair and a wiry frame stood in the doorway. The smattering of freckles across his nose gave him an innocent appearance but his blue eyes betrayed it. They seemed as haunted as the eyes of a combat veteran.

His gaze fixed on Sam. "Ms. McCaffry said I should show the new kid around and she needs to talk to you."

"How come you're here early?" Sam asked.

"My social worker picked me up from school to talk to me. She just left."

At Sam's frown, the kid shrugged and said, "I doubt she'll stay interested. It's the first time I met with her this year."

Why was having a social worker do their job a bad thing? Were they hiding something?

Sam looked at me, then motioned toward the other guy. "This is your roommate, Sneaker."

Huh? What mother names their kid after a shoe?

Sneaker smirked. "It's my street name. The staff here lets us use them."

Sneaker must have read my surprise. After all the time I spent working on keeping my expression neutral, it was another discouragement to add to the mountain of them today.

"What's your street name?" he asked.

"I don't have one."

"Shouldn't have said that." Sam grinned. "He'll stick you with one."

"I'd rather choose my own."

Sneaker stepped inside the room. "That's not how it works. You have to take a label someone wanted to hurt you with and make it your own. It's the ultimate payback."

Sam looked at his watch. "Sneaker will give you the tour and answer your questions. Let me know if you have any problems."

Sam seemed nice, but I was still suspicious of him. "I'll be okay."

He gave me a nod before limping out. I turned to Sneaker. "How did you get your street name?"

"Our administrator here, Ms. McCaffry, thought the fencing would keep kids from running away, but I've been in institutions a long time and sometimes need a break. My last group home didn't even report my disappearances since they knew I'd show back up in a few days." Sneaker smiled. "When I proved Ms. McCaffry wrong, she called me a sneak, among other things, so everyone started calling me Sneaker."

Hmm. Could I convince him to share the best ways to escape? "Someone did label me earlier today. They called me Maverick."

"I like it. It fits you."

"You don't even know me."

Sneaker chuckled. "No, but showing up in a group home with $300 jeans and custom boots tells me you aren't afraid to be different."

Sneaker was dressed in shorts and a t-shirt whose faded colors betrayed them as well worn. I hadn't known where I was headed when I chose the duffel of clothing packed for the Bureau's camp.

Heat flushed my cheeks. "I didn't pick out the clothes. My tutor said I needed to dress for success."

He cracked up laughing. "Do you think it's working?"

I laughed too. "I'm here, aren't I?"

As Sneaker waved at one of the lockers and said, "That's for your things," I spotted the puckered white line of a scar that ran from his wrist to his forearm.

"My bag will be dropped off later. Do we get a lock?"

"No. Keep anything valuable on you."

"I consider it all valuable since it's all I have."

"I get it, but carrying it will make you a target. They don't normally steal clothes. Keep cash and jewelry on you, but don't keep your wallet in your back pocket. There are more pickpockets in here than San Quentin."

Dad taught me to carry a wallet only as a decoy. My ID and cash was in my front pocket. It was still nice of Sneaker to warn me.

We traipsed back into the hall. The heat blasted me as we exited the air-conditioned cottage.

"Guys are assigned one of the five cottages." As we walked toward the main brick building, Sneaker motioned to it. "On the first floor is the cafeteria and the offices for the staff and nurse. The second floor is where classes will be. The girls' rooms are up there too. We only have a couple girls since it's easier to find foster homes to take them."

We turned down the side of the building and passed some vending machines. Sneaker stopped at a patch of concrete with a basketball hoop without a net.

"This is our basketball court."

"Impressive."

"So what brought a rich kid here?" he asked.

Did he think I'd share everything within minutes of meeting? "I'd rather not talk about it. What about you?"

"My parents are in prison serving life sentences."

"Really?"

Sneaker chortled. "I have no idea. They relinquished me when I was a baby, so it's not like I remember them."

When we moved behind the main building, he pointed to a low area on the grounds that held a puddle of water. "This is our pool, but it's only here if it rains."

"Lovely." There was another structure in the back of the property. It had a screen of trees around it, so I couldn't tell much. More fencing separated it from the rest of the grounds. I caught a glimpse of a guard inside the gate. "What's in that building?" I asked.

Sneaker rubbed the back of his neck, usually a sign someone's not sure how to answer. "That's not part of our group home. It has nothing to do with us."

Why would there be a shared drive and a gate that allowed access between the properties? And why was the lanky guard who searched my belongings there? Was Sneaker intentionally lying? Was rubbing his neck a tell?

"So who owns it?"

"A gun club. You'll hear shooting sometimes."

The building was mostly hidden, but I saw satellite arrays on the roof. I pointed to them. "Why would a gun club need satellites?"

"Maybe they play hunting games on the internet. Anyway, it's best not to get too close, or a stray bullet might find us. I've got something else to show you."

He took us around the front of the building and across the grounds to a big oak tree located close to the fence, not far from the front gates.

He jumped to grab a branch and swung himself up. "Come on."

When I climbed up behind him, he inched his way out onto the limb. "You've got to admit this is an amazing view."

Yeah, I could even see beyond the fence. A bus was parked in front of the gate, and kids were scrambling off. They lined up to be searched by the guards. After the search, they sauntered down the drive.

"No one ever looks up." Sneaker pointed toward the kids. "They won't see us."

"Why are they bald?"

"All of them aren't. Just those first ones. Most kids in here belong to a group. Like our street names, someone labeled them something, and they embraced it. The Hicks shave their hair, the Freaks dye theirs, the Dreads are mostly African-American, and the Tinos are Hispanic. Just stay out of their way and don't tick them off, or you could get hurt."

A knot of fear twisted my gut, shaming me. Dad said being afraid wasn't wrong, it only signaled danger. These kids' hostile faces, rough clothing, and tattoos set them apart from anyone I'd been around. My first impression of them screamed delinquents. The type of kids who might kill someone for fun. Still, I should be able to handle them. Yes, any one of them. But a gang? And what if they came at me while I slept?

Dad said being fearless was doing whatever you needed to, regardless of the danger. I wouldn't let them stop me, but I'd take precautions and be ready.

The kids wandered off the drive to other parts of the grounds. Looked like each group claimed a different area.

"Are you in a gang?" I asked Sneaker.

"No. And don't let anyone else hear you call them that. Gang involvement isn't allowed at Fallentier, but you can't stop kids from hanging out in cliques with their friends. Every school has cliques."

Hmm. Did they? "So what group are you in?"

"They call me a Misfit. The only thing Misfits have in common is we don't want to join another group."

Most of the kid's below now appeared to be smiling. "They seem happy."

"You'd be, too, if it was your last day at that school."

What? Before I could ask more, a dinged up SUV pulling into the drive caught my full attention. A chill ran up my spine. I dreaded the news Connor might be bringing. I could only hope with all my heart Dad remained free.

Chapter 10

Beloved Family

"Family gives us roots. Storms can't destroy things with deep roots." Dominick

Derrick

Perched in the tree, I watched Connor stop his SUV to talk to the guards. One guard strode around the vehicle and climbed into his passenger seat.

I pointed toward the SUV. "They'll be looking for me."

"Who is it?" Sneaker asked.

I didn't know what cover story Connor had given, and I didn't want to compromise it. "Not something I want to share."

Sneaker blew out his breath. "You're sure tight-lipped."

One of Dad's rules was Intel wasn't shared unless someone absolutely needed to know. "It isn't something you need to know."

After I shimmied down the back of the wide trunk, I approached the drive as the SUV drove down it.

Connor stuck his arm out of the open window and, motioning me closer, looked at the guard. "That's the one I need for the meeting."

I reached his window and asked, "What meeting?"

The guard scowled. "It doesn't matter since your attendance isn't a choice. Now, get in."

What a jerk, but I wouldn't get answers by refusing to go. When I jumped in the back, my duffel was still there. I unzipped it enough to see the pellet I'd placed on top. Maybe Connor hadn't ransacked it. He turned and drove back to the guard shack.

The guard got out, then flung his thumb toward me. "If you have any problems, let me know."

"We'll be fine. Thanks." After Connor raised his window, he glanced in his rear view mirror. "Buckle up."

Connor's tone was as stiff as his posture. I put my seatbelt on. "Are you going to tell me where we're going?"

"Not now." Connor drove out of the gates and down the lane.

I drummed my fingers against the front of the seat. At my signal, my pet Sugar Glider slipped out of Connor's suit pocket and under the seat to me. I tucked him into my hoodie pocket.

"Did you dry clean?" Connor asked.

I couldn't be sure I'd found every listening bug, especially without Pip. "I tried, but I didn't have a detector."

Connor leaned over to open his glove department. He pulled out what looked like a microphone and flipped a switch. It began to beep.

"Use mine." He stuck it over the seat.

Pip still carried Dad's newest and supposedly undetectable bug. This would be a good test. I ran the detector all around myself. The beep never changed.

"I'm good." I handed his detector back.

After slipping the detector back inside his glove department, he pushed the switch. When the secret panel slid open, he took my holstered weapons out and tossed them to me.

"The people we're going to meet will be armed, and they'll expect you to be," he explained.

I buckled my gun holster to my ankle and my knife sheath to my belt as Connor pulled on the main road and passed the truck stop.

He tossed a mechanical knife over the seat to land beside me. "That's Company issue. We owe you one, so you can keep it."

"Thanks." I slid the mechanical knife into my hidden heel compartment.

"One more thing." Connor reached into his center console and brought out a small paper sack. Mouthwatering aromas wafted as he passed it to me. "Shen insisted I bring your dinner to you."

Inside the sack, I found a foil package, a napkin, and chopsticks. A lump rose in my throat. Our Chinese cook had been with us since I was a baby.

"What will happen to Shen now?"

Connor blew out a breath. "You don't have to worry about Shen. The way he cooks, he could be working at a five star restaurant."

"What about the rest of our staff?"

"Your dad only hired quality people, and most of them had several job offers. They won't have any problems landing on their feet." He motioned to the foil package. "You should eat. Dinner at Fallentier might be over when we return."

I unwrapped the package to find thin slices of Peking duck, along with some dumplings. Two of my favorite dishes. Dad's too. Too bad he wasn't here. My stomach knotted. I couldn't eat. I closed the foil package and put it back in the sack.

Connor turned onto the highway entrance. "Your dead drop is in this underpass. There's a couple hundred dollars for emergencies. I'll put your weapons and that detector in when we're done. Anything else you need?"

A false ID would be nice, but did I want Connor to know my alias? "Thanks. That should cover it." I'd never been in debt before. "And I *will* pay you back when I can."

"I know you will."

Connor took the Reagan National exit, but before the airport, he turned into the parking lot of a boarded-up restaurant, drove to the back, and pulled beside a black limousine parked there.

"Aren't you going to tell me who we're meeting?" I asked.

"Your family. They flew from LaGuardia to see you and could offer you a home."

What? That couldn't be right. "Dad said he didn't have any family."

Connor opened his door. "He's an orphan, but your mom wasn't."

Confusion filled me as I sat gawking at the limo. How come I'd never met them? They must be distant relatives. Would I even like them?

Connor had climbed out, but he stuck his head back in and barked, "What are you waiting for? Get out and act nice."

My resentment flared, and my chest tightened. "I never knew going to a group home meant I joined the army."

Connor's eyes sparkled, and he chuckled. "Okay. Please get out and act nice."

I clambered out. The Limo's driver had come around the car. "Good to see you again, Connor."

"Thanks, Anthony. This is Derrick."

"Nice to meet you, Derrick. They're expecting you." After opening the middle door of the Limo, Anthony motioned toward the opening.

Connor got in and scooted over. When I slid in next to him, Anthony closed the door. Three men sat across from us in the facing seat. They shared some similar features like their thick black hair, high cheekbones, and tan complexions.

The center man's dark hair was speckled with gray, like quartz, and he wore a suit. The one on my left was young, probably around my age, while the one on my right was a little older, maybe early twenties. The younger men were dressed less formally in slacks and dress shirts, but their vests bulged on one side. Pretty obvious where their guns were.

All three of them had maple eyes, but the older man's were as sharp as glass and glinted while he scrutinized me. "The pictures didn't do him justice, Connor."

He'd seen pictures of me? My skin crawled under their combined stares. "Who are they, Connor?"

The older man's gaze finally turned to Connor. "Tu non gli hai detto?"

He'd spoken Italian fluently when he asked what Connor had told me. "He only said you were famiglia, so are you a distant cousin or something?"

"Derrick—" Connor flung a hand toward the older man "—I want you to meet Dominick Amato, your mother's father and your grandfather." Connor pointed to the man on the right. "This is Sergio—" he pointed to the youngest one on the left "—and this is Lucca. They *are* cousins, but not distant."

My mouth gaped open. I closed it and looked at my grandfather. "Then why didn't you even come to Mom's funeral?"

He winced. "When my daughter fell in love, I investigated and learned Victor's career choice. We eventually came to an understanding. He agreed not to personally get involved in investigations against us, and I agreed we'd keep our distance. I loved my daughter enough to allow her to leave us, but it broke my heart."

Investigations? "Are you criminals?"

"We're men of honor, who do whatever it takes to care for those we love." My grandfather's eyes hardened. "Costa nostra would not be necessary if we could trust governments to protect our famiglia."

Lucca's hand waved in the air. "The government might call us criminals, but who stole your assets?"

Sergio's jaw clenched. "They're the criminals."

Okay, got it. They didn't like the government, so why were they friendly with Connor. "What's your connection to Connor?"

My grandfather shrugged. "In exchange for a favor, he agreed to give me information about my daughter and her children."

My spirits plummeted. Was the close friendship with Dad a sham? Connor wouldn't meet my gaze. "Did my dad know?"

Connor's shoulders fell. "No."

Dad and I considered Connor family, so his treachery hurt. As if a chunk had been ripped out of my heart, leaving a gaping hole. "Do you always betray those you say you love?"

"I don't blame you for being upset," my grandfather said. "We also value loyalty. Connor, leave us."

Connor got out, abandoning me. Was Connor a puppet with my grandfather pulling his strings?

My grandfather turned to me. "A group home isn't a place for an Amato. You should come home with us. Everything you need will be provided—a home, cars, cash, girls—" He leaned forward, and his eyes pierced me. "—but to join the family isn't a matter of blood alone. You'd have to vow to be loyal to me and do whatever I ask. And it's not something you can take back. Anyone who betrays our family will die."

A lump grew in my throat. I'd have a family again and a home. I wanted that, but would they expect me to commit criminal acts? Maybe even kill people? Not to protect our country, but for personal gain. Dad wouldn't want me involved with the mafia. "I don't want to be anyone's puppet."

"Everyone has a price. What would it take to gain your loyalty?"

Agents sometimes needed to ally themselves with people they didn't like to complete a mission. The double A. Adapt to gain Advantages. I'd already promised myself I'd do whatever it took to help Dad and Deidra. "You'd have to find my sister, reunite us, and clear my dad's name. That's the only way I could agree."

My grandfather smiled. "We're not that different. We both would do most anything for our family. If you join us, I'll promise to do what I can to find Deidra, but I won't clear your father's name. Not after he failed to protect my daughter."

How could he blame Dad for the accident? "Then I can't join you."

"The world can be cruel without family, so you may want to reconsider. I'll leave the offer open, but until you join us"—he pointed a finger at my chest—"you need to remove the Amato necklace and give it to me."

Memories surged up. Brakes squealing. Our car flipping over and over. Mom pinned and bleeding. Her whispered words, "Take my necklace off." Reaching into the small gap to remove it and reading the inscription on the back of it aloud, "Amato Famiglio—beloved family." Her last whispered instruction. "Wear it, my Amato figlio." Her beloved son.

Help came too late to save her. When the doctors tried to remove the necklace that had frozen to my skin, I fought them. I was only six, then, but the necklace meant just as much to me now.

I slid my hand down to my ankle holster and pulled my gun. I leveled it at my grandfather.

Chapter 11

Disappointed

"The most valuable and rarest friend is the one whose loyalties don't change." Victor

Derrick

I hadn't thought out pulling my gun, but my grandfather needed to back down. He wasn't taking my necklace.

My cousins grabbed their guns to aim them at my face.

Grandfather said calmly, "You might kill me, but you'll die too."

I glared at him. "I won't shoot to kill, only to shorten your spine. If you want to take Mom's last gift to me, you have too much backbone."

He snorted, then laughed. My cousins chuckled.

Grandfather's expression turned serious. "You've proven to me you're an Amato, but keep that necklace hidden under your shirt."

"He hasn't earned the right," Sergio exclaimed.

My grandfather slashed the air with his hand. "Enough." He leaned forward. "Derrick, I need you to promise you won't let anyone see it."

"Why?"

"The most important reason is that our family has enemies. If they see it, they'll strike."

"Okay. I promise."

He glanced at Sergio, then me. "Put the guns away. No one needs to know Derrick pulled his."

My cousins holstered their weapons, so I did too.

"When you change your mind about needing your family, an associate will come for you." My grandfather extended a slip of paper to me. "Just call this number."

I didn't think I'd ever call it, but I took it and stuck it in my pocket.

Grandfather grabbed the back of my neck and kissed my forehead. "I look forward to you joining us."

Sergio extended his hand. I took it and shook hands with him, only Sergio didn't let go—he kept squeezing harder—until it hurt.

"Normally," Sergio's tone was hard. "If someone pulled a gun on the Don, I'd break their hand. If anyone else knew you threatened him, I'd have to." He finally released me.

I resisted the urge to flex my throbbing hand. "Normally, if someone held on to my hand that long, I'd rearrange their face."

Lucca chuckled. My grandfather gestured to the door. "You can return to Connor, but I'd rather you didn't kill him. He comes in handy."

That he spoke so matter of fact about killing someone chilled me. Did he value life? I climbed out, then jumped in Connor's back seat.

Connor tilted his head toward the seat beside him. "You can sit up front."

"I'm fine where I am."

Connor shifted the car into drive and pulled out on the road. "I'll need your weapons back to put them in the drop."

Without a word, I tossed my weapons in the front seat.

"I know you're angry, Derrick, but…"

I cut him off. "You told me the Mob was on the decline since the RICO act imprisoned so many. Is it 'declining' when they're promising homes, cash, and cars? They even own a CIA agent."

"Things change. After 9-11, agents were pulled from investigating organized crime to focus on terrorists. The mob's responsible for more deaths, but those seldom make the news. So they rebounded and grew powerful again." His tone turned angry. "But they don't own me."

"Then why are you aiding them?"

"The Company needed Intel on terrorists making purchases

through the black market. I traded for that, but it wasn't really betraying you. If I hadn't kept your grandfather updated, he'd have hired someone else, and they might not have been as careful about what information they shared."

How could Connor say what he did wasn't wrong? I didn't even want to look at him. I gazed out the window at the scenery of trees and fields speeding by on the side of the highway.

I took a couple of calming breaths. "When I told you I didn't know if I could work for an agency who used practices like torture, do you remember what you said?"

"Yes. I told you, 'To catch demons, we need to pretend to be evil. We can't cross the line and think evil isn't wrong, though, or we could lose our soul. Soulless agents aren't an asset, but a detriment.' I also said, 'With the right people on the inside, those types of practices could end.'"

"If it wasn't a betrayal, then why didn't you inform Dad? You crossed the line, Connor. I'm not just angry, I'm disappointed because I don't think you know where the line is anymore."

When Connor pulled into the group home, a guard opened the gate, then came to the window to say, "We won't need to search Derrick since he was with you. The administrator wants him to come to her office, so drop him at the main building." He glanced at me. "It's past the cafeteria, last door on the right."

Whatever cover story Connor used had worked to gain their cooperation. He drove down Fallentier's drive and, after coming to a stop at the main building, turned in his seat to face me.

"Whether you believe it or not, I care about you and Victor, and I'm trying to help."

My resentment surged. "If that's true, why didn't you defend him?"

"I can't defend Victor to people whose minds are made up. That will only put me under suspicion too." His tone turned pleading. "There are some battles you can't win."

I grabbed my duffel and got out of the car. "Maybe, but I'd rather lose on the right side than win on the wrong." I slammed his door.

He turned the SUV around and drove away. Even though I wasn't happy with Connor, seeing his car grow smaller as it left Fallentier made me feel as if I'd been abandoned. An overwhelming desire for a familiar face and surroundings welled up inside me. I wanted to chase after him, but I shook off my misgiving and hiked up to the door of the main building.

I couldn't help wondering what the administrator wanted with me. Would it be more bad news? Was it to do with Dad?

Chapter 12

Unwanted

"Most foster kids are unwanted, abandoned by both parents and society." Sam

Maverick

When I reached the administrator's office, I peered in. A lady with short red hair sat behind a long rectangular desk.

"Derrick Connor Costa?" she asked.

My heart pinged. I used to like that Dad named me after Connor, but I couldn't feel the same pride in that name after he sold us out to the mafia.

"Yes," I answered.

"I'm Sherry, your caseworker." She smiled. "They're letting me borrow this office, so come in, close the door, and take a seat."

When I took the chair that sat on this side of the desk, she pulled a pen and paper out of a briefcase. "I'm sorry I missed you yesterday. I went to the house, but you'd already gone." She wrote something on the paper before asking, "How do you feel about living at Fallentier?"

Should I tell her the truth? What could it hurt? "I'd rather be on my own or at least staying with Connor. So what if he's gone a lot. I don't need someone with me all the time."

She put her pen down. "I agree you don't need constant supervision. I was told Connor was your dad's choice for guardian, so I did the initial background check on him. It came back clean, so I'd have approved him if he'd been willing to take you. He wasn't."

A cold fist squeezed my heart. Connor hadn't wanted me, and he lied to me about it. Why? Because there was no money now? There was a land line phone sitting at the end of the desk. I picked it up.

"What are you doing?" Sherry asked.

"Calling Connor." Several buttons were lit up on the phone. I hit one that wasn't. The phone was dead, so I pressed the nine and got a dial tone.

"I don't think that's a good idea," Sherry said.

"I do." I punched in Connor's private number and listened to it ring.

Connor finally answered, "Who is this?"

"It's Derrick. I just learned I could have stayed with you. Why did you lie about it?"

"There's a good reason I didn't take you."

"Yeah, there's no money now."

"No. I had two accidents happen in the last month. My brakes failed, and there was a gas leak at my house. I didn't tell you because I thought you had enough to worry about. They could just be accidents, but...."

The icy fist squeezing my heart cracked. Even with how Connor had disappointed me, I couldn't forget the good memories he was a part of. Worry for him filled me.

I choked out, "Coincidences don't exist."

"Exactly. You know the response."

If an agent suspects someone is after them, they should distance themselves from those they care about so they don't bring the trouble to them. That would explain why Connor hadn't been around much recently, before things fell apart.

Connor's tone was solemn. "I don't know if this is connected to you and your dad's problem, but if we're all targets..."

Then protocol would be to spread out. Make it more difficult for an enemy to catch us in one place.

"You should have told me. Lying to me makes it difficult to trust you."

"I'm sorry, lad. If those problems hadn't happened, you'd be with me."

He sounded sincere, and that sent my concern flaring again, twisting my stomach. My dad's motto came to my mind. Stay smart, skillful, and safe.

"Connor, remember your S's."

"You too."

I hung up and sat across from Sherry again. "Sorry, but I needed an explanation."

"Did you get one?"

"Yeah. He has a serious health concern he's dealing with."

"I hope he'll be okay."

"Me too."

"All right, let's get back to you. To make the transition to a group home easier, it might help to be able to talk to someone about your problems. I could set up some therapy appointments for you."

Our problems weren't something I could ever disclose. "I don't need help dealing with my situation. I'm fine."

She wrote on her paper again. "Do you have any goals for the future?"

"I plan to attend college."

She frowned. "Hmph."

"I wasn't aware having goals was a bad thing."

"It isn't, but sixty percent of teens who leave foster care get convicted of a crime. One-third of inmates in our state prison say they've been in the system. And no one's kept track of the number of foster kids who aged out and died on the streets. I don't want that to happen to you, so we need realistic goals and a plan."

After writing something down, Sherry pulled a pamphlet out of her briefcase. "This is a brochure on aging out, and since you have less than a year, you need to be prepared."

I took the pamphlet from her. "Don't you think college is a realistic goal?"

"Did you score high on your SAT test?"

My tutors hadn't ever said anything about it. "I haven't taken one. Is it necessary?"

"You won't qualify for admission to most colleges without a good SAT score, not to mention scholarships or loans. Typically students with college aspirations spend months just preparing to take the SAT, so no, I don't think it's a realistic goal for you at this point."

My heart sank to my toes. Could she be right about my college plans being unlikely to be met? What did Dad say when I was feeling discouraged? *If you keep trying, today's obstacles will be tomorrow's accomplishments.* I *would* continue trying.

"What if I take the SAT and score high?"

"Then college might be a good goal, but it can't be your *only* goal. In one year's time, you'll have to provide for yourself and pay for rent, food, and utilities not to mention any college expenses all while attending classes. A few of my kids have managed it, but think about what skills you have that can be used to get employment because it's something you'll need."

I had skills that were useful to a select group, but they would no longer touch me.

She looked at her watch, then passed me the paper she'd been writing on. "Sign this, please."

It said that she had met me, I declined therapy, and we'd discussed goals and a plan.

After I signed it, she tucked it in her briefcase and handed me a business card with her name and phone number.

"I have to go, but if you need anything, you can call me."

I couldn't help worrying about Connor as I walked back to the cottage. Was there a connection between Dad being framed and Connor's *accidents*?

Chapter 13

For nothing

Derrick

When I entered the cottage, Sam, Sneaker, and a couple of other kids were sitting around watching TV.

"Yo," Sneaker said upon seeing me.

I gave him a chin lift.

Sam smiled at me. "You missed dinner. Are you hungry?"

"No." My stomach was too knotted to want any food.

"Okay, if you change your mind let me know. I have a few sandwiches in my mini fridge."

"Thanks."

"Would you like to join us?" he asked.

What I really wanted to do was to curl up and forget this day had happened. "I'm tired. I'd rather go to my room."

One of the kids gasped. He looked up from the TV to point at me. "It's him."

All their gazes flicked between me and the TV. The station was announcing about Dad being wanted and showing the footage of me in Connor's vehicle at the CIA headquarters. My heart sank to my toes. Even with my sunglasses and hood pulled up, it was still obvious. I even had the same clothes on.

The TV announcer started talking about the rise in juvenile delinquents, and how another girl had put a guy in a coma. Sneaker pointed at the TV. "Hey. That's Gina. She went to our camp."

Instead of looking, I used the opportunity to avoid questions and escape down the hall. When I reached my room, I sat Pip down, filled his bowl with pellet food, put in an apple slice, and sprinkled in vitamin supplement. After I placed it in his shoebox with water, I slid the box under the cot.

Pip scurried around the room, investigating, then climbed in his box and snatched some food. As usual, he threw some around, but the box would keep the pellets from getting all over.

While Pip ate, my thoughts returned to everything that had happened. There were so many unanswered questions. What was I missing? My exhaustion weighed my thoughts.

I collapsed on my cot. My phone was digging into my butt. I pulled it out of my pocket and laid it on the locker next to my bed. I still couldn't get comfortable. This lumpy cot wasn't anything like my bed. I wanted to go home. Tears leaked from my eyes. I wiped them away. Pip climbed up on the cot and nuzzled my ear.

"Hey, little guy. You trying to cheer me up?"

Pip settled on my pillow between my shoulder and neck. I closed my eyes.

A soft chitter sounded. Pip's warning. I snapped my eyes open. They felt gritty, and my mouth was dry. I must have slept some. Pip ran under my cot as the door creaked open, and Sneaker strolled in.

"What up?" he asked.

"Just sleeping." I checked my watch. "It's already eleven o clock."

"Yup, and eleven's our curfew." Sneaker kicked off his shoes. "In a minute, Sam will stick his head in, then switch the light off."

He took off his shirt and pants and let them fall to the floor. Dressed in his boxers, he pulled back the sheet and jumped in his bed across from me, flipping over a couple of times.

I needed to call Dad soon, but the Company might be listening for radio transmissions from here. I should leave so it would be harder for them to hijack.

When Sneaker had settled, I asked, "If you were going to sneak out of the grounds, how would you do it?"

He propped his head on his arm. "I don't usually share my escape routes and risk the guards learning them."

How could I convince him? "It's really important. I give you my word if you help, I won't share what you tell me."

"There's something else you should know about Fallen kids. We don't help unless there's something in it for us. You ain't going to get something for nothing."

I rose from my bed. "I have very little money, and none I can spare, so I'll find a way myself."

"Hold up. We can trade for something else, like your expensive phone over there."

I picked my phone back up. Should I tell Sneaker? He'd learn it didn't work when he tried to make a call. "My service was canceled. And even if I could, I wouldn't restore it since the government is probably tracing it."

Sneaker smiled. "I don't need service to sell it, and it doesn't have to go to a friend."

Relief filled me that he still wanted it. "You tell me how to sneak out, and it's yours."

Sneaker sat up. "Behind that tree we climbed, there's a fence section that's cut on the bottom and will pop out. Make sure to put it back." He grabbed his pants and pulled out a roll of silver tape. "Use this to hold it together." He tossed it to me. "Wait for Sam to do his check before you leave, and go through the fire door." He smirked. "The alarm and the camera back there keep malfunctioning."

My heart leapt in anticipation of speaking to Dad. I threw him the phone. "Thanks."

He caught it. "Just don't get bagged."

Chapter 14

Prowlers

"Suspect the unexpected." Victor.

Derrick

I snuck down the dark hall to the fire door. The alarm's steady light showed it as operational. I could deactivate it, but that would take time. Sneaker had claimed it didn't work. I took a chance and cracked the door open. No alarm broke the quiet, and I didn't see anyone outside. The camera above the door faced the grounds, and it, too, displayed a green light. To be certain my picture wouldn't be taken, I dug a black sock out of my duffel and slipped it over the lens. After scooting out, I kept in the shadow of the cottage.

I crept around the back of the building and scurried from tree to tree. I didn't see the guards. When I got to the fence, I pressed the top of my watch to activate its light. 11:30 p.m. Not much time. By the glow of my watch, I found the taped fence section. After I undid the tape and pulled the fence back enough to throw my duffel through, I shimmied through after my bag.

Outside the fence, I entered the woods, and the canopy of leaves cut off the light of the moon and stars. The darker shadows of tree trunks and limbs hulked around me as I stumbled over roots and forced my way through brush.

"Ouch." Another thorny vine scratched me. I needed to see them to avoid them. The red lens of my flashlight wouldn't be very noticeable. I pulled it from my duffel and turned it on. Even with the light, I couldn't travel fast through the woods, and I needed to get farther before transmitting.

I cut out of the woods to the lane and jogged up to the main road. A dog barked from the neighborhood there, so I ducked behind a tree.

A guy hollered, "Shut up, you yappy mutt." The dog quieted, and he ordered, "Get inside." The dog must have gone in because the door slammed.

I checked my watch. 11:55 p.m. I probably wasn't even two miles from the group home, but I didn't have time to go farther. Hopefully, I was far enough away to throw off anyone listening for transmissions.

Pip squirmed in my pocket. Sugar Glider's had excellent night vision, so I let him down so he could run around and use the bathroom if he needed. After I slipped off my duffel, I let it fall to the ground.

I set my flashlight in the crook of the tree's trunk and pointed it toward my bag. I found my portable ham radio, as well as the rods of my Slim-Jim antenna, and quickly assembled it. Once I attached my antenna cable and parachute cord to it, I threw the cord around one of the tree limbs to hoist my antenna higher. I turned my radio to the setting for privacy and found the frequency 94.8. Thankfully, I could transmit and decipher Morse code quickly and was familiar with most abbreviations.

I used my tones to identify myself, *K-24,* put in *HR* for here, and *CLG* for calling, then *N14.* Silence answered my transmission. Oh no. Had Dad been caught? For repeat, I toned *RPT,* then *K-24 CLG N-14.*

When the sound of tones came back, relief filled me. I deciphered them. *N-14 HR. R U OK K-24?*

I put in *C* for correct, then asked *R U?*

C. Correct. The tones sounded again. *QTH OC.*

QTH was location, OC was old chap. After I pinned Connor in our last wrestling match, I'd teased him about being too old. Dad must be asking if I was with Connor, so I transmitted back *N* for negative. I toned *OC HUNTING U.* After a second, I added *OC RAT 2 MOMS FAMLY.*

He toned *PLS HV NIL 2 DU WID TT FAM. K?*

Dad was saying to please have nothing to do with that family, and he wanted to know if I understood? I entered CFMD for confirmed, put in *QTH* for location, and sent out tones until I spelled *GROUP HOME.*

SRI.

He was sorry. Not his fault. *UNC S FROZE ASSETS.* I asked him how *HW CAN I AID U?*

NEG. FOCUS ON U. B 3 S.

Be smart, skillful, and safe.

U 2.

GG 8 U.

GG meant going. 88 stood for love and kisses so 8 must be love. He was leaving, and he loved me. I didn't want our conversation to end, but he was being careful. The longer our transmission lasted, the more risk of someone detecting it. I wanted to tell him I loved him, too, so I sent one more and hoped he'd receive it.

8 U 2.

I packed up, collected Pip, and hightailed it back to the fence. As I approached, I heard a muffled pft, pft in the distance. A gun with a silencer. I barely heard the shots, so they weren't close enough to threaten me. Could it have come from what was supposed to be a gun club? As if members of a gun club would be shooting at night with silencers. At least the shots had stopped.

I didn't see anyone, so I crawled through the fence and secured it again with the tape. I made my way across the grounds and down the side of the cottage to the rear corner. As I turned it, I caught sight of several shadows moving at the rear of the grounds. My mind screamed to hide. I dodged back around the corner to peer out. The gate of the so-called gun club stood open, and four shadows came through it. One walked with a limp. Sam? A light mounted on a pole at the gate lit their faces long enough for me to confirm that it was Sam, along with Sneaker, a bald kid, and a kid with a red Mohawk.

Hmmm. Had they been the ones shooting? But why shoot at night? Maybe they wanted to hide their activities from the other kids? Whatever was going on, the staff and guards must be aware of it.

The group separated. Sam and Sneaker headed toward our cottage, while the other two guys turned toward another.

If I tried to go in before they did, the light over the door would make it easy for them to spot me. When they got closer, I heard Sam's voice. "So what's your impression of your roommate?"

"Hard to buy that he's a hardened terrorist when his face was as wet as any other kid who's surprised to find himself here."

My embarrassment heated my cheeks.

Sam spoke softly. "My gut tells me the same thing, but I need to know for sure."

"He's not going to open up unless I gain his trust." Sneaker sounded defensive. "Giving him that escape route might help do that."

Seriously? I should have suspected Sneaker's aid came too easily.

"I didn't say you were wrong," Sam said as he and Sneaker arrived at the back door of the cottage. "Just that you should have alerted me quicker so we could have learned where he went." They traipsed inside, and Sam's voice drifted back. "Now we'll have to wait for the next time he escapes." The door shut behind them.

What would they do? Use a GPS tracker? Follow me? I needed to find out who pulled Sam's strings. If I investigated that other building, I might find out. I'd have to look at it tomorrow.

I waited several minutes, then crept to the door. My sock was still on the camera. Sam and Sneaker must not have noticed it in the dark. I slid inside and reached back to remove my sock.

When I reached my room, Sneaker had the blankets wrapped around him. His breathing was too fast to convince me he was asleep. I'd let him think he'd fooled me.

Was it safe for me to rest? My eyes burned from exhaustion. Even waking from a dead sleep, I could handle Sneaker, but what if more kids showed up? I'd have to take a precaution. I stowed my duffel in my locker, then grabbed my hair conditioner and spilled a little in front of the door. After I kicked off my jeans, I slipped into bed.

Pip slipped out of my pocket and climbed under my cot. I closed my eyes. A chirp that sounded like a locust woke me. Pip's warning.

Chapter 15

Reconnaissance

"Always scrutinize your surroundings for possible threats and escape routes." Victor

Derrick

It took a second for my eyes to adjust to the darkness before I spotted Sneaker in front of my locker. Why did he have my duffel out?

"What are you doing?"

Sneaker jumped. "You scared me to death."

I sat up. "Dead people don't talk, but I could get *really* scary if you don't explain why you're messing with my stuff."

"Sorry, I was looking for an aspirin." Sneaker rubbed his temple with two fingers. "I have an awful headache and didn't want to wake you."

"Isn't there a nurse here?"

"She says we better be dying if we wake her, so do you have any?"

If he'd *really* been looking for an aspirin, he'd have found it. I got up, took my first aid kit from my locker, and pulled out the little bottle of aspirin. "Here."

Sneaker grabbed it. "Thanks. I really appreciate it."

I wouldn't appreciate the time I'd spend with Pip tomorrow searching for any GPS trackers he planted.

Sneaker took a step toward the bathroom, but stumbled over my duffel. With his arms flailing, he crashed into me.

As we fell back, Pip barked, then ran out and launched himself at Sneaker's back.

"Eek," Sneaker screamed. "A rat!" He jumped to his feet and fled toward the door, but slipped in my conditioner and fell. He thrashed trying to remove Pip.

"Hold still and I'll get him." When Sneaker froze, I picked up Pip and stroked him to calm him.

"What in the...." Sneaker hollered.

"He's my pet Sugar Glider. He thought you were attacking me." Pip's soft purr rumbled while I petted him. I turned on the light. "Look, he's friendly."

Sneaker rose to his feet and huffed, "We're not allowed pets here."

Fingers of worry clawed my gut. I couldn't lose Pip.

Sam's voice came through the door. "Are you two all right?"

"Fine." I jumped back on my cot and hid Pip behind my back.

"Why the commotion, Sneaker?" Sam asked as he cracked open the door.

I pleaded with my eyes for my roommate not to tell.

"Sorry, I fell out of bed from a nightmare," Sneaker said.

"It's time to get up anyway. If you're late to class, you'll be washing dinner dishes for the next three days." Sam closed the door, and his uneven steps retreated.

Sneaker twisted his body around to see the scratches on his back. "Are you sure that thing won't attack me again."

"He didn't mean to hurt you, only scare you. I keep his nails short, but they'll still scratch bare skin." I had to convince Sneaker not to snitch. I held out my hand with Pip toward him. "If you pet him, he'll know you're a friend."

Sneaker tentatively reached his fingers out to stroke Pip, and his face scrunched. "He's kind of cool looking."

He seemed far from convinced. Maybe Pip could change that.

"Sugar Gliders do more than look pretty." I got up, grabbed another one of my sweatshirts, and held it out. "Throw this on so he doesn't accidentally scratch you, and I'll show you."

He pulled my sweatshirt on. "Is that why you've been wearing hoodies even though it's hot?"

"The material's light on my sweatshirts, but yeah. I wear these because they have a front pocket and that's where Pip likes to hang out." I backed up over by the bathroom. "Tap your elbow with your fingers."

Sneaker hesitated. He finally tapped his elbow. Pip leapt off me and glided over to Sneaker's arm to alight on it.

"Wow, he flies."

"Actually, he glides." I rolled my finger. Pip leapt in the air, flipped, and landed back on Sneaker's arm. "Sugar Gliders are acrobats, too, and can climb anything."

"Neat." Sneaker stroked Pip. Pip snuggled into his arm, nuzzling him. "You like me, don't you? But you'll have to stay hidden if you want to stay."

Pip adored affection. Was he winning Sneaker over?

"He's nocturnal, so he mostly moves around at night," I explained. "He's perfectly content sleeping in my pocket during the day. It shouldn't be hard to hide him."

"What about the gate searches?" Sneaker asked.

Pip jumped off Sneaker's arm and sailed over to my bed. "He can glide over the fence to meet me on the other side."

"That might work, but I wouldn't tell anyone else about him. There are a lot of snitches in here."

"Do I need to worry about you telling anyone?"

Sneaker blinked a couple of times. "I swear I won't say anything if you do the same for me." His eyes lit up. "I want to get me one."

Yes. Pip had done it. "It's a deal. Sugar Gliders do love company." I held my hand out. "If you're not going to take any of that aspirin, I'll put it away."

Sneaker grinned and gave the bottle back to me. "Pip must have cured me."

Pip could do a lot of things, but healing headaches wasn't one. I lit my watch. "It's 7 o'clock. When do classes start?"

"8 a.m., so if you want breakfast and a shower, we'll have to hurry."

My stomach growled at me. I missed too many meals yesterday. "Are there any school supplies I'll need?"

He shrugged. "Beats me." He ran a hand through his hair. "This is the first day we've had classes at Fallentier. I'm guessing they'll provide everything, if they want us to do much."

I hoped we wouldn't need anything with me short on cash. "So why did they stop sending you to public school?"

"Too many hassles. No school wanted us *delinquents*. They kept redistricting us and charging Fallentier a ton of money to bus us. Finally, Fallentier decided they'd educate us here."

What would classes here be like? I guess I'd find out soon. I grabbed clothes and my shower kit before I went in the bathroom. After I quickly showered, I dressed in my gray tank and black jeans. When I left the bathroom, I took my washcloth and towel with me.

While Sneaker showered, I used my washcloth and towel to clean and dry the floor where I had spilled the conditioner. Then I pulled on my boots and a hoodie. Pip jumped on my arm at my soft whistle.

"Good boy." I petted him, and his soft purr rumbled. I slipped the elastic band with the camera and listening equipment over his head.

Sneaker dressed in a t-shirt and shorts reappeared from the bathroom. "Ready?"

"Yeah." I put Pip in my front pocket, and we headed over to the main building. On the side of the building, the vending machines caught my attention. "Pip eats fresh fruit and vegetables with his protein pellets. Is there any fruit in those machines?"

"No. The cafeteria provides healthy choices, but hardly anyone eats them. No one will say anything if you take extra. Hulk is always stuffing food in his pockets, and not just the healthy stuff."

"Don't they allow snacks?"

"Sure they do, but Hulk's last foster home thought he needed to lose weight, so they put him on a starvation diet. Hulk wasn't fat before, he just has a big frame. When they got through with him, he looked like a skeleton. He's almost back to normal now, but after something like that, it's hard to convince yourself there's going to be food tomorrow, you know?"

I nodded although I'd never experienced a shortage of food. When we trooped into the cafeteria, only a few other kids sat at the tables eating breakfast.

"Where is everyone else?" I asked.

"Most would rather skip breakfast and sleep late."

Not me. This might be a good time to do some snooping with so few around. My stomach grumbled again. First things first. I followed Sneaker up as he grabbed a tray. A couple of older ladies wearing hair nets stood behind the counter. Containers of milk, juice, breakfast rolls, cereal, and selections of fruit were lined up buffet style. There was even a container of blueberries and strawberries to put in the cereal.

I took some strawberries for my cornflakes and put some blueberries on my tray for Pip. We sat at a table by ourselves. The other kids eyed me, but didn't say anything. I finished quickly and checked my watch. 7:40 a.m. I slipped the blueberries in the cellophane that my plastic silverware came in and put them in my jean pocket.

I stood and asked Sneaker, "The classrooms are upstairs?"

Sneaker's mouth was full, so he gave me a nod and mumbled, "Uhum."

"I forgot something. I'll meet you there." After putting the tray up, I headed out the door and around the back of the building toward the supposed gun club. When I got close to the gate, I slipped behind a tree to keep out of sight of the two guards. I pulled Pip out.

A twinge of worry assaulted me. I tried to shake it off. Hadn't I trained Pip for this? Yeah, but he didn't always get it right. Sugar Gliders can learn to recognize word commands like *come*, but Pip responded better to signals and sounds like clucks, whistles, and tapping. Even using them, he wandered off course occasionally.

I snaked my hand, the signal for reconnaissance, pointed to the building, and cast him off. Pip latched on to the limb above me, before he soared over the fence line to another tree.

I put my sunglasses on and untucked the two flexible arms. I adjusted them so the ear bud lay near my ear, and the microphone sat at the corner of my mouth. Pip might hear me without the Mic., but I wasn't taking the chance. If I spoke too loudly, the guards might detect me.

I pushed the button on my sunglasses, and a screen popped up inside the lens to show the view from Pip's camera. I urged Pip on with a soft hiss. He glided to another tree, then over the roof. I clucked quietly once, and Pip descended to land at the rear of the building. He'd made it.

His camera showed me the grounds behind the building. They had several sheltered shooting stands with a raised berm. I'd expected that, but not the posts rising to the west of it. Was that a net hanging between them? Some trees blocked a better view. Could it be part of an obstacle course?

I pursed my lips and made a soft kiss. Pip climbed down over the roof and the side of the building to a window, giving the lens an unobstructed view of what lay inside. I caught sight of a stove and refrigerator. A kitchen? At another kiss, Pip descended to the first floor and looked in another window.

The room held workstations lining two walls with several office chairs and computers. And in the center, a big conference type table. At my quiet cluck, Pip scrambled to the left until he found another window. I recognized a treadmill and other gym equipment in the large room beyond. Gun clubs don't need gym equipment. This must be someone's training facility, but I still didn't know whose or how they used kids from the group home. If it were for a JROTC program or something like that, it wouldn't be kept secret.

I'd have to figure it out later. It must be getting about time for class. To recall Pip, I whistled softly into the Mic.

Pip glided his way from tree to tree until he landed on a branch above me. His camera showed me a glimpse of a guard staring at him.

"Look," the guard exclaimed. "A flying squirrel."

Oh no. Pip had been spotted. My breath caught. Would the guard come over to take a closer look?

Chapter 16

Hard choices

"Just once, I'd like to say something in my life was easy." Gina

Gina

I lay on one of the cold, hard metal benches bolted to the concrete floor in the holding cell and rubbed my eyes. I hadn't slept all night. Who knew jail would be so noisy? Between doors clanging, the footsteps of guards, the inmates who snored, cried, or even wailed, there wasn't a second of quiet in here. The smell wasn't pleasant either. The heavy scent of some cleaning agent didn't completely mask the odor of urine, vomit, and sweat. A steady thumping began as one of my cellmates, who sat on the floor, banged her head against the cement wall.

Like my mom. I couldn't think about that. Not here, not now, or I might cry.

I took the coarse blanket they'd given me, stuffed it into a ball, then marched over and slid it behind her head. She grabbed my hand and looked at me with eyes that were glazed. Shouldn't any drugs be out of her system? She'd joined us early last night.

I murmured reassuringly, "Sheila, it's me. Remember, I'm Gina."

"Oh." She blinked several times before meekly saying, "Hi."

The other older woman sharing the holding cell, Candy, who hadn't had a problem sleeping, opened her eyes. "No sense trying to talk to her, kid. She's off her rocker, like my old cell mate, Margo."

Not another prison story. Candy had taken seriously the detective's instruction to share hers and had regaled me with tons yesterday evening.

"I remember, one time, my toothbrush disappeared." Candy pressed her finger up to her lip, which accented her missing front teeth. "You see, Margo was quite the klepto. Most people in prison are, and toothbrushes can be filed for a weapon. Anyway, I was sleeping, and I already told you how you have to sleep with one eye open, didn't I?"

I sighed. "Yeah. You told me."

"Well, it was a good thing I did that night because I caught Margo trying to stab me with my own toothbrush. I fought her and got it away from her. She cried and kept saying she had to kill the demon. A couple nights later, I woke up and found Margo hanging in our cell, dead, her blanket wrapped around her neck." Candy sat up. "Can you believe they thought I killed her? I finally convinced them she offed herself." She winked at me, and her voice turned creepy. "Never relax your guard in prison, kid. Never."

Goosebumps rose on my arms. Maybe she did kill her cell mate.

A couple of cops came to the front of our cell. "Gina, your attorney's here."

My heart leapt. Maybe she'd been able to secure my release. They unlocked our door and handcuffed me. One of them escorted me to a room, twin to the one I was interviewed in yesterday, except this one didn't have a mirror.

My state-appointed attorney sat stiffly at the table. She wore a black pantsuit and her hair in a severe bun. If she wanted to make herself appear older, it didn't work. She still looked fresh out of law school. I was probably her first case.

"Go ahead and sit, Gina," she ordered in a no-nonsense tone. When I did, she turned her attention to the cop. "Remove her handcuffs."

I turned in my chair so he could reach them. As he took them off, I informed my lawyer, "They didn't separate me."

The cop straightened. "The law just says we should make a reasonable attempt to separate juveniles whenever possible. It's not possible when we're overcrowded. You shouldn't have picked such a busy time to commit a crime."

My attorney's lips pursed. "My client's guilt hasn't been proven." She pointed to the camera. "Make sure that's off before you leave."

I massaged my wrists as he left, then I sought the answers I craved. "Did the interview work?"

"No." My attorney's shoulders slumped. "I'm sorry, but I warned you it was risky. Instead of garnering support like we hoped, they painted you as a kid gone bad. A *mean* girl. The news station ran the clip in a story about juvenile delinquents and included some footage of a terrorist kid."

My heart plummeted. "You should have let me speak, instead of talking for me."

"That might have been worse. Look. The facts are that you hurt someone seriously enough that he's in a coma, and there's an eyewitness who places you at fault."

Ugh. "Mary wasn't even in the garage. Fred must have told her to say that."

"Regardless, she's willing to testify. Maybe you should reconsider the option you rejected yesterday."

My chest tightened. "I won't claim I'm nuts so I can be put in a psychiatric hospital." That wasn't being released. Just a different prison.

"If you won't see a psychiatrist, this is the best offer I can get you." She took a paper out of her briefcase and slid it over to me. "Read that. I'd advise you to consider it carefully."

If I pleaded guilty, I'd be charged as an adult, but they'd reduce the charges from felony-malicious wounding to felony-unlawful wounding. Instead of facing a minimum of five years and a maximum of twenty, I'd face a minimum of one year and a max of five.

My heart plummeted at the thought of being behind bars for at least a year. "What kind of chances do I have if we go to court?"

"With an eye witness, it's not impossible you could walk away, but improbable."

Should I risk it? There was another option that would make the charges disappear, but could I live with myself?

Chapter 17

Blending in

*"Disappear into monotony. The boring person gets
overlooked." Victor*

Maverick

I peeked out from behind the tree to see if the guards were coming
closer.

"You have a squirrel brain," one guard said scornfully to the
other. "There's nothing there."

"I can't help that you're blind," the other snapped.

The guards were looking at each other, now, not the tree. I tapped
my fingers against my hoodie, and Pip climbed down the tree to
scamper inside my front pocket. Staying in the shadows, I made my
way back around the main building before I whispered, "Good boy."

I moved out of the shadows and inside. Kids were rushing through
the door and up the steps to the classroom.

I joined them, and in the press clomping up the steps, I
accidentally bumped into a scrawny kid with thick glasses. "Sorry. It's
kind of crowded here."

"No worries. I'm Jinx. Sneaker told everyone your street name,
but I forgot it."

Apparently, I had a street name now. "Was it Maverick?"

"Oh, yeah."

Sneaker could have called me something worse, so I didn't object
to the name.

Jinx motioned to the herd of kids around us. "When we went to
public school, it was really crowded. You're lucky we're not going

there anymore because they sure wouldn't have liked you.

"Why?"

The kid with the red Mohawk said from behind us, "You're too dark. You Hispanics might ruin their image and affect their property values."

With my tan and Italian heritage, I could easily pass as Hispanic. I'd let the assumption stand for now.

Jinx whispered. "That's the Freaks leader, MB."

I had an online friend who went by MB. "What do the initials stand for?" I asked.

"He won't say, but some think Mad Butcher."

Definitely not the same guy. Sam was standing beside an open door with a stack of papers in his arms.

"Go on in and take a seat," Sam instructed.

I streamed through with the others to a small room. There were two larger 'teacher type' desks pushed together in the front with a wooden chair behind each. On the other side of the room were shelves lined with books, and against the back wall was a table with three computers. Crammed into the rest of the floor space were six rows of six smaller desks that kids were plopping into.

It looked like the kids with the dyed hair they called *Freaks* were taking the seats on the right. The bald *Hicks* were clumped in the center. The *Dreads* sat on the left, and the *Tinos* were gathering in the rear. Each of their cliques appeared to hold between five and seven kids.

Jinx had stopped beside me. "Usually the Misfits sit in the front row since no one else wants to sit there."

Sneaker was already seated at the second desk in the first row. He pointed to the third desk next to him. "Here. Maverick."

Did he think I was a dog? I smothered my resentment. He was trying to be helpful. Maybe I'd appreciate it more if I thought his efforts to befriend me were sincere.

I ambled over and sat, cramming my legs into the desk. My knees brushed the top. It was a good thing I wasn't any taller.

Jinx plopped on the other side of Sneaker and said, "I was telling your boy how people that live around here hate Fallentier."

It irked me to be referred to as someone's boy, but I bit back a scathing response as Dad's words filled my mind. "A good spy doesn't make waves or do anything to stand out. They blend in."

Sneaker was nodding his agreement. "Yeah. They tried to keep Fallentier from opening, but couldn't since we're on government property. Now they just swap wild stories about us."

A bald guy in back of us who had a round face with a crooked nose that screamed *fighter* growled, "We didn't name ourselves Fallen kids, they did."

It sounded as if people assuming the worst of them was a sore spot. At least no one had accused them of being a terrorist and put them on the watch list like me.

"That's Bullet, the Hicks leader," Sneaker said. "The guy on the left side of the room with the skull cap is the Dread's leader, Hulk. The Tino's leader, Blade, is on the right with the red t-shirt."

After Sneaker's story about Hulk being starved, I expected his thin face, but the rest of him fit his street name. The dude was huge. He must be 7 foot tall, and he did have a large frame, but Sneaker was right, I only saw muscles, not fat. He was spilling out of that little desk, and must be uncomfortable.

Blade was a lanky, slender guy. His nose and cheekbones that protruded sharply from his face fit his street name, "blade". Both of his arms had colorful ink sleeves with exploding asteroid fields. Whatever artist did his tattoos did an amazing job. The asteroids seemed so realistic with craters and everything. Wait. Were those craters actually scars? When I realized I'd been staring, I tore my gaze away from his arms and back to his face. His cold brown eyes were chilling as they met mine. I turned back to Sneaker.

"So when did Fallentier open?"

"Last year when they transferred the kids that the other homes didn't want." Sneaker fidgeted in his chair. "Before then, Fallentier was some kind of convent. The church closed it, and it sat empty until the government bought the buildings and grounds."

"Is it owned by the Federal government or State?"

"Don't know, don't care." Sneaker's eyelid twitched.

He really needed to work on his tells if he was going to lie to me.

"I think it's Federal," Jinx said.

I was coming to the same conclusion, but what interest would the Federal government have in a group home?

I caught the group leaders from Fallentier watching me. "Why are the leaders checking me out?"

Sneaker glanced back. "Probably considering you for their groups."

Blade stood, then strolled over to stand in front of my desk. "Hablo espanol?"

Should I inform him I spoke Spanish? "My heritage is Italian, not Hispanic."

"I've made exceptions before. If you spoke Spanish, I might consider letting you join our group."

The entire room quieted. Were they all listening? I felt the heavy weight of stares. "I don't think I want to join."

Blade's head tilted to the side as he studied me. "Belonging means you don't face anything alone. Everyone wants to join."

That wasn't what Sneaker said. I shook my head. "The Misfits don't."

Bullet laughed from his seat behind me. He leaned forward over his desk to say, "Not don't, can't. They would jump at the chance if invited."

Crimson lit up Sneaker's cheeks. Hmmm. Maybe they would, but if I were in a group, it would mean more people watching me.

"I'm a loner, so don't expect me to jump at the chance."

At a soft rhythmic thumping, I twisted to see Bullet's leg bouncing as his foot tapped the floor. "No one's invited you, but it won't be long before you wish someone had."

Was that a threat? Blade sauntered back to his seat as Sam's voice came from outside the door.

"Thanks for coming. You're just in time."

"We'd have been here sooner, sir, but our flight got delayed," somebody replied in the hall.

Sam came into the room with a pretty red headed lady and a guy wearing glasses that gave him a scholarly appearance if you ignored his fit body. Both strangers were fairly young, in their mid to late twenties. They paused inside the door and stood rigidly while Sam limped to the desk. Did they have a military background too? Sam put down the stack of papers and faced us.

"If you aren't aware, the public schools decided educating Fallentier students was problematic and, between your constant fights and terrible grades, we had to agree. We have decided not to continue with what was obviously a dismal failure."

Someone snickered.

Sam shook his head. "Remaining ignorant isn't anything to be proud of. It takes education to succeed." The sound of a hammer banging somewhere made it difficult to hear his words.

He raised his voice. "Unfortunately, it's going to be crowded and noisy for a few weeks while we turn some of the unused girls' dorms into a computer room and another classroom for you." Then Sam motioned toward the strangers. "I'm going to let your new teachers introduce themselves and tell you more." He limped toward the door. "Good luck," Sam touted as he passed them to leave the room.

The teachers came inside further. The man stuck a thumb in his chest. "You can call me Mr. Potter."

The woman waved. "And I'm Ms. French. We'll—

A kid with crooked front teeth who Sneaker had called "Pinch" whistled.

"Enough," Mr. Potter barked. "There will be serious consequences for those who can't treat us, those around you, and the equipment with respect." He moved to the desk and sat in one of the chairs. "You may continue, Ms. French."

She pulled a notebook and pencil out of a small purse she carried. "We'll start by going around the room and learning your names"...she pointed at Jinx... "Let's begin with you."

After Jinx and Sneaker relayed their names, they came to me, and when I replied, "Derrick," the screech of a power saw smothered it.

"Can you repeat that?" Ms. French asked.

"His street name's Maverick," Sneaker announced loudly, giving me a smirk.

She pointed her pencil at me. "Is that what you want to be addressed as?"

The new name might be a better fit for this chapter in my life, and it had grown on me.

"Yes, Ma'am."

As her pencil scratched on her paper, kids snickered at my use of Ma'am. I'd been taught to use honorifics when addressing my tutors. Apparently, they didn't use them in public schools.

When we finished introducing ourselves, Mr. Potter stood. "Today, you'll each be taking an assessment test so we can learn what you need. After today, you'll start every morning in foreign language class, then you'll work on your own." He uncrossed his arms. "Once the computer room is ready, each of you will have a computer assigned to you. After lunch, you'll have physical training in the martial arts since we believe they increase fitness, and that's important for our student's health."

Hmmm. Why were they teaching kids to fight when they had rules against it? There were plenty of other ways to keep fit.

Mr. Potter continued, "Does anyone have any questions?"

Kids' hands shot in the air. When Blade raised his, all the other hands lowered. Were they intimidated by him?

Ms. French looked down at her notebook, then back up. "Yes, Blade. What's your question?"

"I already speak two languages." He scowled. "I think that's enough."

Ms. French's lips pursed. "It's good that you speak two languages, but America is a multi-cultural country. Many of our companies are global, so each language you learn will give you more opportunities."

Dad deemed foreign language fluency important as well. To ensure Deidra and I learned several, he'd hired an international staff, but it seemed strange that Fallentier would prioritize foreign languages if these kids were having trouble in their other classes.

Mr. Potter marched around the desk to stand in front of it. "Fallentier considers education essential, so none of this curriculum is optional. Shirking any of it will result in severe consequences." He clasped his hands behind his back. "Any other questions?"

I raised my hand.

"Yes, Maverick?" He must have a good memory if he already remembered my name.

"My social worker says I'll need to take an SAT test to attend college, so can you give that to me?"

"We can schedule an SAT…when you prove to us you're prepared to take it," he said condescendingly, but then he winked. His tone implied he didn't think I was capable, but what did that wink mean?

Ms. French moved around the room and put a slip of paper on each of our desks. "These have the day and time when you will meet with one of us weekly to get individual help."

I glanced at mine. It read, "Tuesday 10 a.m."

She walked back to the front of the room. "We don't want you working together on assignments. Each of them will be different and tailored for your needs."

Mr. Potter picked up the other stack of papers Sam laid on the desk and said, "Most of you will find you're able to complete the same work you did at your old school within a few hours."

"What if you can't?" Sneaker asked.

"Then you better have a good reason." Ms. French had a melodic voice, but her tone was hard. She softened it with a smile.

After Mr. Potter placed a stapled packet on my desk, Ms. French handed me two pencils from a box of them.

"Skip any questions on the test you don't know," she instructed. "When you finish, turn it over on your desk."

My hands trembled as I picked up a pencil. I needed to go to college. I had to pass this test.

Chapter 18

Aspirations

"Changing identities is like borrowing a suit. The trick is convincing yourself you own it." Victor

Maverick

Sneaker had been right. We didn't have to worry about school supplies. I put my name at the top of the test and read the first question to myself. "How do you find the square of a number?"

Seriously? I circled c. *multiply the number by itself.* I read it again to make sure it wasn't a trick. It wasn't. All the questions were easy. Relief poured in.

I only hesitated over a few questions. It had been so long since I'd learned most of it. And it was hard to concentrate with kids shuffling, the papers rustling, and pencils scratching. At least this test didn't take much thinking. Maybe the SAT wouldn't be difficult either. When I finished filling in the last answer on the last page, I turned the test over.

Mr. Potter picked up my test and put down another stapled packet with a blank piece of notebook paper. "Read this and follow the instructions."

As I read the reasons a foreign language could be useful, Mr. Potter continued to pick up tests and take them to Ms. French who seemed to be grading them. She picked up one and glanced at me before handing it to Mr. Potter. He examined it, his eyebrows shot up, then they both looked at me.

What? When he frowned, I dropped my gaze. Had they been examining my test? But their reactions seemed to be almost staged.

Like they already knew my capabilities and were only acting surprised. Maybe I was just being paranoid. I turned to the next page to read how important it was to also learn foreign customs to avoid giving offense. At the bottom of the page were two lines of instructions. "Write at least a paragraph in each foreign language you're fluent in and describe the customs of that country. If you're only fluent in English, use it to list what you know about any foreign countries."

When I filled up one side of my notepaper, I peeked to the side. It seemed as if all the other kids had finished the tests and were now writing. I turned over the paper and continued on the back.

Ms. French began moving around the room. She stopped at kids' desks to quietly ask them to answer a question in Spanish. After they answered, Ms. French would mark something on her pad. Then she stopped beside Hulk. "Are your parents from Nigeria?"

"No, my grandparents but they died when I was little, so I only know a few words of Yoruba.

When she came to me, Ms. French glanced at my paper. "I thought you might be Italian. Your English is very good."

Her words didn't ring as sincere, but regardless, I'd play along. "That's because I'm an American who speaks other languages."

She picked up my paper, then turned it over to scan it. "You speak seven?"

"No. I'm considered fluent in seven—Arabic, Chinese, Farsi, Irish, Italian, Russian, and Spanish, but I speak nineteen conversationally. Twenty if you count Latin, but I usually don't since it's a dead language."

Sneaker kicked me in the shin.

What did he do that for? I glared at him.

He mouthed, "Shut up." His eyes darted around the room.

I followed his gaze. A bunch of kids were scowling at me. Why? Did they consider it wrong to answer questions? Regardless of what these teachers knew about me, I had to either confirm or prove I'd pass a SAT if I wanted them to schedule it. I couldn't do that by hiding my knowledge.

Ms. French put her finger on the side of my paper. "List in the margin each language you speak."

When I finished, she took my paper to Mr. Potter, and they both examined it.

Mr. Potter's brow knitted. "Answer us in the language we use." Then he and Ms. French took turns shooting questions at me in different languages. After I answered six times, Mr. Potter switched to English. "Have you ever seen the test we gave you before today?"

"No. My tutors gave me lots of tests, but not that one."

He and Ms. French exchanged glances before she said, "Well, congratulations. You got a perfect score, so we'll need to figure out a more advanced curriculum for you."

The kids were giving me the stink eye again. Why? Maybe I should be glad I'd never taken classes with other kids.

"Does that mean you'll schedule an SAT for me?" I asked.

Ms. French's eyes twinkled. "Yes."

"Woohoo." I pumped the air with my fist.

Mr. Potter's lip twitched as if holding back a smirk. "We're going to begin with teaching Arabic. So for today, you can help Ms. French demonstrate those customs while I meet with Sam."

If they *really* wanted to teach language skills that would be in demand by corporate America, they should start with Chinese since we exported the most goods to China. Arabic countries weren't even on our top ten export list. One more thing that didn't add up at Fallentier.

When Mr. Potter left the room, Ms. French motioned to me. "Come up here, Maverick." When I did, she said, "Now, pretend we were in Saudi Arabia, and I introduced myself." She extended her hand toward me. "Hi, I'm Ms. French. How would a Saudi respond?"

"He probably wouldn't. Unrelated men and woman in the Saudi culture don't greet one another in public, and they wouldn't touch. But since you're an American, he might make an exception and put his hand over his heart." I put my right hand on my heart. "Then he'd tell you his name, his father's, and grandfather's."

We explained several other Arab customs when Ms. French said, "Thank you, Maverick, you may return to your seat now."

When I did, she began to pass out some more papers. "These are the customs we discussed. I expect you to memorize them by tomorrow." After Ms. French moved beyond me, a spitball came flying toward me. I batted it away.

Someone coughed out, "Teacher's pet."

Someone else hissed, "Suck up."

Ms. French turned. "Is there a problem?"

Tattling would surely make it worse so I shook my head, no. Ms. French resumed passing out papers.

When she finished, she looked at her watch. "It's time for lunch. Remember, there will be martial arts training afterwards, but you can go now."

Kids bolted from their chairs. It sounded like animals stampeding as they ran out of the room and down the steps.

What was the big hurry? I waited until they'd all crammed through the door before I followed, trailing out last.

Sneaker waited outside in the hall and fell in beside me. "Do you have a death wish?"

"No, why?"

"You don't have a clue?"

I just shrugged.

"First, you wear designer clothes and show everybody how much better off you had it than most of us. Then when they consider asking you to join their groups, you turn up your nose and say you're not interested. And then you act like a *know it all* who has to prove how much smarter you are than them. You gave people an awful lot to resent."

I guess I hadn't exactly blended in like Dad recommended. "I wasn't trying to show off."

"That's how it was taken, and that means trouble for you, dude."

Was there anything in my life now that didn't mean trouble? When we got to the first floor, I followed Sneaker into the cafeteria to get behind the other kids in line. As they moved forward, we came to a counter with stacks of trays.

Sneaker took a tray, then spoke softly, "We normally eat outside when we can, but it would be better for you to stay inside so you don't get jumped."

"I'm not going to hide from them."

"Then I guess I'll have to save you. Good thing I like you."

I smothered the laugh that almost escaped me with a cough. I'd seen Sneaker without his shirt. The kid was a beanpole. Pip had more muscle than him.

I straightened my face and grabbed a milk. "How are you going to do that?"

He said softly, "When we go out there, loudly thank me for getting you the test answers. Then I'll say I appreciate the payment, and it's been nice doing business with you." He picked up a straw and napkin from the dispensers. "Then after today, you act stupid."

"If I act stupid, the teachers might decide not to schedule my SAT." I put silverware on my tray. "I'd rather fight than act stupid."

"Then you're going to end up in a hospital, if not a cemetery."

His concern surprised me, but he didn't know about my martial arts training. We came to a line of plates. Sneaker picked up one. It held some type of meat, a sauce that might be apple, something green that looked like creamed peas, and a roll.

"What is that?"

"Your state approved nutritional lunch."

I took a plate with the mystery food. "I know how to defend myself, Sneaker."

"Against several kids at once?"

Sneaker turned toward the doors that led outside were the Fallen kids where spreading out on the grounds to sit on the grass with their cliques.

He paused in front of the doors. "So are you going to stay in?"

"No, I'm going to sit out on the grounds behind that big oak tree so I can let Pip run around."

"I'll sit with you, but if you get into a fight, I won't jump in to help. I can't risk another strike."

I hadn't expected Sneaker's aid. We walked out the doors, and I blinked as my eyes transitioned to the sunlight. When I could see, I caught the stares of the other kids, but ignored them.

After we moved past them, I cut behind the bushes and over to the thick trunk of the oak. It would shield us from sight. With my back against it, I sat and put my tray down.

I took Pip out and let him run around. I pulled the cellophane with blueberries out of my pocket and dumped them in the grass for him.

Sneaker was cutting his meat in sections, then began devouring it.

I pointed to his tray. "So what kind of meat is that?"

Sneaker prodded it with his fork. "I think maybe meatloaf."

Humph. "Do you often eat things you can't identify?"

Sneaker chuckled. "All the time. It beats hungry."

I stirred my applesauce with my spoon. The consistency was too thin, almost like soup. Should I try it?

Sneaker's tray clattered as he tossed it aside. "Uh, oh."

"What?"

He pointed behind me. I swiveled to peer around the tree trunk. A police car was coming up Fallentier's drive.

Chapter 19

Choices

"There's no such thing as too many skills. An ill-prepared agent dies." Victor

Maverick

The police car pulled to a stop on the drive, not far from where Sneaker and I peered out from behind the tree.

A police officer got out and opened his rear door. A handcuffed girl emerged to stand defiantly. She tossed her head, and locks of long black hair swung in front of her heart-shaped face. "I need my stuff."

The officer grabbed a garbage bag out of the car as Fallentier's administrator, Ms. McCaffry, came out of the main building to move toward them.

He dropped the bag at the girl's feet. "I have a new transfer for you."

Why was her face so familiar? Snap. She looked like the younger pictures of my mom. Could it be Deidra? Had I found my missing sister here, of all places? My family picture was in my locker. I should check the picture against this girl's face.

The officer was speaking. "Stay of trouble, Gina, or your next home will be Juvie."

So this girl went by Gina. Whoever kidnapped my sister would have changed her name. My heart wanted to believe it was Deidra, but to have her show up here right after I arrived?

Maybe her resemblance to Deidra was a coincidence. No. Coincidences didn't exist.

As a terrorist suspect, the government would want me watched.

Were they trying to use people I'd be likely to trust to get close to me? Was Gina a plant? They already had Sneaker nosing around, but maybe they were trying to create a floating box and have surveillance on all sides. Or there could be more than one agency targeting me.

Wasn't that girl in trouble on the news called Gina? Maybe she'd cut a deal? I'd need to be cautious around her.

Gina huffed at the police officer, "I got the message the first time." Her eyes narrowed. "Now, get these cuffs off." If her tone wasn't so defiant, her melodic voice would sound like my mom's.

"You better have gotten it." The officer unfastened her cuffs. She rubbed her wrists while he addressed Ms. McCaffrey. "She's all yours. I hope I never see her again."

As he got back in his car, Gina called out, "You won't if I see you first."

"We're serving lunch now." Ms. McCaffrey pointed toward the main building. "The cafeteria's through those doors. I'll have someone show you your room after lunch."

Gina scowled at her. "I'm not hungry, but if that's what passes for a welcome here, it definitely needs work."

Ms. McCaffrey's hands moved to her hips. "That smart mouth attitude will only get you in trouble, so I'd suggest dropping it."

Gina's eyes got cold. "I am smart. Glad you noticed." She grabbed her bag and strolled onto the grounds.

Ms. McCaffrey's lips pursed. She shook her head and marched back in.

"Smoking hot and feisty." Sneaker stared at Gina. "I'm in love." Then he glanced at me. "You can quit glaring at me. I know I don't have a shot with her."

I hadn't realized I'd been glaring, but if there was a chance that was my sister, I didn't like the idea of guys leering at her.

Pip scampered up my leg to return to my hoodie pocket. When I petted him, he curled up to sleep.

I focused on Sneaker again. "You said you know Gina from camp?"

"Yeah. Last year someone had the bright idea of sending the kids who'd been in the system forever to a camp."

"What was the camp like?"

"You know—swimming, canoeing, archery, crafts."

No, I didn't know. That was nothing like my camp.

"It was only two weeks." Sneaker took a drink of his milk then smashed the empty carton. "Uh, oh." He pointed. "Cuk's coming this way."

A beefy guy with greasy hair and jeans that hung so low they dragged the ground was striding toward Gina. He grabbed her wrist. "About time my bae came."

Was she his girlfriend? Didn't matter. Dad said real men protect women, they don't harm them. There were two exceptions. If a woman was trying to kill you, or if they were a trained agent. Dad pitted me against a female operative once, and she kicked my butt. If Gina was untrained, I needed to help her, but Pip could get hurt.

I pulled off my hoodie carefully so I didn't dislodge Pip and held it out to Sneaker. "She needs help. Will you hold on to Pip for me?"

"Yeah," he took my shirt. "Cuk is cray cray, so be careful or he might kill you."

I might kill him. Most of my training concentrated on taking an enemy out quietly with sudden and lethal strikes. But that could mean a murder charge here. I'd have to try not to hurt him too much.

Gina was yanking her arm trying to break the guy's hold. "I don't even know you, so let go of me.

Cuk pulled Gina closer and rasped, "My bae needs to treat me extra *nice*."

She dropped her bag and kneed Cuk. He bent over, releasing her.

She snapped, "Like my *nice*?"

Cuk hissed. "You'll pay for that."

If Gina had training, she'd have followed through, and he'd be unconscious. A bunch of other kids from Fallentier were moving toward them.

Sneaker grabbed my arm. "You should let Bullet help her. Cuk will listen to him."

Would he? I'd wait a second to see.

Chapter 20

Not Alone

"Instincts are valuable assets, so don't ignore them." Victor

Gina

I hadn't even been in this place five minutes before some jerk confronted me. You'd think he'd stop spewing threats after I kneed him.

"Better watch out, Cuk. Gina will bust your head open." That was Bullet's voice.

I spun to see the same old Bullet, leading the charge toward me with some other kids I'd met at camp. There was MB who hid his brains behind a tough guy image and flamboyant red Mohawk. Blade, as graceful and deadly as a panther was followed closely by the gentle giant Hulk, and Felicity, the fiery Hispanic girl who'd refused to be brushed off and insisted she was my friend. That only lasted until camp ended and I found out once again how temporary friendships were. Should have figured they'd be at Fallentier since they'd been in the system for years too.

Felicity yelled, "Gina," before running up and throwing her arms around me.

I didn't like anyone touching me, and Felicity had abandoned me. I stepped back. "You said you'd keep in touch."

"I wanted to, Chica, but my phone got stolen."

Hmmm. So that was why she didn't answer when I called. I turned to the others. Blade's ink sleeves had been finished. I knew Felicity was an amazing artist, but she outdid herself.

I motioned to them. "Your tats turned out wicked."

Blade's mouth turned up just a little into one of his rare smiles. "Yeah, they did."

I lifted my chin to give Bullet a nod. "What up?"

Bullet shrugged. "Living the dream. Saw you on the news. Figured you'd be doing time."

I should never have done that stupid interview. "I didn't kill Fred, just put him in a coma. They probably thought sending me to Fallentier was punishment enough."

The guy who I'd kneed sputtered, "You won't be acting so tough after I finish with you."

Bullet's chest puffed out, and he glared at him. "You need to back off, Cuk. She's my girlfriend, and she'll be choosing to join the Hicks." He took a step closer to me.

"Whoa. First him, now you. I think I'd know if I had a boyfriend, and I don't."

Bullet frowned. "I told you I liked you."

"And telling someone you like them makes them your girlfriend? Not hardly. And if you liked me so much, why haven't you called me?"

Bullet blushed. "I've been busy, but you're here now, so we can talk whenever you want. But first you need to join my group so you won't have any more problems. We don't risk strikes unless you belong."

MB grinned at me. "Why would you want to join the Hicks when you can join the Freaks? Bald isn't beautiful."

Felicity touched my arm. When I flinched, she dropped her hand and said, "I'm with the Tinos. Blade will let you join us."

I knew better than to think I'd get something for nothing. "So what do I have to do if I join?"

"Same as everyone else." Blade smirked. "Whatever the leader tells you."

"He doesn't tell me much." Felicity stage-whispered to me. "No group wants to lose a girl when there are only three in Fallentier."

Didn't matter. I didn't take orders. "I can take care of myself."

Bullet put his finger under my chin. I jerked back. His face fell, but he covered it with a wink. "You're smokin, so you're going to attract trouble. Too much to fight alone."

"Hey," a boy hollered as he pushed kids aside to break through the ring that had formed around me.

Wow. The guy shoving his way like a wrecking ball toward me was really hot. Wavy black hair, brown eyes, a classical face, and muscles that strained against his tank top.

"Teacher's pet, what you doing?" MB taunted.

Hot guy's jaw tightened, and his toffee eyes fixed on MB. "The name's Maverick, and I came to help Gina."

He came over to help me? I couldn't help but stare at his mesmerizing eyes. The toffee color was rimmed at the edges with lighter gold flecks, streaking outward in a starburst pattern. I finally tore my gaze away.

"I think Gina likes you," MB said. "I'll let you both join if she chooses the Freaks."

Bullet scowled as MB turned to me. "Both the other girls at Fallentier have boyfriends here. That still leaves thirty guys who will want the only girl who's not taken. That's too many problems to handle alone."

I'd handled plenty of problems before on my own, but this Cuk seemed as crazy as my mom, and crazy people weren't reasonable.

"You don't have to join one of their groups," Maverick said. "I'll help you if you want."

Bullet snorted. "Do you think we'll let you start your own group?"

Maverick shook his head. "I'm not doing that."

MB's arched eyebrows and Bullet's sneer left no doubt they didn't believe him.

If I let hot guy help me, what kind of payment would he expect. I crossed my arms. "I won't do whatever you want in return."

"I don't want anything," Maverick replied.

"Then why help me?" I uncrossed my arms. "And don't lie, cause I'll be able to tell."

"My sister was forced into a vehicle by a kidnapper." A heavy breath escaped him. "I wish I could go back and stop him from manhandling her. I can't, but I *can* help you."

"Are you sure about that?" MB asked.

Maverick's biceps bulged as he balled his hands into fists. "Yes."

There was no hesitation. He believed it. I wanted to believe him too.

"Come on, Gina." Bullet gave me a saucy grin. "Join the Hicks. I know you want to."

Not hardly. I looked at Maverick. "I'll take your help."

Maverick gave me a smile that lit his eyes. Then his penetrating gaze locked on Cuk. "This is your only warning. Don't touch her again."

Cuk snickered and grabbed my arm. I tried to yank away, but couldn't break his hold. He sneered at Maverick. "What are you going to do?"

Maverick lunged forward to punch Cuk's cheek. Cuk's head snapped away, then he recovered and swung wildly at Maverick.

Maverick sidestepped and hollered at me. "Get back."

Without thinking, I retreated as Cuk charged. Maverick ducked under Cuk to flip him over his shoulder and away from me.

Maverick pounced on him, driving a fist toward Cuk's throat. His fist stopped an inch before it hit Cuk's Adam's apple.

"Stay down," he snarled.

When Maverick turned away from him, Cuk lunged up. He threw an uppercut which landed on Maverick's ear. Maverick recoiled, and his hand flew up to cup his ear. It was probably ringing.

Cuk was drawing his fist back to hit him again.

I flung myself at Cuk and jumped on his back. He grabbed my leg and tossed me off. I tumbled on the ground, and my air rushed out with an oomph. I lay gasping for breath.

Maverick had spun around, and he threw a right cross to Cuk's jaw. Cuk crumpled in a heap.

Maverick leaned over Cuk. "Just knocked out." He straightened, then flexed his fingers on his right hand. Did he hurt it? He hurried over to where I was still lying on the ground.

His eyes roamed over me. "No blood," he whispered under his breath. He extended his left hand to me. "Are you okay?"

"I'm fine."

I didn't like other people's touch, but he'd helped me so I took his hand. Instead of the normal revulsion, warmth surged through me as he pulled me to my feet. When I was steady, he let go. It felt as if I'd lost something crucial. Like the first time I tried to ride a bike without training wheels. How crazy was that? I wasn't one of those girls who fell in love with every hot guy I saw.

Cuk groaned. He fingered his jaw.

Maverick stalked back to him. "You got off easy... this time." There were a lot of kids around us, and Maverick's gaze pinned them all. "I'm warning all of you. Don't mess with me or her."

Bullet rolled his shoulders. "Everyone's not as easy of a fight."

Maverick balled his fists. "You want to try me?"

"Yeah, but not here, not now."

Sneaker came up and handed Maverick his sweatshirt.

When Maverick took it, the other girl called, "Don't cover that ripped body." She fanned her face with her hand. "I like the view."

Felicity giggled. "Me too."

When Blade gave Felicity a glare, she shrugged. "Nothing wrong with looking, only touching."

Red flushed Maverick's cheeks.

"Scramble, Sam's coming," MB hissed in warning.

Footsteps pounded against the ground as kids rushed away from the adult heading our way.

"Come on." Sneaker took a few steps back.

I moved to follow. The adult, Sam, pointed at me and Maverick. "You two, stop."

Maverick froze. I halted, too, but Sneaker kept going. Sam strode to where Cuk was picking himself off the ground.

"Are you okay?" Sam asked.

"Yeah." Cuk glared at Maverick and me. "No thanks to them."

Maverick narrowed his eyes. "Then don't manhandle girls."

Sam's tone turned cold. "All three of you just earned a strike for fighting. That's your third strike, Cuk, so you're going to Juvie. I'll take you to your room so you can gather your things." He pointed to me and Maverick. "After martial arts training, go to Ms. McCaffry's office."

Ugh. Would we be receiving a lecture or worse?

Chapter 21

Sparring

Maverick

When Gina and I joined the other kids in the cafeteria, the tables had been folded down and stacked against the walls, and Mr. Potter and Ms. French were laying mats on the floors.

When they finished, Mr. Potter asked, "Have any of you had fight training?"

Several kids' hands went up. Normally, my training wasn't something I divulged, but I couldn't protect Gina if I didn't convince these kids that I wasn't someone to mess with. I raised my hand.

"Okay," Mr. Potter said. "Everyone put your hands down except those who learned boxing."

I kept my hand up. Hulk and Bullet had their hands up too.

"Okay what about martial arts?" he asked.

I left my arm up. So did Bullet. MB and several others kids raised theirs.

"You can put your hands down. Those of you that have had no training will go with Ms. French so she can teach you some basic defense moves."

After Gina and several other kids followed Ms. French to the back of the room, Mr. Potter continued, "The rest of you will split up but stay in the front half of the room. Those who trained in martial arts will partner up to spar with each other. Those who trained in boxing will do the same. Bullet and Maverick, since you both had mixed training, you'll partner together. I don't want anyone putting force behind any strike. This is training, not a fight." He motioned to the mats. "We wouldn't be using them if we wanted you hurt."

Bullet shot me an evil grin, then moved toward me. Would he ignore that last part and pull his strikes? Better if I didn't find out.

"I hope you like kissing mats," he taunted.

With his flat-footed, narrow stance, I could easily knock his legs from under him. I rose to the balls of my feet and shifted my weight. With a roundhouse kick, I struck. He toppled.

"I wasn't ready," he snarled as he picked himself up.

"Are you ready now?" I asked.

His answer was a grunt as he put force behind a punch he threw at me. I dodged, and his fist whistled by me. I pivoted to kick the back of his knee. His leg gave out, and he fell, catching himself on the mat to spring back up. He charged me, ducking his head into my gut.

I grabbed him around his neck and twisted my body, then pushed him past and down on the mat.

His face and neck were beet red as he lunged up.

"Enough," Mr. Potter hollered.

I glanced up. Everyone in the room had stopped sparring and were staring at us. Hmmm. Had they been watching long?

Mr. Potter pointed to a spot next to the door. "Bullet, go sit on the floor over there and cool off. You won't be sparring more until you learn not to use force. Maverick, I'll partner with you." He glanced at the other kids. "I'd tell you to ignore us, but I know that won't happen, so I'll let you watch. You might pick up a few pointers."

He turned and bowed to me. I returned his bow. Then he circled me. I moved with him. He front kicked and shouted, "Ei," but I blocked it with my arm. He blocked my hammer fist, then my heel strike yelling, "Toh."

Our sparring sped up to a flurry of arms and legs moving to strike and block one other, but nothing landed. He punctuated his strikes with shouts, but I'd been taught to fight in silence to keep any nearby enemies from hearing.

I struggled for breath, but so did he, his shouts a whisper of what they were. One of his arms dropped, leaving me an opening. Was that a feint? I threw a hook. He ducked it and came inside my guard, moving to strike my chest with his elbow. Ready for that, I grabbed his upraised arm, twisting around to jab his kidney.

Mr. Potter dropped his arms. "That's a point for you. We're out of time, so I'll concede today's match to you. Congratulations."

That one jab would have never ended a real fight. "Thanks. You're a formidable opponent."

"Likewise." He bowed to me.

I bowed back.

"Class is over for today, so you're all dismissed except you, Bullet."

"Why do I have to stay?" Bullet grumbled.

"Because you need to pick up the mats and put the tables back. Call it punishment for ignoring a teacher's instructions."

Bullet shot me a glare. Was he going to blame me for his own actions? His eyes narrowed even more as I quickly moved to join Gina, who had headed toward the door. I needed to figure out if she was my sister.

"I can show you where Ms. McCaffry's office is if you don't mind me walking with you?"

She shrugged. "Be my guest."

I opened the door for her, then motioned to it. "After you."

When she walked through, I followed her, then pointed to the hallway leading to the offices. "This way."

She appeared nonchalant as we hiked down the hall. I'd never been sent to a principal or administrator's office before. Was my concern needless?

Chapter 22

Nosy

"If you have hope, you have the key ingredient to succeed." Victor

Maverick

Ms. McCaffrey looked up from some papers as Gina and I came to the open door of her office.

"Derrick and Gina." Her surly tone made it clear she wasn't happy with us. "It didn't take you long to start breaking the rules."

"Some jerk grabbed me, so I needed to defend myself." Gina flung her hand toward me. "He was just helping me."

Ms. McCaffrey pointed to the two chairs at the front of her deck. "Sit down." When Gina and I squeezed into the chairs, Gina put her garbage bag in her lap.

Ms. McCaffrey leaned over her desk toward us. "Besides both getting a strike, you'll receive a punishment because you decided to fight instead of going to the staff for help. You can sit in the hall and wait for Sam, who will show you what those consequences will be."

"Oooh. I'm so worried," Gina snarled as we walked out.

When Gina plopped in one of the three chairs sitting outside the administrator's office and placed her garbage bag in front of her, I sat next to her. This was my chance to find out more about her.

"How long have you been in the system?" I asked softly.

"Seven years. You?"

"Two days." I took a breath to calm myself. "How old are you?"

"I turn seventeen next week." Her green eyes studied me. "How old are you?"

Deidra would have just turned sixteen since we were one year and two days apart, but wouldn't a kidnapper try and convince a kid of a different birthday?

"I just turned seventeen. Do you remember your parents?"

"Nosy much?" Her pert nose wrinkled. "Why would my parents be your business?" Her fractious tone left no doubt she didn't want to discuss it. Her question was valid. What would it hurt to answer?

"My sister was six years old when she was kidnapped. She's still missing, and you look just like her. So do you remember your childhood?"

"Yeah. My mom abandoned me when I was eight years old, then died of an overdose. I'm not your sister."

"Maybe she wasn't your mother but your kidnapper."

She rolled her eyes. "She wanted drugs, not kids."

"My father would have paid any ransom for my sister, and that would buy a lot of drugs."

"Then why wouldn't she have turned me over?"

"Maybe she got scared after all the press." There was a way to know for certain if I could find someone to run it. "Would you be willing to take a DNA test? All it would take is a few strands of your hair."

"I'm not your sister, so I don't see any point unless there's something in it for me."

Not with all our assets frozen. "Only my thanks."

"Then no."

She twisted in her chair to move closer. "So how did you end up at Fallen?"

Like she didn't already know. "My dad went on the run after he was framed for something he didn't do."

"That must suck." Her voice softened. "Isn't there any way you can join him?"

Was she trying to learn whether Dad was nearby and if I could contact him? "Who sent you here to spy on me?"

Her eyes widened and she spat out, "No one."

Could I be wrong about her? "So how did you get out of jail?"

She hesitated then said, "Wasn't enough evidence to charge me."

Could be true, but her tone was far from convincing. Before I could ask anything else, Sam stalked up to us with his left leg dragging heavily.

"The two of you will be joining Cuk soon if you keep getting strikes."

"Am I not supposed to defend myself?" Gina snarled.

"Maybe you should think of a different solution than fighting while I talk to Ms. McCaffrey. I'm sure you'll want one after you learn the consequences.

How much worse could it get?

Chapter 23

Consequences

"How can one be certain any fear isn't a paranoid delusion and evidence of insanity?" Gina

Gina

When Sam left us to talk to Ms. McCaffrey, I opened my garbage bag and checked my stuff. My phone was on top, and everything appeared to be there. The police must have left it alone. Good. I didn't want to lose any of it.

I caught Maverick staring at my garbage bag. I blushed then got angry at myself for being embarrassed over what some spoiled rich kid thought.

"We all can't haul our stuff around in fancy suitcases," I griped. "You've probably never even gone hungry."

His brown eyes pierced me. "I've been through things worse than being hungry, and I think you have too."

"You don't know anything about me."

"But I will." He reached over and snatched something off my shoulder. He had a couple of loose pieces of my hair. I grabbed for his hand, but he pulled it behind his back and mouthed, "Finders keepers."

I glared at him. "I didn't say you could take them."

I barely heard his soft reply, "What are you going to do, snitch to Sam?"

If I did that, it would prove to him that I was a rat. "No, but I'm going to be mad if you run my DNA."

He grinned at me, flashing his perfect teeth. "You may thank me later if it turns out you're my sister."

Ugh. This guy might be hot, but he was delusional. My cheeks heated with anger. I looked away, ignoring Maverick.

Sam emerged from Ms. McCaffrey's office. "Now you'll learn the consequences of fighting. Come on."

Even with Sam's limp, I had to take two steps to each of his strides as Maverick and I followed him down the hall in the main building. Why was Sam in such a hurry?

He paused when we came to the steps. "Maverick, go change into clothing that stains won't hurt, then meet me back in the kitchen in five minutes. I need to show Gina to her room."

Maverick nodded, then jogged away. I turned back to find Sam already half-way up the steps. I rushed after him.

At the top of the staircase, a hallway led in two directions. The sound of hammering came from the right where a line of construction tape blocked it off. Plastic sheeting lay on the floor, with a toolbox on top. The banging stopped, and a big guy walked out of an open door and over to the toolbox.

He did a double-take when he saw us. "Oh, hello sir, I mean Sam. We're almost done. The drywall's finished, so we'll start painting." He dropped a tape measure inside the toolbox. "After that, you'll be good to go."

"Great. Our kids will enjoy having the new computer room and classroom."

He laughed. "Not if you're teaching any classes."

Sam chuckled too. "I'm not." He waved at me. "I've got to show a new transfer to her room, so we'll leave you to it."

"Roger that."

That was strange. This Sam guy didn't act like a teacher, and that worker spoke like a soldier. Sam turned to the left, and I followed him.

"Fallentier kids share rooms," he said. "You'll be in with Felicity."

At least I knew her. He stopped at the second door and opened it.

There were two narrow beds with lockers between them. Felicity must sleep on the left since that bed had her stuffed kitten, "Tigger," lying on top. She had dragged that stuffed animal to camp too.

"Put your stuff away, change, and meet us back in the kitchen in five minutes." Sam instructed before he left.

I threw my bag on the bed and sorted through it until I found an old t-shirt to wear. No sense in unpacking, but I better grab my phone before I shoved the bag in my locker. I looked in my bag. Where was it? I dumped everything out on the bed. It wasn't there.

My heart plummeted. I needed my phone and my contact numbers. Did it fall out without me noticing? Doubtful. Could Maverick have taken it?

Chapter 24

Revelations

"Trusting blindly can get an agent exploited, imprisoned, or killed."
Victor

Maverick

I let Pip down to run around my room while I searched for a baggie. After dumping my toothpaste out of one, I slid in Gina's hair and zipped it closed. I pulled out her phone and the slip of paper from my pocket.

A twinge of guilt struck me for taking Gina's phone. But this was important and could help her. I took a deep breath, read the number on the paper, and made the call I never thought I would.

A guy with a low voice answered on the first ring. "Is this Derrick?"

Hmmm. Was I the only one with this number? "Yes. I wish to speak to my grandfather."

"Just a minute, I'll patch you through."

A minute later my grandfather's voice came through the phone, "Derrick?"

"Yes. I think I might've found Deidra."

"Where?"

"At the group home. I know it seems weird, but it could be her."

"So what do you want me to do?" he asked.

"We need to run a DNA test."

"I told you it takes more than blood to be family. If you've changed your mind about joining us, I'll help you, but you've got to commit. You can't expect to gain our aid while you sit on the fence."

After the callous way he'd spoken about killing Connor, there's no way I wanted in. "I'm sorry. I thought you'd want to know. It was a mistake to bother you."

I hung up, deleted the number in Gina's phone, then tore up the paper with the number written on it. I wasn't going to let myself be tempted to call again. Whatever happened now, I was on my own.

I hurriedly changed into my workout clothes, gathered Pip, and headed back to the main building's kitchen. I checked Gina's contacts on the way. She didn't have many, less than ten. I found two names—Parker and Jax—that were agent's aliases. Jax was FBI, Parker was CIA. Both knew me since they had taken Dad's training courses, and Parker had been with Connor when I'd been forced to leave our home.

The whole situation angered me. To pursue this witch hunt, the government was utilizing resources that should be spent on catching the real bad guys, not wasted on us.

When I reached the kitchen, Gina was at the sink filling up a bucket with soapy water as Sam looked on.

I held up her phone. "I found this. Did you lose a phone, Gina?"

"Yeah, it's mine." She rushed over to take it from me and stuffed it in her pocket. "Thanks for returning it."

"That's enough water." Sam motioned to Gina's bucket. "Let Maverick fill one."

After I added soap and water to a bucket, and Sam led us outside, I whispered to Gina, "Tell Parker and Jax I said hi."

She blushed a furious red. "You had no right."

"When it concerns me, I make it my right. You should have told me who you were working for when I asked nicely."

***

I dipped my scrub brush back into the pail of soapy water. I wouldn't mind dumping the bucket over myself to wash the sweat away. Whoever painted over the tier so it read "Fallen Group Home" had done too good of a job. The paint wasn't coming off easily. Neither had the dirt on the floor or the walls that Gina and I scoured in the cottages this afternoon.

Gina looked as uncomfortable as I was. Sweat glistened on her face and plastered her hair to her head. When she caught me looking, she sneered. Yeah, she was still angry with me.

She wasn't a very good spy. Even with her cover blown, she should be trying to gather more Intel on me. Maybe she was roped into doing it. It might be better if I stayed away from her, but I couldn't until I found out for sure whether she was my sister. Besides, what if one of these guys tried to strong arm her again? I couldn't let that happen. I needed to stay close to her.

Gina looked at her watch, then defiantly over at Sam, who stood watching us from under the shade of a tree.

"You said our punishment was three hours of chores." She dropped her brush in the bucket. "Three hours is up."

Sam crossed his arms. "If you had worked faster, you'd be done."

I tried a nicer tone. "The sign's not going anywhere. If we finish it tomorrow when we're not so tired, we could probably do a better job."

Sam harrumphed. "All right, but you will *do* better tomorrow." He pointed to the buckets. "Dump your water, then rinse the buckets and put them away before you join everyone else."

"Our punishment wasn't supposed to be tomorrow too." Gina picked up her bucket.

Sam shrugged. "You'll finish tomorrow like Maverick suggested."

"Thanks, Maverick," Gina snapped, then she flung her bucket so the dirty water spilled and splashed my shoes and legs.

So she wanted to play that game? I tossed my water toward her.

She jumped to the side, but not fast enough to avoid getting soaked. She sputtered, "You..." Then she clamped her lips shut.

Had the no cursing rule saved me an earful? I laughed. "You shouldn't play with water if you're afraid to get wet."

She threw up her arms and hollered, "Ugh! Look at me!" Then she pivoted and stomped up the lane toward Fallentier.

As we rushed to catch up with Gina, Sam chuckled and said, "Your social skills need work, Maverick."

When the guards opened the gate for us, most of the other kids were hanging out in their groups around the grounds. Everyone stared at us. Must be Gina. Beauty like hers drew attention like a flame drew moths.

Sam turned toward the cottage as Gina and I headed to the main building. After Sam limped inside, Sneaker rushed over with some kids trailing him.

"I've got good news, Bro." Sneaker waved to the kids with him. "All the Misfits want to join our group, and so do some of the kids in other groups."

If that many kids were around me, it would make it difficult to disappear when I needed to snoop or leave the grounds.

"I told you I'm a loner. If you want a group, fine, start one, but I'm not joining."

Gina had already ducked inside the building. I opened the door to do the same.

Sneaker waved the other kids off. "Wait for me out here. I need to talk to Maverick." He followed me in and stage whispered, "The leaders of the other groups already think we're trying to form another group, so they want to beat the crap out of us." His voice cracked in desperation. "We might avoid that if we have enough kids to stop them."

Most Misfits seemed small or scrawny like Sneaker, which is probably why they hadn't been chosen for a group. I'd just have more to protect unless I taught them to fight, and that would take a while. Each of them would be a rope tying me down.

I traipsed through the cafeteria to the kitchen. "I don't want a group."

The staff hadn't started fixing dinner yet, and the kitchen appeared deserted except for Gina who stood at the sink.

She finished rinsing her bucket and handed me the sprayer. "Thanks to you, I need to change." She left the kitchen.

Sneaker moved over to the sink. "What do you expect me to do?"

I rinsed my bucket and hung the sprayer up. "You're free to do whatever you like."

His shoulders drooped. "You mean I'm free to get my head smashed in for being your friend."

After I put my bucket in the closet, Sneaker trailed me out of the cafeteria. I looked over at my shoulder at him.

"Here's the thing. I know you're not my friend. I'm your assignment."

"If you were only an assignment, I'd quit now and have nothing more to do with you," Sneaker mumbled as we headed out the front door.

I blinked in the bright sunlight and paused to let my eyes adjust. The Misfits were waiting over by the vending machines, but I wasn't going over there. "Then leave me. You said you can't risk strikes, so tell everybody we aren't friends. That should protect you, and isn't that what you care about?"

"Yeah, but I said that before I considered you a friend, and a friend doesn't bounce if their friend needs them."

It would be nice to have a *real* friend. Except Sam told Sneaker to befriend me. How could I trust this wasn't an act?

Sneaker moved toward the Misfits. "I'll tell them you don't want them."

"Good." The sky darkened as clouds moved to blot out the sun. Must be going to rain soon. After all the scrubbing today, I stank. I wanted a real shower with soap, not a rain shower, so I hiked back to my room. After I cleaned up, I sat on the cot, and before I knew it, nodded off. Growls from my stomach woke me. I checked my watch. 5:25. Fallentier served dinner from 5:30 to 6:30.

Pip was in his box sleeping. He should be all right if I left him in my room. When I headed out of the cottage to go back to the main building, I shivered. The temperature had dropped considerably. Hard to believe how hot it was earlier. The gray sky, wet grass, and puddles showed that the storm must have come and gone while I slept, cooling things off.

Most of the Fallen kids filing toward the main building for dinner wore hoodies or jackets. When I reached the doors, I hung back from the press of bodies streaming through, then trailed them inside.

At the counter, I filled my tray with fried chicken. One of the staff said, "Everyone will be eating in the cafeteria tonight since several of you didn't return your trays after lunch and left them outside."

I looked for a place to eat. Each group claimed a table, and kids sat with the group they belonged to. Several staff members filled another table. There weren't any empty tables.

Sneaker waved at an empty chair at the Misfits table. "Over here, Bro."

The rest of the Misfits looked at me as if I could fulfill all their wishes—like I was Santa with a bag of gifts. Did they think I'd change my mind about forming a group? Sitting there might add to their delusion.

I walked to the closest table, MB's. He scowled at me, then glanced at the staff before stage whispering, "This is for Freaks only. You can't sit here."

The entire cafeteria had gone quiet, and my reply seemed to echo. "Wouldn't want to. I like a better view."

After I hooked the backs of two empty chairs with my free arm, I took them over to a window. I sat in one and propped my tray on the other. I ignored the other kids and concentrated on devouring my fried chicken.

Shuffling steps alerted me. Sneaker carried a chair and his tray toward me. "I like a view too."

"I'm fine alone. You don't have to sit by me."

Sneaker plopped down his chair and sat. "The other Misfits want to come back too. If I wave, they'll know it's okay."

No wonder they were staring again at me with longing. And they weren't the only ones watching. The eyes of the entire room were on us, and the group leaders' stares weren't friendly. "Don't."

Chapter 25

Stuck up

"Only in fairy tales do girls get rescued by princes." Gina

Gina

The Tinos were mostly speaking Spanish at their table, so I didn't understand them, but Felicity had asked me to sit with her. Too nervous to be hungry, I picked at my food and let my gaze drift around the cafeteria. My breath caught when I found Maverick sitting near the window. Like a perfectly sculpted museum piece, Maverick's muscular frame was cold perfection. His ebony hair a striking contrast to his toffee eyes and bronze skin.

Felicity nudged my arm, drawing my attention back to them. "Guys, you're leaving Gina out. Speak English."

I wish she hadn't done that. Now they were all staring at me.

"I'm fine." I glanced at the room. "Just checking things out."

Felicity laughed. "Not things. Maverick."

Sneaker smiled at something Maverick said. When Maverick's attention turned from him, Sneaker's face fell. The kid might seem happy go lucky but it was a thin façade. He was as haunted as the rest of us, only he bottled up his anger and despair until it burst out and consumed him.

I turned back to Felicity. "Did anyone warn Maverick about Sneaker?"

"No, and you shouldn't either," Blade replied curtly. "If Sneaker wants to tell him, he will."

"What if Maverick wakes up to the same nightmare we did?" I huffed.

Felicity touched my arm. "Sneaker's not having issues now."

"Everyone thought he was fine at camp too."

Blade pointed his fork toward Maverick. "Your boy's stuck up. He comes from money, so he's not interested in you, or Sneaker, or anyone else here. You're chasing the wrong dude."

Heat rose to my cheeks. "I was only curious because everyone else is watching him."

"Because they know he doesn't belong," Blade said sharply. Was he jealous of Maverick? All the leaders probably resented Maverick for becoming the center of attention.

Could Blade be right when he pegged Maverick as stuck up? Maverick sure didn't act as if he cared what anyone thought. That made him even more intriguing.

Now that my cover was blown, he wouldn't want near me. Usually, I was the one avoiding unwanted attention.

His searching eyes landed on me again. His head tilted a little as if trying to figure me out. I wanted to hide to keep him from learning more, only I was trapped in his hypnotizing gaze.

My heart skipped. Warmth flooded my cheeks as my hand fluttered to the base of my throat.

Then Maverick shook his head. His focus left me to wander the room again.

Blade swallowed his last mouthful of food. "You're wrong. Only half of these dudes are watching Maverick. The rest are watching you watch him."

Felicity nudged him. "Gina's beautiful. Of course, guys are interested."

The guys here didn't have much to choose from. Felicity was just being nice. Maverick sure didn't act as if I were beautiful.

Blade finished guzzling his milk and threw his carton on his tray. "Yeah, but maybe she thinks she's too good for Fallen kids too?"

No, but I refused to open myself to more heartache when I'd need to leave here as soon as they learned about me. Ratting to staff could get you beaten up, ratting to cops might kill you. No one would forgive that.

"I'm not too good, and I'd like to keep my old friends." But I knew I wouldn't.

Felicity grabbed my hand and rubbed a hidden note against my palm. "Old friends are there for each other."

I curled my hand around the slip of paper. Blade checked his phone, then grabbed his empty plate and stood. "Time to go."

Felicity and all the Tino's jumped up. "Do you want to go to town on the bus with us?" Felicity asked.

"What do you do there?"

"Shopping and an arcade."

Hmm. Maverick was still sitting, and I should try to keep an eye on him. "Probably not."

"Okay." She waved as she followed Blade. "See you later."

"Later." After they headed out the door, I opened the note Felicity had passed me and read, "Warn your boyfriend they're going to jump him."

Oh no. I had to tell Maverick. He and Sneaker were returning their trays to the counter, then they headed toward the door.

I rushed over to catch them. "I need to talk to you, Maverick."

Sneaker kept moving but tossed Maverick a wave. "I'll meet up with you later."

I handed Maverick the note. "Felicity gave me this."

He read it. "You told her I'm your boyfriend?"

"Of course not, but that shouldn't be what you're worried about."

He shrugged. "If they want a fight, I'll give it to them."

Ugh. "Are you stupid?"

"I don't think so." The clang of a dropped tray grabbed his attention.

When he turned back to me, I said, "You act like it. Everyone in this room was watching you."

"So?"

"So, kids here admire one thing, who's toughest. After you knocked out Cuk and won that martial arts match against Potter, everyone thinks that's you."

He waved the note. "The leaders don't admire me."

"No, they're too worried that if you let kids join you, Fallentier could end up with only one group—yours."

A couple of kids were trying to get out the door we were blocking. Maverick retreated a couple of steps to let them through and motioned to me to do the same.

After they left, he said, "That's too much drama for me."

If he let other kids join him, he probably wouldn't get jumped. Surely he must realize to fight alone, meant losing. I blew out my breath. I couldn't fix stupid.

He reached into his hoodie pocket. "There is something I wanted to show you." He drew out a family picture of a woman and man with two kids.

He pointed at the woman. "That was my mom." His finger moved to touch the little girl's face. "And this is my sister, Deidra. Now tell me they don't look exactly like you."

They resembled me some, but there was no way I was his sister. I didn't know every detail of my early childhood, but I knew the hunger pains were always there. And before mom abandoned me, she told me she'd be better off without me. She wouldn't have stolen a kid she didn't even want.

Should I let him keep his delusions and the hope shining in his eyes? Had everyone been doing me a kindness when they fed me fairy tales? Telling me I would go to a nice home and get a new mom and dad who'd love and take care of me. No. It was cruel since the longer someone believed in happily ever after, the more it crushed them to learn it was a lie.

"I admit they look like me a little, but not exactly."

He waved the picture. "Look at my mom's eyes. Look at Deidra's. Those are your eyes."

"They have green eyes. Lots of people do, but they're not like mine. They're a lighter shade and rounder."

He examined the picture again. "This was in the studio under lots of lights. That's why they look lighter."

I'd love to believe I didn't have a crazy lady's genes, but I couldn't put hope in fairy tales. And neither should he.

"I'm not your sister." I walked out the door of the building and Maverick followed. The cool air hit me, and I shivered. In just a few hours, fall had arrived. I stuck my hands under my arms to warm them.

Sneaker was talking to some Misfits. He broke away and came over to us. "You still want to go into town, Maverick."

"Are there shops where I can buy a phone?"

"Yeah."

"Then yes."

Sneaker scuffed the ground with his shoe and mumbled, "It might be safer for you to stay here."

"I'm not hiding."

"Okay, I'll go too." Sneaker glanced at me. "What about you, Gina?"

"I'll go." How else would I learn what Maverick was up to?

Chapter 26

Surprises

"For an agent to be surprised is a failure on their part to anticipate an outcome." Victor

Maverick

The flashing lights, dings, and buzzers were hard to ignore as I perused the games in the arcade. Some of them appeared interesting, but I didn't have money to waste. Could we leave? Sam was the chaperone for our excursion to town. I strolled over to where he stood playing a car driving game. His car crashed.

"You have to brake going into those turns," I explained.

"I've been driving longer than you, Maverick, but if you think you can beat me…" Sam pointed to the other steering wheel on the game console. "Play against me."

I'd won that game before on my computer, but it wasn't what I should be doing. "I need to go to that electronic store I saw."

Several other kids piped up that they wanted to go to different places too.

"All right, but not alone," Sam said. "Go in groups and stay out of trouble. We'll meet at the electronic store in an hour."

"I'll go with you, Maverick," Sneaker announced.

Felicity and Blade were already moving toward the door with Gina in tow. Would Blade protect her? He didn't earlier, so I called out, "Gina, I want you to come with me so you'll be safe."

"Trouble magnet like you." She rolled her eyes, but she stopped and waited. "With you is probably the least safe, but I'll try to keep you from harm."

When we reached the electronic store, I browsed the phone displays. Most of the phones were hundreds of dollars. The few that weren't had a sticker below the price, "with a two-year contract."

"Don't they have any cheap burner phones?" I asked Sneaker.

"No, but the truck stop does."

Several other Fallen kids were in the store. Blade was playing with a 3D electronic game. Hulk was trying on a flashy watch. Bullet was scrolling through the options on an expensive phone. MB's fingers flew as he typed on one of their demo laptops.

When those four took their selections up to the check-out line, I asked Sneaker, "How do they get the money for that stuff?"

Sneaker rubbed the back of his head. A sign that he didn't want to answer me. "Um, we get fifty dollars a month allowance from the state to buy clothing and stuff we need. They must have saved up."

I didn't believe it, but I doubted Sneaker would reveal more if I pressed him. It was one more thing to add to a long list of things that didn't add up. I'd keep playing along for now, but I intended to find all the pieces that would let me figure out this puzzle.

After we left, Sneaker pointed across the street to a coffee shop. "I want a latte."

Sounded good, but I couldn't afford frivolous purchases. "I don't have money to waste, so I'll wait for you outside."

Sneaker practically skipped as we crossed the street. "I know you and Gina haven't got your allowance yet, so it'll be my treat."

I didn't accept charity. "No, thanks." I stopped at the door.

Sneaker shook his head, but I shooed him with my hands. "Go on."

"We'll get them to go and be right back." Sneaker opened the door, and the bell tinkled.

Gina hesitated, then followed him in. I looked through the lacy curtains on the windows to see her and Sneaker get into a line at the counter. MB's group was in there.

"Been looking for you, Maverick," Blade called.

I turned to see Blade and his group running across the street. "You found me."

The coffee door sprang open, and MB and his group came out.

My heart raced as both groups spread out around me, encircling me. They must be really afraid of me to combine forces like this.

They all rushed me, and I got in several punches before the sheer number of foes overwhelmed me. They dragged me between the buildings to the back where dumpsters sat off an alley. They threw me to the ground, pinning my arms and legs. I struggled to break free.

Someone said, "This doesn't seem very fair."

I craned my neck around my attackers to see a half dozen teens coming up the alley. The guy in front was white, but some of them were African American. One of the kids had braces on his teeth and they all wore name brand clothing. They didn't fit my idea of thugs, and I didn't see any gang symbols.

"What's it to you, Lenny. You friends with Maverick?" MB asked.

"No, but we have something in common. We don't like you. Now let him up."

Bullet snorted. "Do you seriously think that I'm afraid of you?"

"You should be. Lenny lifted the tail of his shirt to reveal his waistband. He had a gun tucked into it.

"Let him up," MB ordered.

When they released me, I shakily got to my feet. Lenny let his shirt fall back over his gun.

I gave him a nod. "Thanks."

"No problem. I never cared for the losers at Fallentier."

"He's at Fallentier too." Bullet cracked his knuckles. "And this isn't finished. Only postponed."

Lenny frowned, then looked at me. "I don't think you belong at Fallentier. I have some friends that'll give you a job and place to stay."

"What kind of job?"

"We help them with security."

Who would hire kids for security? Maybe people like my grandfather.

MB shook his head. "You don't want to go with Lenny. The last Fallentier kid who left with Lenny ended up dead in an alley."

"Yeah, and you could be the ones who killed him, so quit pretending to care." Lenny motioned to my face. "Would your nose be bleeding if they cared about you?"

He had a point. A man's head poked out from the back door of the coffee shop. "The back of my store ain't no hang out. You kids better find somewhere else to be, or I'll call the cops."

The Fallen kids took off toward the front. When I moved to follow them, Lenny and his friends trailed after me. As we rounded the corner, a black limo moved slowly down the street in front of the cafe. Was that my grandfather? I couldn't see through the tinted windows. It couldn't be him, could it? Didn't he return to New York?

The Fallen kids headed across the street as Gina and Sneaker came out of the café carrying cups of coffee. Gina caught site of me and hurried over.

"What happened to you?" She looked at Lenny. "Did you hurt him?"

"No. He helped me." I sounded like Donald Duck with my nose pinched.

"Now I know why Bullet wanted to pound you." Lenny smirked. "His girl is into you." Lenny lowered his voice to a stage whisper." I know she's hot, but..." He circled his finger by his temple. "She's cray cray. You don't want any of that."

Gina turned her sparking emerald eyes on him. "I'm not Bullet's girl. And I'm. Not. Crazy."

"Yeah, lots of girls put a dude in a coma," Lenny snipped.

She put her hands on her hips. "He attacked me."

"Not what I hear." He turned back to me. "You coming with me?"

Dad said to choose my fights and avoid impossible odds. It was tempting to just disappear and leave Fallentier, but I couldn't bail on someone who might be my sister.

"I might be interested later, but I've got things to take care of before I leave Fallentier."

Lenny shrugged. "If you live long enough to change your mind, come find me."

He and his friends sauntered off. Gina, Sneaker, and I moved toward the arcade where the bus was parked.

"How do you know Lenny?" I asked.

Gina took a drink of her Latte, her eyes dancing over the rim of her cup. "He hangs out in my old neighborhood."

Sneaker glanced back. "I know him from our old school. His dad's rich like yours, but I heard that when Lenny dropped out of school, his dad kicked him out of the house."

"So he joined a gang?"

Sneaker chortled. "That ain't no gang. They're just a bunch of runaways that pretend they're something." He looked at me. "But he's still bad news, and you don't want him as a Homy unless you want to be dead like Shorty."

Everyone kept warning me I'd die. Could I be in over my head?

Chapter 27

Battling a war

"Battles are everywhere, but only some are worth fighting." Connor

Maverick

I turned on my flashlight and swung the red beam toward Sneaker on his cot. He didn't stir and his breathing deepened to a snore. Last night's lack of rest must have caught up with him. After returning from town, he'd fallen asleep in seconds.

Remembering the chill outside, I threw my denim jacket over my sweatshirt and put on gloves. Since I shouldn't be gone long, I'd leave Pip in his warm box under my bed. I grabbed my duffel, turned off my flashlight, and crept from our room and out the back of the cottage.

After slipping through the fence gap, I cut through the woods to the lane. With the sudden cold snap, the drone of insects couldn't be heard anymore. The woods were too quiet, creepy. Goosebumps rose on my arms.

"Whoo."

I jumped, and my heart lurched. A shadow swept over me, and I recognized the form. Just an owl. I'd over-reacted. I jogged down the lane to the main road. There wasn't any traffic, so I crossed it and dashed through the yards of a couple of homes.

Behind the neighborhood, a path led toward the freeway overpass that spanned a creek. Even at this time of night, traffic rumbled above. Connor had stashed my weapons in a dead drop near the footings. I was only radioing Dad, so I wouldn't bother retrieving my gun. I ducked under the overpass, dodging the concrete supports. The water in the creek wasn't that high. My boots should keep my feet dry.

I waded through, then climbed the bank to the truck stop. The lights from the gas pumps were bright enough to see my wet boot tracks as I crossed the parking lot and entered the store.

Two teens around my age perused a clearance rack of hats and gloves. One kid was white, the other African American. They seemed to be the only customers. Why were they whispering and keeping their backs to the surveillance cameras? Were they planning to shoplift? They were dressed in name brand clothes. It seemed as if money wasn't a problem, so why would they steal?

I hurried over to the display of burner phones. The most reasonable low-tech slider was $35, but it included 200 minutes. Most of my cash. I could contact Dad by radio, but to speak to anyone else I'd need a phone. I took it up to the register.

The heavyset middle-aged lady rang me up with barely a glance away from the magazine she read. She handed me my loose change. Thirty-two cents. That and twelve dollars was all that remained of my money unless I dipped into the cash Connor left in the drop. I'd prefer to save it for emergencies.

I discarded the packaging, scrolled through the phone's options to turn the locator off, and slipped it in my pocket. I checked my watch. 11:45pm. Roving signals would be difficult to trace. Before I radioed Dad, I should hitch a ride, hopefully without the driver knowing. I could jump out later when the driver slowed or stopped at a light. I moved out the door on the other side where the diesel fuel was and trucks normally parked.

There wasn't much to choose from. Only one decrepit box truck parked near the gas pump. Beggars couldn't be choosy. I picked the simple lock on the door and slid the bar back. I about gagged at the strong smell of ammonia coming from a stack of barrels inside. Just my luck to get a truck hauling fertilizer. Could I stand being cooped up in there? Probably not. I'd have to wait for another truck to come. Voices broke the quiet.

"We're going to be famous."

I glanced back. The two teens from inside were heading toward the truck. Oh, no. They'd spot me. There was nowhere to hide except one place. I jumped inside the truck, putting my arm over my nose and trying to breathe shallowly. My eyes watered from the overpowering smell of ammonia and diesel fuel. I pulled the door closed except for a crack. The kids walked to the cab and climbed inside.

The roar of an engine sprang to life. One of those teens was driving this? The truck lurched forward. Since I was already here, I could stand it long enough to make a radio transmission. I shut the door and pressed my watch. A glow lit the face. Five minutes to midnight. The corner of my eye caught something shiny in the light. I pointed my watch face toward it. Blasting caps and wires! Oh no. My heart leapt to my throat. I was inside a bomb.

My head spun. What were they planning on blowing up? Maybe a school? Most school bombings were done by lone students. Maybe they belonged to a terrorist organization and were after one of the government buildings. They hadn't spoken with a foreign accent and sounded local, but that didn't eliminate them. Foreign terrorist organizations recruited from every state. And Americans of all ethnic and economic groups joined them and converted, so there wasn't an easy way to detect them. Whatever these guys intended, lives could be lost. I had to stop them. Contacting Dad would have to wait.

I took off my gloves to flick the catch on my boot. I grabbed my mechanical tool, then put my gloves back on. Good thing I wore them. I didn't need any bomb investigators finding my fingerprints anywhere in this truck. I crawled forward carefully. Should I flip open my phone to use its light? No, a cell phone battery can create static electricity which could cause a spark to ignite the gas fumes and set this thing off.

Sloshing sounds revealed the drums to me. I crept to one and felt along it until I got to the top and found a wire. There better not be any fail safe. I drew in a deep breath. Would it be my last? With trembling hands, I cut the wire. No explosion came. My breath rushed out in relief. I cut the next and the next.

Once the wires were all snipped, I pulled out my cell phone, and using the camera, took pictures of the barrels, the caps, and wires. I moved to the door and opened it a crack. Enough to recognize the freeway.

I sent the picture files to Connor, then texted him, "A black panel truck that's been made into a bomb is heading North on the George Washington Freeway and just passed mile marker 155. You need to stop it."

What if he was asleep? I could call 9-1-1, but would they believe me? How long would it take to convince them?

My phone beeped with a return text. "Who is this?" Connor asked.

I typed in, "Someone trying to save lives. I've cut the wires, but it might not stop this truck from exploding if it hits something."

The message scrawled across my screen. "We're on the way. What's the ETA and destination?"

I typed, "I don't know. They just passed mile marker 152."

"Can you give me a plate?"

I texted, "Too dirty. Wait a sec."

I laid on the floor of the truck in front of the door and stuck my head and hand out to swipe at the plate. It didn't have numbers. It was only a rectangular piece of metal.

I sat back up and typed, "It's a blank."

"Can you slow them?"

Even if I jumped out and managed to shoot a tire, the blowout and collision could cause it to explode. "No." I blew out a breath and typed, "I'll get the caps out."

My screen read, "Be careful, lad."

I'd never heard Connor call anyone else *lad*. He must suspect I was the one texting him. I knew it was a risk to call his private number. Just how many people would have it? Couldn't think about that now. I needed to get the caps out of here.

I took off my denim jacket, wrapped the caps in it, then knotted it. If I jumped out, the door would be left open. Would the barrels start sliding out? That might be okay, but what if they hit other vehicles and caused accidents? I grabbed the line out of the other heel of my boot and wrapped it back and forth from one side to the other in front of the barrels.

There, that should keep them in. The truck slowed, and I heard the clatter as it drove over the bridge. Good. Now was the time.

I flung open the door. Car lights lit the area behind us, but it was far enough back to give me some room. *Please let me get this right and hit the river.* I flung the jacket as hard as I could toward the rail. I didn't hear a splash. I jumped after it.

I hit the ground hard, and the shock reverberated through my ankles as I dropped and rolled. Lights bore down on me as I recovered and lunged to my feet. My left ankle bit, letting me know I might have sprained it. I ignored it and ran for the side. The honk of a car freaked me out. Its passenger-side mirror brushed me, partially spinning me. I recovered my balance as the car sped away following the taillights of the disappearing truck.

I limped down the road's shoulder toward where I'd thrown my jacket. It had snagged on the outside railing of the bridge. I leaned over to grab it and shook it, casting the caps into the water. I drew my jacket up and hobbled over the bridge as fast as I could. Sirens wailed in the distance coming closer.

Finally, but I didn't want them to find me. They might think I was involved in the bomb plot. I reached the end of the bridge and ran awkwardly through a strip of grass to some trees as the sirens screamed by.

Beyond the trees was a neighborhood. I sought cover behind sheds and garages as I cut through yards. A few dogs barked, but I avoided the fenced yards, and no one poked their heads out. The first sirens faded, but more approached in the distance. The thump of helicopter blades added to the din. In the strip of businesses ahead, some college-age kids walked unsteadily out of a tavern. There were two guys as beefy as defensive football players, and a couple girls who looked like cheerleaders, except one had a purple streak in her hair.

I circled to approach from behind, then left the shadows, swaying a little to emulate them. With my ankle so painful, I didn't have to fake a clumsy gait.

"Hey, if any of you can give me a lift home, I'll pay you." I thumbed my finger toward the bar. "They won't let me back in, and I can't find my ride."

The guys were looking at me as if I were a bug to squash, but the girl with the purple streaked hair smiled as she gave me a once over. "You seem too young to drink."

I threw her a smirk. "That's what the bartender said after he figured out my id was fake."

She laughed. "You're cute. I'm D.D tonight." My confusion must have shown since she explained, "Designated driver, and I can take you home along with these other bozos."

"Claire, we don't have enough room for him," the taller of the two guys griped. "And what if he's dangerous?"

"There's four of us to him." She waved at me to follow as she led the way to a mustang in the parking lot.

I handed Claire my ten dollar bill. "Is this enough?"

She took the bill. "Yeah, squeeze in."

The other guy jumped in the front seat with Claire, but Shelly scooted close to Lenny in the back, leaving me enough room to crowd in. Claire adjusted her mirror, then glanced at me. "Where to?"

I gave her directions to the neighborhood near the group home. I'd pick a house and pretend it was mine. As Claire drove, they kept up a lighthearted banter. How different they were from me. I could never be that carefree.

I'd been upset to learn how difficult it would be for me to attend college, but I'd discovered my training had value too. I'd been on the front lines of the war on terror tonight, and these guys didn't even know a battle had been waged. If I hadn't been willing to take a few risks, innocent people like them might have been killed. Wasn't that as important as attending college?

I had only wanted to go to college so I could be hired by the Company. But tonight proved I didn't need them. I could do this on my own if I wanted. After what the Company did to Dad, I was better off on my own.

When Claire dropped me at my imaginary home, I limped back to Fallentier, squeezed through the fence, then crept across the lawn. The curtain to Gina's room was open. She was pressed against the pane of glass, staring at me.

Should I sneak up there and try to convince her not to tell anyone I broke curfew? Why bother? Hadn't I already revealed myself by texting Connor?

Chapter 28

Right Thing

"Determining what's right is difficult when everyone has a different view." Gina

Gina

I shouldn't have turned on our room light. I could see better outside without it, and Felicity was sleeping. I flipped the switch, plunging the room into darkness, and hurried back to the window to peer out. Moonlight spilled across the grounds, making it easy to find Maverick again. He was slipping around the back of his cottage. Was he headed to his room?

My stomach twisted. Why did he have to be out after curfew, breaking the rules? Had he been on a terrorist mission? Were lives at risk?

Maverick's face flashed into my mind. Those soulful eyes, him moving in front of me to protect me from Cuk, and that crazy grin after he soaked me. My heart lurched. What would those government agents do to him?

Just my luck after guarding my heart for so long, I'd get attached to a kid who was a terrorist. But I had to make the call, didn't I? Maverick might even plant bombs here. I wouldn't just be keeping myself out of prison, I could be saving the other Fallen kids. Wasn't that the right thing?

I opened my phone. The screen light bathed the room in an eerie glow. Felicity turned over on her bed. Was she awake enough to overhear me? It didn't really matter. Once I fulfilled my side of the bargain, those agents would move me.

I pushed my contact's number. Even as late as it was, Parker answered on the first ring.

"What have you discovered?"

"Maverick was out after curfew, but I don't know where he went. And he knows I'm ratting on him. He stole my phone and found your contact, so I don't think I'm going to be able to get anything else."

"We never expected your cover to hold up, but he won't be able to resist you since he thinks you're his sister."

"He took some hair from me to run a DNA test, so he'll figure out I'm not related. I've done what you asked. Now keep your end of the bargain and get me out of here."

"Maverick isn't going to hurt you."

"If he'll blow up people for kicks, who knows what he'll do?"

"We feel completely confident of our threat analysis of the situation. If you want to stay out of prison, just keep doing what we ask until we're ready to pull the plug."

Seriously. Would these guys ever be finished with me? "I'm not going to Narc for you forever." I hung up the phone.

Felicity sat up, swinging her legs over the side of the bed. "I can't believe what I just heard. You're ratting to the cops?"

"I only ratted on Maverick because he's a terrorist, and I was helping them save lives."

Felicity jumped up. "I never took you for stupid before. Maverick's no more a terrorist than I am."

Could she be right? Did I get played? My heart sank to my toes. If Maverick were really a dangerous terrorist, wouldn't Parker be worried about my cover being blown?

Felicity paced around the room. "Is that all it takes, Gina? For the cops to make up some label like 'terrorist' or 'gang banger' for you to help them bring us down." She came to a stop in front of me. Her eyes grew wide with fear. "Who's next, me or Blade?"

"No. I wouldn't do that."

"I don't believe you." Felicity threw her arms in the air. "You pretended to like Maverick to get dirt on him so you could send him to prison in your place." Her lip trembled. "I'm not going down too."

She waved her finger at me. "After this, don't talk to me. We're not friends, and you better watch your back, girl. We both know what happens to a cop nark."

Was she threatening me? I shouldn't be surprised. Most kids in the system weren't worried about breaking laws, only getting caught. Sending us all to camp together had even taught me a few tricks. Felicity had been one of my teachers, but now she was afraid of what I might divulge. And Blade loved her. What would he do if he felt I was a threat to her? Slit my throat?

Chills ran up my spine.

Felicity marched to my locker, grabbed my garbage bag of belongings, and tossed it on the floor. "I don't care if it's after curfew. You get out of here and take your stuff. And don't ever come back, or I'll jack you up."

Felicity was barely five foot tall. Compared to my five-foot-six frame, she was tiny, but I didn't want to fight her. I'd rather not give the Tinos more reason to come after me. Besides, she was right. My heart told me Maverick couldn't be a terrorist and that their label was a lie, but I'd burned him anyway to save myself. Disgust for my actions welled in me. I picked up my bag and plodded toward the bathroom.

Felicity ran in front of me and threw her hand up. "Oh, no you don't. You ain't using my bathroom."

I tugged at my pajama top. "I'll leave, as soon as I change."

She pointed to the door. "You're leaving now. You can change somewhere else."

"Fine." I picked up my bag, grabbed my shoes, and shuffled out the door into the dark hallway.

Felicity slammed the door behind me. Ugh. That should alert everyone that someone was breaking curfew. I could go down the steps to the lobby, but the doors would be locked and alarmed this time of night. If I hung out in the lobby, it would be easy for anyone to spot me. Would the doors to the rooms they were remodeling be open?

I ignored the "do not enter" sign and slipped under the construction tape to creep down the hallway. The plastic sheeting over the floor crinkled under my feet. I came to the door on the left side and tried the handle. It was locked. I tiptoed across the hall to the other one. *Please open.* I grabbed the handle. It turned.

When I opened the door, a strong odor of fresh paint wrinkled my nose. I activated my phone light. Paint cans stood near a wall, and there were strips of plastic over the wood floors, but otherwise the large room was empty. After I darted inside, I dug around inside my bag for jeans and a shirt. I threw them on over my pajamas and slipped on my shoes.

I felt a little more prepared to face this day. I crept over to the window. It was cracked open a tiny bit. Probably to let the paint fumes air out. Outside the window, I glimpsed the metal rungs of a fire escape.

Hanging off a building by those rungs didn't particularly interest me. Heights frightened me, but I needed to leave Fallentier before I learned how far the kids here would go to protect their secrets from a rat.

But before I left, I needed to warn Maverick. I owed that to him. Then he could bounce, too, and avoid the mess I'd caused.

I pulled the window completely open and peered down. Didn't look to be anyone moving. I knotted the top of my bag and tossed it through the window. A soft splat sounded as it landed. Okay, now for me. I backed through the window, held on tight to the ledge, then lowered my feet until I felt a metal rung and moved down cautiously. I balanced myself on the ladder and pushed the window shut.

As I perched on the thin rungs on the side of the building, I took a look down. I froze. It was a long way. What would happen to me if I fell? My legs trembled as my heart pounded in my ears. The air felt too thin as I gasped for breath. I shook my head in an attempt to pull it together.

I finally forced my foot to move. One step, one hand. Slow and agonizing, step by step, until one foot touched the ground. I'd made it. Relief welled up in me.

My sack of belongings would be safe behind the dumpster for now. I headed toward Maverick's cottage to talk to him.

Chapter 29

Caught

"Life is full of mine fields, so step carefully." Sam

Maverick

Pip's warning chirp in my ear startled me awake as he dived under the cot. A knock sounded, then Sam opened the door and flipped the light on. His gaze moved immediately to my bed, as if checking to make sure I was there.

"Maverick, get up and follow me."

I was groggy from exhaustion, so I couldn't have slept long. Did Sam know I broke curfew? I'd need my wits to pull off the innocent act.

I tried to shake myself awake. "What for?"

"If you get up, you'll find out."

I shielded my eyes from the light with my arm. "What time is it?"

"It's o-four-thirty," Sam replied sharply.

"You couldn't wait until the sun rose?" I asked.

"No," he snapped.

"Fine." I sat up and grabbed my clothes off the floor.

Sam's foot tapped impatiently. "What happened to your ankle?" he demanded.

I glanced at it. The elastic bandage I'd wrapped around it last night was still secure. "I twisted it."

"Humph," was his only reply.

Sneaker's blue eyes blinked open. He pulled his blanket up over his head.

I couldn't stop a yawn from escaping. "I need a few minutes to get dressed and use the bathroom."

"You have two minutes." Sam opened the door. "I'll be out in the hall." He left, slamming the door.

I stood, testing my foot. Only a little sore when I put weight on it. I must not have hurt it too badly. I stuffed my legs in my pants, pulled on my boots, and threw on my tank. My hoodie moved a little. Pip must have returned to my pocket. Apparently, my pet didn't want to be left again. I slipped my sweatshirt on carefully. Maybe I should record the conversation with Sam. I grabbed the band that held Pip's listening bug from my locker, turned it on, and maneuvered it over Pip's head.

After I used the bathroom and threw water on my face at the sink, Sam called, "Two minutes is up."

"I'm coming already."

Once I moved into the hall, Sam opened the door to his room. He motioned me to go in first.

His room was larger and had more furnishings. There was a round table with two chairs, a small flat screen television hanging on the wall, a mini-frig and microwave, even a coffee pot. It looked like a motel room. The spread was pulled back on the full size bed. Had Connor called and woken him up?

The only personal touch in Sam's room was a framed picture. It showed him and three other guys in jumpsuits standing in front of a plane on a desert runway with some rocky hills in the background. Maybe Iraq? They stood rigidly as if at attention, even though they weren't in uniforms. Probably a military special ops unit. I recognized two of the guys in the picture as Fallentier guards. Hmm. Could everyone here be ex-military and connected somehow?

Sam waved to a chair. "Sit down."

I pulled it out and sank into it. There were files on the table. The one on top had my name on it.

"You want something to drink?" Sam's tone had lost some of its curtness.

"I could use some coffee."

"Me too." He strode to the refrigerator. "Chilled okay?"

"Sure."

He grabbed two bottles and handed one to me. An iced mocha. I uncapped it and took a swig. A blend of sweet sugar and chocolate with the sharp kick of coffee swirled around in my mouth. I downed half the bottle while Sam fidgeted with his, picking at the label while the silence stretched.

My patience ran out. "You mind telling me what this is about?"

Sam uncapped his bottle. "You broke the rules last night when you went AWOL. That's two nights in a row, plus the fight with Cuk." He took a drink. "That makes three strikes."

My gut clenched. I'd run before I let them lock me up in Juvie or somewhere worse. The door was closer to me than him. I got ready to spring, but something didn't seem right. Where were the guards?

Sam picked up my file. "There is another option."

I sank back. "I'm listening."

"My job here is a cover."

Duh. "Who are you working for?"

"Myself." He took another swallow of coffee. "There are some things the military and agencies won't do, but there's a demand for someone that will. Private contractors take on most of those jobs, but there are some no one will take. So I put together people to tackle the impossible. The missions everyone else failed at or didn't want, I get."

"What kind of jobs?"

"My newest contract is to infiltrate and gather intelligence on terrorist groups who are recruiting kids. Terrorists suspect adult agents. Teens that are age seventeen can join the military and go to war, so I didn't see any reason why they can't fight in the war on terror too. When I decided to enlist kids in the system, it wasn't only because a group home would make a good cover, I wanted to give them direction and help them like I was helped."

"So what's that have to do with me?"

"Every agency wants to learn whether those terrorists last night have ties to an organization and if there are any more bombs. I need those answers."

"I can't give them to you."

His eyes pierced me. "Is that because you won't incriminate yourself or you don't know?"

"Both. But if I did know about more bombs, I'd tell someone."

He leafed through my file. "According to this, you like thrills. I don't think there's anything as thrilling as pulling off a successful operation like you did, do you?"

I grinned. "I won't incriminate myself."

"I think you'd enjoy doing it again. But to do that, you need a team, and my team needs a leader. I'm not sure you're the right choice, but most of the kids here look up to you, so I'm willing to offer you the job."

Last night proved I didn't need anyone, but my curiosity was piqued. "How much do you pay?"

"A thousand dollars a month will be put in an account in your name, plus performance bonuses of up to a hundred dollars."

My jaw dropped open. "You think that's worth risking my life?"

He shrugged. "You have no living expenses, and it's better than the alternative."

"Are you saying if I don't accept this offer, I'll end up in Juvie?"

Sam closed the file. "I don't want to have to do that, but yes."

I could disappear, but what about Gina? And working with them would give me more resources. Maybe I could negotiate for the things I really wanted.

I released a heavy breath. "I should probably consider it a compliment your bosses consider me dangerous enough to try to control me, but the rest of this conversation needs to be with them."

The corner of his mouth lifted in a partial smile. "I told you, I'm the boss."

He couldn't even claim it with a straight face. "We both know the people who hired you have some say over this team. Call the Director and set up a meeting."

Sam smiled. "He was right."

"Who?"

"Never mind." Sam stood and limped to his refrigerator to grab two more bottles of mocha. "We'll need this and our coats, so get yours."

When I crossed the hall to my room, Sneaker sat up in bed. "So are you joining the team?"

I grabbed my leather coat. "We're negotiating." I switched Pip to my coat pocket and zippered it up. "You look like you're dying to ask me something?"

"It's just… I'm wondering if I made a mistake getting involved."

"You did."

"What do you mean?"

"Don't tell me they didn't give you any stats before signing you up."

Sneaker rubbed his hand through his hair. Sam's voice boomed through the door, startling us.

"Maverick, let's go."

Grrr. "You should have been informed, but I don't have time to explain now."

"Yeah. Sam hates waiting." Sneaker extended his fist. "Take care of yourself, Bro."

He must know that there was a chance I wouldn't be coming back. I bumped fists with him. "You too."

We double-timed it down the hall and out the front door. Someone rushed toward us out of the dark. The light above the door caught a face. Gina.

"I knew it." She leveled a scowl at Sam. "You're taking Maverick to Juvie, aren't you?"

"It's not decided yet." Sam waved toward his car. "Maverick, get in."

"Can you let me talk to him for a minute?" A tear ran down her face. "It's really important."

Sam blew out his breath. "One minute."

He climbed in the car as she grabbed my arm to tug me a few steps away. "I'm really sorry."

In the few days I'd known her, this tough girl had faced some bad situations and never shed a tear. "What's going on?"

She sniffed. "You're going to hate me."

"Just tell me."

"I shouldn't have believed them about you. But I didn't want to go to prison so I ratted on you." She swiped at the tear on her face angrily. "I wanted to warn you so we could run, but it's too late."

"You wanted to run away with me?"

"I can't stay here. Felicity knows, and she's already threatened me. You wouldn't want to leave with a rat anyway."

"I gave myself away, so whatever you told them didn't matter." I leaned in. "I don't want to lose someone who could my sister. Can you hide out for a little while? I'll be back to help you, one way or another."

Her hand fluttered in front of her neck. "Parker didn't care that my cover's blown. Why do you?"

Sam lowered his window to holler, "Now, Maverick."

Anger surged in me at Parker. I blew out my breath. "Brothers don't forget their sisters."

I jogged the few steps to the car and glanced back to see Gina wave at me. I lifted my hand to wave back.

Worry for her churned my gut. I hoped she'd be all right until I could return. I had to go for both our sakes.

Chapter 30

Negotiations

"The sign of a great agent is the absence of any. No one knows them, or what they've done." Maverick

Maverick

When I opened the back door to his sedan, Sam motioned to his passenger seat. "You can ride shotgun if you'd like."

If I rode in front, he might notice Pip squirming in my pocket. "Nah. I like to sprawl out."

After I climbed in, Sam handed me back another iced mocha, then drove to the gate. The guards snapped to attention, then waved him through.

"Are you the one really in charge here?" I asked as we drove down the road.

"It didn't take you long to figure that out." Sam pulled onto the interstate.

With the traffic light at such an early hour, we soon left the burbs and entered the city proper. I pulled out my phone and called Connor.

"Hello, Derrick."

Not surprising, Connor knew my number after last night. "Did you know Parker's running an operation on me?"

"Yes. Director Deputy Johnson assigned him, although I told him it would be a waste of time."

"Parker's threatening Gina with prison. Can you find out if it's a possibility?"

"I owe you one after last night, so I'll check. Just a sec." A minute later, Connor returned to speak in the phone. "It's not. Her foster mom gave an affidavit detailing abuse, so the charges against Gina were dropped."

My anger rose at Parker. "Is the affidavit in the police report?"

"Yes. I'll leave you a copy in the stash, only you didn't get it from me."

"Thanks." I hung up and admired the sunrise filling the horizon with brilliant bands of mauve, blue, and yellow colors. Sam left the freeway and turned on a decrepit road with several scruffy looking warehouses. At the end of the road sat one with boarded up windows. It looked abandoned, but the surrounding fence was newer. It must be a front.

Sam pushed an automatic opener on his visor, and the gate swung open. When he drove in, the gate closed behind us. He pulled the car to a stop by a door where two men dressed in black suits stood.

Seeing the suits sent my anger soaring. When our government needed anything, my dad had always stepped up. Be it training, equipment, or an operative. Because he did, he got burned. I wouldn't get roped into putting their needs over ours now.

"You should probably let me go in alone."

"Why?" Sam asked.

"Dad said an agent's duty was to protect every citizen. My dad's a citizen, but they put me on the watch list because I wouldn't betray him. If they still expect that, they'll be disappointed."

"That's not why you're here. And I'm going in to support you, not condemn you."

As we climbed out of the car, I took a deep breath to calm myself. This meeting could be crucial. Dad and Gina needed me to keep my wits about me.

When we got to the two suits, one opened the door. "He's expecting you."

The other suit followed us in and motioned to the left. "This way."

He stopped at the fifth door, then opened it to show a plain office with a desk and some files. I recognized the man behind the desk as the Director of Intelligence from the official photos I'd seen.

"Hello, Director Williams," Sam said as we strode in. "This is Derrick."

"It's good to meet you, Derrick." Director Williams extended his hand. After I shook it, he motioned to some chairs across the desk from him. "Please, take a seat."

The suit who escorted us moved behind the desk to stand beside the Director while Sam and I sat. Director Williams met my gaze. "I understand you wanted to see me before deciding whether you wanted to join the team."

"I think it's obvious you need me, but I need more than what Sam offered."

"You want more money?"

"No. I want my sister's case reopened." I pulled out the baggie with Gina's hair. "You can start by having Gina's DNA tested. And regardless of the results, I want you to secure Gina a good foster home placement. Plus, I think you know my Dad's no terrorist, so I want a public announcement that you are calling off the hunt for him, retracting the warrant and reward, and unfreezing his assets."

Director Williams leaned back and crossed his arms. "You don't want much."

I snorted. "Think of what you spent to get Saddam Hussein and tell me again I'm asking for too much."

"How do we know you can deliver?"

I didn't have to tell them that last night's success was due to luck. "I already proved I can."

He blew out a heavy breath. "The President is the only one who can pardon your dad."

"Dad hasn't been convicted of anything, but if Potus can stop this witch hunt, then call him."

The glare he gave me made it clear what he thought about that.

I shrugged. "You can make the call now or later after some kids' get another bomb through."

He stood up. "I'll call, but not in here." He left the room with the suit following.

"To prevent eavesdropping, there's a disrupter in here," Sam explained.

I nodded. I wasn't going to reveal the bug Pip wore would work. Maybe ten minutes passed before the door opened.

Director Williams came back in and sat again. "This is what we'll agree to. We'll announce we have heard from reliable sources that your dad is dead, and we'll retract the reward. But only if he leaves the country and remains outside of the US. If he enters our borders, we'll announce our sources were wrong and do our best to apprehend him."

He leaned back in his chair. "As far as your assets, we'll unfreeze your trust once we see results. Your dad's accounts will stay frozen until we have evidence of his innocence or death. It's the best Potus will do when so many are convinced you both could be a threat. If you want better than that, you'll have to prove his innocence."

I planned to. "What about testing Gina's DNA?" I needed to learn if the Company was using Deidra or someone who looked like her.

The Director's eyebrows knitted. "Gina's been mistaken for Deidra before, but her fingerprints aren't a match."

Dad and Connor lifted fingerprints off Deidra's toys the day she'd been taken, so Gina wasn't Deidra. A sudden sense of relief filled me. Why, when I hadn't found my sister?

"I've been considering Gina for the team," Sam said.

Her beautiful face flashed in my mind. I still felt the overwhelming need to protect her.

"No. She deserves somewhere where she'll be safe."

The Director's head tilted, and his gaze pierced me. Then he gave me a curt nod. "All right. And we'll do what we can to find your sister, including have the Bureau reopen her case. So do we have a deal?"

"Can I get it in writing?"

"No. There won't be any paper trail. After today, you'll never see me again. If it ever comes out a contractor of ours used kids, we'll deny we knew. Do you understand?"

"Yeah. I'm going covert."

"Worse. You'll be so deep, you won't be able to reach out to other operatives for help. No one—not the Bureau, not the Company—will know about you. And you'll be naked."

Naked meant I'd use my real identity. That could come back to haunt me, but it held one advantage. My cover would hold up because there wasn't one.

Director Williams frowned. "If a terrorist cell you're investigating gets arrested when you're with them, you could end up in Gitmo. And if you die, your name won't grace any wall." He crossed his arms. "The reason we're using Fallentier kids is that you're disposable. If you disappear, everyone will just think you ran away." He shrugged. "You're easily forgotten."

"Then how do I know you'll keep the bargain if something happens to me?"

Sam put his thumb to his chest. "Me. I'm your contractor. You have to trust me."

"I've known you for a few days, and I'm supposed to trust you? I want to talk to Connor."

The Director's brows shot up. "What?"

"You should stop underestimating me. I know Connor's the operations officer in charge of this."

Director Williams uncrossed his arms to wave at a suit. "Get Connor."

When Connor walked in the door, Sam shook his head. "You told him."

"I never even hinted, but I told you Derrick's too talented for any deceit to last." Connor handed me a couple sheets of paper. "Here."

I glimpsed affidavit written across the top. I rolled them up and stuck them in my back pocket. "If anything happens to me, will you make certain they search for Deidra and don't resume hunting Dad?"

Connor met my gaze. "I promise I'll do everything I can to make sure."

Should I trust him? Everything in me replied yes. I'd leave my recording of the meeting sealed in the stash. With that, Connor should be able to ensure the agreement was kept.

"All right. I'll lead your team until I find the terrorists who killed Kurt and framed Dad, but I'm not signing up for life. Agreed?"

Director Williams answered tersely, "Agreed."

Connor put a hand on my shoulder and gave it a squeeze. "Victor would be proud of you, and so am I."

Connor's advice on how to act during a mission came back to me. *If you befriend your sources, you'll get better results, but don't get too attached. Like in a chess game—play every piece to your advantage and be prepared to lose some.*

Did he consider this a mission? Was his praise sincere, or was I another pawn on the game board?

Chapter 31

Evaluations

"People's actions are hard to predict since they refuse to be consistent." Maverick

Maverick

While Sam drove us back to Fallentier, images of Gina flashed through my mind. Her defiant stance when she faced Cuk, her glittering eyes when she drank the Latte, her tears this morning. My heart pinged.

I scooted to the front of the back seat to talk to Sam. "Felicity thought you were taking me to Juvie. When I come back, everyone's going to think I'm a rat, and they already know Gina's one. I've come up with a cover story."

"Which is…?"

"To tell everyone I called in my dad's attorneys for me and Gina. They were able to get Gina cleared, and they convinced Fallentier to give me another chance."

"Sounds plausible to me. I'll back you on it."

"Thanks, and one other thing. I want to inform the team of the risks. If they want out, I'd like you to let them."

"You act as if these guys are either naïve, or I forced them into joining."

"Yeah, you gave them a great choice, between this or Juvie."

He blushed. "I never had to threaten anyone but you. They jumped at the chance for the money and the excitement."

"So you won't mind if I hear that from them."

"Fine."

I settled back in the seat. Right before we reached Fallentier's gates, Sam drove off the road.

My pulse raced, and I yelled, "What are you doing?"

He chuckled. "Just wait."

We were headed toward some bushes. Shouldn't they have shadows at this time of day? Aha, it was a panel painted to look like bushes. The panel slid open to allow us entrance to a tree-lined dirt drive. Must be a motion sensor. The panel closed as we drove down the drive to the brick two-story building that I'd glimpsed from Fallentier through the screen of trees. Sam parked the car by a small door.

We got out, and Sam punched in a code on a security panel. When the door opened, florescent lights bathed the entrance while the overbearing scent of new paint and carpet choked me. The chilled air from the vents only circulated it. Fighting the desire to open the heavy shades and windows for fresh air, I forced myself to follow Sam over the multi-color Berber carpet and into a large room.

A long rectangular table stood in the room's center, and a large television screen was mounted on the front wall. To the right sat a printer, copier, and fax machine. Across from us were a couple of doors. At the room's far end, a floating desk ran down the wall where Sneaker, Bullet, MB, Blade, and Hulk sat in office chairs in front of computers.

The Fallen kids glanced up at us from their monitors that displayed social media sites and chat rooms.

"They're fishing for terrorists?" I asked.

"Casting lures," Sneaker answered.

"Any luck?" I sauntered over to look at his monitor.

"A few bites." Sneaker was typing between several chat screens.

"Seems like more than a few."

Sneaker shrugged. "Sam says only a few are real threats, but there's no way of telling which for sure."

MB sat next to Sneaker, and his finger's moved furiously. I checked his monitor. A chat screen popped up with a new message. "I want to blow up something."

Whoever sent that wasn't very smart since they used an email linked to their provider, and that wasn't an international company.

I pointed to the chat screen. "Are all the bites homegrown?"

"Yeah," Sam replied. "But most of the terrorist attacks on our soil came from people who weren't affiliated with any foreign group, so it's just as important to find them."

"These are mostly kids who want to be terrorists." MB sent a photo of a bomb exploding. His screen showed his IM name as ARI. He typed, "I can teach you how to build a bomb."

The message came back. "Great."

My mouth dropped open. This was unbelievable. "You're not really going to teach them how to build a bomb, are you?"

"There are tons of places on-line they can get that information. If they get it from us, we leave out some necessary ingredients." MB typed in, "If you give me your address, I'll send you a package with everything you need."

An address scrawled across the screen. "Now we send him a kit," MB explained. "If he's serious and sets off the bomb, it will only smoke. If that doesn't give him away, the signal it sends to us will."

"Then we have the evidence for a conviction." Sam came over to look at the monitor. "Great job, MB, reeling another one in. Now, print that chat."

"I think I may have talked to you on line," I said.

MB swiveled his chair around, his eyes wide. "You bit on a lure?"

"Not like that. My on-line name is Spook."

"Oh." He chuckled, then twisted in his chair and hit print. "Did you ever get by your dad's system?"

"Yeah, thanks for helping me hack it. I figured you for an MIT student since your computer skills are phenomenal."

"Don't tell anyone else that." Sam took the paper out of the printer. "We don't want people knowing what MB can do." He waved at a chair. "Here, Maverick, sit. Everyone else close down and come over."

I plopped in the chair as the other kids turned off their computers and unplugged their power strips.

Sam noticed me watching. "We follow the protocols to prevent electronic eavesdropping."

As they scooted their chairs over to the table, MB grumbled, "I put so many security measures on these, it would be nearly impossible to hack us."

"I prefer impossible." Sam waved at me. "Maverick has been given the job of leading your team, so he'd like to talk to you."

Everyone here was a leader except for Sneaker. A lot of captains and few sailors can sink a boat.

"Is this the entire team?" I asked.

"Yes." Sam sat at the head of the table.

I looked at Sneaker, then glanced at the others. "I wanted you to know about the risks so you can decide whether to continue."

Blade played with a throwing knife similar to my own. He kept flipping it, then catching the hilt. "It's not like we aren't used to risks."

I'd have to spell it out. "Foreign terrorist organizations kill eight out of every ten Americans they recruit. They pit them against each other, or murder them just because they hate us. The chance of surviving an operation like this is slim."

"That's only if they leave the country." Sam frowned at me. "They probably won't need to do that."

"Bull. Without going to a foreign training camp, they'll only get rhetoric, an issue of a terrorist magazine, and encouragement to target things on their own. They won't be trusted enough to pick up any Intel. The government wouldn't have funded a fancy op center unless they felt you could succeed."

Hulk rolled his shoulders as he scowled at Sam "Is he right?"

"I plan to do it differently. We'll get their attention so they contact you without anyone leaving the country."

Bullet's feet tapped the floor, and he fidgeted in his seat. "Is your Dad really a terrorist? Is that how you know so much?" he asked.

How much should I divulge? If I wanted them to believe me, I had to tell them some things.

"Dad's not a terrorist. He was framed. He used to be a CIA

agent and made equipment for spies. I wanted to be a field agent, too, so I learned everything I could."

MB asked, "Do you think what Sam plans will work?"

"Both the FBI and CIA already tried infiltrating these foreign terrorist groups. Each of their skilled agents was killed, including my friend Kurt." I rubbed my chin. "Makes me wonder why they believe kids could succeed."

All of us looked at Sam.

"Terrorists recruit kids because they're easier to subvert, and it helps them avoid spies." Sam rifled his stack of papers. "The agents that were killed lied about how old they were. One of the operatives sent a message out saying they were going to test his age."

Hmmm. "X-rays can't give you an exact age, only a range."

"We're not sure if there could be another way of testing someone's age."

"Have scientists been able to produce a DNA test for age?" I asked.

"Not that we're aware of. But if it wasn't a western scientist, we might not know."

"Being the right age won't guarantee anyone's success." Were the Fallen kids so determined because of the money? "You can't spend money if you're dead."

"You act as if we're morons," MB huffed.

They were far from stupid, but the job of a spy required more than brains. "Do any of you know the Quran?"

"I know some." Hulk stiffened. "I was raised Muslim." His jaw clenched. "Are you going to accuse me of being a terrorist?"

"No. Every religion has extremists, but they're a tiny minority. "Kur"…I choked on his name as memories flooded me. I pushed my grief aside. "Kurt could recite most of the Quran and spoke Farsi, Urdu, and Arabic fluently. He could kill someone with his bare hands several different ways, but he's…he's in a coffin now." A sigh escaped me. "If you try to do this, you'll be in one too."

"Maybe that's why he got caught." Bullet leaned forward over the table. "Everyone says American's are stupid. Too smart could be a giveaway."

What more could I say to convince them to quit while they were still breathing? "If I only had four bullets in my gun and started shooting, would the five of you just stand there? Because that's what you're doing."

Hulk crossed his arms. "At least if we survive this, we'll be set for some time."

This wasn't working. And with the glares Sam was shooting me, I'd better give it a rest.

"Okay, it's your decision." I released a heavy breath. "If you're really determined, I'll try to train you. But you'll have to do what I say if you want to have any chance of surviving."

While we'd been talking, Sam had been writing "FFF" across the top of the papers the team had printed when they were fishing.

I pointed to the 3 F's. "What does that mean?"

Sam tapped the pen on the table. "It's the code name for this group."

"I figured that, but does it stand for anything?"

Sam stopped his tapping. "When I originally pitched my idea of using teens from a group home to Wells and Connor, Wells said it would only teach aspiring criminals useful tricks and have zero chance of success. He said such a team should be called *future felons who'd fail*—he shortened it to 3'F's. But he was wrong, and this team will prove it."

"Wells from the Bureau?"

"Yeah," Sam answered.

Sounded about right for him. At the Bureau's camp, he never gave sympathy to anyone lagging behind and always said *only the best of the best should expect to be recruited.*

"That code name sucks. Can we change it?" Sneaker asked.

"It can't be changed now, but the meaning can." Sam put the pen down. "No one else even knows what the 3 F's meant. So what starts with an F that you think represents this group?"

Even though I'd just told them the risks, no one had wanted out. I suggested, "Fearless."

Blade twirled his knife. "Fallen."

Hulk uncrossed his arms. "Everyone wants to forget us, so

Forgotten."

Sneaker's eyes lit up. "Yeah, I like that. *Fearless, Fallen & Forgotten.*"

"Sound's good to me." Sam stood up. "How about we give Maverick the tour?"

I rose and followed them to the gym a pro sports team would be happy with. Sam pointed to another door leading outside. "There's an obstacle course and a gun range out there." We climbed some stairs. "I made sure we'd have a great op center and if anyone needs to bunk here, they'll be comfortable."

We walked into a living area furnished with a couch and chairs along with a flat screen television on the wall. On the other side of an island stood a kitchen with a fridge, stove, and dishwasher.

Sam opened the refrigerator to show me sandwich meats, cheeses, pudding, and fruit cups, plus several types of drinks. "You can help yourself to the stuff in here, but everyone cleans up after themselves."

The kitchen wasn't the one I'd spied from Pip's camera. There must be more than one.

Sam waved toward another door. "Behind that is a hall with three bedrooms and two bathrooms. Like at Fallentier, there are two beds in each room, but they're a little larger. That's all that's up here. We can go downstairs, now, and I'll show you the range."

There was no way this was everything on this floor. Was Sam planning on expanding and having more teams? It made sense if you expected a high mortality rate. That's probably why he recruited the leaders first so they could encourage the others to join.

"If you can't talk about something, say so, but don't lie to me, Sam, because that will convince me not to trust you."

"Even if it's something you'd rather not know?"

"I'll take hard truths over fantasy. Do they sugar coat things on special force teams?"

His shoulders sagged. "No." He motioned for us to take the steps. "But we tread very carefully." When we reached the first floor, Sam moved us down the hall to the back door. "We'll show you the courses now."

Birds were chirping as we emerged out the rear of the building, but my exhaustion clung to me, weighing me down as I walked beyond the screen of trees to the obstacle course. Not much like Dad's. First were rubber tires, then a net wall, followed by a wooden bridge with gaps to leap, next came a hill of sandbags to get over, then a choice of maneuvering between barbed wire fencing or going underneath through a ditch filled with water.

"Is your ankle too sore to try it?" Sam asked.

I flexed my ankle. Just a little twinge. "I could, but I'd rather observe the team doing it so I can assess their skills." I sat under the shade of a tree and reclined, propping my head on my arms.

Sam nodded, then bellowed. "All of you get changed into work-out clothes and meet us back here in ten minutes."

My jaw almost dropped open. When they left, I confronted Sam, "We'll be wearing street clothes on missions, and that's what they should be training in."

"I guess that makes sense." His tone was apologetic, almost sheepish. "I usually have them run the obstacle course and then practice firing their guns."

"Have them do both three times today."

He mumbled, "They're not going to like that."

I shrugged. "I don't care if they like it as long as they do it."

Sam scratched his head. "They might not."

Was he kidding? Did they think it a game? If they didn't even care enough to give their best in training, they'd die for sure on a mission.

When the guys returned, Sam checked his watch. "Let's show Maverick what you've got. Go."

Sneaker was the only one that ran. The others kind of jogged.

I let my eyes close to slits and got comfortable while I watched their pathetic performance.

Sam growled, "I guess they're not worried about impressing you. I should have given them an incentive."

Sam seemed embarrassed by their performance. He should be. It took them thirty minutes to go through easy obstacles. These guys would be killed if I didn't convince them to quit. Giving them the statistics hadn't worked. At camp, most kids refused to sign up for courses that were taught by jerks like agent Wells. Maybe I just needed to act like a jerk.

When they finished, Sam asked me, "Do you want to go over to the gun course?"

The firing line was about 25 yards away. Their targets were set up 25 yards down range of that.

"I can see what I need to from here."

When they left, I pulled out my glasses and put them on. I pressed the catch on the bottom until the lens zoomed in enough where I could see the targets clearly.

They shot eight rounds. Bullet actually put a few rounds in the bullseye, but the others never got close and only had a few rounds hit the silhouette. Blade's silhouette had no bullet holes. Had he shot his gun?

As they walked back toward the obstacle course, I scrutinized them. They weren't even sweating hard, and they dragged their legs worse than Sam with his limp. I adjusted my glasses to normal view.

Sam spoke in a cajoling tone, "Yes, I'd like you to do it again, but this time, I'll give you $20 for every obstacle you complete, $100 to whoever completes the course first, and $100 to whoever shoots best."

No wonder they had money for stuff at the electronic store. This time they all ran when Sam told them to. They barely got through each obstacle, and it still took twenty-five minutes.

"I can't believe you pay them for this," I told Sam.

"They fight authority, so orders and threats don't work. Money is the only thing they respond to."

Was that so different from what Dad did with me? I had to earn my allowance, and I needed a good report from my tutor to get it. But Dad never had to reward me to train. I wanted to be the best, so I'd have trained all day if Dad hadn't set limits. And what kind of response was five minutes shaved off their time?

They plodded back to the targets and shot again. This time I watched Blade. I was right. He never raised his gun so he wasn't even shooting. Bullet placed two rounds in the bullseye again and everyone else only hit their silhouettes a few times. Sam brought them back toward me.

"No." Hulk's raised voice carried. "I'm not doing it again."

Bullet waved his hands in the air. "Maverick ain't even watching. He just wanted us to do it three times so he could sleep while we sweat."

Sam shook his head. "He's not sleeping."

Blade's voice turned sharp. "I don't care what he's doing, I'm not working while he relaxes."

I sat up. "Is that what you call working? I call it the most pathetic attempt to run a course that I've ever watched."

"It's more than you've done," Bullet snarled.

"Even if I agreed to do the obstacle course with you, I doubt you would since Sam had to pay you last time."

"You don't get something for nothing," MB quipped.

"Fine, how about if we up the stakes. Anyone who beats me through the obstacle course gets a thousand dollars. I wouldn't call that nothing, would you?"

Sam's eyebrows shot up, but he didn't contradict me.

The Fallen kids put their heads together and whispered. The way they kept sneaking glances at me warned me they must be planning to take out their competition, me, then split the money. I didn't let my smile show. This should be fun.

Chapter 32

Failing

"Lifting an elephant would be easier than bearing the fault for harming a loved one." Maverick.

Maverick

I stood and walked to the starting line to toe it. Bullet moved up on my left as Hulk crowded in on my right.

Sam hollered, "Ready. Set. Go."

Hulk and Bullet both jumped toward me as I leapt back. When they collided with each other, I helped them fall by plowing into them. A laugh escaped me when I spun and took off around them.

The other kids were almost to the first obstacle, and they were actually moving fast. When I reached the tire obstacle, they'd completed it. I pumped my feet like pistons through the tires, then raced past Blade and waved.

MB was behind Sneaker when we reached the wall of net. I climbed it quicker than MB, and scampered down to cross the bridge with only Sneaker in front of me. I moved up to stay even with Sneaker, conserving my strength for the finish. His face reddened, as he put on a burst of speed before slowing to tackle the sandbag hill. I kept his pace until the barbed wire.

Holding the wires gingerly, Sneaker maneuvered through them while I rolled under them into the water. When lifted myself out, I'd gained the lead. Yes!

Sneaker's footsteps faltered, then quit. I glanced back. He walked toward Sam and the other Fallen kids. He didn't attempt to complete the course. I sprinted to the finish line, then jogged back.

"What was my time?" I asked Sam.

"Five minutes."

"Exactly?"

"No, four minutes 55 seconds."

I'd completed five obstacles in less than five minutes, which is what Dad expected from agents, but these weren't even tough. Usually, I had better competition pushing me.

"If we outshoot you, will we get the thousand dollars?" Bullet asked.

"Not if you shoot me to win. If you do it fairly, yes."

We lined up at the firing line. The Fallen kids started shooting at the targets except for Blade.

"Why aren't you shooting your gun?" I asked.

"I don't need a gun." Blade pulled his knife and threw it at the target. It hit dead center. Hmm. Good thing this contest wasn't a throwing one.

When the Fallen kids finished shooting, Bullet had placed four of his six rounds in the bullseye and his other two were in the next ring. Not bad. The other guys got three rounds apiece in the silhouette.

Bullet held out his gun and smirked at me. "Beat that."

I took it from him and checked the weight. It felt comfortable. I loaded the clip and shot one round to check my sights. A little low of the center. I adjusted and shot five more rounds in quick succession. All of them hit the bullseye. I slid out my clip, put in another, then switched the gun to my left hand.

"You should learn to shoot with either hand." I emptied the clip again. Every bullet hit dead center. Yes! I released the clip, opened the barrel, and held out the gun.

"I wouldn't take any of you on a mission." I sneered at them. "You couldn't keep up. If things go bad, you'd die."

Sam took the gun before Bullet could. "Then train them to do better."

Why should I put these guys at risk when I already had the skills necessary? It would be better to keep being a jerk so they'd quit. Then Sam could just use me.

"They don't even care enough to put any effort into it. You want them to commit suicide, load that gun, and let them shoot themselves. I can't train morons."

All of them glowered at me. MB snapped. "We're not morons, and you never gave us a chance. You weren't able to break your dad's system on the first try."

"I gave you three chances, and you idiots performed horribly on all of them."

Bullet curled his hands into fists. "I don't care if Sam is here. You call us another name, and we're going to throw down."

"Fine, but you wouldn't win a fight against me either."

Sneaker shook his head. "I used to think of you as a friend, but you're a jerk. We'd be better off without you on the team."

"You're right." Sam flicked a hand at the building. "Go in and change into your street clothes while I talk to Maverick."

My jaw dropped as I turned to him. "You've got to be kidding?"

Sam waited until they entered the building before he answered. "I've worked for weeks to build their confidence, and in just a few hours, you've taken that away. So no, I'm not kidding. I don't think you're who we need."

"You've seen my performance and theirs. Any mission would have a better chance of success with just me."

"There are reasons we consider a team absolutely crucial for this operation. I read your Bureau assessment. They rated you exceptional in tradecraft, but poor in social skills. I agree. Your social skills suck. You'd be an asset for a solo operation, but it would be a disaster to have you lead a team you've completely alienated. I'll call Director Williams to tell him to forget making the announcement. The deals off."

My heart plummeted. "Wait. Why do you consider a team necessary?"

"We're running a false flag operation where we claim to be a terrorist organization. That's how we'll avoid leaving the country and get them to come to us."

What was that screen name they were using? "Ari?"

"Yes, one of our fake acronyms. Americans Rising for Islam."

He was right. For that kind of sting to work, it would take several people.

"I admit I messed up, but you should have told me a team was crucial. Let me talk to them and see if I can fix this."

"The director's press conference is scheduled for noon. You have until then."

That was in thirty minutes. I jogged inside the building.

The Fallen kids had finished changing and were heading for the door. Sneaker glanced back at me. "Tell Sam we're leaving."

"Wait, can we talk?"

They stopped, but Sneaker replied angrily, "So you can tell us again how we're nothing?" He shook his head. "We don't have anything to talk about."

Sam had come in, but he went in the gym. He wasn't going to help me. A shadow under the door revealed he stood close, probably listening.

MB's eyes narrowed at me. "We don't need you so why should we listen. There's nothing in it for us."

"There is something in it for you. If you give me two minutes, I'll explain."

Bullet sneered. "I'll give you two minutes because after the way you treated us, I want to hear you grovel." He walked over, plopped in a chair, and stuck his feet on the table.

The others followed him over, except for Sneaker, who grabbed a chair and rolled it away from the table to a computer to peck at the keyboard.

Bullet waved his hand in the air. "Go ahead, Maverick, beg."

"I acted like a jerk because I thought I'd be protecting you if I convinced you to quit. The truth is that each of you has skills that could be an asset to a team. Bullet's shooting, MB's computer knowledge, Hulk's strength, Blade's knife throwing skills, and Sneaker's ability to hide. You aren't morons, and I shouldn't have called you that."

Hulk crossed his arms. "So you don't think we'd be committing suicide?"

"What I said about the odds is true, but odds have been beaten before. I can teach you things to help you survive, but you have to care enough to work on learning them."

Blade flipped his knife in the air and caught it. "How does running some stupid obstacle course help anyone?"

"If we're fleeing for our lives, the quicker we get around any obstacles the better."

Bullet took his feet off the table and put them on the floor. "I'd rather shoot the person who wants to kill me than run away."

"Me too if there's only one, but if there's several, the best chance of survival is to run. Now I know I messed up, but I really *do* want to help you. I think I can if you're willing to let me?"

Bullet gave me an evil grin. "I haven't heard you beg,"

For my dad, I'd beg. "I really need this to help my dad, so please, I'm begging you to give me another chance."

Bullet pounded his chest. "Kind of gets to me right here." He dropped his arm. "Not. I don't feel sympathy for someone who thinks they're better than us."

MB frowned at me. "You only want to return to your old life. Fallentier doesn't matter to you, but this is our reality. Why should we let you stomp on it and us?"

Hulk's face was set like stone, unforgiving. "You disrespected us."

Sneaker's fingers had quit pecking, but he didn't say anything.

"I *would* like to be your friend, Sneaker."

He spun his chair around. "I don't think you know how to be a friend."

"No, but I'd like to learn if you'll teach me."

"Like you said, there's no sense trying to teach morons. Sam might call you a leader, but you never earned it." He waved at the others. "They did so I'd follow them, not you."

"So how do I gain your respect?"

"The same way we did." Hulk cracked his knuckles. "You fight for it."

I stood and pulled my sweatshirt with Pip in it over my head. "Fine. Which one of you wants to fight me?"

Bullet shook his stood. "Your two minutes is up." They all rose.

Wait. What was this? "You're afraid to fight me."

Bullet snorted. "I told you the other night we weren't finished.

We'll fight, but we decide when, not you."

"No." I moved toward him. "I need this to happen now."

Blade lifted his knife in the air. "Take one more step, and I'll throw this. And I don't miss." They backed toward the door.

I couldn't let them go. I needed to stop them.

"Don't move." Sam barked as he rushed out coming between me and them. He held his hand out to Blade. "Give me the knife, then you can leave. Maverick's not going to do anything because he knows it won't help him. Right, Maverick?"

I nodded. That was the best I could do with the lump that rose in my throat.

After Sam took the knife Blade handed over, Sam lit into him. "You know you're not allowed to threaten other people with your weapons or carry them outside the training facility unless you're on a mission. If it happens again you could find yourself off the team."

Blade shot me a glare that let me know he believed the reprimand was my fault. Then he and the other Fallen kids trudged out, taking all my hope.

I messed up, and that could kill Dad. I felt as if I couldn't breathe. I collapsed back into the chair. Sam's look of pity broke me. I threw my hands over my face and put my head down on the table to hide my streaming tears. I hated crying in front of Sam. Was it too much to wish that he'd leave?

Tones sounded as Sam punched numbers on his phone. His voice rang out in the room, "Connor, we've had some problems with Derrick's ability to lead the team, so at this point, I don't think we should go forward with his deal."

My heart ached as if I'd been stabbed.

"It's probably not a good time to talk to him," Sam said. "He's pretty upset." After a pause came, "Okay."

I heard the door open and footsteps sound. Who was here? I lifted my head to see Connor with his phone in his hand. Grrr. How could he have gotten here so fast? He must have been really close. I was too upset to ask why he'd been nearby, and I didn't want to see the disappointment that was sure to be in his eyes. I let my head fall back on the table.

"I don't think this can be fixed." Sam's voice penetrated my despair. "But I've been wrong before. Maybe we could give Derrick 24 hours to see if he can resolve the problems."

Hope sprang up in me. I lifted my head to take in Connor's grim face.

His frown was deep. "Derrick, you're not 'shadow man.'"

Shadow man was dad's code name. I didn't think it was possible to feel worse, but Connor's words crushed me. My anger at myself spilled out.

"Do you think I don't know that Dad wouldn't have failed? If you plan to rub in how much I messed up, don't bother. I'm aware of it."

"It was Vic and I that messed up when we encouraged you to act like him. He is good at being invisible because that's natural for him. Long before he became an agent, people overlooked him, but you're more like your mom. And your mom was responsible for getting us more Intel than Vic."

My jaw fell open. "Mom was an agent?"

"No, but she traveled a lot with Vic on his business trips. People were drawn to her, and they'd let stuff slip they shouldn't have, especially with Vic nearby. Of course, he'd pass on what might concern us." He pulled out a chair and sat. "What I'm trying to say is forget about doing things like Vic. People are drawn to you too, so you can't hide in the shadows. But you don't need to. Your mom was just as effective when she befriended everyone."

"How did she do that?"

"Simple. She cared about people. I can't tell you all the times she went out of her way to help someone. Everyone loved her." He pulled out his phone and spoke into it, "Yes, Director. We'd like you to delay the announcement by 24 hours." Connor pushed his phone's speaker button and held it toward Sam. "He wants to know if that will affect next week's mission?"

"No, they'll be ready regardless."

Connor turned his speaker off and returned his phone to his ear. "Yes, Director."

Connor hung up and pocketed his phone before meeting my gaze. "Thanks to Sam, you have 24 hours to turn this around."

"I'm not sure I did him any favors." Sam's solemn tone sounded as if he regretted his suggestion. "I should just transfer Derrick to another group home. They won't fight him fairly. He could really get hurt."

"Derrick, what do you want?" Connor asked.

Last time I fought Fallen kids, I escaped relatively unscathed only because of Lenny. My stomach knotted with the realization that next time it could turn out differently, but I'd risk any amount of injuries to help dad.

"Even if the chances are slim, I need to try." I used my sleeve to wipe my face. "What mission?"

"It's *need to know*." Connor stood and walked toward the door. "At this point, you don't need to know."

Sam motioned to me. "We have to return to Fallentier too. Since we left in my car, we'll go back the same way."

As we walked out the door, I glanced back at the training center. Would this be the last time I saw it?

Chapter 33

Firsts

"The first attempt is the most thrilling." Maverick

Maverick

Sam drove out of the training center and back to Fallentier. He had barely brought the car to a stop before Gina ran out from behind the corner of the main building.

When I opened my door, she grabbed the top and called to me breathlessly, "Are they sending you to Juvie?"

"Nope." I climbed out.

Sam cleared his throat. "You two have a sign to finish cleaning, but I'll give you a few hours to relax. Meet me in the kitchen after lunch."

I checked my watch. 9 a.m. It seemed like it should be later, but a lot had happened.

"Thanks, Sam." Kids were milling around the grounds. I turned to Gina. "Is there somewhere we can talk?"

"Follow me." She led me toward the main building. After checking to make certain we were alone, she ducked behind the dumpster.

When I slid in behind her, she jumped and grabbed the rung of a fire escape ladder. She clambered up it ever so slowly.

She crept to the second story window, then slid it open, and crawled inside. I raced up the ladder after her and grabbed the ledge. When I vaulted inside, I landed on plastic sheeting in a large empty room.

Gina whispered, "The construction guys don't work on the

weekends, so no one should come in here."

I asked softly, "Did you lock the door?"

"Yeah."

I leaned back against the wall, sliding down to sit on the floor while I studied Gina. Now that I knew she wasn't my sister, it seemed so obvious. Had I let my obsession to find my sister cloud my judgment? Gina had some classic Italian features like high cheekbones, but her face was softer, and her eyes had an exotic cast. They were darker than moms. A deep green that mesmerized me. She was stunning.

Gina sat beside me and twisted the cuff of her jeans nervously. "What did you want to talk about?" she asked.

"First, I wanted to tell you I'm sorry, but you were right. You're not my sister."

"I'm not sorry because if you were my brother, I couldn't do this." She leaned over to softly brush my lips with hers.

My heart knocked and my blood pounded in my ears. Her lips felt as soft as butterfly wings. The taste was sweet as a raspberry.

She pulled back, and her eyes tentatively met mine as if asking if I was okay with the kiss.

I wanted more so I put my arm around her shoulders to bring her closer, then crushed my lips to hers. She met my exuberance with her own, stealing my breath. When she pulled back and broke the kiss, I felt woozy.

"Wow!" I grinned at her. "Now there's a third thing I need to talk to you about."

She blushed. "Let's start with the second."

"Okay. Can I use your phone? I don't want Parker to have my number."

"You're going to call Parker?"

"Yeah. Do you trust me?"

She handed her phone to me. I pulled the affidavit papers from my pocket. "You might want to read this." I found Parker's number and called it.

"Gina?" Parker asked.

"No, it's Derrick. You knew the police weren't pursuing any

charges against Gina. Plus, you left her twisting in the wind when her cover was blown. How do you live with yourself?"

"You know the job, Derrick."

"Yeah, I do. It's protocol to yank out anyone who's compromised. You put her at serious risk with the Fallen kids, so don't even think about contacting her again."

"I followed my orders."

"To leave an innocent in danger. That doesn't fly. You need to stop trying to run ops on me. Dad never pitted me against you in training because you wouldn't be a challenge, so don't make me your enemy." I hung up Gina's phone and held it out to her. "We should get you a different phone, but he shouldn't bother you anymore. If he does, let me know."

Gina's hand trembled as she took the phone. "Just who are you?"

"I don't know what I should tell you, and there are some things I can't. I'm trying to fix our situation, so I don't want us to run away. Can you give me 24 hours?"

"Felicity has kicked me out, so I don't have anywhere to stay. Fallen kids don't like rats."

"Can't you sleep here tonight?"

"What about meals?"

"They aren't going to do anything in front of the staff. Everyone's mad at me, too, so we can be hated together."

"And if you can't fix it, we leave?"

"Yes, and I promise I'll keep you safe, okay?"

"All right."

"Thanks, now for the third thing. I can't believe I thought you were my sister. I mean, I felt a pull from the moment I saw you. Now I know that connection wasn't because we were related."

"You don't feel brotherly toward me anymore?"

Heat crept up my cheeks as my embarrassment rose. I'd already admitted I was wrong. Maybe I should share my lack of experience.

"Not at all, but I've never had a girlfriend or anyone I felt this strongly about before."

She smiled. "That's hard to believe."

"I wasn't allowed off the grounds of the mansion except to go to camp, and the girls there were trying to kick my butt, not kiss me."

She laughed a sweet musical laugh, and her face that normally bristled with defiance softened. She beamed a smile at me that lit up her eyes and my heart.

"I haven't had any boyfriends either."

I scoffed. All the guys watched her.

"I've been asked out, lots, but I didn't want to get attached." She frowned. "Not when I knew I'd probably be moving in a month."

I couldn't keep a grin off my face. "So we can be each other's first."

Her cute little nose scrunched. "Are you asking me to be your girlfriend?"

Had I been too reckless again? "Yeah, is it too soon?" I blew out my breath. "I really don't know what's normal."

"It's probably not normal, but neither is living in a group home." She smiled. "So the answer is yes, I'll be your girlfriend."

Joy surged up inside. The most beautiful girl I'd ever seen, and she was mine. I reached over and touched my lips to hers, and the sparks flew.

Time stopped for a few minutes until she pulled back. "I'm not having sex with you."

"What? I may not have had a girlfriend, but I know how to treat one. I'm not going to push you for sex."

"Okay." She yawned. "I need to sleep before we have to clean that sign. I'm exhausted."

I was too, so I laid back on the floor and propped my head on my arm. "Sleep sounds good."

Gina walked over to her garbage bag and started digging in it. She brought out a throw and two pairs of sweatpants.

She balled the sweatpants and handed one to me. "Use this for a pillow."

"Thanks." Then she lay next to me.

"I only have one blanket so we'll have to share," she said.

It wasn't that cold, but I wasn't going to complain when she backed closer and threw one side of her throw over me. I put my arm around her and breathed the sweet honeysuckle-like smell of Gina.

"Maverick?" she asked.

"Yeah?"

"Those things you couldn't talk about. You're not a bad guy are you?"

I wanted to be truthful with her. "That would depend on your definition of bad." I chuckled at the memory of the garter snake in Francine's bed. "Some of my tutors would tell you I was really bad." I stiffened. "But I'm no terrorist. I wouldn't kill innocents. Dad taught me to protect them."

"Most Fallentier kids aren't innocent."

They weren't combatants engaging in the art of war—not yet anyway. "You are to me."

"And you wouldn't lie to me?"

"I want you to be able to trust me, so I won't lie to you."

"Okay," she yawned again, and her eyes closed.

She didn't say she wouldn't lie to me. Would she?

Chapter 34

Chances

"When betting on your life, stack the odds." Victor

Maverick

I dumped the bucket of cleaner and examined the Fallentier sign. The graffiti was gone.

"We're finished."

Gina nodded. "Yeah, let's go eat."

My stomach growled in response. We arrived at the cafeteria to hear Sam make an announcement, "After dinner, I'll take anyone in the bus who wants to go bowling. Fallentier has graciously agreed to pay for it."

Gina and I pulled two chairs over by the window to avoid the other kids and propped our trays on our laps to eat.

I swallowed a bite, then glanced at her. "I'm going with Sam, but it might be safer if you stayed here."

She shook her head. "If you go, I'm going."

Blade's group walked by. Felicity sniffed dramatically at Gina. "I smell a rat."

I stood and moved between them. "If I really were a terrorist, you could have been killed. Gina thought she was protecting you. Yeah, she ended up being wrong, but haven't you ever made a mistake?"

Blade shifted Felicity behind him. Did he think I'd hurt her? She peeked around his arm to say with venom, "I've never ratted."

Sam and the other staff were staring at us, but they didn't come over. They must figure no one would fight with them watching. Who'd risk a trip to Juvie?

I pointed at my temple. "If someone put a gun to Blade's head, would you call the cops to save him?"

She placed a hand on her hip. "It's not the same."

"It is the same. Gina thought she was saving people, and as soon as she realized she was wrong, she warned me."

"She warned you?" Felicity moved out from behind Blade.

"Yes. And now no one has anything to hold over her."

Felicity twirled a strand of her hair. "We heard you called your dad's attorneys to help her. She's lucky you did that."

"Yes, I am." Gina stood. "Thanks for setting me straight so I could warn Maverick."

"Someone needed to." Felicity eyed her. "Well, Maverick's the one you hurt, so if he forgave you, I guess I can. But you better never be that stupid again."

"I won't be."

"All right. I'll let you move back in." She grinned. "Tigger misses you."

Gina rolled her eyes. "Now I need to set you straight. That stuffed cat's not real."

Felicity covered her mouth, but a laugh escaped. "Don't hate on Tigger."

Blade's group left the cafeteria, so Gina and I returned our trays, then walked outside to join the Fallen kids climbing on the bus. We sat in the first seat, away from the others. They ignored us while Sam started the bus and drove to a business area with a large sign advertising bowling.

When Sam parked at the bowling alley, he glanced back at me and his forehead creased. Was he concerned about something happening? I was more worried about nothing happening. Time was running out to change the Fallen kids' minds.

"No wandering the town tonight," Sam said as we filed off. "I don't want anyone getting lost."

When we entered the bowling alley, kids rushed to the counter to get their shoes. Bullet sidled up to me.

"In ten minutes, meet me out back if you still want to prove yourself." He sauntered off, the kids from his group following.

No sense in me getting shoes or selecting a bowling ball. I walked around the place with Gina to check it out. It held twenty bowling lanes. Some Fallen kids had claimed some and were preparing to bowl, but both Bullet and MB's group strode into a room with old-school arcade games. On the far wall was a door with an exit sign. I took a seat at the end of a lane near the arcade room.

Gina was still standing. "Do you mind if I go talk to Felicity?" she asked.

"No, but if anyone gives you trouble, holler."

She strolled into the game room, and Sneaker plopped next to me. "None of the Misfits will help you. They say you were too good for them yesterday, so they're too good for you today. I won't help you either since we're not friends."

"All right, but you like Gina. Can you keep her inside so she'll be safe?"

He sighed. "Yeah. I can do that."

Gina came out of the game room and rushed to me. "I heard rumors that you're going to fight."

"You shouldn't believe everything you hear." I glanced at my watch. Almost time. I stood. "I'm going to the bathroom."

Gina's voice followed me. "Don't fight."

The men's bathroom had a high window that wasn't very big. I could probably maneuver myself through it. After making sure I was alone, I stood on my tiptoes to peer out the window. A drive led around the building to a much smaller paved area. In the dark I could barely discern a few parked cars, probably employee vehicles. Behind the cars was a lot for a large brick building which was completely dark. Looked like some kind of factory.

I cranked open the window, but it only partially opened. With my mechanical knife, I unscrewed the rods that prevented it from opening farther. I pulled myself up to the window ledge, then twisted myself through to jump down on the pavement.

To the side of where I landed, a dim light hung over the building's rear exit and let me pick out the kids huddled there. Bullet, MB, Hulk, Blade, and several others. Must be a dozen.

MB's voice broke the quiet. "I don't think he's going to show.

Maybe he chickened out."

Bullet snorted. "He'll show." He motioned. "Everyone backup so he can't see us until he comes out. Then we'll jump him."

I snuck behind them. How many could I take out before they'd catch on? I'd been taught to quietly slit throats, but I didn't want to kill anyone. The kid with crooked teeth who's street name was "Pinch" stood in the back. I punched him in the temple, and he collapsed.

"What was that?" Someone exclaimed.

The bowling alley door cracked open. I caught a glimpse of Gina looking out.

I couldn't let them jump her. I moved into the light. "Stay inside, Gina."

The group spun toward me.

I stood my ground. "I'll fight you, but one at a time."

Bullet shouted, "Get him!"

Aargh.

Chapter 35

Blood Rubies

"Symbols can be so powerful that people willingly give their lives for them." Victor

Gina

Oh no. My heart raced as I peered out the cracked door. Maverick had hollered for me to stay inside, but a bunch of Fallen kids were trying to jack him up.

I had to help. As I yanked the door open, Sneaker stopped texting behind me and shoved the door to close it. I stuck my foot in the crack to keep it open. Sneaker wedged himself against it.

"Let me out," I demanded.

"No. He'll be all right. And he doesn't want you out there. I don't either."

Whatever. Maverick could be in trouble.

A small rectangular window with a grid of x's at the top of the door gave me a better view than the crack. Maverick punched a guy in the jaw, then kicked another in the chest. Several of them charged him. Maverick reeled back as fists landed on his face. They grabbed him, ripping his tank shirt and exposing his chest as they dragged him to the ground. Maverick bucked to get them off, but they held onto his arms and legs, crushing him to the pavement.

Someone cried out, "Help."

I had to do something. "Sneaker, if you don't let me out, I'm going to..."

Sneaker's breath hit my cheek as he peered out the window too. "That wasn't Maverick."

Pinch wobbled into the light and stalked over to where they held Maverick down. "That guy blindsided me." Pinch reached down to finger Maverick's necklace. "So I'll take this."

"No." Maverick yelled. He got one arm out and punched Pinch in the face. Pinch reeled back while some other kids jumped in and forced Maverick's arm down. Then Pinch came back, spitting blood out of his mouth. His foot slammed toward Maverick's face.

Maverick jerked his head to the side, and Pinch's foot glanced off his cheek, hitting the pavement.

Pinch hollered. He must have hurt his foot. Some Fallen kids laughed.

I shoved my shoulder into Sneaker. When he staggered back, I flung the door open and ran outside. I darted between two of the kids surrounding Maverick as Pinch drew his arm back to punch him.

"Stop." I shoved Pinch.

He fell, then jumped back up with murder in his eyes.

"Leave. Gina. Alone." Maverick struggled and lifted his shoulders partially off the ground. They forced him down.

Bullet grabbed me. I clawed at his hands.

"Quit fighting." Bullet's arms wrapped around me, pinning me.

I stomped his foot.

He lifted me a couple of inches in the air. "I don't want to hurt you."

"Stop, Gina," Maverick shouted.

I couldn't get loose. I went limp to wait for Bullet to relax his guard.

MB grabbed Maverick's necklace. Maverick struggled, heaving against those holding him.

"This must be valuable the way you're fighting to keep it." MB jerked it over Maverick's head. He examined the medallion, then his eyes widened. "Let him up."

"Why should we?" Bullet held onto me even tighter.

MB dangled Maverick's necklace in front of him. "He's an Amato, and his medallion has rubies."

I sucked in my breath. Was my boyfriend an Amato? Maverick had said he couldn't tell me some stuff, but this...

Bullet released me as everyone unhanded Maverick and backed away as if he had the plague. I took a step back too. Being near an Amato wasn't healthy.

"What's an Amato?" Pinch asked.

Maverick touched his face gingerly. "Amato is a common name in Italy. Lots of people have it."

"Including the most vicious mob family out there." Sneaker came out the bowling alley door. "Those Amato's wear a medallion with their name in blood rubies to represent the blood they'll spill if you cross them."

Bullet handed Maverick his necklace. "Is it true that Amatos have to kill an enemy of their family to get a medallion?"

Maverick eyed the medallion and his face scrunched.

"Maybe it's not his," Pinch whined.

"He wouldn't be breathing if he stole it." MB held his hand out to Maverick. "Let me help you up."

Maverick slipped his necklace back around his neck and let MB pull him up.

It irritated me that Maverick hadn't told me. "Why would an Amato be at Fallentier?" I snapped. "And why did you hide it?"

Maverick fingered his split lip. "I'm at Fallentier because I don't want anyone controlling my life, and my grandfather asked me not to reveal my medallion."

Bullet squinted at Maverick as if trying to identify his features. "Who's your Grandfather?"

"Dominick Amato."

"The D-don," Bullet muttered. "Just shoot me now."

"That can be arranged."

I jumped at the voice. It came from beyond where the overhead light cast its circle of illumination. A couple of guys stepped into the light. One of them was huge—probably seven foot tall—and muscular like a body builder. The other guy was normal sized, and he carried a large shopping bag.

Maverick frowned at the guy with the bag. "What are you doing here, Anthony?"

"The Don hasn't washed his hands of you," answered the big

dude. "He's concerned."

Maverick's brows shot up. "Who are you?"

"He's Enzo, one of your family's eliminator's." Anthony waved at Maverick's face. "They resolve problems like this."

An eliminator wasn't someone I wanted to be around. All the Fallen kids were sidling toward the door, and I joined them.

Enzo barked, "None of you move."

I froze, and so did the other kids.

Maverick wiped his face with his sleeve. "The problem's already solved."

Enzo poked Maverick's arm, then held up a bloody finger. "Not when an Amato's blood is spilled."

"Why is it taking so long to collect my cousin?" A guy with dark hair and brooding eyes came around the corner. Dressed in a fancy suit, he looked like he should be strolling down a fashion runway. When he spotted Maverick, he rushed toward him.

Maverick took a step back. "I don't want to get you dirty, Lucca."

Lucca's eyes flared. "That's not dirt. You're bleeding." He looked over his shoulder. "I told you, Sergio, we shouldn't have left him."

A guy emerged holding a phone to his ear. Sergio looked like Lucca except he had a mustache and his eyes were harder, more steely.

Lucca appeared to be our age, but Sergio seemed to be a few years older. Both of them resembled Maverick some. The angle of their jaws, the high cheekbones, the thick dark hair. Maverick's angles weren't as sharp, and his eyes were softer. But all three of them had the same magnetism.

Felicity elbowed me. I hadn't even seen her come outside. She whispered, "Those guys are off the scale hot, but now I know what other animals feel like when a lion walks through the jungle."

Yeah. Everyone had wanted Maverick's attention, but Lucca and Sergio scrutinized us as if we were prey. No one in their right mind would want those guys' focus.

Lucca's arms waved in the air as he turned to Anthony. "How could you let this happen?"

Anthony's Adam's apple bobbed up and down. "We didn't get

the call until just now. When we got here, they were all on top of him."

Lucca pulled a handgun out. "Then maybe they should all die."

My mouth flew open. Did he plan to commit mass murder?

Maverick jumped between Lucca and us. "We were just messing around. I bet them all that they couldn't keep me down, and someone's foot clocked me accidentally."

With a flick of Sergio's hand, Lucca lowered his gun. Relief flooded me.

Sergio's steely eyes trained on us. "Is that what happened to Derrick?"

To have someone call Maverick by another name seemed weird. Maverick must have thought so too.

"I go by Maverick now. That's how they know me, and it's the name I prefer."

Sergio's eyebrow arched. "Is that what happened to *Maverick*?"

"Yeah, we were messing around." Bullet patted Maverick on the shoulder.

Sergio smirked. "I thought you might have been jealous. Amatos are born leaders, and there's always a few who can't accept our destiny." He walked over to where MB and Bullet stood by Maverick. "So you must have already accepted Maverick as your leader?"

They looked at their feet, shuffling them. "Yeah."

Sergio pinned us all with his gaze. "Is everyone giving Maverick the respect due?"

Some kids nodded.

Lucca lifted his gun again. "I'm not convinced."

The rear door of the bowling alley flung open and Sam limped out. "Are any of you going to bowl?"

His eyes widened as he took in Lucca waving the pistol. "There's no need for guns." He barked, "Put it away. Now."

"There is a need when you let my cousin get harmed," Lucca spat out.

Sam flicked two fingers at Maverick. Was that a signal? Was he asking if Maverick could take two out?

Maverick flashed him his palm, then turned to Lucca. "It was just an accident." He ran his fingers through his hair. "Why are you here?"

"We came to take you to a party," Lucca said.

Maverick moved closer to me and laced his fingers with mine. "I'm not leaving Gina."

Surely the Fallen kids wouldn't come after me now for ratting. "I should be okay, Maverick."

"Should isn't good enough." Maverick squeezed my hand. "I gave you my word you'd be safe."

"She'll be safe— if you go with us," Sergio retorted.

Was he saying I wouldn't be if Maverick didn't?

Maverick's face clouded. He stared at Sergio with narrowed eyes. Wasn't he intimidated by these guys at all?

Sergio blinked first and motioned to Enzo. "Stay with Gina and guard her until Maverick returns." He snipped at Maverick, "Any other problems?"

I didn't want to hang out with their eliminator, but I wasn't sure how to get out of it.

Sam moved over to us. "Yes, there's a problem. You can't just take Maverick."

Sergio pulled a paper out of his suit pocket and gave it to Sam. "A judge approved our family visits with Maverick."

Sam looked at the paper. "Even if you have a judge in your pocket, he'll have to reconsider when I tell him you guys were waving a gun."

Sergio sprang like a tiger right up in Sam's face. "I think you're mistaken." He glanced over at the other Fallen kids. "Did any of you see a gun?"

They all shook their heads, no. They weren't going to cross the Amato's.

"Be careful about making wild allegations." The threat in Sergio's voice was unmistakable. "They can be costly."

Sam released a heavy breath. "All right, one two-hour visit, and if any harm comes to him… I'll shine a huge spotlight on the Amato's."

"You're threatening the wrong people," Lucca snarled. "Look what your punks did to my cousin's face. Tell my why they shouldn't look similar?"

Sam barked, "Sneaker, get the first-aid kit off the bus." He made a shooing motion. "The rest of you kids get inside."

They fled as Sam turned to Maverick. "You need to come in too so I can treat you before you leave."

Sergio moved toward the door. "We'll *all* go in so Maverick can clean up."

Maverick tugged me with him inside. The din of bowling balls rolling and striking pins assaulted my ears, and the flashing lights of the arcade games seemed too bright.

The kids in the arcade room left when they spotted us. I barely heard Sam over the din as we moved into the hall with the restroom. "I'm going to check on the kids while you wash up, but I'll be back."

As Sam limped away, Sergio pointed to Maverick's chest. "You can't party in those clothes."

Maverick's cheeks flushed red. "I have other clothes at Fallentier, but not here, and I don't have the money to be going out."

Lucca beamed. "Nonno's paying and he already bought you a suit."

Anthony held the bag he'd been carrying out to Maverick. "Here."

Maverick wouldn't take it. "I can't accept gifts or Grandfather paying my way."

Lucca's eyes flashed. "Do you think you're too good for Nonno's money? Or maybe you think he's some poor schmuck that can't afford to buy his grandson a suit of clothes?"

"Neither. Dad says accepting charity is asking for misery since it harms your pride. Birthday's and Christmas are the only times I didn't earn what I received." He crossed his arms. "I may be in a group home now, but I'm not a charity case. I *will* pay the state back for my keep."

Lucca's brows knitted. "All Amato's are prideful. I don't want to hurt yours. Birthday and Christmas gifts are okay?"

Maverick nodded once. "As long as they don't have strings attached."

"Good. Your birthday was five days ago, so the clothing and everything else tonight will be a late birthday gift—no strings."

Maverick took the bag of clothing from Anthony. "As long as

Grandfather considers it the same."

Sergio slapped his shoulder. "The Don will say Happy Birthday."

Sneaker came carrying the first aid kit and handed it to Maverick.

"Thanks." Maverick looked at me. "Will you be around when I come out?"

I gave him a nod. "I'll be where we sat earlier."

"I'll keep her safe," Enzo said.

When Maverick entered the bathroom, not only Enzo but everyone followed me to the chairs near the arcade. I sat, and Sneaker plopped next to me. Not sure why he'd stay around the Amato's, but it was a little less scary with him here. So I threw him a smile as Lucca and Sergio sat on my other side and Anthony and Enzo stood behind us.

The other Fallen kids were bowling. Felicity was four lanes away and tossed a ball that wobbled toward the gutter.

Lucca glanced at them, then turned his disdainful sneer on me. "You're not good enough for an Amato. Break up with Maverick."

His superior attitude irked me. They weren't kings, just glorified thugs. When Maverick couldn't be intimidated, Sergio backed down. Maybe I should show some courage too?

I smirked at him. "Maverick thinks I'm good enough…" I changed my tone to snarky. "And you ain't God, so don't dictate to me."

Sergio's cold eyes met mine. He spoke so softly I barely heard the words, "My parents were killed in front of me and Lucca. Not by the men holding guns on them, but by the Don in the crossfire. He was right to shoot. If he'd dropped his weapon like those men wanted, we'd all be dead. Associating with Amato's can get you killed."

I shut my open mouth. If that story was meant to scare me, it was kind of working. "Maverick wouldn't be at Fallentier if he wanted to be around your family."

Lucca smirked. "It's not what Maverick wants that is important, but what the Don wants."

Sergio's phone beeped again. He read a text, then showed it to Lucca who frowned and wrinkled his nose at me. "You're wasting your time with Maverick. He's engaged."

Heat flooded my face. Had Maverick been playing me? "I can't believe he didn't tell me."

"He doesn't know yet," Lucca said. "The Don just chose her."

I'd heard plenty about the Amato's but never this. "Your grandfather chooses your wives?"

Sergio shrugged. "Another family won't declare war on us if their daughter's in ours."

"It won't be hard for Maverick." Lucca's tone was testy. "I know his fiancée, Maria. You can't compete. It would be like comparing a dandelion to a rose."

"Shouldn't Maverick be the judge of that?" Sneaker asked stiffly. "He won't like you talking trash about Gina."

I shot Sneaker a grateful look. It took guts to stand up to an Amato.

"Neither of you will tell Maverick if you don't want an accident." Lucca slashed a finger across his own neck. "Capiche?"

Sneaker and I nodded. I didn't want to be the one to tell Maverick his family chose his fiancé, anyway. Why were they so confident that he'd accept her? Did it matter? Did I really want to be with someone connected to the Amato's? I didn't need any more problems, did I?

Chapter 36

Bizarre

"Bizarre can seem normal to someone crazy." Gina

Maverick

The new shoes were the right size. I slipped them on and looked in the mirror to put antibiotic cream on the gash by my lip. I barely recognized myself. The red tie accented the dark suit nicely. Strange that everything fit me perfectly. The cuffs ended at my wrists, and the pants were hemmed right below my ankles. Dad had measured me a few weeks ago when he ordered my new wet suit. Could Connor have gotten those measurements and given them to the Amato's?

Connor wasn't the only one informing on me. Someone told them I was in a fight. My cousins had gotten me out of a bad situation, but I didn't want anyone keeping tabs on me. They might discover my radio messages to Dad. With the court order, I'd have to go with them tonight. But this would be the last time. I would convince the Amato's to leave me alone.

Sam came in the restroom with his phone in his hand. He held it out to me. "I called Connor to tell him about the Amato's court order for visits with you. He wants to talk to you."

When I put the phone to my ear, Connor's voice came through as if he were standing there. "I need you to get close to your Grandfather."

Wasn't it risky enough to infiltrate terrorist groups? Now he wanted to add the mafia? "Haven't you already done that?"

"The Don says he no longer needs my reports, but we still need to know whose buying arms and explosives. So act friendly tonight and try to get those contacts."

"Dad wouldn't want me to do that."

"You're not working for your dad, now, but us. You want us to make that announcement, don't you?"

I fought to tamp my rising temper. "Director Williams clearly stated that I wasn't working for you. I'd say I'm working for me since I negotiated my contract, the one where I agreed to help catch terrorists, not play nice with the mafia. So stick to the agreement and don't threaten me because that makes it *even* harder to trust you."

"Okay. No threats, but I'm asking you to *please* do what you can."

"Do you really think I have any control over them? I'm not going to give up my soul, and Grandfather won't just hand over that Intel because I ask."

"Then we're going to have to convince him."

Like that would be easy. I tugged at the tie around my neck to loosen it a little and blew out my breath. "All right. I'll try."

"Good. But be careful, lad. Remember your S's."

No kidding. I pressed the button to hang up, then handed the phone back to Sam. I stuffed the clothes I'd changed out of into the empty clothing bag on the floor.

"Where can I put these until I get back?"

"I'll have someone take them to the bus with the first aid kit."

I put the cream back in the kit, then handed it and my bag to Sam. "Thanks."

"No problem."

I left the bathroom and moved toward Gina. Hmmm. Sergio and Lucca were sitting by her and Sneaker. Her stiff shoulders showed she wasn't happy, even as she turned to smile at me.

Lucca beamed. "That Zegna suits you. Now you look like an Amato."

I'd heard of the Italian fashion brand, but I'd never worn anything of theirs. I could only guess the cost.

Gina jumped up. "You do look fantastic."

"Thanks. Did I miss anything?"

"No." Lucca grabbed Gina's thigh. She jerked away as Lucca

announced, "We were just getting to know your girlfriend."

A red hot-streak of jealousy surged up in me. "Don't. Touch. Gina."

"Aww, you don't like to share?"

Sam snarled at Lucca. "You shouldn't be touching any Fallentier kid." He tapped his watch. "I expect Maverick back before ten when we'll be leaving, so if you want to spend any time with him..."

"Anthony, bring the car around to the front," Sergio ordered. Anthony double-timed it toward the door as Sergio stood. "This has been fun, but we have better things to do. Let's go, Maverick."

I squeezed Gina's hand. "You sure you're all right with me leaving?"

She nodded. Enzo handed me a slip of paper. "Here's my phone number if you want to check on her."

I put the number in my contacts as I followed Lucca and Sergio. When we strolled past the lanes with other Fallen kids, Sergio glared at them.

It worried me. "You aren't planning some payback, are you? I don't want them hurt."

"That's up to the Don. He might let it go since they didn't know who you were. But if anyone were to harm you again like this..." Sergio pinched my swollen nose making it ache. "I can guarantee they'll feel our wrath."

I jerked my face away. "Except you."

Sergio laughed. "Yeah, I'm allowed." He lowered his hand and voice. "You'll feel a lot more pain if you ever lie to me again to cover someone else's mistake."

I hissed, "I never asked to join the family."

"No, but you chose to wear the family medallion. Now that others have seen it, there is no going back."

My heart sank at the thought of losing my mom's necklace, but I couldn't live with the guilt of people getting harmed because of me. "What if I give the necklace to Grandfather and ask him to wash his hands of me?"

Sergio grinned wolfishly. "I don't think you know what you're asking. When the Don washes his hands of someone, there is a hit and they die."

Well, that wasn't an option. We trudged out the door into the parking lot, and Anthony brought the Limo up. He jumped out and opened the middle door for Lucca and Sergio and the rear one for me. I scooted in to sit across from my cousins.

When Anthony pulled out of the bowling alley, Lucca leaned forward. "I'm sorry if I upset you when I touched Gina. I didn't think either of you'd mind."

"I told you she was my girlfriend."

"She was flirting with Sergio before you came out, so I didn't think you two were very serious." Lucca shrugged. "She didn't know Sergio's married."

What? Was Lucca even telling the truth? He didn't exhibit any of the normal signs of lying. Maybe he was an accomplished liar.

I shook my head. "I don't believe you. She looked pretty unhappy to me."

"That's because I turned her down." Sergio cracked his jaw. "Those kids back there are like so many other people we deal with. Leeches and snakes. They only want you for what you can give them. Favors, money, connections. But once they get what they want, they go to the next person."

My heart felt like someone had hammered it. Could he be right? I didn't want to believe it, but I knew the Fallen kids' mantra. *You don't get something for nothing.* Had Gina just wanted me for what I could do for her?

I didn't want to think about it anymore. I glanced at Sergio. "Are you really married?"

"Yes, and Lucca's engaged. We don't wear rings because our enemies don't need reminders that they can go after someone else to get to us."

Wow. Lucca was my age. "I'm nowhere near ready to be married."

Sergio chuckled. "It's not that difficult." He leaned forward in the seat. "I don't understand why you're going by *Maverick*. You should have chosen Rico."

I fingered my necklace. "That was my mom's nickname for me."

"I know. Grandfather's full name is Dominick Rico Amato. Your mother wanted to name you Rico after him, but your father wanted you to have an American name. They compromised on Derrick." Sergio crossed his arms. "We will call you Rico. Everyone should. It will make the Don happy."

I didn't even like Dad telling me what to do, and I loved him. I'd known these guys for a few days. What made them think they could boss me?

"Both Rico and Derrick belong to a different life." I lifted my chin. "I go by Maverick now. You can call me anything you want, but I'll only answer to Maverick."

A black sedan pulled alongside us, and the tinted window in the back rolled partially down. I glimpsed part of a face and black hair. Then the barrel of a gun.

"Gun," I yelled and dove into the seats.

My ears rang to the sound of gunfire. The window shattered under the impact of bullets, raining glass on us. My heart careened as Anthony floored the gas pedal, and our car rocketed forward.

My cousins swore in Italian. They had dived across the seats, too, and had pulled out their pistols to shoot back.

The car swerved. Anthony must be changing lanes. Then the car turned, tires squealing, and turned again, throwing us the opposite way. I pulled myself up enough to look over the back seat. I didn't see the other car.

The window slid open in the partition that separated us, and Anthony said, "I've lost them for now. Is anyone hurt?"

For now? Would they be back?

I sat up, shaking off the glass, and examined myself. I hadn't been hurt, but I felt anything but all right.

Lucca bounced in his seat. "We're okay, but we should have driven our car here from New York so we'd have bullet proof glass."

"Should we still go to the club?" Anthony asked.

Were they kidding? Shouldn't they call the police?

Sergio had laid his gun in the seat and was texting on his phone. "The Don says yes. There are more men at the club," Sergio answered calmly. "Maverick, could you identify any of the people in that car?"

"I only got a glimpse of the top half of the shooter's face, but I'd probably recognize him if I saw him again."

Sergio texted some more. He acted as if people shooting at them were nothing, while Lucca seemed if he'd just drunk a gallon of highly-caffeinated coffee.

Sergio stopped texting and his phone rang. He answered, "I'll put you on speaker, Nonno." He angled his phone toward me.

Grandfather's voice came from the phone speaker, distant and tinny, but his authoritative tone unmistakable. "Tell me what you saw."

I leaned toward the phone. "The shooter had black hair, a wide forehead, thin brows with a scar on the left one, brown eyes close set over a strong nose, and a lean face. I couldn't see his mouth or chin. The lines around his eyes weren't deep, so I'd guess mid-thirties. The gun was a 45 semi-automatic, and he shot 4 rounds."

Lucca's jaw dropped open. "All I saw was the gun." He bounced in his seat again. "Ricardo has a scar like that. He must not be happy about his sister's engagement."

"We have to retaliate." Sergio's tone was ice cold. "We should wipe out the Russo family."

"We're not going to resume a war if Ricardo acted without his family's consent." Grandfather's voice rang forcefully. "I'll give them the chance to wash their hands of him before we act. Now stop talking about it," he barked. "Anthony, how long until you arrive at the club?"

"Five minutes, sir."

"Good." A click came from the phone.

Not soon enough for me. This whole situation was beyond bizarre. Apparently, they were involved in some feud with another family, but I had no interest in becoming a part of it.

Lucca still bounced on the seat. He needed tranquilizers or something. Sergio had gone back to texting calmly. They acted completely opposite from one another.

I turned my focus back to searching for the other car. My hair whipped in the wind as it rushed through the destroyed window, and chills raced up my spine. Would the shooter find us?

Chapter 37

Celebration

"Make the most of today. There might not be a tomorrow." Victor

Maverick

Anthony slowed the Limousine and slid open the partition window. "Should I go to the back door?"

"No." Sergio stopped texting. "I don't want anyone thinking Amato's can be cowed."

Sergio pocketed his phone as Anthony pulled the car over in front of a stately brick building with the sign *Baldoria* which basically meant *good time* in Italian. The people in the line that snaked from the door didn't look my age. It must not be an underage club.

"Are we allowed in here?" I asked.

Lucca laughed. "Our family has a controlling interest, so yeah."

My neck prickled when four guys in suits moved toward us. "Is that trouble?"

Sergio gave them a quick perusal. "No. Those are ours."

Anthony opened our doors. The guys in suits surrounded us as we climbed from the car and headed toward the club.

One of the bouncers standing behind some ropes announced loudly, "This club is now closed for a private party. Invitation only. Everyone else, please leave."

Several people moved from the line and walked away together. In their midst, I glimpsed the back of someone with short blonde hair. They moved around the corner, cutting off my view. Could that have been Jake? Probably not. There were tons of tow headed guys.

Sergio glanced at me. "Only friends of our family got invitations. Some flew in for this."

The bouncers motioned us past the line and lowered the ropes. A few people grumbled. A glare from Sergio shut them up.

We traipsed in the door and into a foyer that opened into what could easily pass as an elegant ballroom. Thick draperies covered the windows, but soft globe lights dangled from an embossed ceiling to light the band playing on stage. Although the lyrics were in English, the music seemed to be a mix of Sicilian pop and folk. The haunting strains of a bagpipe, hand drum, and accordion blended with an electric guitar and crooning vocals.

In front of the stage, about a dozen people danced, but most of the few hundred occupants sat around small round tables with servers moving between them. The crowd consisted mainly of adults with a few teens scattered in, all dressed formally. Many had telltale bulges revealing they were armed.

Sergio paused inside the foyer to ask one of his men. "You kept Maria here?"

"No," the guy replied. "The Don said to let her go, but she hasn't tried to leave."

"She always did have courage." Lucca's lip turned down. "But her guards should have made her."

I didn't have any idea what they were talking about, but they moved on into the club. Everyone rose to their feet as they noticed our appearance. The band screeched to a halt.

"Thank you all for coming." Lucca put an arm around my shoulders. "Tonight we are celebrating my cousin Maverick's 17th birthday. I hope you will help us make it special."

The lead singer in the band began belting out the lyrics to the birthday song. He hollered, "Everyone help."

A roar shook the room as everybody joined in enthusiastically. When they finished, Lucca shouted, "Let's party!"

People rushed over to shake our hands. It was hard to hear over the music, but several of them wished me, "Happy Birthday," or said in Italian, "Buon complenna."

Coming from strangers, it didn't mean much. After we shook several hands, Sergio and Lucca moved toward a table where a girl sat with several bulky guys. Must be guards. Her black hair was pinned up with a glittering hair clip in some fancy hair-do and sparkly jewelry draped her dress.

"Hello, Maria." Lucca smiled at her. "You look beautiful as always."

Her guards stiffened, but she returned his smile. "Thank you, Lucca." She stood and asked, "Aren't you going to introduce me to your il cugino?"

Hmm. She pronounced cousin in Italian fluently. Was it her native language?

"Of course." Lucca waved a hand at me. "Maverick, this is Maria Russo. She's not only gorgeous, but brave as well."

My breath caught. Russo? She must be related to the guy who shot at us.

"Lucca, you are too kind." She extended her hand to me. "Buon complenna, Maverick."

I took her dainty hand, which felt as smooth as silk, and gently shook it. "Thanks."

"I'm going to leave now." She glanced at Sergio. "I just wanted you to know that I don't approve of Ricardo's actions." Her head was high as she walked away regally, her guards surrounding her.

"What did you think of Maria, Maverick?" Lucca asked as his eyes followed her.

He was obviously enamored with her. Sergio had said Lucca was engaged. "I don't know her well enough to offer an opinion on who you marry."

Lucca's chuckle sounded forced. "She's not my fiancé."

Then maybe he was engaged to the wrong person. Sergio's phone buzzed. He pulled it out and looked at the screen. "Let's sit down."

All the tables looked full except the one she'd just vacated.

"Here?" I asked.

"Up there." Sergio pointed to a balcony that overlooked the dance floor and stage.

I followed Sergio and Lucca to a staircase. Across the first step was a rope with a sign, "No admittance." One of the uniformed employees stood blocking it, but he opened the rope at our approach. Sergio motioned to his men who'd been following us. "Stay here."

They took positions at the bottom of the steps as we started up. When we reached the top, the landing opened on the left to the balcony where a horseshoe-shaped leather sofa looked out on the action below. A low marble table stood between the couch and the railing and held a selection of sandwiches, snacks, and a birthday cake. A waitress hovered over the cake cutting slices. She was the only one in the room before we stepped onto the plush carpeting.

There was a small mahogany bar against the back wall, left of it stood elevator doors, and to the right a bathroom. Sergio and Lucca sat on the sofa. Lucca patted the cushion next to him, "Maverick, come, sit."

Why did people keep trying to command me as if I were a dog? I'd told Connor I'd try to act friendly, so I bit back a sarcastic retort.

When I perched on the couch, the waitress asked, "What can I bring you to drink?"

"A coke will be fine."

Sergio snorted. "You're not drinking coke. Bring us a bottle of good Campari."

They could place it in front of me, but I wouldn't drink alcohol and let my senses be dulled. After the waitress poured us each a glass, she retreated to the bar.

The elevator dinged. The doors slid open, and my grandfather strode out. "Buon complenna, il nipote."

Even with his thick New York accent, I translated his Italian as *Happy birthday, grandson.*

Both my cousins stood to greet him. I rose, too, and asked, "Why didn't you tell me you were coming?"

Grandfather's flinty eyes sparkled. "I wanted to surprise you."

"You did." I tugged my suit jacket. "Thanks for the clothes." I waved at the table of food. "… and everything else."

"It's nothing." He flicked his hand in a shooing motion at the waitress. "We won't need you anymore."

"Of course, Mr. Amato." She rushed down the steps.

Grandfather turned to me. "Sergio wasn't sure you'd come, but I figured Connor would make you once I cut him off." He frowned. "So you're working for him now?"

Grrr. Grandfather had set a trap, and I walked into it. "No. I make my own decisions, but terrorist attacks threaten everyone. If your information might stop them, you should do the right thing and hand it over."

He moved toward the bar and grabbed a bottle of wine. Grandfather screwed a corkscrew in and popped out the cork.

After pouring two glasses, he came back to hand me one. "Sit down, relax."

When I perched on the couch, again, he sat next to me and said, "I can't give Connor that information."

I put the glass of wine on the table next to my full glass of Campari. "Why? Is doing the right things against some code for criminals?"

"You have the wrong idea. The Amato family isn't comprised of terrible *criminals*." He swirled his wine. "What we sell is information. If someone needs something, they pay us a commission, and we set up a meeting with our contacts."

I had doubts whether that was all they did, but it was still illegal. "That's conspiracy."

Sergio laughed. "The CIA collects and distributes information too."

Grandfather took a sip of his wine. "The only names we gave to Connor are the ones who didn't pay our commission." He set down his glass. "If I double-cross those who did pay, no one would trust us, and we'd become everyone's target. I won't start a war where we'll be wiped out. Being an enemy of one family is bad enough."

"The Russo's won't be our enemy after we eliminate them," Sergio said frostily.

Grandfather shot him a glare before turning his focus back to me. "As soon as others saw your necklace, you became a target as well. I can't protect you at Fallentier. You have to go home with us."

I shook my head. "I don't mean to be rude, but I don't think you can protect me anyway."

Grandfather sighed. "We are more equipped for these situations there, and punks know better than to touch an Amato."

"You aren't going to hurt the Fallen kids, are you?"

One of his dark eyebrows arched. "Are they your friends?"

"I'm working on it."

"I'll let it go this time." He stroked his chin. "So if Gina's your girlfriend, she must not be your sister."

Warmth rose in my cheeks. "Her fingerprints didn't match."

"Is that why you want to stay?" Lucca asked.

"She's a bonus, but I'm staying because the chances of clearing Dad are better from Fallentier."

"I hope you change your mind soon." Grandfather's tone sobered. "We don't want to attend your funeral."

I glanced at the crowd below. That short lady with long black hair. Could it be?

I gasped as she turned, and I recognized the familiar face of my tutor, Angela. But what was she doing here? Dad thought she set him up. Was she a terrorist? Wait, why did she look like she'd gained twenty pounds? Could she be wearing a bomb?

I needed to get down there. Now!

Chapter 38

Threats

"Life will drag you down if you don't keep moving." Victor

Maverick

I had to stop Angela, but I couldn't let her see me coming. My heart pounded as I jumped up and snatched the knife the server cut the cake with. Then I vaulted over the balcony railing toward Angela below.

When I landed next to her, the shock traveled up my legs. As I grabbed desperately for the remote detonator in Angela's hand, my injured ankle gave. I careened into her, holding the knife up so I wouldn't stab her.

She gasped as she fell on her butt, and I crashed across her legs. The remote flew from her grasp, sliding across the floor. I scrabbled after it. Angela leapt after it too.

I scooped it up first and waved the knife. "Stay back, Angela. I don't want to kill you, but I can't let you blow this place up."

Angela's mouth set in a grim line. "I have to, or my family will die."

She lunged toward me as I scooted back. The sharp retort of a gun sounded. A hole opened in Angela's head, and blood splattered me as she collapsed on top of my feet.

My grandfather and cousins rushed down the steps of the staircase. Sergio's gun was drawn.

The sharp scent of blood and gunpowder choked me. My

body trembled like a phone set to vibrate, and I couldn't stop. Angela was dead. A tornado spun in my gut and nausea rose in me.

Several other people in the club drew their handguns and leveled them at me. Would they shoot?

"I'll handle this," Grandfather shouted as he and my cousins raced to me.

I lifted the remote to show him. "She's wearing a bomb. There may be another remote, so you should get these people out and call the bomb squad."

Grandfather held out his hand. "Give it to me."

When I placed it carefully in his palm, Sergio pulled out a knife and cut a slit in Angela's dress, revealing dynamite strapped to a vest.

"Get her out of here," Grandfather ordered.

When a couple of his men picked up her body gingerly and headed for the door, I climbed to my feet.

Grandfather put his other hand on my shoulder. "If we called the police, they'd just twist this, and Sergio would be standing trial for murder." He glanced at the crowd and raised his voice. "Put your guns away. My grandson's quick thinking eliminated the threat."

After the guns disappeared from sight, my gut churned again. I fought to keep the bile down.

"I'm going to be sick."

Grandfather squeezed my shoulder. "Amato's must smile, even when they feel sick." How was I supposed to convince my stomach of that?

He dropped his arm and motioned to Sergio. "Take Maverick to a restroom."

After Sergio showed me to an employee bathroom, I retched until my stomach was empty. The image of Angela's bloody body haunted me. Another person I knew and liked was dead. I wanted to sink in a ball and cry, but I needed to pull it together. When I opened the restroom door and peeked out, Sergio stood there texting. He pocketed his phone.

When I emerged, he reached a hand out and flipped my tie. "You should have said something before you jumped."

"I didn't think I had time."

He yanked on my tie. Not so much that it choked me, but it was uncomfortably snug. "One word. Bomb. If you had given me that, I could have gotten the Don out."

"It happened so fast. All I could think of was stopping her, but you're right. I should have warned you."

His voice was low and deadly. "Don't forget again that our family puts the Don's safety first." He let go of my necktie and smoothed it.

I grabbed his wrist and spun him so I was at his back twisting his arm. I flung my other arm around his throat. "Don't forget this. If you have something to say to me, do it nicely. Threats make me angry enough to want to defend myself."

"Well said." Grandfather's voice came from behind me. "Now release him."

I did. We both turned to face the Don, who shook a finger at Sergio. "I keep telling you, threats aren't always needed. Your cousin may have saved our lives, so I think both an apology and congratulations are in order."

The red running into Sergio's neck and cheeks was unmistakable. He gritted his teeth. "I'm sorry, cousin, for threatening you, and congratulations on earning your medallion's rubies."

The rubies? "I didn't kill anyone."

Grandfather smiled. "Rubies are earned when you do something to save the life of a family member. That could be by killing someone, but it doesn't have to be."

That made better sense. I couldn't picture the mom I

remembered killing anyone.

Grandfather waved a hand at Sergio. "You can go. I want to talk to Maverick."

Sergio protested, "I don't want to leave you without protection."

Grandfather turned to me. "If someone came through those doors waving a gun, would you act?"

"Absolutely," I answered.

Sergio snipped, "He might act with them if it's cops. Remember, he's sworn no oaths."

"You forget your own," Grandfather barked. "Go."

Sergio stomped away like a sulking toddler.

I almost laughed. Grandfather smiled. "You have to forgive him. He takes his job a little too seriously, but he has good reason."

That sobered me. One evening with them had made that crystal clear.

Grandfather grasped my elbow and led me to the nicest employee break room I'd seen with an elegant marble table, chairs upholstered in teal fabric, and a gleaming stainless steel kitchenette.

His eyes twinkled as he pulled out one of the chairs. "Your Nonno is an old man, so let's get comfortable." After we sat he asked, "So are you feeling any better?"

His warm tone that dripped concern wasn't easy to resist. "Some," I answered truthfully.

"Good. How did you know that woman?"

The words hit me like a punch in the gut. But I owed him an explanation, so I forced it out. "She used to be my tutor…" I took a deep breath. "She left before everyone came after Dad." I ran a hand through my hair. "He suspected she was involved in framing him."

Grandfather rubbed his chin. "Doesn't explain why she'd

bring a bomb here, unless she's acting on a vendetta against your family."

"I doubt that since she seemed surprised to see me. But terrorists do like to make statements by bombing places where there's a crowd."

His face and shoulders drooped. "Sometimes I think I'm getting too old for this." His spine straightened. "They could have killed us, so I'm reconsidering giving you the list of those who bought materials that could be used in terrorist acts."

I sucked in my breath as I recalled Connor's words, *we'll have to change your grandfather's mind.*

Could Connor be behind this?

"I thought of that too." Grandfather's grooves in his forehead deepened.

What? Did I slip and say that aloud? Or was Grandfather just good at reading me?

"Connor being a federal agent won't protect him from my anger if he's responsible," Grandfather said.

My breath hitched. Would he hurt Connor? "I can't believe Connor would do it."

"You don't think Connor is capable of such an act?"

"There's a lot I'm not certain about with Connor, but I know he cares about me. I can't believe he'd have a place bombed where I'm at without warning me."

"You're certain."

He was good at reading me, so I couldn't lie. "No. My gut says he wouldn't do it, but everything I thought I knew has been turned upside down lately. There's a lot of people treating me like a puppet and yanking my strings. When I figure out which are trying to harm me or my dad, I'll cut their strings."

Grandfather pulled a pen and small notebook from his shirt pocket and started writing. "This is a list of those I suspect might be terrorists and the materials they received. I'm trusting you not to cause a mob war by revealing how you got it.

His pen paused it's scratching. "The names are probably aliases, but I'm including the shipment addresses. It may help you clear your dad, but I want who tried to kill my family in return. Capiche?"

"Capiche."

Grandfather tore the paper from his notebook and handed it to me. "This is for you, not Connor. If they're not terrorists, I don't want them exposed." When I folded it and stuffed it in my pocket, he stood up. "We're done here, except for one thing."

"What?"

"I owe you a debt for your actions tonight. If you need something, let me know." Grandfather's voice rose several decibels. "Sergio's very loyal, but he could use a few more brains." Grandfather jerked open the door, and Sergio stumbled into the room. "See."

We both laughed as Sergio glowered. "If you two are done bonding, we're late returning Maverick. Enzo just called, so I told Anthony to bring the car around."

Grandfather patted him on the shoulder. "Good. But you should remember when I spend time with one il nipote, it doesn't mean I love the others less."

Sergio nodded once. "Apparently, our bomber forged an invitation. It was close enough to the original that she must have seen a real one. The bouncers remember her if you want to speak to them."

Grandfather moved out the door. "After we escort your cousin to the car."

Lucca rushed up to say excitedly, "D called from Europe. One of our shipments was stolen, and they suspect terrorists."

Grandfather put his finger to his lip for quiet. He moved aside to reveal me.

"Oops," Lucca said sheepishly.

That sounded more like something Connor might be behind. And it confirmed they didn't only sell information. Is that why didn't they want me to hear it?

Chapter 39

Busted

"It's difficult to cross the ocean if you refuse to board the ship."
Victor

Gina

Butterflies were playing havoc in my stomach. Could something have happened to Maverick? His family was supposed to bring him back before the bowling alley closed, but he wasn't here.

Enzo shifted his legs again. These bus seats weren't big enough for the Amato's eliminator. His frame overhung the seat into the aisle, but he took his assignment to guard me seriously. So when Sam told us to load up on the bus, he came with me.

The air was stuffy, so I cracked open my window as far as it would go. The night air was perfect, just a little crisp. Several kids followed suit and opened their windows too. The din of kids chattering quieted when Sam turned in the driver's seat.

"We're not waiting any longer." Sam picked up his phone. "I'm going to call the police and report Maverick missing, and then I'm taking the rest of you home to Fallentier."

Enzo's phone buzzed with another of those texts he kept reading. "They're here."

The black stretch limousine that had taken Maverick pulled alongside the bus. A sheet of plastic taped on a window billowed. What caused the broken window? One of the doors popped open, and Maverick jumped out. His voice carried in the stillness of the night. "Don't bother getting out, Anthony."

Enzo rose to his feet stiffly, then moved off the bus and over to

Maverick. "Gina's fine."

Maverick smiled. "Thanks for guarding her."

"I should be thanking you for doing my job. I don't know if I'd have caught what you did. If you ever need a problem fixed, call me."

Then Enzo strode toward the Limo as Maverick climbed on the bus.

Sam closed the door, then asked, "What happened?"

Maverick replied softly, "Later."

A bunch of the Fallen kids were giving Maverick glares. Why? He sat next to me and grabbed my hand. "I'm sorry about my crazy family."

My voice came out shaky. "They don't like me."

"I do."

MB moved to sit behind us, then lightly kicked the back of the seat where Maverick was sitting. "You called your grandfather to help you?"

So was that what they were upset about? They must think Maverick ratted.

Maverick frowned. "He didn't learn from me. Ask Sneaker how my grandfather knew."

MB snapped his fingers. He pointed at Sneaker, then the seat beside him.

When Sneaker slid into it, MB confronted him. "Maverick says you ratted to the Don?"

"What?" Sneaker leaned forward, his tone indignant. "I can't believe the Don told you that."

Maverick glanced at him. "He didn't have to. Whoever called them wasn't busy fighting, but saw it going down, and you know an awful lot about my family."

Sneaker ran a hand through his hair. "Everyone knows about your family. Gina watched the fight, too, and she already ratted you out once."

My temper flared. He was trying to pin this on me. "I didn't do it, and I saw you texting someone."

Maverick pointed to Sneaker's phone. "You want us to check that, or are you going to admit it?"

Sneaker held up his palm. "All right, but it's not like I had a choice. They told me if I didn't call and anyone hurt you, they'd hurt me."

MB growled, "And you didn't care whether you got some of us killed?"

Sneaker blanched. "I didn't think they'd go that far."

"What should we do to him?" MB looked at Maverick.

"Did you mean it when you said you were willing for me to lead?" Maverick asked.

"No, but after you jumped in front of your cousin's gun, you proved you care about us. That earned our respect. So there's only one group in Fallen now. Yours."

Maverick's face lit up. "Thanks." Then he locked eyes with Sneaker. "Misfits are welcome to join my group if they can be loyal, even if that means risking themselves. Do you still want in?"

"Yes."

"Then you can't rat on us," MB said.

Maverick smirked. "Oh yes, he can, but only what we tell him to say."

"But if I get caught telling them stuff that's not true…"

MB snorted. "You might die. Isn't karma sweet?"

When we got to Fallentier, Sam parked the bus, and we filed out.

"Are you going to stay with Felicity?" Maverick whispered as we lined up to be searched by the guards."

"Yeah," I answered. "We're good."

Sam looked at his watch. "Ten more minutes to curfew, so after you've been searched, head for your rooms. Except you, Maverick. I want to talk to you."

Maverick's jaw set. "After I walk Gina to the main building, I'll come."

Sam didn't look happy about the delay.

I whispered to Maverick. "You don't have to walk me."

His breath tickled my ear as he said softly, "Humor me."

Sam stalked away as the guards patted us down. When they finished, Maverick grabbed my hand, and we walked across the grounds.

"You seem down. Is something wrong?" he asked.

I have a mafia boyfriend who's engaged to someone else. My brain told me it was an impossible situation, but my heart felt differently.

"Just tired. It's been a long day with too little sleep."

He stiffened. "I agree today's been tiring, but that's not what's wrong. I don't want to hear more lies, so I won't ask you again."

I was so busted, and it was obvious he was angry. He opened the main building door for me. "Goodnight."

When I traipsed in, he jogged off toward his cottage. Had I just blown it with Maverick? My heart faltered. Maybe it was for the best. Wouldn't it be asking for more heartache to stay in this relationship longer?

Chapter 40

Silence

"The absence of sound is terrifying since it means alone." Gina.

Maverick

Explanations weren't something I wanted to waste time on. I needed to radio Dad, but Sam had been insistent. I stopped by my room to check on Pip, who climbed up on me.

"Miss me, Pip?" I stroked him as he chittered excitedly.

"Okay, I'll take you." I slid him in my pocket, then went across the hallway to Sam's room to softly knock.

Sam opened the door and waved me in. "What happened with the Amato's?"

"We went to a club and celebrated my birthday."

He crossed his arms. "Are you on my team or your grandfather's?"

"I'm on *my* team."

"You might lead the team, but I'm your boss. If you're going to hold back information, this isn't going to work."

When I first came to Fallentier, all I wanted was to be left alone so I could fade into the shadows like I'd been taught. It almost lost me the opportunity to help Dad. Here, it was crucial to work with others. But he was asking me to trust him. Could I?

"Do you know what a spy's training consists of?" I asked.

"No, but I imagine it's a lot like Special Forces."

"Maybe somewhat. We have teams, and we're given objectives like capturing the other team's flag. Every team has a mole planted, who tries to sabotage it. I didn't trust anyone, so I was good at finding the mole and gaining our objective first. Dad said Special Force teams are loyal and don't turn on each other. So who do you consider the team you owe your loyalty to? Us or those who hired you?"

"I owe some loyalty to those who hired me, but I put this team together so their interests *will* come first."

"So if I ask that what I say goes no further, will you honor that request?"

"As long as it won't harm my team or country, I'll keep it confidential."

"Would you mind if I sweep the room before I talk?"

"I sweep it every day, but have at it."

Had he taken precautions to prevent his own electronics from being hijacked? "Do you have your television and laptop unplugged?"

"Yes, and location and cloud are turned off on my phone."

I pulled Pip from my pocket. Sam's eyes widened, but he didn't say anything as I gave Pip the signal and cast him off. He glided to a lamp. Then ducked under the shade and chirped. I went to the lamp and pulled off the bug. I showed Sam, then put it on the floor and smashed it. Pip climbed down from the lamp to scurry around the room. He came back to me without another chirp.

"Good job, Pip." I sat back down. "We're clear."

"What is that?"

"My pet Sugar Glider. He's very good at detecting bugs."

"You're full of surprises. Now, what happened?"

I quickly gave Sam a rundown of what occurred. I checked my watch. It was 11:25.

"So I have the list. But if I give it to Connor, it could mean a mafia war, and I don't want to do that anyway. People in the Company framed my dad, so the only way I can be sure that the list gets checked out is if I do it."

"I agree."

"You do?"

"Yes. When our team gathers leads, we should be investigating them so that we get the credit if we find anything."

"What about Angela and the bomb?"

"I'm sure no one will find her body or the explosives. An

investigation won't go anywhere without them. No agency would risk bringing attention to an operation without good reason, and neither can we."

I checked my watch again. 11:35 p.m. I moved toward the door. "I'm tired."

He smirked. "Yeah, get some rest. You'll need it tomorrow."

When I got to the woods and set up the radio, I sent out the tones over and over, but didn't receive anything back from Dad. My heart was in my throat. Had a bounty hunter caught up to him? Maybe Dad was just busy, or he wasn't where he could transmit. I knew it was risky to keep sending the tones, but I didn't want to stop. At 12:45 a.m., I had to concede he wasn't going to answer. I was only going to get silence.

With a heavy heart, I packed up the radio and jogged back. But I couldn't stop worrying about Dad. Had the deal I arranged come too late to help him?

Chapter 41

The Deal

"The most frightening thing about having a loved one disappear is the not knowing." Maverick

Maverick

I picked at a second bagel while I watched for Gina. Several kids came into the cafeteria, but not her. When they finished serving breakfast, I gave up and moved out the door. Gina and Felicity came around the corner of the building carrying a donut package from the vending machine.

I moved to intercept Gina. "I missed you at breakfast."

Before she replied, Sneaker rushed up to me. "Sam wants you, Maverick."

"I'll see you later." Gina sounded relieved as she moved away.

What was up with her? I didn't want to believe my cousins' claims that she had flirted with Sergio. Only, last night when she talked to me, she wouldn't meet my gaze and blinked several times. She wasn't a good liar, but it irritated me she'd tried. So I called her on it. Now she seemed to be avoiding me.

Sneaker waved a hand in front of my face, "Dude, are you listening? We're supposed to go to the training facility."

"Sorry," I turned toward the back of the building.

Sneaker grabbed my arm. "Not that way." He let go of me. "This way." He led me to our cottage and into Sam's room where he went to the bed and slid his hand under the rail. "There's a button here, but we don't let anyone who's not on the team know about this."

A small click sounded as the bed rolled away from the wall

leaving a gap. A panel slid open in the floor.

Sneaker jumped into the opening. "Come on."

I peered in. Sneaker was descending stone steps into gloom. I climbed down after him and heard a whir. The panel above us slid shut, leaving it pitch dark. My heart sped up. Florescent lights along old brick walls flickered to life. When I reached the bottom, I discovered a large tunnel fashioned from those bricks, some of them crumbly looking. I choked back a sneeze. The damp air smelled of mildew like in an old basement.

"Who built this?"

"We don't know. Sam learned about the tunnel when they bought the property, but it wasn't used for anything but storage then. It runs beneath all the cottages and both of Fallentier's buildings. Sam thinks maybe the original purpose was to hide slaves, and that it could have been part of the Underground Railroad."

Sneaker moved down the tunnel, but I hesitated. "I hope it's safe."

"It is. Sam had an engineer friend of his check it." Sneaker glanced back at me. "Don't tell me you're like MB?"

"What?" I asked as I passed another set of steps. Must go to one of the cottages.

Sneaker snorted. "He's claustrophobic and hates using the tunnel. Did your parents lock you in a closet like his did?"

"No, but that must have been awful." My complaint about Dad not letting me leave the grounds seemed petty in comparison. "And I don't mind using the tunnel now that I know it's not going to fall in."

"Good since Sam prefers we take it. He doesn't want kids that aren't on the team to know about the training facility, so he'd rather they didn't see us going back and forth."

Another tunnel branched off to the right, but Sneaker passed it. Must go to the main building where the cafeteria and offices were.

After a few more minutes, we came to another set of steps where the tunnel ended. Sneaker practically skipped up them until we were blocked by a brick wall. He pushed on one brick that seemed a little more sunken than the others. The wall slid open. We stepped through into a dark room, filled with black shadows. Sneaker flicked a wall switch, and light flooded the training center's gym. We moved through it to the conference room.

Sam sat in one of the chairs pulled up to the table. "Take a seat. The others will be here shortly, but you won't want to miss this."

When we sat, he flicked the button on a remote, and the big screen came to life. Sam flicked through channels to stop on the local news.

A reporter excitedly announced, "We have some breaking news about the hunt for Victor Costa. We're going live to a press conference with the Director of Intelligence."

Director Williams stood in a room in front of a sea of reporters. Flash bulbs popped as he cleared his throat. "I've called this Press Conference to announce that law enforcement agencies have called off the search for Victor Costa. As some of you have already reported and reliable sources have confirmed, Victor Costa has been killed."

To call off the hunt, Director Williams told me they'd claim Dad had died, but since I couldn't reach him by radio last night, the words squeezed my heart. Could it be true? Was Dad dead?

"What about his minor son? Is he still a terrorist suspect?" One of the reporters asked Director Williams.

"He continues to be a person of interest, but we have no evidence that he ever engaged in any crimes."

"Is it true he has hired a team of lawyers to force the government to unfreeze his trust?"

They must be planting a cover story so when they did release my trust, no one would consider it suspicious.

"We are considering releasing his funds since we found no evidence of wrongdoing. That isn't a result of any litigation."

"In a written statement to the press, Costa's son said his father was an innocent man slaughtered by the US government to silence him and then steal his company, the new technology he'd developed, and the rest of their assets. How do you answer those allegations?"

I never wrote that. But for me to infiltrate terrorist groups, everyone had to believe I had a grudge.

Director Williams faced flushed red. "They're lunacy. I'm disappointed you'd repeat the rant of a grieving kid who wants to place blame anywhere but where it belongs...on Victor Costa's shoulders." His eyes snapped at them. "It's irresponsible to give fodder to the conspiracy theory nuts, regardless of whether it boosts your ratings."

Director Williams was a good actor. I couldn't find any revealing tells.

"I'll only take one more question," he huffed.

"According to the minor son, the wrongs against his father must be addressed, and he intends to do it. Doesn't that worry you?"

"Anyone that threatens to deliver their own brand of misguided justice worries me. That's all the time I have. Thank you for coming." He turned, giving the camera a last shot of his back as he left.

Sam turned off the TV. "I guess its official, Maverick. You're part of the team."

Yeah, and Dad wouldn't be hunted if he were still alive. I had to believe he was, even if my gut clenched with worry.

My phone rang. Connor's number flashed across the screen.

When I answered it, he asked, "What did you think, lad?"

"I don't remember making that statement."

Connor chuckled. "Funny how that works."

"Yeah." I had to ask, "Connor, are there any real reports of Dad being dead?"

He released a heavy breath. "There have been a few from people looking to collect the reward, but I don't believe they're credible."

My heart sank.

I heard a voice in the background. "I've got to go, lad." Connor hung up.

Those reports had to be false. I couldn't—I wasn't going to believe otherwise. But Dad's radio transmissions stopped… Would I ever learn if he did die?

***

I looked around at my team. They'd found the mock bombs that Sam and I had placed around the grounds. This was the last rotation, so everyone had tried to disarm all the different ones.

The buzzer sounded again. Time was up, but smoke furled from where Bullet was working.

He threw his wire cutters down. "I can't do this."

He was too hyped. You had to stay calm and not allow your hand to tremble. After all my training hours, I was only considered competent, so I wouldn't waste more time on it. Everyone had the basics now. Sneaker did the best by far. I'd ask Sam to get Sneaker some training with a bomb disposal expert because we needed one.

Sneaker sidled up to me and whispered, "Bullet has problems hearing your instructions when you're speaking softly. Try to keep him on your right. His step dad punched him too many times in his left ear so he's deaf on that side. It's also why he has so many anger issues."

No wonder Bullet was frustrated. Just how many instructions of mine had he missed? I wished they told me sooner. Did the team have other problems I should be aware of?

"Okay, we're done with this," I said. "Everyone get a drink before we do the obstacle course again."

No one gave me any argument, even though I'd been pushing them since this morning and it was coming up on late-afternoon. What a difference from yesterday. MB said I earned their respect, but did he say that to save face because they were afraid of grandfather? I wanted them to respect me, but I'd take their cooperation any way I could get it.

Sam came out of the building. "That's enough training for today. I just got a call, and Gina's placement was approved. Her social workers on the way. Maverick, you can go with me to tell her."

"What kind of placement?" Bullet asked.

"She's going to a politician's family who wants to offer a foster kid the advantages they might not otherwise get." Sam glanced at me. "I think that meets the deal requirement of a *'good'* placement, wouldn't you agree?"

Even though she was avoiding me, I didn't really want to let Gina go. Only, that was selfish. She'd be so much better off there.

"As long as they treat her well, and it's not just a resume builder," I grumbled.

As Sam and I took the tunnel toward Fallentier, my heart felt heavy, and my steps dragged. I could find a way to visit Gina. It wouldn't be the same, but shouldn't I still act happy for her sake?

Chapter 42

Abandoned

"Hope is like trying to keep a lightning bug. If you try to hold onto it, it will die." Gina

Gina

I was done crying. When Felicity questioned me, I'd spilled out what Sergio said. She was right. I had to break up with Maverick. He was engaged, even if he didn't know it. And his family was too scary to cross. But I didn't want to do it. Instead, I avoided him this morning.

Felicity nudged me. I looked up to see Maverick and Sam crossing the lawn.

"Gina, we need to talk to you," Sam called.

"What about?" I reluctantly moved forward to meet them.

"We have good news." Sam beamed at me. "We were able to get you a placement with a politician's family."

Maverick's smile didn't reach his eyes. "You'll be safe now."

My mouth dropped open. "What did you do? Give them your kidney?"

He grimaced. "Nothing that bad."

It might be easier to get over my heartache if I didn't have to see Maverick, but no rich politician was going to be happy with me.

"Don't you think you should have asked me?" I snapped.

Sam stiffened. "You'd be crazy to pass this up. With your record, you won't get another opportunity like this." He waved toward the main building. "Your caseworker is on the way. You should get packed."

I crossed my arms. "Maverick would fit in better with a politician's family. He should go."

Maverick shook his head. "I want this for you. Besides, I can't go."

Was he going to live with his grandfather? Or was Sam taking him to Juvie?

"Why not?" I demanded.

"Not here," Sam said curtly. "We'll talk inside."

I trailed them to Sam's office. There were two desks with chairs behind them and a few more chairs against the wall. A file cabinet sat to the side.

"We cottage parents share an office." Sam motioned to the chairs. "Sit."

When we did, Sam leaned back against the desk. "Maverick's going into the military."

Maverick glared at Sam.

I choked past the lump in my throat. "I won't even be able to visit you." I had to know. "Was that to help me?"

Maverick's mouth set in a firm line. "I'm doing what I'm doing because I want to."

He didn't say military. Parker said Maverick was on the watch list. Would they let him in the military?

I wiped my tears away angrily. "What branch?"

Maverick didn't answer. He said he wouldn't lie to me, but Sam apparently would.

I narrowed my eyes at Sam. "Unless you tell me what's really going on, I won't take this placement. You can forget it."

Maverick arched a brow at Sam.

Sam sighed. "All right, but if you don't keep this to yourself, Maverick could be killed."

Killed? Was he going to work for the Amato's? What if he had agreed to rat on them?

I locked eyes with Maverick. "I won't tell."

He took my hand and laced his fingers with mine. "Some other kids and I are going to be working undercover to capture terrorists."

Relief flooded me. It didn't have anything to do with the mafia, but he would be doing something really important, something good.

"I want to do it too," I declared.

Maverick squeezed my hand. "No. I need you to be safe."

"When people harass me, I fight back. I'll get blamed until I run away or go to Juvie." I pulled my hand from his. "My mother probably told herself I'd be safe if she abandoned me." I leapt up and stomped to the door.

I glanced back. "I wasn't safe. Just alone."

I slammed the door behind me.

Chapter 43

Jungle

"Every mind is a jungle, so find a way to look beyond the trees."
Victor

Maverick

My chest felt as if three people sat on top of it, crushing me. I could barely breathe as I watched Gina shove her garbage bag of belongings in her social worker's car. She turned to the Fallen kids, who had gathered to see her off.

Felicity gave her a hug. "Text or call me, but keep in touch."

"I'll try."

Bullet bumped her fist. "Stay strong."

She nodded at him. One by one she exchanged a few words with them. I approached her last, holding out the slip of paper I'd written my phone number on.

"Call me anytime." I was choking up, but I didn't care. "And if you have any trouble, let me know. I'll get there."

She let the slip fall to the ground. "I was going to break up with you anyway, even before this happened."

What? Her rejection felt like a fist squeezing my heart. Why had she given me grief about abandoning her when she was going to break up with me? Had Sergio and Lucca been right about her? The Fallen kid's motto rang through my mind. *You don't get something for nothing.*

My temper flared. "You don't need me anymore, so you break up with me?"

"Think whatever you want." She got in the car and shut her door.

Sneaker punched my arm. "Dude, you really blew it."

"He sure did," MB's mohawk bobbed as he emphatically nodded his agreement. "If Gina had been interested in me, there's no way I'd be sending her away."

My heart sank to my toes as I watched the car go down the drive. "She wasn't that interested. She broke up with me."

Felicity stomped her foot. "After what your scary family told her, I would too."

The car passed through the gate, and it closed behind them. "What did my family say?"

"Nothing, I ain't crossing the Amato's either." She put a hand on her hip. "But she didn't break up with you until you abandoned her."

"I wanted her safe."

Bullet frowned. "Haven't you learned yet there's no such thing as safe?" He waved his hand around us. "The world is a jungle we fight to survive, and every predator out there thinks Fallen kids are prey."

Could he be right? I ran toward the fence, throwing my denim jacket over the razor wire. I climbed the chain link, vaulted over the wire, and jumped down. I grabbed my jacket and ran down the lane. The guards yelled at me to stop, but I sprinted down the lane. Where was the car? I raced past the last curve. They were idling at the stop sign, waiting for a gap in traffic.

I yelled, "Gina!"

The car pulled out, then zoomed down the road, leaving me only an exhaust trail. I sank to the ground.

I'd messed up.

The sound of another car came from behind me. It was Sam. I stood as he pulled to the side of the road.

Sam rolled down his window. "Better get in."

I looked to where the car had disappeared. "They were right, Sam. I blew it. I should have never sent Gina away."

"No, you shouldn't have." That was Gina's voice.

My heart soared as I twisted to see the woods that her voice had come from. A stick cracked, then Gina emerged from the trees carrying her garbage bag.

I ran to her, picked her up, and twirled her around. "I'm glad you didn't leave."

"Put me down, Maverick." Her voice shook. "I'm not your girlfriend anymore."

My heart fell, but I tried not to show it as I sat her down. "What were you doing in the woods?"

"I bailed at the stop sign and ran into the trees in case she noticed."

"Why would you do that?" I asked.

"I wasn't going to fit in with rich people. I might have lasted a day before they sent me to Juvie."

My breath caught. "You weren't coming back to Fallen?"

"I hadn't planned on it until I heard you admit you messed up. I'll go back if you let me help you catch the terrorists, but I'm not going to be your girlfriend again. We're done."

Her rejection stung. "What did my family say to you?"

"It isn't important. You abandoning me is."

"I was trying to help you, but you were going to abandon me, too, over a family I hardly know."

"The Amato's are crazy."

I arched my brow. "So was your family, according to you."

Her face grew red. "Yeah, *was*. They're dead. They aren't picking my wife." She gasped, and her hand flew to her mouth. "Please, Maverick, don't tell them I said that."

I wanted to give the Amatos an earful, but I wouldn't put her at risk. "I won't."

"You have a dad and a grandfather. Sooner or later, you'll leave us, so I'm not getting attached." She picked up her bag. "Now do you want me to help you with those terrorists, or should I take off?"

If she joined the team, I could watch out for her. I'd just have to make sure she didn't do the risky stuff.

"If you'll follow my orders, I'll agree to you joining if Sam will?"

Sam was waiting with his window still down. Had he heard?

"She was already on my short list to recruit, so it's fine by me." He thumped the top of his car with his hand. "You two should get in. We can go over the details later."

As soon as we did, Sam made a U-turn. "We need to get back,

and I'll have to call Gina's social worker."

It was wonderful to have Gina returning with us, but I wanted more than that. Could I convince her to be my girlfriend again?

Chapter 44

Extreme Risks

"Risk assessments are only a guess, so even when they're low, prepare for the worst." Victor

Maverick

I woke with a start. I must have dozed off. Did I miss my chance to call Dad? A glance at my watch gave me the time, 11:35 p.m. I could make it.

Sneaker was sound asleep and didn't even crack open an eye when I turned on the light and threw on my black jeans and hoodie. I grabbed my duffel with my radio and antenna, gathered Pip, flipped the light off, and slid out into the hall.

"You don't have to hide it anymore." I jumped at Sam's voice and found him standing in the door of his room. "I suspected from the beginning your father's out of the country and you use a ham radio to keep in contact."

"I'd prefer if you kept that confidential." A quick glance at my watch showed 11:45 p.m. I rushed out of the cottage and across the lawn.

After I slipped through the fence, I broke into a run. If Sam suspected, others probably did too. I zigzagged through the woods and crossed back on my trail. At 11:58, I stopped in a clearing. I threw down my duffel and began to assemble my antenna.

A stick cracked.

My heart pounded in my chest as I swung my flashlight to see only trees.

"Turn it off." That was Dad's voice. Joy bubbled up in me as I switched off my light.

"Come here," he ordered.

I followed his voice into the trees. My spine tingled. What if it was a recording and not really Dad?

A shadow glided toward me. It might be dark, but I knew that form. Tears formed in my eyes. "It's really you?"

Dad embraced me. "I'm here, son."

I returned his hug. He stepped back and motioned toward the trees. "Come on."

We moved farther into the woods. Dad stopped at a large tree and grabbed a branch to swing up. He lowered a hand to me.

I grasped it and climbed up after him. He scrutinized the woods around us. Nothing moved.

He whispered, "Okay, I think it's safe to talk."

Fear for him rose in me. "You have to leave the country. My deal's only good if you stay out of the US."

"Slow down. Tell me everything that happened since I talked to you last."

I filled him in quickly on what had occurred. When I finished, he swore in Italian again. "We've got to move. Now."

We scrambled down the tree. "Running off so soon, Vic."

Crap. That was Connor's voice. Did he have a team with him? Would they try to take my dad?

Dad pulled me behind the trunk of the tree and drew his gun.

"Are you alone, Connor?" Dad called.

"I'm alone, and you can put the gun away. I'm only here to talk."

Was that true? How I hoped it was.

"I'll put the gun away when I find out whether you're armed and if anyone's with you," Dad said sharply. "Derrick, check the perimeter."

Dad must be sending me away so I'd be safe if a firefight ensued. My gut clenched at the thought since I loved them both. I didn't want to go, but we did need to know if anyone was with Connor. I moved into the woods to circle around them. I pulled Pip out and sent him out to scout too. He chirped once above Connor, but that was it.

I rammed my boot against a trunk. When my heel compartment slid open, I removed my mechanical knife. It wasn't much, but I could hurt someone with it. Only I didn't want to, especially Connor. I moved up behind him.

I called to Dad, "I didn't find anyone but Connor, and he doesn't have his gun out."

"Connor," Dad ordered. "Raise your hands and come toward me." When Connor got about ten feet from him, Dad barked, "That's far enough. I have a good bead on you, and there's no way I'd miss. Derrick, stay behind Connor, but remove all his weapons."

I grabbed the gun from Connor's shoulder holster and the one from his boot. When I searched his pockets, I found a knife, several zip ties, and some other tools that could be used as weapons, so I took them. Then I patted him down and found a couple more knives. I unbuckled his belt and removed it.

"Secure his wrists," Dad ordered.

When I grabbed Connor's arm to bring it behind his back, he yanked it away. "You don't need to do that."

I wanted to agree, but he'd betrayed Dad's trust. Nothing could have convinced Dad to double cross someone he considered family. So when it came between listening to Connor or Dad, I'd choose Dad.

"Connor, if you don't cooperate, I'll shoot you," Dad warned.

Would Dad really do it? Connor must have thought so. His shoulders drooped, and he let me bring his hands behind his back and zip tie them.

"Take his stuff in the woods and stash it, Derrick."

"Come on, Vic." Connor's voice rose in protest. "I'm tied. There's no reason to take my stuff."

I swallowed my own objection after Dad replied, "We'll give you the location of your things once we're gone."

I slipped into the woods to the willow I'd seen and lodged Connor's belongings in the crook of its trunk, minus his boot gun, which I slipped into my belt. When I trotted back, Dad had Connor sitting.

"Derrick," Dad called. "Shine your flashlight on him while I ask him a few questions."

We might be able to detect Connor's tells by lighting his face. The red beam gave it an eerie glow.

"Does anyone else know you're here?" Dad asked.

"No one." Connor's eyelids didn't drop.

"Did you come here to try to take me in?"

"No, Victor. I came because I want to help you both."

He sounded sincere. Dad must have thought so too. "Derrick, you can turn the light off."

I switched it off. "How did you know he was coming?"

"Tell him, Connor," Dad ordered.

"I knew when your dad heard the news, he'd know you'd struck a deal so he'd come to take you with him."

"Why?"

Dad snorted. "Because they wouldn't offer that deal unless it was an extreme-risk op. He knew I'd never let you sign up for something like that."

I shook my head at Connor. "You told me Dad would be proud of me."

"I am proud of you, but I don't want you doing that type of mission. Connor probably wanted you to so it would flush me out of hiding. And it worked. Now I want to know why."

"You're wrong, Vic. The only reason I'm here is to keep Derrick from making the mistake of going with you. Why should he live on the run when he can be here doing what he loves?"

"There's no agency support," Dad said gruffly. "It's suicide."

"I was worried about involving him, too, but he kept proving me wrong. He will survive, and he'll learn who framed you. He might even locate Deidra." Dad harrumphed, but Connor persisted. "It's what he wants. And it's the only way he'll get the chance. No agency will touch him. Let him do what you trained him to do."

"You sold us out." Dad crossed his arms. "I don't care if Director Williams ordered you to. There are things you don't do to your family."

"What do you want me to do? Quit. I could, but then who'd be on the inside to help you?"

"What help?" Dad asked sarcastically.

"I've been dropping hints about things not adding up. But if I'm blatant about my support, I'd be sorting mail. I wanted to be where I could help Derrick, even if I can't do much for you."

I wasn't really paying that much attention to their conversation. Not when a big question kept intruding. I turned to Dad.

"Do you really want me to go with you?" I asked.

"Yeah, Derrick, I do."

The longing to be with him filled me. But if I ran out on my deal, everyone would think we were terrorists. Is that what I wanted?

"I don't want the people who killed Kurt to get away with it. Connor's right. I need to stay and accomplish the job."

"You don't have to be here for us to keep investigating."

"Maybe not, but I gave my word. You said a man doesn't break that. Only you need to leave the country so you're not being hunted. With this deal in place, we can talk on the phone."

Dad let out a heavy sigh. "I don't want to lose you."

"Trust me. I *am* your son. I can do this."

"All right, you can try. But if at any time you feel the risk is too great, I want you to promise me you'll get out."

"If you promise you'll leave the country."

"You've got yourself another deal." I could hear the smile in Dad's voice.

Connor rolled his shoulders. "I know a private plane leaving tonight I can get you on."

"Quit trying to escape those ties," Dad snapped. "And I'll find my own ride, not one going to an overseas prison." He pulled a phone out of his pocket. "Derrick, in ten minutes, release Connor and tell him where his stuff is." Then he handed me the phone. "Put your number in there."

I did, then found his number and memorized it. When I gave his phone back, he pulled me in and hugged me. "I've missed you."

"I missed you too." I felt my duffel shift on my back. Dad must be placing something inside.

He let me go and turned back to Connor. "If you fail us again...." With that warning he slipped into the night.

"Release me, Derrick," Connor barked.

I lit my flashlight and checked the time. "Not until ten minutes are up."

His shoulders jiggled. Why was he so determined to free himself? I took his gun from my belt and pointed it at him. "I won't shoot to kill, but I can guarantee it will hurt." I lifted the flashlight to his face. "A few minutes shouldn't matter unless you want to call someone to tell them to move in on Dad."

His eyelid dropped. I gasped. "You do."

"No, but I do need to check in, or they'll come looking for me."

I wasn't sure whether to believe him, but I'd give him the benefit of the doubt.

"Fine, we'll get your belongings." I helped him through the woods to the willow and grabbed his phone. "I can hold your phone up so you can talk to them. What number?"

"Speed dial 1."

I looked at my watch. "What time's your check in?" He hesitated, confirming my suspicion. "So there isn't one."

"No, it's one o'clock."

"That's fifteen minutes. You can call after I let you go." I put his phone back in the crook, grabbed his arm, and led him toward Fallentier.

After taking him partway, I let go. "We can stop here." I pointed the flashlight at him again. "I've been wanting to ask you, 'Were you responsible for the bomb at my grandfather's club?'"

His eyes widened, as he fired out, "What bomb? Was anyone hurt?"

"It's not important now." I didn't think he was behind that. I checked my watch, then flung his gun into a bush. "That shouldn't take you long to find." I slid behind him. "Be still so I don't cut you." I took my knife out of my pocket. "Once I free you, you'll need to hurry to that willow if you really have a check-in." With one quick slash, I cut his ties, "Goodbye, Connor."

I raced into the trees, then back to Fallentier. When I got inside the cottage, I couldn't resist shining my flashlight into my duffel to see what Dad had given me. Wow. A couple of Dad's newest toys, spy equipment that very few people knew about. A squawker and a couple of zee shooters. I could have used them yesterday.

The need for them might come again all too soon.

Chapter 45

Cutting strings

"Ties of love are what holds a family together, not blood." Sam

Maverick

Everyone around me was gulping for breath as we ran the obstacle course. At least they were doing better at keeping up with me. Gina put on a burst of speed and passed me, giving me a challenging look. I sprinted all out, but couldn't take back the lead until we came to the net wall. She couldn't climb it as fast as me, but she gritted it out.

She gained ground as we raced to the finish line. I beat her by a half stride. After she flashed me a grin, she grabbed her side and sucked in air.

None of the Fallen kids crossed the line over a minute behind me. They congratulated Gina. "You almost beat Maverick."

Yes, she did. She was a natural, but I hated how good she was getting since it would be harder to justify keeping her from missions.

I caught sight of a napkin fluttering on the ground. Next to it lay a cookie. When I picked them up, Hulk hung his head. I needed to talk to him, and I should let everyone catch their breaths.

"Good job, everyone. We'll switch to shooting now, so head for the range. Hulk, walk with me."

The Fallen kids moved toward the gun range without any complaints. Were they too breathless to voice them, or had they finally realized the importance of training?

I hung back a little with Hulk and spoke softly so no one else would hear. "When we go on missions, put the food you carry inside a zippered compartment of your backpack because we can't leave a trail or any evidence like this." I handed him the cookie and napkin.

He stuffed it back in his pocket. "So I can take food?"

"I want you to if it makes you confident. I just don't want it left behind."

"Okay."

We joined the others, who had lined up at the firing line and were waiting for my instruction.

"Eventually, I want you to be able to shoot even when running, but for now we'll concentrate on a locked position." I demonstrated. "Stand to the side since it makes you a smaller target for anyone firing back. Stretch out your arm, look through your sights, then fire. All of you try it. You too, Blade. Bullets travel further than a knife so you need to learn to fire guns too. Now empty your clips."

The shots rang out. When they stopped firing, I pressed the catch on my sunglasses to switch to binocular view to see their targets. Sneaker, MB, Hulk and Blade had missed. Gina had shot almost as well as Bullet. Three of her rounds hit the center.

"Clear your weapons and drop your clips, but hold your positions," I ordered. After the clips hit the ground, I went down the line to Hulk. "You're holding your gun sideways. That looks great on gangster shows, but it'll mess up your accuracy." I adjusted his hand so the gun was positioned correctly, then I moved to Sneaker and pulled his shoulders back. "Don't lean forward. The gun doesn't need help to fire bullets." I went to MB. "You're too tense. The recoil isn't that bad." I sidled over to Blade. "Breathe. Stop holding your breath." I moved off the firing line. "Load your next clip and try again."

After they did, I examined the targets. Everyone had at least one shot in the center, but Blade dropped his gun, bent with his hands on his knees, and started retching. Bullet holstered his gun. He patted Blade's back while he murmured something to him. I couldn't hear what was being said, but my teammates were casting dirty looks at me.

"What's wrong with Blade?" I demanded.

"Do you think the smell of smoke might bother you if you'd been burned with cigarettes by your mom?" Hulk asked.

Geez. I had thought his asteroid tattoos covered scars.

"Yeah. But if anyone ever told me these things, I might be more sensitive."

Gina's green eyes sparked. "It's not always easy to bare your soul."

"I know, but I can't find a way to avoid problems if I don't know about them."

Blade straightened and picked up his gun. "There isn't any problem. I just prefer knives."

I heard a footstep. It was Sam.

He motioned to us. "Everyone clear your weapons, and come in."

When we trooped inside, Sam unlocked the weapons room, then used another key to open one of the gun cases against the back wall, the one for pistols. The locked cabinets against the side walls held gear like Kevlar vests and gloves, but Sam was the only one with keys.

I took off my holster and went to the table with the cleaning supplies. When I pulled out a chair and sat, the team joined me. I slid my pistol from its holster. Connor had removed my gun from the dead drop and given it to Sam. That hadn't thrilled me. I liked the familiarity of my own weapon, but now I couldn't access it easily. I could break in, but it would take time. I applied the cleaning liquid to a cloth and slid open my gun bolt.

Sam sat beside us. "We have two more days before our operation, but if you can't trust one another, you'll fail. All of you have to think differently. Not how do I succeed, but how can I help the team succeed?"

"What do you suggest?" I asked as I shoved the cloth inside my gun.

"My Special Forces team members are my family. My brothers and sisters will always have my back, and I'll always have theirs. You're all at Fallentier because you lack family, so become one. Promise you'll have each other's backs, you'll put each other first, and you won't betray each other or your team. Is everyone willing to do that?"

Gina blew some powder out of her slide, then rubbed at the

remainder with a cloth. "Maverick has way too many families. He doesn't need another one."

After the Amato's tried to destroy my relationship with Gina, I certainly didn't need *one* family. I set my gun down, and pulled out my phone.

"I don't want anything to do with the Amato's, and I'll prove it."

"What are you doing?" Sam barked.

"I'm cutting my ties. The Intel isn't worth dealing with them. I'll never allow them to control me, and having them coming around is going to get us exposed."

"You could be right," Sam frowned. "But I don't think Conner will like it."

I shrugged. "Not really too worried about what Connor thinks when it has to do with the Amatos."

Gina chewed her bottom lip. "I'm sorry, Maverick. I shouldn't have said that." She picked up her clip. "My mom was crazy, but I wish every day I still had her."

"It isn't the same." I dialed the number.

"Maverick?" Grandfather answered.

"Yeah, I'm calling in the debt."

"What do you need?" he asked.

"You to forget me. I'm never going to join your family, and I don't want you getting reports about me. You can have the medallion back. We're done. Capiche?"

"Is this about Gina breaking up with you?"

I gave Sneaker a glare, then answered, "No, this is about what I told you. If I learned someone was trying to hurt me, I'd cut their strings."

"I wasn't trying to hurt you."

"Yes you were, but you thought your needs were more important than mine."

"I don't want to do this," Grandfather spoke solemnly. "But I'm a man who honors his debts. Anthony will pick up the medallion, and we'll leave you alone. But taking it off doesn't mean our enemies won't come after you."

"I understand."

I hung up my phone, then turned to Sneaker. "You told them Gina broke up with me."

Sneaker set down his clip. "I had to, dude, so they'd leave her alone."

"You shouldn't have done that without checking with me."

Sam pointed at Sneaker. "Maverick's right. One of the most valuable gifts we give is trust, so breaking that gift can destroy a team or family beyond repair."

I slipped the necklace I'd worn for so many years off my neck. I'd always remember my mom, with or without it. "*Derrick* might have had a lot of families, but I'm not Derrick anymore. I'm *Maverick,* and I could sure use one, at least until I get my Dad cleared."

Sam smiled. "I wouldn't expect this new of a team to make promises for life, only while on the team. So who's willing?"

I stood. "I promise while I'm on this team, you'll be my family. I'll put us first, I won't betray you, and I'll have your back."

Each of them stood and repeated the same promise.

Sam beamed at us. "Good. Now keep your word. Don't ever break the trust of your brothers or sister so you'll always have something to be proud of—your family."

When our guns were clean and the clips loaded, we holstered them before going to the cabinet and hanging them on our hooks. Sam came over and locked the cabinet.

Pip squirmed in my pocket, so I put my hand in to pet him. He nuzzled me.

Sam's gaze flicked to my pocket, and he smiled. "Since everyone's family now, you should introduce the other member of the team."

I wasn't sure I wanted to take the chance, but I didn't have a choice now. I pulled Pip out.

"Yo, Pip." Sneaker tapped his shoulder, and Pip glided over to him.

All the Fallen kids stared at Pip.

"What is that?" Hulk asked.

I tapped my arm, and Pip soared back to me. "Pip is my pet Sugar Glider. He's already been helping me and Sam check for listening devices, and he can do a lot more." I stroked Pip as the team huddled around me to get a closer look. "He'll be a valuable asset, but no one else can know about him."

I hoped they meant their family promise. There were people who would want to get their hands on Pip if they learned his capabilities. Would any of these guys rat him out?

Chapter 46

Babying

"My training's tough because I care about agents." Victor

Gina

My feet sank into the mat that lined the floor of the gym as I faced Maverick.

"Get him, Gina," Bullet called from where he and the others sat watching. Each of them had already tried to take Maverick down and failed.

I kicked out at Maverick.

He jumped back, then grabbed my leg and yanked. I fell back, my arms flailing. He caught me. "Is that your only offensive move?"

Being held in his arms flustered me, but he released me as soon as I straightened. "It's the one that works best on guys."

"Not if they've had training."

Maverick turned back to the other kids. "Now, practice the six basic defense moves on each other. MB and Bullet, Gina and Sneaker, Hulk with me."

"When will you teach us your strikes?" Hulk asked.

"Defense first because some strikes are lethal, and you'll have to soften those blows when you practice on each other."

Sneaker got up and came over to me. "When Maverick does that, I'm not teaming with you."

I threw a punch at him, and he blocked it. "Are you afraid of a girl?"

"No, but you don't know the meaning of soften." He motioned toward Maverick. "You're more gung-ho than he is."

One defensive move required he run toward me, but Sneaker only did a slow jog. I grabbed his clothing around the chest area, dropped down, and used his natural momentum to send him over my body. He face planted in the mat.

"Maverick says fighting nice gets you dead, so stop it." I snarled at him. "I'm as capable as any of you."

He picked himself up. "We know that."

"Then why won't Maverick consider me for the mission?"

"He doesn't want you hurt." Sneaker threw a slow punch.

I blocked his fist. Ugh. "Maverick, I want you."

He came over and smirked at me. "I know I'm hard to resist, but right now?"

All the guys laughed. Maverick was beginning to sound like the rest of these jerks. I gave him a glare. "I mean as a training partner. Sneaker isn't even trying."

Sneaker put his hands up. "Hey, I'm trying... not to hurt Maverick's girl."

All the guys laughed again. My temper flared. "I'm not his girl."

"Gina and Maverick, I want to talk to you." Sam said from behind us.

He was almost as good at sneaking up on people as Maverick. Since Maverick didn't react, he must have known Sam was there.

Maverick called out to the guys, "Keep practicing."

We followed Sam out of the gym and into the operations room where he sat at the conference table. "Gina's right, Maverick. You're not helping her by babying her. If someone comes after her, she won't be prepared."

"I can protect her," Maverick said.

Ugh. "I don't need your protection." I kicked the back of his chair. "Stop treating me like glass. I'm not going to break."

Maverick glanced over his shoulder at me. "If I take the gloves off, you could get hurt."

Sam leaned forward, resting his arms on the table. "Tonight, I'm sending the team on a training exercise to prove to Director Williams you're ready for missions." Sam pointed his finger at Maverick. "But this isn't going to be a cake walk. Some friends of mine will try to prevent you from reaching the objective." Then his eyes flicked to me. "No one's off limits."

Maverick clenched his jaw. "She doesn't have to go."

No, Maverick did not just say that. "I'm going."

Sam gave me a nod. "You'll be going. Connor expects a report on how each individual does. He'll want me to drop anyone who can't handle the job because that could hurt the team. Since he's right, I will."

Would I be dropped? No. I'd prove I deserved a spot.

Maverick ran a hand through his hair. "All right, I'll tell everyone no more babying." He locked eyes with me. "Don't get yourself hurt and make me regret it."

Chapter 47

Tested

"Tests should be looked at as an opportunity to shine." Victor

Maverick

The noise of the chopper made it difficult to hear anyone. My team sat in back while I was in front with Sam who piloted. I tried to study the terrain we were flying over, but in the dark, all I could see were the tops of trees. I'd take woods over the desert. More cover.

With so little warning, I'd worked furiously to prepare my team for this test. They were doing better, but we'd be pitted against friends of Sam who were likely with Special Forces. I'd need to use everything I could to get us through this.

Sam reached out to press a switch on the helicopter dash. He glanced at me, and my headphones crackled as his voice came through.

"A couple minutes more."

"Are your friends already there?" I asked.

"Yes."

"They'll hear us coming."

"They'll give you five minutes before they pursue."

"Will you be helping them?"

"No, I'm only observing." Sam pointed down at a clearing.

Our chopper descended. The skids hit the ground softly, and he cut the engine. While the blades came to a stop, he handed me a map with a black X for where we landed and a red X circled with both coordinates written on the side.

"The red X marks your flag. Its four clicks from here. The exercise ends at sunrise, so you better get going." Sam smiled. "Watch your six."

"Always." I jumped down. "Everyone out." As soon as their feet touched the ground, I hollered, "Follow me," and ran for the cover of the woods.

Once we hit the trees, I slowed to a trot. When I was certain we were deep enough to hide from any watchers, I stopped, brought Pip out, signaled reconnaissance, then cast him off.

"They'll be using thermal imaging goggles to see us in the dark." I drew the plastic sheeting from my duffel that I had borrowed from the rooms they were painting at Fallentier. "These will hide our heat signature. I cut slits in them so we can wear them like a poncho." I handed them out, then pulled mine on. I found a muddy spot and bent over to grab a handful. "Mud will keep our face and hands cool, so quickly rub some on them."

Pip chirped not too far to the North. Probably someone watching to learn which way we headed into the woods.

"Our flag is about two and a half miles due west." I turned on my flashlight with the red lens that wouldn't broadcast as far, then pulled out the map. "Everyone memorize these GPS coordinates." They came over to huddle around me. "Pip located a combatant about here." I pointed to the map. "He'll be in a tree with night vision goggles, so it will require stealth to take him out. Sneaker, you think you can handle it?"

He was leaning over the map. "Yeah, I can do it."

"They'll be using paint guns, but I don't know whether they have any rifles or just pistols like us. When you finish, head for the flag coordinates. If we fail, it will be up to you to get it." I grabbed the map and shut off my flashlight. "Let's go."

We tried to keep to a trot, but it wasn't easy in the woods. I didn't want to risk even my red light revealing our position. Our eyes did adjust some, and my team was tripping over the roots less. Pip came back and glided over us, but he wasn't detecting anyone.

Special Force teams were good at concealment. If Pip couldn't see them in the dark, I wouldn't be able to. Ahead of us, cliffs rose to the North and South. Anyone on foot would want to take this route where the ground was level so it would be the perfect place for an ambush. I didn't want us to walk into one, so I stopped.

"Turn off your phones and anything electronic you have on you." I brought out the device Dad had given me.

"What is that?" Gina asked.

"It's one of my dad's toys—a squawker," I explained softly. "It transmits disruptive radio waves at several ranges, including 800 megahertz, so it causes cell phones to squawk. A lot of other electronic equipment too. Shoot at any noise."

I switched the squawker to my left hand so I could hold my paint gun in my right, then pushed the button. Three squawks came from in front of us. I ran toward one. I shot at the small pile of leaves behind a log where it seemed to originate from. The leaf pile moved as someone threw a tarp aside. I shot again and hit the guy in the chest. Other shots sounded. I ran toward them.

"Any of you get hit?" I asked my team.

"No." Bullet laughed. "But Gina nailed one of theirs, and I got another."

"Great job, but anyone around will have heard that. We have to move."

Pip gave out another chirp. It came from behind us. "Bullet, can you check that out. It might be Sneaker, so look before shooting."

"Aww, you're no fun."

The sky was starting to lighten. "Catch up if you can. We can't wait."

I jogged away, taking point. MB, Hulk, and Gina scrambled after me. There was the creek. All those memorization lessons were paying off. I didn't need to look at the map again to know in less than a half mile we'd be where the flag was. Pip chirped twice. Just a little to the South.

"Hulk and MB, can you take care of those?"

"Yeah," they peeled off, and Gina and I kept running.

We jumped the creek and put on a burst of speed. I spotted the flag in a large clearing. Sam had set down the helicopter on the far side.

"Gina, I'll try to draw out whoever's protecting the flag so you can circle around and get it. Use the helicopter for cover."

"Okay."

I stomped forward, stepping on sticks to draw their attention. Pip chirped in front of me and I dove, sliding and shooting under some leaves. A guy swore, then emerged with paint on his butt. I leapt up and ran behind a tree as shots rang out from my South. Paint splattered the trunk.

I ran, zigzagging toward where the shots came from, returning fire.

A guy stood up. "You got me."

Gina raced out from behind the helicopter. Someone grabbed her ankle, but she shot as she fell, marking them with paint. She jumped up and sprinted for the flag.

After grabbing it, she waved it the air. "Woohoo, we did it."

"Yes, we did," said Bullet, as he, MB, Hulk, and Sneaker came out of the woods. Bullet slapped Gina on the back. "Awesome shooting, girl. Looks like you picked up a few things from me."

The sky was really lightening now. I needed to get Pip. I slid behind a tree and whistled. There were a bunch of birds whistling at the new day dawning, but Pip distinguished mine and glided over to land on my arm. Then he scurried into my pocket.

I stroked him and whispered, "Well done, Pip."

When I moved from behind the tree, Sam's friends were talking to him.

One of them complained, "I can't believe we didn't tag any of them, but they had an unfair advantage."

MB shook his head. "How do you figure that when you had twice our number?"

"We didn't get a jammer..." he crossed his arms "...or a drone." When we all cracked up laughing, he demanded, "What's so funny?"

"Inside joke, Dirk," Sam replied. "I'm sorry I couldn't give you the same equipment. It's experimental, but I *really* appreciate you helping us with this exercise."

Dirk uncrossed his arms. "No problem, but we've got to get back to our real work now." They faded into the woods.

Sam limped toward the chopper. "We need to go, too, so you can sleep before you take your SAT's."

Bullet groaned. "I don't see why that matters when I don't plan on going to college."

"It matters because the tests have to go in the system for your alibi, and we're not giving anyone scores they don't deserve. Now get in."

Everyone jumped in, and as Sam started the chopper, a sense of accomplishment filled me. We proved we could handle missions. But on a real mission, they wouldn't be shooting at us with paint guns. Could I get the team through them without anyone getting hurt?

Chapter 48

The Mission

"Taking risks loses its thrill when people you care about could get hurt too." Maverick

Maverick

Sam drove the bus up to the depressing high school building. Four stories of dingy grey concrete only interrupted by glass windows.

"This is it." Sam said as he parked and opened the door.

Before we could unload, a guy dressed in a suit came out the glass doors. "Are you here for the SAT exam?"

"Yes," Sam answered. "From Fallentier. We appreciate you letting our kids take the test."

"It's no problem. We have students from several schools here, but they will have to show a government ID before they can take the exam."

"They have them."

"Are you leaving?" he asked.

"No. I'll wait in the bus."

When we climbed off, the guy in the suit said, "I'll show you the way to the auditorium where the test will be given."

I glanced at the camera recording us as we went into the school. When we reached the auditorium doors, four adults sat behind a table with a line of kids in front.

"You'll need to register here," the guy said before he left us.

I pulled out my ID and waited. When it was my turn, a woman wrote my name and school and examined my ID, then she issued instructions.

"Once we start, the doors will be locked. If you need to use the restroom, do it now." She pointed, "They're down the hall. Then go in the auditorium and take a seat."

"Thanks." I made my way to the restroom doors and waited.

Once my teammates joined me, MB pulled out his laptop. With the schools schematics up, he directed us through a door that said janitorial staff only, past shelves of cleaning supplies, and out a side exit where a truck with a fiberglass camper shell waited. Gina slid behind the wheel as the rest of us climbed in the back. My adrenaline soared. Step one was completed. With Sam's contact inside, our tests would end up with everyone else's, and we were on camera going into the school. We had an alibi.

Now for the mission.

***

I stopped crawling and looked out the screen of brush to study the fence and the cars going by. Butterflies fluttered in my stomach. This was a bad idea.

"What do you think?" Sneaker whispered.

I'd already voiced my concerns about sneaking into a guarded facility during broad daylight, but I was overruled by Sam. He felt it was important we have an alibi if anyone cast suspicion on us. I glanced behind me. My team members blended in with the foliage since they'd dressed in camouflage, but I picked each out—Sneaker, Blade, Hulk, Bullet, and MB—and all of them wore concerned expressions.

Now wasn't the time to shake their confidence even if my own nerves were telling me not to go through with it because someone in those cars would spot us. I took a deep breath to calm my pounding heart.

"We can do this." I forced certainty into my tone. "We just have to time it right."

MB drew his laptop out of his backpack and began to type. "I'm in. I shut off the cameras back here."

"Good, I'll go first." A break in the traffic came. I couldn't see any cars, so I straightened and ran. When I heard the hum of a vehicle approaching, I dove into the tall grass that lined the roadway and crawled to the chain link fence. There were two strands of wire across the top. I stood and crimped the wires together with a clip, giving us a larger space between the wire and fence. I moved down the chain link, standing only long enough to add two more clips to the wire so there was enough room for us all to go through. When another break in the traffic appeared, I waved.

My team rushed headlong over to my side of the road. We scaled the fence, slid under the wires, and jumped down. We scurried into the woods beyond, slipping through the trees until we came to a neighborhood of ranch homes. Military housing. We crawled to skirt them, then rose to a crouch to run parallel to the street until we came to some buildings.

Were these the deserted ones? No one was moving around. I sprinted for the largest—a brick monstrosity that took up most of the block on this side of the street. When we drew closer, I could see some windows had panes missing while the rest were blackened by dirt and time. This must be the old factory that hadn't been used since World War II.

My team's gasps for air meant they needed a breather. After leading them to the shadows behind the building, I put my glasses on to view Pip's camera. I brought Pip out of my pocket—snaked my hand toward the broken panes—and cast him off.

Pip glided in the window and landed on the sill. A little light spilled in from the windows but not much. As Pip scurried in farther, it was pitch black.

Sneaker whispered, "What do you see?"

The base of my neck prickled as if someone were watching. Could there be someone in there? "It's too dark for me to pick out anything."

I softly whistled, and Pip climbed out and scampered to me. I put him in my pocket and turned to face the others.

"Stay here. I'm going in."

Sneaker shook his head. "That wasn't part of the plan."

I had to satisfy my conscience. "There could be a squatter in there. I have to know it's empty."

Blade grabbed my shoulder. "No one's going to squat in a

government installation."

I shook off his hand. "I just need a few minutes to make sure."

Hulk scowled. "Then we're going with you whether you like it or not."

My team's mouths were set in firm lines as they nodded in agreement.

MB had pulled out his laptop again. "Our fish aren't far. They should be at the gate in a minute."

We'd told our fish—the wannabe terrorists from the internet— they should smuggle in any materials they had and join the action. With them so close, there wasn't any time to argue.

I blew out my breath. "All right, you can go with me, but we'll have to be quick about it."

I moved toward the back entry. A small volunteer tree grew through a crack in the concrete steps leading to the door. I maneuvered around it and tried the door handle. It was locked.

"Sneaker, can you pick this?"

He bent over the old lock. "Yes, unless it's too rusted. Just give me a sec." He shoved a couple of pins into it and twisted them back and forth. A click sounded. Sneaker shoved the door.

"Open sesame." It swung open with a creak. Sneaker's smile beamed as he waved a hand toward the dark opening. "You want to go first?"

"Yes." I pulled out the flashlight from my backpack. The others drew out flashlights, too, except MB, who held his laptop.

"MB, stay here by the door and be our lookout," I ordered. "The rest of you can come with me."

Our beams of light picked out old manufacturing machines as we moved through the huge open space of what must have been the factory floor. I fought the urge to sneeze as we disturbed the thick dust covering. Boot tracks already marred it, but a thin layer of dust coated them so they couldn't be recent. There wasn't any other sign of anyone, but the boot prints climbed the stairs off to the side of us.

"Since we're here, I could set the explosives inside," Blade said. "It will mean less chance of being seen."

My neck still prickled. I couldn't get rid of the sensation that someone watched us. "Okay, you and Sneaker take care of that while the rest of us check upstairs. Be careful. I'm not sure this building is safe."

As we moved up the stairs, our steps echoed in the large space. When we came to the top, my flashlight picked out another big room. I heard a rustling. What could it be?

I took one more risk and called out, "If anyone's here, come out now. This building is about to blow."

A riot of flutters sounded as shadows dived toward us. I jerked my flashlight up to see bats. They must have been what I'd sensed. There were at least a hundred. I threw my arms in front of my face to fend them off. They swooped by within inches of me to fly out the broken windows.

Aargh. The guards couldn't miss that. "We've got to get out of here."

We fled down the steps and across the floor to where the others waited.

I called, "Blade, did you finish?"

"Yeah," he replied.

"MB?"

"The fish are in the net," he said as they ran out the door with us.

When we reached the trees, I skidded to a halt. I'd rather we were farther away, but I couldn't wait.

"Blow it, Blade, before anyone comes to investigate."

As Blade pressed the remote, Hulk aimed his phone toward the building to get it on video. A huge explosion rent the air, flames leapt up the sides of the building, then dust billowed as it partially collapsed in on itself.

The distant wail of sirens sounded. I made a slashing gesture across my neck. Hulk pushed the button on his phone to stop taping.

"Run," I ordered.

When we got to the military housing, people had come out to stare and point at the clouds of soot and dust. I dropped to my knees, using the brush for cover, and whispered, "Crawl."

When we were out of their sight, I stood and raced toward the fence. People had pulled their cars over to see.

I dove to the ground, then peered out over the grass to spot the truck. Gina had pulled it to the side, too, but how could we get through the fence without anyone seeing us?

We needed a distraction.

Gina flicked her lights once. She'd seen us. Her door opened and she got out of the truck.

She wasn't supposed to leave the truck. She began gesturing wildly, and every gaze swiveled toward her.

"It's an alien invasion," she yelled. "They're bombing us. Look." She pointed up the road. All those eyes followed.

Sneaker let out a snicker. I had to suppress my own laughter.

"Go," I whispered. As one, my team and I scaled the fence and dropped to the other side. I stood back up long enough to grab the clips off the fence.

Gina ran up the road waving her hands like crazy. "Get out of here aliens. This is our planet."

I opened the camper shell window above the tailgate, and we dived inside.

I heard Gina yelling again, "Oh, they're huge, and they have big heads. I'm getting out of here."

Footsteps pounded the pavement. She must be running to the truck. The door opened and shut, and the bed rumbled as the truck started. A hard thump came from the wall of the cab. I rapped back five times. One for each of us. The truck swayed, and we heard the slap of tires on pavement as it pulled onto the road. MB's fingers tapped on his laptop.

"Have you turned the camera's back on?" I asked.

"Yeah." He pointed to his blue tooth headpiece. "I'm listening to their transmissions. They've locked down the gates, and they're searching every vehicle. It's only a matter of time until our fish are pulled in."

"Good." I glanced back to see a helicopter flying near the bombed building. I rushed to peel off my camouflage clothing and change into my jeans and sweatshirt from my backpack while my teammates did the same.

Hulk handed MB the phone with the video. Gina turned the box truck off the road and hit a pothole.

MB hollered, "Crap," as he caught his laptop from flying.

We must be at the alley we'd chosen. When the truck stopped, I popped open the camper shell window. Yes, we were at the back of the old gas station. We jumped out and switched to the mini-van waiting there. Blade got behind the wheel. His driver's license was real, not fake like Gina's.

The whup-whup sound of helicopter blades beating the air came closer. My heart raced. Could they be on to us?

Chapter 49

Shark bite

"Nothing good can last forever." Gina

Gina

My mouth dried and my heart pounded. If we were caught…

When the helicopter flew beyond us to the government installation, relief flooded me. I shifted slightly from where I sat wedged between Sneaker and Blade in the front of the mini-van to see the guys in the back.

MB tapped on his laptop. "They've arrested our fish, and I've sent the video and our message so ARI gets the credit."

"Woohoo," Maverick hollered. "Great job, everyone."

Giddiness bubbled up in me. I laughed. "I can't believe we bombed a government installation."

"We did more than set off a bomb." Maverick grinned. "We earned a reputation for ARI and got some homegrown terrorists busted."

MB looked at his laptop screen again. "It's all over twitter already. It seems as if everyone's talking about us."

Maverick leaned forward. "We owe you a big thanks, Gina, for distracting everyone."

My heart soared. "I told you I'd come in useful."

"Yeah, you were hilarious." Sneaker chortled. "I could barely climb I was cracking up so much."

From past experience, I had figured it would work. "Crazy gets attention."

A corner of Maverick's mouth dipped. "I hope no one got you on video."

I hoped not either. "I didn't see any phones. I think they were too shocked."

Blade passed another vehicle like it was sitting still. The speed was making me nervous.

"You should slow down,"

Blade sped up even more. "We need to get back. It doesn't take forever to take the SAT."

Maverick checked his watch. "We've got time, and I think we'd all prefer it if we arrived safely without a trail of police."

Blade snorted but eased off the gas pedal. A few minutes later, he pulled over in an alley behind the school.

Maverick opened his door. "I'll go first, then follow one at a time."

After he jumped out, he strolled casually toward the school until he disappeared from view. I waited five minutes before I climbed out so it wouldn't look like we'd all finished the exam at the same time. Although I wanted to run, I forced myself to walk normally. We'd taped the lock on the rear exit door of the school. I cracked it open and crept inside. I shuffled through the halls and arrived at the school's front door where the guy in the suit stood.

"How did your SAT go?" he asked.

"Fine." I strolled out and over to the bus.

Blade came last after handing the keys to whomever Sam had disposing of the van.

MB whispered to us, "We got a shark bite."

Wow. A foreign terrorist group was reaching out to us.

Maverick fist-pumped the air. "That's great news."

Was it? Today had been scary. Were we ready for a shark? Even the thought was terrifying.

***

I finished reading the section on World War II and closed the textbook. Why did they have to make text books so boring? It seemed pointless anyway. How could learning more about an old war help me? But Fallentier had strict rules about completing school assignments. Working independently didn't mean we had a choice on whether to do it.

Felicity chewed on her eraser. "What do you have scheduled tonight?"

Fallentier didn't want us having too much time to get in trouble, so everyone was assigned a schedule, a peer group, and a staff member to oversee us. Felicity was awful nosy about my schedule. Probably because Blade had the same one. But our team's assignments were code words that meant training.

"After homework, I have a peer counseling session and community service for my chore."

She made a face. "Picking up roadside trash again?"

The team was supposed to meet for the mission debriefing. I'd have to lie again. "Yeah."

"At least you get to be with Blade, and Sam doesn't seem too bad. I wish they would have given us the same peer group."

That wasn't likely to happen unless Sam added her to our team. "I won't hit on him."

She smiled at me. "I'm not worried. I know you like Maverick. You should get back together with him now that the Amato's are leaving him alone. He's a really good guy."

That's what they all said now. Maverick had changed since he became leader. It wasn't just our team he went out of his way to help, but everyone that needed it. He must be tutoring half the kids in here, and they all loved him. Too bad he wasn't going to stick around. I checked the time on my phone and stood.

"I've got to bounce."

She gave me a wave. "Have fun picking up trash."

I went down the steps to Ms. McCaffry's office where she sat behind her desk. When she saw me, she rose and waved me in, closing the door behind us.

"One second, Gina." She went back to the desk and pushed the button underneath. The wall slid back revealing the steps to the tunnel that only the team and the staff knew about. I descended the steps.

When I exited the tunnel in our training facility gym, I turned on the lights. Strange that no one else was here yet. I went through to our operations room. It was dark too. I reached for the switch.

I screamed when I brushed another hand. The room flooded with light.

"Surprise," my team members yelled.

They laughed, and Sneaker pointed at me. "Look at her face. We got her good."

"You guys," I sputtered. Then I noticed the streamers and balloons. And in the middle of the conference table a cake said, *Happy 17th Birthday, Gina*. Beside it, there were wrapped packages.

My heart melted. It had been a long time since anyone did anything to celebrate my birthday. I had given up on expecting it. That just led to disappointment.

Maverick gave me a grin. "Families celebrate birthdays."

Families did, but I hadn't had one in a long time. I never thought I'd have another. But now... My eyes misted.

Blade grabbed a package. "You have to open your gifts." He held it out. "This one's from me."

I'd never received this many gifts. It was overwhelming.

Maverick motioned to a chair in front of the gifts on the table. "You can sit to open them."

I took Blade's package and collapsed in the chair. The guys huddled around me.

When I picked at the tape to unfasten it, Blade reached over and ripped the paper off. "Here."

I lifted the box out of the package, then opened it. Inside was a pair of knives.

"They're weighted for throwing." Blade eyes gleamed. "I'll teach you how to use them."

"Thanks, Blade."

One by one, I opened their gifts. MB gave me a tablet, Bullet a laser sight. Sneaker's gift was running shoes, I received Nun chucks from Hulk, and Sam handed me $50.

Maverick touched my arm. "I didn't have any money for gifts, but I made the cake."

Neither of us had received our monthly pay yet since we hadn't been on the team that long. "Cake is a great gift."

He handed me a piece of paper that had been folded. "I do have one other thing for you, but I'd like you to read it when you're alone."

"Okay." I slipped the folded note in my pocket.

Maverick lit the candles on the cake, and everyone sang the birthday song to me.

"Make a wish," Sneaker said.

What could I wish for? I'd already received what I had wanted— a family. *I wish our family would always stay together*. I knew it was unlikely, but no one besides Maverick had anyone either. Maybe the rest of us *could* stay together.

I blew out the candles, and Blade sliced the cake. When we finished eating, the guys refused to let me help clean up. Afterwards, Sam debriefed us. He dismissed us, and since it was late, everyone headed back to Fallentier. Before going into my room, I pulled out Maverick's note and unfolded it to see a heart drawn on it.

Underneath the heart, he'd written, "I've given you my heart. I'm waiting and hoping one day you'll give me yours. You already own mine."

Tears welled in my eyes, and I swiped at them. He owned my heart, too, and it was going to break when he abandoned me again.

Chapter 50

Expansion

"Life's most important lessons don't come from a textbook." Sam

Maverick

When I trudged into foreign language class alone, Mr. Potter glanced at me. "You're excused to meet with Sam. He has another project for you."

All I ever did in foreign language class was help the teachers, so I didn't mind missing it. I went to Sam's room and knocked.

He hollered, "Come in."

Sam sat at his table with two stacks of files. "Help yourself to a drink out of the fridge and join me."

I grabbed one of his mocha coffees and sat in the other chair. "Is this about Sneaker?"

"No, did he disappear?"

Should I rat on him? Sam would learn all too soon, and I was worried. "Yeah, I wasn't concerned when his bed was empty last night, but he never came back this morning."

Sam shrugged. "He will in a few days."

"And you're okay with that?"

"Not really, but I accept it. I grew up in the system, too, and most of the kids that do are troubled. Like these kids, I learned to ignore my friends' flaws and love them regardless. Sneaker has seen psychiatrists and therapists. If they weren't able to affect his need to escape, I doubt we can."

"So you're saying I can't change it?"

"You already have. He went much longer than normal. He told

me a while back he needed a break, but he wouldn't *bounce* while you needed his help. Just don't expect miracles."

Sneaker's disappearance still bothered me and discussing it wasn't helping so I changed the subject. "What did you want me for?"

"After you proved teens could pull off a mission, Director Williams gave the go ahead to expand the program, so I could use your help."

"What kind of expansion are you talking about?"

"Eventually, we plan on five more teams."

Wow. "I know we've had a lot of bites when we fished for terrorists, but there aren't that many from this area. Is this because you think there will be casualties?"

"This isn't for the DC area alone. Fallentier will be our base, but teams could be deployed anywhere in the country. We have a helicopter, a plane, and a few safe houses already."

"So what do you want me to do?"

"Help me select, recruit, and train them." Sam waved to one stack of files. "These have the backgrounds of every Fallentier kid who is either age seventeen or will be soon." He pointed to another much larger stack. "This has the backgrounds of all the foster kids that age in the state." He took two files from the first stack, and handed me one. "We'll start by checking the Fallentier kids to see if any might be a good match."

Hmm. Did I want to help Sam put more kids in danger? Like he had said, they could join the military at seventeen, and they'd be at risk there too. And didn't terrorists threaten everyone's safety, theirs included? Wait a minute, they were teaching them other languages.

"Are you planning on sending them into other countries that have terrorist organizations recruiting kids?"

"It's a possibility."

My heart sank. Then they'd be in even more jeopardy, and it had to be more than a possibility. An operation that included safe houses didn't get planned yesterday. It would go forward with or without me. Except if I helped, I could make certain they were trained well.

"I'll help if I get to tell them the risks up front."

Sam was examining a file. "Fine, but it will just make them more determined to do it. These kids like excitement."

Maybe he was right. Yet if I were to take part, I needed to know that they were aware of the danger.

I leafed through the file he'd handed me to see a criminal record, a medical and psych report, a social service plan with placement reason, school records, and even an assessment that listed each kid's strengths and weaknesses. Whoever compiled these records had been thorough.

"I could have avoided some problems if I'd known my team's issues. Why haven't I seen their files?"

"Because I promised your team I wouldn't let you see them. They said they'd tell you their problems when you gained their trust. Aren't they sharing?"

"Yes, but slowly." I took a sip of my coffee and motioned to the stacks of thick files. "This is going to take a while."

"We have until this afternoon to select twelve kids for our next two teams, then we'll talk to them so tomorrow we can start training."

Great. Another rush job. I skimmed through the file. This kid had shot another. That meant he could shoot, but his assessment listed him as antisocial, with anger issues. Not what we needed. I put the file aside and picked up another.

This kid hacked into his school's computers. Hmm. I handed it to Sam. "We need guys with mad computer skills."

Sam looked at it only for a few seconds, then put it aside. "He won't work. He shouldn't have even been transferred to Fallentier."

"Why?"

Sam opened the file and pointed to the placement reason. "Removed from parental custody due to their drug addiction. Parents are undergoing treatment and working toward reunification."

"He has family that apparently cares," Sam announced glumly. "If something were to happen to him, they'd raise a fuss and we don't want the attention. We need the kids who don't have family in the picture."

Like me. My dad was supposed to be dead. There was no way he could raise a public outcry, so I was one of the disposable ones. I didn't matter. My heart sank.

Why was I feeling sorry for myself? Agents risked their lives to keep our country safe, and I had wanted to do that. Weren't we doing something equally important? Yes. I took a calming breath.

Sam closed the file. "I'll have him transferred. Eventually, the only ones at Fallentier will be kids on our teams."

I leafed through several more files, examining the psych evaluations. Each one revealed a problem.

A frustrated sigh escaped me. "I don't see how kids this messed up will be able to do the job."

Sam looked up at me. "Ever seen a stained-glass window?"

"Yeah."

"They take all those rough, jagged, and stained pieces of glass, and mold them together into something beautiful, something whole. We've got to do the same."

Easily said, but could it be accomplished?

Chapter 51

Fishing

"Training others is the most difficult thing I've done, but if I fail, they'll die." Maverick

Maverick

Sweat stung my eyes as I moved out of the gym at the training facility. I swiped my sleeve across my forehead. I needed to make sure our teams were prepared, but the schedule I had set myself had my feet dragging. It wasn't even noon yet. After a few hours of school work at Fallentier, I ran the obstacle course with team Charlie, then sparred with team Bravo. Now I needed to work with my team, Alpha.

When I walked into our operations center, the team was sitting at the computers, fishing. They glanced up from their monitors.

"Our turn to spar?" MB asked.

"I need to catch my breath, so I was thinking about helping you fish first."

Sam was writing a report at the conference table. He set his pen down. "That's a good idea. You should learn to fish, and they can use the help."

The door of the training center opened, and Sneaker walked in. All my teammates jumped up and ran over to him.

"We missed you, little dude," Hulk said as he slapped Sneaker on the shoulder.

Gina hugged him. "Yes, we did."

Blade bumped fists with him. "Welcome back."

Bullet thumped his back. "Bout time you came home."

Sneaker shuffled over to the conference table where Sam was. "I know there are consequences for leaving. I've got two days of extra chores coming, right?"

"Try four days."

Sneaker gave him a nod. "Okay. So am I forgiven?"

"Yes. I forgive you."

Sneaker came over to where I was standing. He looked at his feet. "Are you mad at me?"

My teammates had accepted Sneaker back without any condemnation even though he'd disappeared for days. I admired that they were so supportive of each other, but I couldn't do that.

"I'm not mad, but I was really worried about you. Where did you go?"

"Just around," he mumbled.

"Where do you sleep when you leave?"

"Different places."

"Be more specific."

"It depends. A park bench, down by the river, an alley."

"That's really dangerous. I don't want you to do it again."

The rest of the team were shooting glares at me, as if I'd said something really wrong.

Sneaker lifted his head. "I can't help it, Maverick." His blue eyes brimmed with unshed tears. "If I don't go when I need a break, I'll blow up and hurt something or someone"—his voice lowered to a whisper—"probably me." A tear escaped to roll down his face. "I have to go."

That must be how he got the scar on his arm. "All right, we'll figure out something." I reached out and squeezed his shoulder. "You don't know how glad I am to have you back. We need you. I need you."

He brushed the tear away and gave me a sheepish smile. "Thanks."

"Are you hungry?" Sam asked.

"Starved," Sneaker replied.

"Go get a sandwich from the fridge. The rest of you should get back to fishing."

While Sneaker went upstairs, my teammates returned to their

computers. I sat at an open one.

Sam limped over to me, and laid a piece of paper next to me. "That's the user names and IP addresses of everyone that's bitten on our bait in chat rooms and forums. In parenthesis is the fake terrorist group they think they've been talking to. We use several, so remember to respond with the same user acronym they reached out to before. The ones crossed off have been arrested."

I read the fake terrorist group acronyms. ARI stood for American Rising for Islam, PART was Patriots of America Resisting Tyranny, RY meant Radical Youth, and there were a dozen more phony names for fictional groups that might attract people who planned to commit acts of terror.

A message popped up on my computer screen. "We'd like to meet at 3 p.m. today." I checked the on-line name. It was circled and had shark written next to it. "Sam, there's shark written next to this one."

"That's the IP of the foreign terrorists that contacted us after the bombing. Agree to meet them."

"Finally," MB exclaimed. Everyone on Alpha team left their computers to huddle around us.

I typed in, "OK, where?"

When the address displayed on the screen, Gina said, "My old foster home is on that street."

According to my grandfather's list, an address on that street had received crates of automatic rifles and blasting caps bought from the black market.

I swiveled my chair to face them. "Is that where the mafia dropped off the material and weapons?"

Sneaker had come back downstairs and now sat at the conference table with a giant sandwich in front of him. "I checked that place. It was empty."

Gina chewed her lip. "It's not the same number, but it's across the street. Do you think maybe they moved the stuff there?"

Hmmm. "It would be easy to watch from across the street if anyone came snooping."

Sneaker smirked. "No one on that street ever knew I was there."

"Good." Sam leaned back. "Because this one looks legit. It's not another agency setting up a sting, and it's not a wannabe terrorist. With what they bought, they could kill a lot of people."

Would they meet us where they were building bombs? My gut said no. "I don't think the bombs are at either address, but they'll be close."

Sam pointed to the chat on the screen. "Print it."

I hit print, then glanced at Sam. "I should go in alone to distract them while the rest of the team searches the area to find those bombs."

"No," Sam limped to the printer and pulled out the paper with the chat. "You need backup. And two set of hands are better than one."

My chair rolled as I lunged to my feet. "Remember that a lot of these foreign terrorists pit Americans against each other to test their loyalty." I paced the room. "They'll shoot anyone that refuses to do it." I stopped in front of Sam. "I can live with killing a terrorist, but not a teammate."

Sam's jaw ticked, and his eyes narrowed at me. He'd been testy with me ever since I agreed with Connor that he shouldn't go on our missions. But he'd be a liability, and not only because of his limp. His age and military bearing would raise suspicions. Connor didn't want him participating because if we got caught, Fallentier could claim we were runaways. But if a staff member was with us, it could put the group home front and the entire operation at risk. Sam knew we were right, but that didn't make it any easier to wait while we went in.

He frowned and blew out his breath. "Take Gina. Tell them she's your girlfriend. I don't think they'd pit you against a girlfriend."

"No way." I snapped. "You can't be sure they won't."

"The team can monitor and move in if you need them."

Gina narrowed her eyes at me. "I've proven myself again and again. I deserve to go."

My heart lurched. "At the first sign of trouble, they'd probably blow the place up, or start shooting."

Sam crossed his arms. "It's not up to you, Maverick. This is a team operation, and Gina *does* deserve this." His eyes locked with mine. "It's final. She's going in with you."

Grrr. No sense arguing anymore. Sam's mind was made up, but so was mine.

Chapter 52

Nerves

"Waiting prolongs the agony." Gina.

Gina

The tension strumming through me eased a little as I pulled out the Kevlar vests from the training room cabinet and placed them and some gloves in my teammate's duffels. I crossed them off the list.

Maverick strolled in. "Are you packing for everyone else?"

"I needed something to do."

The corner of his lips dipped, and his voice turned crisp. "Waiting's always difficult for me too."

I turned to the gun cabinet and grabbed my pistol. Hadn't he said the terrorists would search us? I put it back on the peg. "I guess there's no sense in us two taking anything."

His toffee eyes softened. "Take your gun anyway. If they find an obvious weapon, they might not look as hard for a hidden one."

"Are we hiding something?" I asked.

"Yes." He opened his hand. In his palm were two small tubes the width of a straw but not half the length. One end looked like the top of a pen.

"What are those?"

"I call them zee shooters. Something my dad invented." He pointed to the pen top. "Just press the plunger after you point it at whoever you want to neutralize. The cartridge will shoot out, and a gas escapes that will put them to sleep for about thirty minutes. There's not enough gas for a crowd, but it will work on three or four adults." He took a small first aid kit out of his pocket and pulled out some adhesive tape.

"Turn around and lift up your hair," he instructed.

When I did, he placed the tube against the back of my neck. A chill raced through me.

"On a pat down search, most people don't go above the shoulders." Maverick's soft breath tickled my neck, and my skin tingled under the touch of his fingers as he smoothed the tape.

"That should hold it, and it won't be too difficult to take off." He held out the other shooter. "Will you put mine on me?"

His attention flustered me. I didn't want to react like that, but I couldn't help it. "Okay."

Maverick turned around. His thick black hair fell straight to his collar and I resisted the urge to run my fingers through it. He reached back and wadded it in his fist. With a couple pieces of tape, I attached the tube to his neck. Goosebumps rose on his skin. Was he as affected by my touch as I was his? Regardless, I couldn't make the mistake again of getting involved with someone who'd be moving on.

I stepped back. "You're done."

"Thanks." He gave me a warm smile. "Pack an extra duffel so we have a spare."

"Do you think I'll forget stuff?"

"No. It's just a good rule. Murphy's Law. A strap breaks. Someone loses a glove. Will you do it, *please*?"

"All right."

His face darkened. "Be careful today, will you?"

"Of course."

His forehead crinkled as he moved toward the door. "I've got to find Sneaker. I'll see you later."

"Sure." I turned back to the gun cabinet.

. . .

I double-checked every duffel. We had everything. I glanced at my watch. Only thirty minutes had passed since Maverick left. Another half-hour before we'd leave. I should give everyone their duffels now. They might want to put some of their gear on.

Sneaker walked in. "Have you seen Maverick?"

"No, I thought he was with you."

He shook his head. "I can't find him anywhere."

My heart dropped to my toes. Had Maverick gone to confront the terrorists alone? Ugh. That must be why he had me pack an extra duffel. So I'd have what I needed to assist the team.

Heat crept up my neck as my temper rose. Did he think I wasn't capable of helping him? That could get him killed. What if he ran into trouble?

My phone vibrated. Sneaker pulled his out too. A text scrolled across my screen from Maverick.

"In thirty minutes, I'll head in. I left my glasses in the van so you can monitor Pip's camera."

Seriously? It would take that much time to get there, and what would the terrorists do when he showed up an hour early?

Another text scrolled across the phone. "I want Gina to lead the rest of the team to find those bombs, but be careful. Use the zee shooter on anyone guarding them."

Maverick had put me in charge of the other part of the mission, so he had to believe in my ability. Pride filled me. Wait. Now that he'd done that, I couldn't leave the others to go help him. Was that his intention?

I took out my phone and pulled up the number I'd copied from Maverick's phone. I made the call he never would.

"This is Gina."

Chapter 53

Traitor

"Victor always said trust can kill. I trusted him, and Kurt was killed." Jake.

Maverick

After paying the taxi driver from my emergency money, I jogged a block over to the dead end street that Gina used to live on. I checked my watch. Time to start in. I snuck through the overgrown yards behind boarded up abandoned homes. The occupied ones with parked cars still had peeling paint and overgrown grass shouting their dereliction. Any of these could be the place where the terrorists were building and storing bombs.

Would Pip and the team be able to find them?

I picked my way over the rubble of fallen bricks and crept behind a brick ranch house with a caved in roof and black char marking the boards that covered its windows. I stopped at the corner of the home to peer around it. The address to meet the shark was two doors away. It was a large ranch style home with wood siding that had mostly turned green from a covering of mold. There was an old white panel van and a small rusty pickup parked in the driveway.

I pulled out Pip. He couldn't go in with me. They'd search me. Besides, he needed to help my team. I pressed on his ear to signal stealth. I didn't want him chirping inside one of those houses if terrorists were around.

I snaked my hand for recon in front of Pip's nose and pointed to each of the houses on the street, leaving the one I was going to last. Worry knotted my gut. Could he find a way into them all or would he get distracted and come find me? When I cast him off, he glided to the next house.

I heard the clink of bricks in the rubble. I pivoted to see Jake stride around the other side of the house. I darted around the corner and waited as his footsteps came nearer. What was Jake doing here? Was Parker having him watch me covertly?

When Jake got close, I jumped out.

He leapt back as I hissed, "Why are you following me?"

His eyes widened. "I'm not."

"If you're not following me, then what are you doing outside a terrorist house?"

Red flamed in Jake's cheeks. He looked at his feet. "Probably the same thing as you."

No way could he know about the team. No agency did, so did he think I was working with the terrorists? 'The same thing as you...' All those times over at my house, he saw the various agents training. And he had access to our home, so he could have framed Dad. He must be the mole.

I rushed him and threw him against the brick wall, pinning his throat with my arm. "How could you help them?"

"I didn't have any choice. They nabbed me leaving school, stuck a gun to my head, and told me to write down every agent I knew if I wanted to live."

Maybe I shouldn't have sent Pip away with his listening device. No one was hearing Jake's confession but me. "You didn't have to give them the correct names."

"I didn't at first, so they broke my finger. That's when I learned they had another informant, and they'd know if I had lied. Since they already had the names, I figured it wouldn't change anything to confirm them. When I did, they let me go, but they had someone watching me. They said if I said anything, they'd kill my dad."

"You were at my house. How hard would it have been to tell me?"

"They let slip their mole was living in a mansion. I thought it was you. Then they said the informant double-crossed them, and they had me go to that club to see if you showed up. I didn't find out it was Angela until I reported back and saw them strapping a bomb to her."

So this was the group who tried to bomb Grandfather's club. I'd agreed to let him know if we found them so I'd have to make a call.

"It looks like I was right not to trust you," Jake said, then tried to push me off him.

I allowed him to break free of my hold, and took a step back. "You could have trusted me before what you did killed Dad. And why wouldn't you trust your own dad or Kurt?"

"When they released me, they'd already killed the Bureau agents. I'd confirmed their names, and the terrorists made deposits in my bank account. How could I convince anyone I wasn't willingly working for them? And I didn't want to get Dad killed. I thought the safest thing was to do what they told me to."

"Safe," I sputtered. "You got Kurt killed."

"I never gave them Kurt's name, and I left a note under the door of your dad's bedroom warning him Kurt could be compromised. I trusted your dad to make sure Kurt got pulled out, but he ignored my warning. He got Kurt killed."

"Dad wouldn't ignore a risk to an agent. Angela must have found your note."

His face blanched, and his body sagged. Then he threw his head back, slamming it into the bricks. A sob shook him and he choked out, "I should have made sure."

"Yeah, you should of." My rage simmered. Jake had failed Kurt and hurt Dad.

When I heard a footstep, I swiveled to see a dark haired guy with a mustache pointing an automatic weapon at us.

"Don't either of you move," he snapped.

His beady eyes, thin mustache and pointy chin gave his face a weasel look, and even though his hands were small, the gun was held rock steady.

Aargh. I shouldn't have gotten distracted with Jake and let this guy get the drop on me.

Two more guys came over from the direction of the terrorist house. It was Lenny and the kid with braces on his teeth who was with Lenny when he stopped the Fallentier kids from beating me up. I noticed pistols tucked in their waistbands. This was Lenny's security job?

Lenny gave me a chin lift. "Hey, Maverick."

Weasel face barked at Lenny, "You know him?"

"Yeah. I told him if he needed a job to find me."

Did Lenny know the people he was working for were terrorists? "I didn't come here for a job. I'm with ARI."

Lenny's eyes widened, but he didn't ask me who ARI was. So he knew what he was involved in.

Weasel face snarled at me. "You're early." His gaze flicked to Kurt. "And you're late." With a tilt of his head, he motioned to Lenny and the other teen. "Search them."

The teen with braces frisked Kurt while Lenny ran his hands over me, even sliding his hands in my boots. When he checked my jean pockets, he found my cell phone. He handed it to weasel face who stuck it in his shirt pocket. Lenny didn't locate the zee shooter or my hidden heel compartments.

When they finished, weasel face ordered, "Take them to the house slowly."

They led us to the back of the white ranch home as weasel face trailed with the gun on our backs. Lenny opened the rear door, and we trudged in.

After a second, my eyes adjusted to the dimness, and I surveyed a kitchen with cracked linoleum and dingy brown cabinets. Empty spots marked the spaces where a stove and refrigerator belonged. The terrorists probably weren't living here, only using it as a meeting place. Lenny motioned us through to the living room where four more adults trained automatic rifles on us.

Weasel face nudged me with his rifle. "We found Kurt arguing with this guy, who says he's the leader of ARI. Lenny knows him too."

Lenny shook his head. "Barely. I only met him once."

A man with a shaggy beard who by the lines in his forehead appeared to be in his mid-forties, and the oldest in the room asked in the Farsi language, "So you are Derrick Costa, the leader of ARI?"

Hmm. We'd been spreading hints that I might be the leader of ARI. They'd apparently worked, but I refused to show any reaction. If they weren't aware I knew Farsi and thought I couldn't understand them, they might reveal more.

Weasel face drove the butt of his gun into the back of my head above where the z-shooter was taped. Pain rocketed through me and my vision filled with spots as I staggered forward.

"When he asks you a question, you answer," yelled weasel face as I recovered my balance. I wanted to fight back, but all those guys with assault weapons were waiting for that.

Bearded guy flicked his hand at Jake. "He's told us all about you, so don't act stupid."

I felt moisture seeping in my hair. Was I bleeding? I put my hand up and found a lump. When I examined my hand, I found a little blood on my fingers. No sense in taking more lumps for things that weren't vital to hold back, but I should choose my words carefully. Maybe I could create the old Double D, dissent and doubt, and get some of these guys to turn on one another.

"Yes, I'm Derrick Costa, the leader of ARI. The same guy you tried to kill, but I don't understand how my death could warrant sending a suicide bomber to the Amato's club while the Don was inside. Did you want to start a war with the mafia?"

"Oh man," Lenny's eyes widened, and he took a step back toward the door. "If you picked a fight with the mafia, we're all jacked."

Bearded man pointed his rifle at Lenny. "You aren't rethinking your employment with us?"

If Lenny admitted that, I was certain he'd die.

Lenny's eyes darted around the room, and he swallowed hard. "No."

"Good." Bearded guy motioned to Lenny and the kid with braces, "Let's show Derrick why we aren't worried about mafia or anyone else."

With weasel face prodding me with the gun, I followed them down the hall past one closed door to an open one which bearded guy stopped at and flicked a hand toward it. "These are our most important soldiers because they will be strapping on bombs to take the war to the infidels. No one will suspect them or want to kill them."

I moved up to see inside the room. Five younger kids around the age of ten sat kneeling on the floor, softly chanting verses from the

Quran about infidels. On a table by the window was an explosive device with a switch strapped to it.

Bearded guy called inside, "My young soldiers."

The children stopped chanting and looked up.

"If we shout blow it up, what would you do?" he asked.

The kids pointed at the bomb. "Run and push the switch."

"Very good." Bearded guy motioned with his hand. "Continue to memorize our teachings." When their heads dropped to resume their muttering, he turned to me. "Now you know how futile it would be for anyone to attack us. If we don't kill them first, our young soldiers will."

Could I kill any of those brainwashed little kids with their innocent faces? I didn't know, but I sure didn't want to.

When bearded guy moved farther down the hall with Lenny and the other teen, weasel face nudged me with the gun. "Go."

They stopped at the third and final door. Four teens sat on the floor inside laughing, and joking while they played a video game on an older console television. They were the same kids that were with Lenny when I met him. Bearded guy motioned to Lenny and the kid with braces. "You may join your friends. We don't need your help to take care of the Ari leader."

The way he said it sounded ominous. Lenny must have thought so too. He frowned, then looked at me and gave me a little shrug, as if to say he couldn't help me, before they entered the room. Bearded guy closed the door, and led us back up the hall.

The wood floor was solid, but my legs felt wobbly as if I were walking a plank. He stopped at the door we had previously passed and opened it to reveal a large room, probably the original master bedroom. Seven more men I'd estimate to be in their early twenties lounged on older sofas and chairs with automatic rifles in their laps. A movie played on a smaller flat screen television, and a couple of the guys were leafing through magazines.

My heart fell at the evidence of even more armed terrorists.

"Some of you go look around," ordered bearded man. "I don't believe the ARI leader would come alone."

Grrr, would they find my team?

Chapter 54

Searching

"I don't have to look for trouble, it finds me." Gina

Gina

Blade parked at the top of the street in my old neighborhood. He'd broken every speeding record getting here, but we needed to find those bombs so we could help Maverick.

"Has Pip found anything yet, MB?" I asked.

MB touched the frame of Maverick's glasses that he wore to watch Pip's camera. He smiled.

"Pip did it. The blasting caps are in a concrete block garage two doors down from where the terrorists are meeting with Maverick. They have jugs of pool cleaner, cans of gasoline, pressure cookers, fishing vests, and dynamite or maybe fireworks. I can't tell how many bombs are assembled in the boxes there."

I sucked in my breath. They had the material for chemical bombs too. Some of them could be pretty unstable.

"Do you think you can disarm them, Sneaker?" I asked.

"Probably."

Probably didn't settle my nerves. "How many guards are there, MB?"

He touched a hand to his ear with the ear bud. "There are three of them inside, one outside."

I'd have to save the zee shooter for the ones inside. "Everyone has their silencers on their guns, right?"

They all nodded. "Okay, Blade, drive down the alley and park one door down." As Blade pulled into the alley, I issued more orders.

"Blade, stay with the van. Hulk and Bullet will come with me to sneak up on the guy outside." Even a silenced gun might alert the terrorists inside. "Let's try to knock him unconscious."

"MB and Sneaker will come with us too, but both of you hang back." I couldn't risk Sneaker since he'd be needed to disarm any bombs. "MB I need you to keep monitoring Pip's camera and listening to his recorder."

When Blade pulled over, I slipped my gun in the back of my waistband as we climbed out. We snuck up to the other side of the garage. I held my palm up to MB and Sneaker. They waited as Bullet, Hulk, and I sidled down the back and peeked around the corner. The guard sat in a lawn chair by the side door, his gun across his lap, but his head had fallen on his chest, and a snore rumbled from him.

Hulk took his gun out of his waistband. He crept up and swung his gun butt down on the guy's head. The guard slumped to the ground. Bullet took his zip ties out and tied the man's hands and feet while Hulk removed the bullets from his gun and threw it all under a bush.

There was a gap between the door and the concrete of the garage floor. I laid down and put my eye to the gap to see shoes. Carefully removing the zee shooter from my neck, I aimed it toward them and pushed the plunger.

Thumps sounded from inside. I waited another minute before I cracked open the door. All three guys were sprawled on the floor. I waved the door, forcing air inside to dilute the gas. Supposedly, it only took a minute for the gas to dissipate, but I wasn't taking any chances.

When I was sure it was safe, I turned to Bullet. "Go get Sneaker."

Hulk and I moved inside and, kicking the guns from the guys on the floor, we secured their wrists and feet.

When Sneaker came in, he rushed to the workbench where pressure cookers, vests, and other paraphernalia were spread out beside boxes.

"Most of these bombs are ready to put blasting caps in, but they haven't finished the last step." Sneaker bent over a box. "This is the only one active." He pulled out his wire cutters. "I'll cut the wires to the switch."

He snipped the wire. MB rushed in holding his ear. "Maverick's in trouble."

"He's not the only one, but your troubles are about over."

I jumped at the unfamiliar voice. Four guys stood outside, pointing automatic rifles at our faces.

Our Kevlar vests couldn't protect our heads. I had messed up not assigning a look out. Despair flooded me.

Pffft. A gun with a silencer. I dove to the floor. The other Fallen kids had too.

Pfft, pfft, pfft. More shots rang out. The terrorist's eyes widened in shock as they crumpled to the ground, bleeding.

Who'd shot them? Was it a friend or foe?

Chapter 55

Hopeless

"Boxes don't have four sides. There are at least six ways to break out of any cage." Victor

Maverick

I heard a scratch as I followed bearded guy back down the hall. Pip's nails. He'd gotten in and was clinging to the light fixture on the ceiling. I better keep these terrorist's focus on me and away from Pip. Was there something I could do to get them to turn on each other since there were so many?

"You were right. I'm not alone. I have supporters among you."

His dark eyes narrowed. "I don't believe you."

"How would I have avoided being murdered by Angela if I wasn't tipped off?"

We reached the living room where he pointed at Jake. "He must have told you."

I laughed. "I wouldn't believe anything he said. Did he even know about the attempt to kill me?"

Bearded guy's neck turned red. "Is it Lenny? Tell me now who's helping you, or I'll kill you."

"You mean who *they* are. I have many supporters. If anything happens to me, they'll release a recording of this meeting on the internet and declare jihad against you."

Weasel face shook his head. "He's lying. We searched him."

"I'm not the one doing the recording." I locked eyes with bearded guy. "But why battle each other? How does that create fear and dissent between Muslims and Infidels?"

Bearded guy raised his gun at me. "We are willing to kill others or die for Islam, but are you?" He pointed his gun toward Jake. "You don't trust each other, and I don't trust either of you. So you'll fight and we'll see who would kill for our cause." He shrugged. "One of you will die or both of you. It will be as Allah wills."

Could I kill Jake? He'd torn our family apart, and several agents died because of him and Angela. Regardless of whether he deserved it, I didn't want to kill him. Besides, I needed Jake alive so he could confess to everyone and prove Dad's innocence.

A sinking feeling hit the pit of my stomach. When I didn't kill Jake, these terrorists would shoot me. There were too many not to have one of their bullets hit me. I'd messed up. Terrorist cells didn't normally have this many members, so I'd expected fewer.

Even if my team tried to intervene, we couldn't handle all these guys wielding automatic weapons. If I were to die, I'd take some terrorists with me, only I didn't want to kill those kids down the hall. Could I neutralize them so they didn't set off that bomb?

Jake growled and rushed at me. He grabbed my left arm and tapped twice while he threw a punch with his other hand. I almost didn't duck in time as I deciphered his signal. Left arm and two taps meant Jake wanted me to take out the two terrorists on the left while he'd take the three on the right. He still believed he was more skilled than me.

Could I trust him? His plan had almost no chance of success. Even if we took out the five in here, the others would come running. His plan was better than doing nothing, but I wanted to do something first. I crossed my fingers, a distraction signal, and glanced toward the hall.

Jake shoved me toward it. I allowed myself to fall back on the floor. As Jake came after me, I grabbed the zee shooter taped to the back of my neck. I curled my fist around it, hiding it. After I angled the bottom of my fist toward the young kid's room, I pressed the plunger. The little pellet rocketed down the hall, hitting their door frame and bouncing in. Since they were little kids, maybe the gas it released would put the five of them to sleep, but it wouldn't affect any other room.

None of the terrorists seemed to notice what I'd done. When Jake lifted his foot like he meant to stomp me, I rolled to dodge and jumped back to my feet. We circled each other warily. Now we could take some of these terrorists with us before we died.

Chapter 56

Stipulations

"Everyone dies, but for their life to be meaningful, they must leave the world a better place." Victor

Maverick

As I circled Jake, I attempted to move closer to the terrorists before making my move. I worked myself within a few feet of one and Jake was close to another but there were five terrorists in this room, four armed with assault rifles and one brandishing a pistol.

I threw a roundhouse punch at Jake that I telegraphed and softened. He ducked it, then jabbed back. When I blocked his jab with my arm, it stung. Why hadn't he softened that punch? Wasn't he faking our fight? Did he figure out his plan to attack the terrorists was certain to fail? When I leapt at them, would he too, or would he just watch while they shot me. That would be a sure way to win the fight that was supposed to be to the death.

Bearded guy yelled, "If I don't see blood soon, I'll create some when I start shooting."

Jake lunged toward me. I skipped back toward the terrorists. One of them shoved me propelling me toward Jake. I kicked out at Jake hitting him in the chest, and throwing him back. When he recovered he came at me hard, throwing punches in a flurry. I blocked them, and fought back.

Someone banged on the front door. "Derrick, where are you?"

That was Gina's voice. What was she doing?

Both Jake and I stopped, heaving to catch our breaths, but the terrorists kept their weapons aimed on us.

Bearded guy motioned to the terrorist with the pistol. "Get that."

He stalked to the door to crack it. "What do you want?"

"My boyfriend. I saw him go in there," Gina yelled. "Has he got another girlfriend? Is that why he's been sneaking around?"

"Come on in." The terrorist opened the door wider.

When Gina walked in, he slammed the door behind her.

Weasel face snarled, "Gina." He stalked over to her.

Gina froze and her eyes widened. "Fr..Fred, I thought you were in the hospital."

"I was released, but Mary left. It's all your fault." He lifted his gun. "You'll pay for that."

"No," I screamed.

Muffled shots rang out from the bedroom. Gina dove behind the couch. She pulled her gun and fired. Fred was hit in the chest and he crumpled.

Shouting came from down the hall as Jake ran toward another terrorist. I kicked the one close to me in the crotch. When he bent, I jerked his assault rifle out of his hands and swung it toward bearded guy.

"Blow…" bearded guy yelled as I shot him.

Bullets sprayed the room as the terrorist Jake had run toward opened up. Jake was hit. I jumped behind the terrorist I'd relieved of his gun. My terrorist shield fell as bullets hit him, only giving me time to dive to the ground. The front door flew open. Bullet and Hulk stood in the doorframe shooting at the terrorists.

They showered the remaining two with bullets. The terrorists crashed to the floor.

I raced to Jake, but he lay with his eyes open in a pool of blood. No. He couldn't be dead. But he was.

Gina moved out from behind the couch. Footsteps raced down the hallway. I pivoted toward the sound. My teammates aimed their guns toward the hall too.

Enzo and some of the men I'd seen at the Baldoria club came into the room with assault rifles. The one in the rear was pulling Lenny with him.

What were my grandfather's men doing here?

"The little kids are unconscious, the adults are dead, and the teens surrendered." Enzo gestured to Lenny. "This one says he's friends with you."

"He helped me out of a bad situation once, but we aren't friends. What will you do to them?"

We won't hurt the little kids, but the teens are old enough to know better than to bomb a club under our protection. We already put the word out about what would happen to those involved." He glanced at his gun. "The Don wouldn't want anyone not to pay that price."

Sneaker, holding a dangling earpiece, ran down the hall. "I deactivated the bomb back there. Our police informant says neighbor's reported gunfire, so they're on the way. We need to bounce."

Neighbor was code for Sam, and *police informant* was code for Connor. Sam had called Connor who sent law enforcement to mop up but they couldn't find us here.

I turned to Enzo. "Just leave Lenny for the cops. That's a price."

Enzo pointed his gun toward Lenny. "Dead men tell no tales."

Lenny's face blanched. "We won't rat on you. We'll say you wore masks."

"Don't kill him," I barked. "After they helped me, I owe them."

Enzo lowered his gun. "Fine, but the Don won't like it. If any of them say anything..."

I moved to Lenny. "We're even now, but you and your friends better keep your mouths shut. You wouldn't be able to hide from both the Mafia and Ari." I grabbed his arm and pulled him down the hall. "And get a new line of work because you're not good terrorists." I opened the door of the room and shoved him in. I turned the lock before closing it, then ran back to the living room.

Enzo and the rest of grandfather's men were fleeing out the kitchen door. I needed evidence to prove Dad's innocence. I couldn't trust the Bureau or Company to divulge any information they found here.

I handed the rifle to Sneaker who had gloves on. "Wipe my prints quickly, then leave it," I ordered.

I rushed to Fred's body and took my phone from his front pocket. When I grabbed their computer hard drive, Sneaker finished with the gun and tossed it. Then my teammates and I raced out the back door to the alley.

How close were the cops?

Enzo and the other mafia guys had jumped into black sedans. Their vehicles peeled out, as Blade drove up in our van. When Blade stopped, my teammates leapt inside. Was that everyone?

Oh, no. I forgot Pip.

I threw the computer hard drive in and turned back around.

Blade beat his fist on the steering wheel. "Come on."

"I have to get Pip." I whistled. Pip glided out of the house as a puppy scampered from under a neighboring porch and scrambled toward us.

"Tuffy," Gina hollered as she jumped out.

She scooped the puppy in her arms as Pip landed on my shoulder. When Gina leapt inside the van with the dog, I dove in after her and slammed the door.

"Go," I shouted.

Blade raced away. When he got a few blocks, he glanced back at Gina. "Sam's not going to let you keep that puppy, and it stinks. I'll pull over, and you can let him out."

"No!" she yelled.

I wrinkled my nose. The puppy did stink but we didn't have time to mess around.

"Keep driving," I ordered. "We can deal with the dog later."

Gina petted Tuffy and crooned, "I'm keeping you."

She wouldn't be able to hide a dog like a sugar glider, and Fallentier had a no pet policy.

Sneaker grabbed my arm. "Dude, did you get shot? Should we take you to the hospital?"

I glanced at the blood coating my hands and shirt. "It's not mine."

We had clothing inside the van in the event we'd need it. I took Pip out of my pocket, then stripped my shirt off and used wet naps to remove the blood. As I threw on a clean shirt, the vehicles with my grandfather's men split off to go a different direction.

Sirens wailed and lights flashed as cops streaked by us, but no one seemed to pay attention to our delivery van.

Tears streaked Gina's cheeks. She whispered to the puppy. "I didn't want to kill anyone."

I hated knowing I'd killed someone, too, but it was them or us. It still terrified me that she'd come so close to dying.

"You shouldn't have come in, Gina. It was too dangerous."

"If I didn't, Jake might have killed you. Besides, I needed to distract them so your grandfather's men could get in the window."

"How did my grandfather know anything about it?"

"I took Enzo's number from your phone and called them before we left." Her chin jutted out. "And it's a good thing I did, or we'd be dead."

Grandfather couldn't have known they were the guys who bombed his club when she called. They wouldn't have learned that until Pip's listening bug was near enough to transmit my discussions with the terrorists, so how did she gain his aid?

"Grandfather doesn't do something for nothing. What did you agree to?"

"I told him you'd allow him back into your life with some stipulations."

My temper flared. "You had no right."

Her cheeks turned red. "You had no right to go in alone. If you'd stuck to the plan, I wouldn't have called."

I resented her reaching out to them, but I understood her concern. I drew a cleansing breath. "What's the stipulations?"

"You'll call him once a week to discuss what's going on with you so he won't need any rats. Plus, once a year you'll visit him on a holiday of your choosing, and he's agreed not to try to control your life. That's it. Speaking a few minutes and spending a few hours together on a holiday. Millions of families do that. You can too."

I could live with that, and she was right. Without all of their help, I'd be dead. "Thank you."

"You're welcome." Gina pulled my medallion out of her pocket. "Your grandfather sent this and said regardless of whether you ever join the family, you should keep your mom's gift. You earned it."

I took it from her and slipped the medallion back around my neck. The familiar weight came to rest on my chest. I'd missed it. We drove a few miles away and met Sam behind the deserted dry cleaners. After taking everything out of the van, we crowded into his car.

Being mashed together would have bothered me when I first came to Fallentier and considered these kids delinquents, but now I admired their toughness and resilience. I didn't know if I could have survived what they had. Although they had physical and emotional scars from the abuse they suffered and they might be messed up individuals, together they pulled off amazing things. They were an incredible team.

People say there are no stronger friendships than those formed in battle. Even though they'd been battling all their lives, I had just joined them. It hadn't taken long for me to consider them not only my friends, but my best friends. If it weren't for them, I'd be dead now. I'd hate to lose any of them.

Chapter 57

Mascot

"A pet takes work, but it isn't much when compared to the love they give back." Maverick

Gina

When we arrived back at the training center, I cradled Tuffy in my arms as we marched inside. MB set to work on the hard drive while Sam debriefed the team.

Surely, they didn't need my help to fill Sam in. If Tuffy didn't stink, maybe I could convince Sam to let him stay. I carried Tuffy up the steps to the kitchen sink. The shampoo I found under the sink wasn't for dogs, but it would have to do. While the guys' voices drifted up to me, I soaped and rinsed Tuffy until the water ran clear.

Sam's voice rose to a shout. "I told you not to go in alone, Maverick. Tell me why I shouldn't throw you off the team for good?"

I gasped, and my heart ached at the thought.

"Because it won't happen again," Maverick answered. "I know now that I need my team to cover my back, and they're skilled enough to do it."

His words filled me with pride even as Sam continued to berate Maverick in a razor sharp tone. "The only reason we're having this conversation is, despite you, we had some success. But if you pull another stunt like that, you're gone."

"I understand," Maverick replied curtly.

The voices below softened to a murmur as I wrapped Tuffy in a towel and snagged some lunchmeat from the refrigerator. When I carried him downstairs, I crooned to him, "Now that you're clean, Sam will see what a great dog you are."

I sat Tuffy on the floor and gave him the lunch meat. While he gulped it down, my teammates came over to check him out.

"He looks starved," Bullet said.

"I found him in a storm drain. I think someone threw him away." Tuffy latched onto the towel, shaking it with his teeth.

Bullet grinned at Tuffy's antics. "What doesn't break you, makes you. You named him right."

Sneaker bent over to pet him. "Who'd throw away a cute little dude like you?"

Sam shook his head at me. "If I let you keep a pet, I'd have to let everyone, and that would cause too many problems. I know Maverick has Pip, but he's a valuable member of the team. I'm sorry, but I have to call animal control."

I couldn't get any words out past the lump that rose in my throat.

Hulk reached his hand out to Tuffy, who licked him. "They could put him down."

"No one cares if we die either," Blade snapped. "But we do. Don't do it, Sam."

I finally found my voice. "What if all of us Fallen kids share Tuffy? He could be our mascot. Please, Sam."

Sam frowned. "What if there's a kid in here afraid of dogs?"

Hulk snorted. "I doubt any Fallen kids fear dogs. We have bigger worries."

Sam drew a hand through his short military cut. "If you get everyone to agree to keep him and share, I'll let him stay."

I turned to Maverick. "I'm sure they'll agree if you go with me to ask. Will you?"

"I'll help you."

Joy bubbled up in me. I threw Maverick a huge smile and mouthed, "Thank you."

MB's hands stopped flying on the keyboard, and he glanced at Maverick. "This computer is only a few weeks old, so this is all recent stuff. Was there another computer there?"

"No," Maverick answered.

MB's fingers resumed typing. "An email they received from an

Aali Amir mentions you. He told the cell to attempt to bomb your grandfather's club while Costa's son was there."

"His name is probably an alias," Maverick said. "Aali means high and Amir means commander in Arabic, so it sounds like what a terrorist leader might call themselves."

"He also sent information on a couple of training camps to send their recruits to, and some plans for upcoming attacks, but there's nothing else about you or your dad." MB swiveled his chair around to face Maverick. "I'm sorry. I know you were hoping for evidence to clear him."

Maverick's shoulders slumped and his face fell. He took a breath and in a hoarse voice said, "Thanks for trying."

Sam limped over to MB. "Yes, good job, MB. Now that we know the terrorist leader who was calling the shots, it may help us learn more. Put that Intel on a flash drive so I can pass it on."

When MB removed the flash drive and handed it to him, Sam turned to us. "Alpha team deserves a break. No training today. Rest, hang out, play games, or whatever. I'll be back."

While the other guys went upstairs to play computer games, Maverick and I took Tuffy to Fallentier to introduce him to everyone. All of the kids agreed to share Tuffy, and no one admitted to being afraid of dogs.

When we returned to the training center, Maverick asked, "Do you want to introduce him to Pip now?"

"Sure."

When Maverick sat Pip in front of Tuffy, they nosed each other. Tuffy licked Pip. He didn't even mind when Pip climbed on his back.

I looked up to see Sam and Connor walk into the training center.

"Is Director Williams pleased?" Maverick asked.

"He's thrilled," Connor's eyes sparkled. "You shut down a terrorist cell, prevented bombings, and provided valuable Intel on a terrorist leader and training camps. Those are great accomplishments, and you should be proud."

"What will happen to those kids?" I asked.

"We think we can reverse the brainwashing on the young ones, and we're trying to locate any relatives." Connor sat in one of the chairs. "It will be case by case with the teens. They claim they didn't know the people they were working for were terrorists. And they only took the security job because they didn't have anywhere else to go."

"They had to know those guys were terrorists when they saw the bomb." Maverick picked Pip up. "Whether Lenny believed their ideology or did it for thrills, I don't know, but he wasn't there out of desperation."

"I agree with you, and so does Director Williams."

"Is our cover blown?" I asked.

"No. They believe a neighbor reported the gunfire, so they don't suspect Ari of informing on them. And they all related the same story about their attackers wearing masks. When Deputy Director Johnson told them he suspected Maverick of killing Jake and that a witness saw a teen fitting Maverick's description fleeing the house, they claimed the witness had to be wrong because even with masks on, they could tell their attackers were men, not teens."

It worried me that the CIA wanted to pin Jake's death on Maverick. Hopefully, Lenny and his friends wouldn't cave under the pressure.

"Did Director Williams believe me about Jake?" Maverick asked.

Connor shook his head. "He'll look into it, but without evidence, I'm afraid your word alone isn't going to clear your dad. He did agree that your end of the bargain was kept, so he's released your trust. Now that you're financially independent, your dad's attorneys won't have any problem securing your emancipation. You can live on your own like you wanted."

My heart flopped to my toes. Always the same old story. Whenever I allowed myself to really care about someone, they left me. They claimed they'd keep in touch, but it never lasted. The calls grew less and less until they stopped altogether. They always forgot me. My heart cracked as I fled the training center.

Chapter 58

Goodbyes

"Goodbye is like saying I don't mind being left." Gina

Maverick

The sun had set when Dad's attorney, Greg Crawford's pulled his car up to the cottage. Fallen kids poured out of the cottages and main building to see me off. Gina was mysteriously absent.

Felicity gave me a hug. "Gina can't stand goodbyes, not since... well, you know. They bring back those memories of her mom abandoning her."

"Yeah, I know."

I bumped fists with the rest one by one. Sneaker came last. "Dude, are you sure you want to do this?"

Between all the calls and meetings these last couple days, I didn't get the time to explain my decision.

"My social worker says I don't qualify for Fallentier anymore since it's for kids who can't be placed. Once people learned my trust was released, they've had tons of offers to foster me. But I'd rather live on my own than with people who want me for my money."

His face drooped. "Yeah, I get it."

"I won't forget my friends. If you need anything or there's trouble of any kind, call me. I'll keep my number the same."

"Going to miss you, Maverick."

"I'll miss you too. Take care of Gina for me."

"Will do."

I climbed in the car, and we drove out Fallentier's gate. When we finally arrived at the familiar lane, I scooted to the front of the seat. It seemed like years rather than weeks since I'd seen this place. With Dad presumed dead, Greg got the government to release the mansion back to the estate.

Legally, I had to have an adult oversee everything until I turned eighteen. It used to be Connor, but Dad had changed his will listing Greg as executor of the estate and my guardian when he found out Connor ratted to the Amato's. Greg considered the position a formality. He knew I was mature enough to make my own decisions.

Now, I was coming home.

Under the floodlights that penetrated the blackest of nights, we stood out starkly. Ivan waved from the guard shack.

He opened the gate and hollered, "Welcome back, Derrick."

Most of our former employees had returned yesterday. I'd put Ivan back in charge of security. We'd already discussed Angela's breach and took new countermeasures. Ivan was the only one I told, besides the team, that Dad wasn't dead.

When I climbed out of the car, I jogged to the house and entered the new door code. As soon as the light turned green, I burst through the door and turned on the lights. Everything looked surprisingly normal. According to Greg, the government had rifled through everything but had taken little, mostly paperwork from Dad's office. Our housekeeper set the place to rights before I arrived.

I wandered upstairs to my room and let Pip out. Contented chirps came from him as he ran to his model house. After filling his water and food bowls, I plopped on my bed. Much more comfortable than my cot at Fallentier, but I couldn't sleep.

I tossed and turned. What was wrong with me? Even Sneaker's snores would be a comfort. I missed people. I didn't want to live alone. Unfortunately, Fallentier wouldn't let me return, and Dad couldn't come home. I could call him. It was better than nothing. I got up, picked up my phone and dialed.

Dad and I talked a long time. When our call ended, the ache in my heart wasn't relieved, but sharper as I sent a text to Ivan. I finally returned to bed, but barely slept and rose at the crack of dawn. My footsteps sounded lonely as they echoed across the marble floors.

I sauntered to the kitchen and opened the refrigerator that our housekeeper had stocked with my favorites. I got out the milk and poured myself a bowl of cereal. What was I going to do all day? Dad's company was being run by Pete, and he knew more about the business than I did. He certainly didn't need me.

After I ate, I wandered down to the obstacle course and ran it. I completed it fast. Too fast. When I returned to the house, I worked out in the gym and took a shower.

Now what? The hours of the day stretched before me.

My phone rang. "Hello," I answered.

Ivan's voice came out of my speaker. "Connor's here and not happy about your new orders."

So Ivan got my text. Good. Connor's days of unlimited access were over.

Ivan continued, "There's another car of people behind him."

"Who?" I asked.

"A guy named Sam and a couple of kids, Gina and Sneaker."

"Okay, let Sam, Sneaker, and Gina through, but tell Connor he's not welcome."

"I doubt it will stop him," Ivan replied.

"Yeah, so be prepared. And FYI, Sneaker and Gina have instant access when they come."

"Okay, boss."

I hung up the phone, pulled my gun, and checked my clip before sliding it back in the holster. I couldn't wait to see my friends, so I hurried outside.

Chapter 59

Above us

"An abundance of skills and resources doesn't always add up to success." Victor

Gina

As Sam pulled into the drive of the grand mansion, Maverick came out a door set between marble pillars. His face split into a big goofy grin, and he leapt off the porch to jog toward us. My heart skipped.

I threw my door open and ran to meet him.

As he picked me up and spun me, joy filled me. "I missed you."

"And I missed all of you." He set me down and bumped fists with Sneaker, who had jumped out of the car too.

Maverick's face scrunched. "Is everything okay?"

"Yeah, everything's fine," Sam said as he climbed out.

"So what are you doing here?" Maverick asked.

Sneaker snorted. "Dude, we're here because we need you. It's not the same without you."

That was an understatement. The team was broken, and so was I.

Sam sighed. "Remember when you thought their performance was pathetic? That was good compared to now. They're all moping."

Maverick arched a brow. "I'd like to help you catch terrorists, but I can't come back to Fallentier. You heard them."

"You can't stay there as a foster kid, but that doesn't mean you can't come back as staff and have a room provided."

"I'm only seventeen."

"Yeah, so we claim you work part-time as a youth mentor. But whatever's going on between you and Connor needs to be resolved because we have to work with him."

Maverick looked at me. Inside I was begging him, *Please come back*, but I couldn't say it out loud.

Sneaker motioned to the mansion. "Dude, this is a sick crib."

"Come on, I'll show you around."

As Maverick gave us the tour, I gaped at the gym and the theater room. Even the guest rooms with their ornate furnishings were fancier than any room I'd been in. Five bedrooms at Fallentier could fit inside. Sneaker exclaimed over everything, but my spirits kept plummeting. We couldn't compete with this. It was way above us.

Maverick led us back outside. "There are two swimming pools behind the house. The salt water one has a grotto design, which is where we practice scuba diving. We also have an obstacle course and guest house back there, if you want to see them."

His nose wrinkled. "What's wrong, Gina?"

Wasn't it evident? "Why would you ever want to leave this?"

"Yeah, dude." Sneaker waved his arm around. "This is paradise."

Maverick smiled. "I'm glad you think so because I've already told the guards to admit you anytime. If you ever need a place to stay, you'll be welcome. That goes for any member of the team."

"Then forget about coming back to Fallentier," Sneaker said excitedly. "Let's move here."

"Fine by me, but you might not want more neighbors." Maverick handed him a key.

"What's this?" Sneaker asked.

"The key to the guest house in the back. I want you to consider it yours and stay there whenever you feel the need to escape."

Sneaker's blue eyes glistened. I hoped that meant he'd use it and give up sleeping on park benches.

"You should tell him you can revoke access at any time." Connor moved across the grounds toward us.

Connor's sudden appearance surprised me, but my heart stopped when Maverick grabbed his gun out of his holster and leveled it at him. "That's far enough, Connor."

I took a step back. Maverick was acting like Mom. Crazy.

"Whoa, Maverick," Sam barked. "What are you doing?"

Chapter 60

Answers

"One answer seldom will give a person the entire story." Victor

Maverick

While holding my gun on Connor, I slid my other hand inside my hoodie pocket to switch Pip's recorder on. Maybe I could get evidence to clear Dad.

Ivan raced into the driveway with the jeep. He threw it in park and raised his shotgun toward Connor. "You're trespassing on private property, so don't give me a reason to shoot."

Connor lifted his hands, palm out, and locked eyes with me. "Lad, what's this about?"

An ache stabbed my heart. My throat constricted as a lump rose and turned my voice raspy. "I never understood how Angela or Kurt could get that training tape when Dad kept everything confidential in the office. They didn't have those codes, but you did."

Connor's forehead scrunched. "They could have hacked into it, just like you."

"Yeah, but Dad never saw that news clip of Kurt being tortured because he was busy fleeing. Last night, I mentioned it to him. He confided that he'd hidden other cameras around the house because he suspected I'd been turning off the system when I didn't want him to know what I was doing. He installed one in the office. Guess who it showed taking the training tapes? You. You framed Dad."

Connor's shoulders sagged. "All right, I admit I took the tapes, but it's not what you think. I didn't give them to the terrorists, I gave them to your grandfather."

My jaw fell open. "What?"

"You know I was giving him reports about you. And he was curious about your training. I didn't think it would hurt anything for him to see some of what that comprised."

"You're saying my grandfather framed Dad."

He shrugged. "I don't know. He says he still has his copy, so I assumed Angela took the original. Maybe someone copied your grandfather's, and he wasn't aware of it."

"Or you made two copies, one for grandfather and one for the terrorists."

Sam shook his head. "Maverick, think. Connor knew about our operations, but the terrorists didn't. He couldn't be working with them."

Connor blew out his breath. "I swear I never intended for those tapes to be used to harm you or your dad. Lad, you have to believe me."

I didn't have to do anything. "Your treachery has hurt us, and you never came clean until you were forced to. I can't trust you. So stay off this property. The next time you come here uninvited, you'll be arrested or shot like any other trespasser." I motioned to the jeep. "Get in. Ivan will take you back to the gate."

As Ivan drove away with Connor, I holstered my gun and turned off Pip's recorder. I had some of my answers, but not enough to clear Dad. I still didn't know who had given that tape to the terrorists and framed him. He would have to remain dead as far as the world was concerned. And I was no closer to finding my missing sister, so the team was the only family I could be with. If I continued working with them, I might find the rest of my answers, but had I blown that opportunity?

I turned to Sam. "That's probably not the resolution you wanted. I'm sorry for any problems it causes, but I needed answers." My heart lurched. "I'll understand if you don't want me on the team now."

Sam frowned. "I told you before, Connor doesn't decide my team. I do, and I still want you to lead it. We need the group home front, though, so do you think you can leave all this behind and move back in?"

I looked at the mansion. When I went to Fallentier, I'd missed my home. But it wasn't home anymore. Homes have a family. I looked at Gina and Sneaker. The Director had been wrong when he said Fallen kids were easily forgotten. I could never forget them, and they hadn't forgotten me. They *were* family. My home was with them.

"Give me fifteen minutes, and I'll be packed."

Tears came to Gina's eyes. "You won't abandon us again?"

This might not be the path I thought I'd take, but it was one I could be proud of. We'd be working to prevent harm to our country just like the other unsung heroes.

"I promise I won't, and you know I keep my word."

"Woohoo. The team is back together." Sneaker pumped his fist in the air. "Those terrorists better watch out cause we're fearless and we're coming to get them."

He was right. We wouldn't let anything stop us.

I laughed. "Yes!" I pumped my fist in the air too. "We are fearless. We are fallen. But we won't be forgotten."

---THE END---

If you want to learn more about my books, visit terriluckey.com. If you enjoyed the story, please consider leaving me a review. Very FEW people leave reviews, but books are often judged by the amount they receive. It isn't necessary to write much. A line or two of why you enjoyed the book is enough. Thank you. Terri Luckey

CPSIA information can be obtained
at www.ICGtesting.com
Printed in the USA
LVHW11s1135230918
591102LV00004B/657/P